TEDD HAWKS

The Caddywampus

An Encounter with a Demon Bear and Its Consequent Chaos and Catastrophes

First edition

ISBN: 978-1-7365059-3-9

Advisor: Earhart Kentworth
Cover art by Sarah McCord

This book was professionally typeset on Reedsy.
Find out more at reedsy.com

Contents

Dedication

Thanks to Jess, Johnny, Josh, and Mary, for whose indefatigable support there are not enough ways to say thank you.

Cast of Characters

The Detectives

Crockett Cook—19-year-old lawyer, prone to displays of both heroism and extreme cowardice

Brontë Cook—19-year-old amateur detective, precocious and very adventurous

The Deutschefaber Inn Guests

Viktor Gestahlt—young Eastern European husband and father; technical wizard

Ambrosia Gestahlt—young Eastern European wife and mother; lover of illuminated insects

Adon & Ava Gestahlt—rambunctious children of indeterminate age

Elsinore Phipps—unanimously loathed American busybody

Greta van der Raaf—pugnacious, stately elder Dutchwoman

Colonel Collin Collanhall—Australian military man; hunter of everything (even those things of improbable existence)

The Deutschefaber Inn Staff

Sylvia Vindrikimmel—young maid with preternatural family senses

Ursula Deutschefaber—large, square innkeeper

Bristol Deutschefaber—large, block-shaped groundskeeper and accountant

Klaude Deutschefaber—???????

The Constabulary

Officer Bunce—affable, joyful policeman whom nothing appears to upset

Officer Bosch—overly-serious, grumpy policeman whom everything appears to upset

Removed from Text Pre-Emptively Due to Concern of Cancelation

Cubsey McGillicuddy—Irish man who speaks in a distinct, backward language

A Letter to the Reader

Dear Reader,

I hope this finds you well, or, as wildly as things are going in the world, mostly fine. Apologies again for the awkwardness surrounding the end of the last book, *Beatrice*. Although Earhart's manuscript of Crockett and Brontë's second adventure on the Mayweather estate was lost, I trust your imagination could fill in those details better than I ever could. If you like, you can still contribute what you believe happened during that murder mystery by visiting www.beatriceunbound.com.

While the Mayweather draft was lost, the text before you is based on a fully drafted novel written by Earhart prior to his death. June Winterbourne, in addition to giving him a full outline of the events in the Beatrice matter, also shared the contact information for Brontë and Crockett, who met with Earhart several times to discuss their further adventures.

Disappointed *Beatrice* did not capture a publisher's attention, Earhart sought counsel on this new novel. He corresponded with his friend, Didiert Piedmont, about the novel's structure and events. (You may remember Didiert as the previously unnamed author of *The Fantastic Death of Captain Discord, Buttled to Death,* and *The Murderer Is the Son.*) The two had an interesting working relationship, more detrimental then constructive (as I outline through footnotes in the following pages). When the two mediocre writers got together and shared craft tips, the result was something chaotically worse than either could have achieved working alone. It's both horrifying and inspiring. As Petrarch would say, "a true dillyfog." As a result, I had to rewrite large portions of the text, leading to Earhart's name being pushed down the title page.

It's also worth mentioning that the store owner who provided me with the original *Beatrice* text sent on diaries and correspondence that were collected around the time Earhart wrote the drafts for this book. I will call out anything of value or note from these documents in the footnotes of the text.

As far as this completed novel is concerned, I'll only say that the grim details of Beatrice's murder pale in comparison to those of the deeds written about here. I should also maybe warn you that Earhart promotes his British-centric worldview via a detrimental portrayal of other nationalities, including Americans (while he wasn't kind to us in *Beatrice,* his character Elsinore "Elsie" Phipps in this novel is offensive in a cornucopia of new ways). That being said, this novel is more of the same in many regards, including in the ongoing relationship between Brontë and Crockett, which continues to flourish as they discover more detective methodology.

Lastly, it both grieves and relieves the author to state that @badgrrlKinzay47 and I have ended our formerly tolerant relationship. After she went on to publish her own mystery story on Amazon (*Space Vampires from Outer Space*) and called me a "poophead" in numerous podcast interviews and social media posts, I asked my lawyer to intervene. I can safely say, with absolutely no shade intended, that I hope she finds some success in this novel-writing endeavor and breaks her streak of ill-imagined, doomed attempts at fame.

Sincerely,
Tedd Hawks

1

The Arrival and Primary Entanglements

Crockett and Brontë clambered off their train in Praktisch station[1], their eyes wild with wonder. They were greeted by the welcoming visual onslaught of decorations for the city's Finnlicht Festival, a three-day event celebrating the hatching of the local fairy light insects. Around them, the walls and stalls in the station exploded with color. Tourists bustled in every direction, their voices lilting, laughing, and bellowing as if in song. Lively banners with images of large golden bugs hung from the roof. They rippled in the August breeze, the bug images catching the light and shimmering like golden flashes of light on water. All manner of stalls were out and filled with enticements for incoming visitors. The festival drew hordes of international tourists from the surrounding region, as the German town was situated near the country's borders of Switzerland and France.

Brontë's eyes skittered between the little bug-themed shops, her gaze taking in maps, advertised excursions, fairy-themed toys, and the most perplexing of all, a large overweight gentleman dressed as a fairy himself. He was barking in several languages, handing out a moonshine beverage

---

[1] The name of the German town has been altered out of convenience. The editor thought the English towns from *Beatrice* were cumbersome, but the name of this town roughly translated from German means "little town on the border with a light festival and a rumored monster also home to a large and very scary castle which has been converted into a prison."

which he promised "Would make you feel like one of the bugs! Your own butt may light up!"

"It's exhilarating!" Brontë could barely contain her excitement. She squeezed Crockett's arm and looked into her new husband's mismatched eyes (one of which was green, the other blue).

Crockett returned her smile; however, it was less authentic than his wife's. His pulse was rising quickly as he took in the storm of tourists and locals; his ears rang with the squeals of brakes indicating more arriving trains. "It's quite a lot," he said. "Petrarch made it sound a bit more…subdued."

Petrarch, the solicitor under whom Crockett worked, suggested their honeymoon to Praktisch when things ended at the Mayweather Estate in their previous adventure. After days of murder, chaos, decapitations, light clerical legal work, and witchcraft, they took a quiet moment in the Mayweathers sitting room to gather themselves. Brontë and Crockett were eager to travel outside of England after their nuptials, and Petrarch suggested the insect light celebration called the Finnlicht Festival. It had been hosted in the little German town for nearly 100 years, starting in 1812 when Baron Turist von Trapp saw the potential. Petrarch and his late wife attended years before and stayed at a family-owned lodge, the Deutschefaber Inn, which the lawyer described as, "a euphoric, wondrous experience."

"The Deutschefabers are a nice family," Petrarch continued. "And the lights! I really can't capture their beauty with words." After he said this, he began doing a set of jumping jacks. (He assiduously exercised, although he retained a rather bulbous body shape.)

"*Guten!*" A woman carrying a lantern with a small toy fairy inside drifted by Crockett and Brontë. She giggled as she pulled a lever on the contraption and the tiny sprite inside went up and down. A series of mirrors inside the machine caused the fairy's shiny body to reflect and sparkle.

"Oh!" Brontë put her hand to her mouth in delight. "Should we buy one, Crockett? Kordelia would find it amusing, I think."

"It may be too banal for your sister." Crockett inspected the device. He then gave Brontë a wink. "She may prefer something which bursts into flames."

"You're absolutely right." Brontë laughed and squeezed Crockett's hand. "Perhaps we'll forgo gifts and only send letters. That should keep everyone safe."

They had little additional time to decide on the purchase, as the massive man-fairy stumbled toward them, nearly knocking down the woman with the lanterns.

"Hullo," he said gruffly. "Want a drink, then?" He shoved one of his bottles into Crockett's face.[2]

"It's a bit early, I think," Crockett said, disturbed by the odd elixir. He thought for a moment. "You knew we spoke English?"

"You've got that pale, sad look all Brits have." The man appeared to give up on the sale. He began drinking from the bottle he'd pressed towards Crockett.

"Do we?" Brontë felt her cheek. Although she did appear like an average Brit—long brown hair, pale skin, and hazel eyes that glowed with the faint light of a colonizer's superiority—she was sure, in this moment, she looked flushed and overjoyed.

"Aye," the man-fairy said. "It's a bit of a compliment. Rather be pale and sad than Irish, as they say."

Crockett and Brontë could find no response to this, so they politely nodded and started to press forward.

"Be careful," the man-fairy said softly. "There's odd things about."

Goosepimples appeared on Crockett's arm. Upon disembarking from the train, he felt something macabre in the air. He had suspected it was a touch of constipation from the travel, but the man-fairy confirmed it may be something more onerous.

"Why do you say that?" Brontë's face now indeed looked pale and sad.

"The week of the festival there's always shenanigans about…too many

---

2   The fist-draft writer, Earhart, with his consultant, Didiert, originally had the man-fairy speak in awkward Spenserian sonnets. It wasn't altogether terrible, but the need for them to fill out the sonnet form for each exchange meant readers were subjected to pieces of his tragic backstory, which grew rather awkward and violent.

people—foreigners." The man-fairy leaned in closely to them. The young couple could smell the mix of morning breath and alcohol pour from his thick lips. "But this year there's death."

"Death?!" Crockett felt his hand go to his heart.

Brontë swallowed. "What do you mean?"

The man belched. He dabbed his mouth with a green handkerchief he had around his neck. "There was talk of canceling the festival after everything going on. The mayor won't entertain the idea, though."

Brontë's eyes roamed over the train concourse once more. This time she picked up on subtle cues she missed in her reverie upon their arrival. The carnival atmosphere was present, but there was something amiss. Vendors who beamed brightly when someone approached grew nervous when left alone. The woman selling the toy fairy lights had ceased giggling; she was anxiously speaking to a young man carrying a satchel of fairy maps.

Crockett also noticed the bizarre atmosphere which hadn't seemed so obvious when they arrived. Droplets of sweat formed on his brow. Despite their recent adventures into chicanery and murder, he was growing fearful that some hex had been placed on them. Everywhere they went there was a trail of blood.

"Could you tell us—" Brontë started, but Crockett quickly cut off her inquiry.

"All right then, we hope you're well. Thank you for the drink offer." He gently pushed Brontë forward.

They didn't speak as they walked down the platform to collect their luggage. Crockett nervously rubbed his hands together. Brontë threw a backward glance at the man-fairy, who had uncapped another of his bottles and was sucking down its contents.

"An eventful week…"

"Brontë," Crockett tried to smile, "it may be best if we don't inquire. With what happened at the Mayweathers, I think we need a bit of a break from nefarious goings-ons."

Brontë flicked her eyes around the station once more. Whereas Crockett felt an impending dread upon their arrival, she had felt nothing but anticipation, a feeling that she wished to hold on to. She also prudently recognized they were far from home and separated from Petrarch, whose wisdom had guided their previous adventures. "Yes," she said pointing to their bags. "You're right. It's our honeymoon, and we need some relaxation."

"We don't want to be like that Ms. Fletcher from Northwest Jubilee-burghampton that Mr. Mayweather told us about," Crockett added. "Everywhere she went there was a murder. By the end of it, no one wanted to invite her anywhere."

Brontë and Crockett collected their bags and made their way to the station's exit. The awkward tension eased as they made their way out of the central terminal and onto the high street. Crockett extended his arm and took Brontë's. He placed a kiss on her cheek.

"Sorry I'm distracted, darling," he said. "I just feel a bit off. It could be the travel." He motioned to a confectionary shop which had a beautiful display of silver and gold candies. He gave Brontë a bright smile and pulled her toward the front window.

As they stood outside the shop admiring the treats shaped like leaves, trees, and little golden bugs, Crockett squeezed his wife's hand. He turned to her with a warm, somber expression. "Is it all right if we take a bit of a break from the adventuring? I just…have a terrible feeling."

"And it's not constipation?" Brontë pressed her hand to his stomach. "You had similar misgivings when we were traveling through France."

"No, I thought the same, but I think it's plain, quotidian dread."

"Well dread is more readily handled than stopped bowels, so I think we are fine." She kissed Crockett on the cheek. "Besides, with you it's all adventure, Crockett! I'd say this trip shall simply be free of murder but full of adventure."

As if on cue, a small, smiling policeman appeared beside them and coughed to catch their attention.

"Yes, officer?" Crockett's hand tremored with growing fear. Their involvement in whatever malfeasance occurred in the town appeared to be an inevitability.

"*Guten morgen,*" the man said. He spouted off a bit more German to which

Brontë and Crockett did their best to express incomprehension.

"Ah!" the officer said. "English?"

"Yes, please," Crockett said. One of the reasons Petrarch suggested Praktisch was his experience that English was understood readily. How a small town on the border of France, Switzerland, and Germany excelled in English was a mystery, but they were grateful regardless.

"Good! The English! So, I have question about death. The man who was *garrgged* in the square. You know?"

"Garrgged?" Brontë turned to Crockett.

"Yes!" The little man giggled as if it were a marvelous joke. "Garrgged!" This time as he said it, he made a violent choking motion. "It happen a day ago—at night. The man garrgged." This time the officer approached Crockett, gripped Crockett's neck, and began to lightly choke him. "You see?"

Crockett jumped away from the officer. Brontë's mouth fell open in surprise.

"Answer 'no,' I think. Thank you!" The officer tipped his hat and whistled a tune as he walked away.

"Oh, dear," Crockett said feeling his neck where the officer's hands had been.

"Is it us, Crockett?" Brontë asked. "Did Beatrice open some...I don't know, a curse? Who would have thought a fish could cause such trouble."

"Some fish obviously cause more trouble than others, but a herring you'd think would be relatively harmless."

They returned their attention to the candy shop, but their eyes lacked the guileless wonder of their initial glances through the glass.

The mood inside the store was muted as well. The old woman who owned the shop appeared distracted when they entered. She smiled and gave them the German names for the candies when asked, but the moment they turned their attention from her, she would bite her thumb and look out the front windows of the store. In the end, they exited a bit sadly, Brontë chewing on a toffee and Crockett sucking on a strawberry-flavored lollipop.

"Crockett," Brontë said looking at a group of jovial children passing by, "why are we so upset? We're on our honeymoon! There has been a murder, but it has nothing to do with us. We are outside its orbit, unlike our previous experiences."

"That's true." Crockett perked up. He took the lollipop from his mouth. "A man was killed in town, but we are staying at the Inn. Petrarch said it's a good walk from the city center."

"Honestly, we're a bit egocentric, thinking murder is following us around. It happens. People die; it has nothing to do with us."

"Nothing!" Crockett felt calm for the first time since he'd stepped from the train. His face brightened as he added, "Misfortune is everywhere. We don't bring it!"

"No! We embrace it and tame it," Brontë said, suddenly feeling the brazen mystery-solving impulse rise in her. Seeing Crockett so elated at the thought of no terror or horror, however, forced her to push it down. "But… now, we simply stand aside and let others take to solving it." As she swallowed, she consciously tried to force her curiosity about the dramatic events in Praktisch further inside.

"It will be a rather quiet, calm vacation, then." To punctuate his statement, Crockett shoved the lollipop back into his mouth.

The candy was no sooner between his lips than a woman ran shrieking down the street. Her pale hands were on her mouth, her eyes wild with fear. She scanned the crowd and ran toward a group of children gathered around a barker on a nearby corner. She reached out and gripped one of the young boys, shaking him sternly once her ringed fists had him in their grasp. The boy, his cheeks ruddy and his eyes wide, pointed across the street to a young girl with pigtails speaking to a vendor holding multicolored balloons. The woman appeared to be the children's very addled mother. She sighed with relief, grabbed the boy's hand, and stormed over to intercept the little girl. In moments, the family was sprinting down the street, the mother haranguing the children in frantic German.

"That mother appears to be tightly wound," Brontë said.

Crockett smiled with the lollipop sticking out of his mouth. "I suppose that's understandable since someone has been garrgged in the town square.

It would set me a bit on edge as a parent."

Brontë laughed, one quick short note. "I suppose that *is* a rather distressing event, parent or not."

They both stood in silence for a moment, watching the place where the woman disappeared into the swelling crowd. When husband and wife were sure the other was not looking, they allowed two different but equally frightened looks to cross their countenances.

No joke, lollipop, or frivolity could hide it. Praktisch was a place bursting with fear.

2

The Deutschefaber Inn

As Crockett and Brontë walked from the town center, their mood lightened. Thoughts of murder, manic mothers, and belching man-fairies were erased by the natural wonders around them. Their path to the Deutschefaber Inn led them away from the town, deeper into the forest. Trees shimmered in the warm, autumnal light. The air was brisk and cool; it felt as if it was blowing away the confusion and fear of the town, bathing them in the calming anticipation of the changing seasons.

Crocket breathed in deeply and closed his eyes. "This is lovely. Petrarch was right after all."

"It's a pity we only have a short week to enjoy it." Brontë let out a sharp breath, pointing into the trees. "Oh! Look, Crockett. What a huge bird!"

The bird, to Crockett, resembled a large crow or vulture, reminding him again of the fleeting terrors and death in town. "Yes, indeed," he said trying to hide his discomfort. "But look at these..." He quickly searched for something to draw his wife's attention to. "Cigarette butts," he said pointing to a trail of gray ash that wound on the trail in front of him. He flinched at his own idiocy.

"There are quite a lot..." Brontë halted their forward momentum and knelt to the ground.

For their wedding, Petrarch purchased the newlyweds a book, a large

9

volume dedicated to the art of investigation. *Detectivating for the Dunce* [3] was a guide to get you from "divan-bound slugabed to dashing detective" in as quickly as a fortnight. While Crockett had put the book aside, Brontë eagerly pored over its pages during their journey across Europe. It was these new skills she put into practice as she examined the trail of ashes before them.

"They appear fresh," she said dabbing the ground with her finger. "They're still hot."

"I'd say so," Crockett said. "I'd say they were dropped forty-five seconds ago."

"That's precise!" Brontë looked up at her husband. "Did you read the scientific analysis section? I haven't quite gotten there."

"The what?" Crockett laughed. "No, they're coming from that little man there." His eyes were fixed on a tiny, ugly man, who was dropping the ashes as he weaved through the trees just fifteen yards ahead of them. He appeared to be in vivid conversation…with himself.

"Rather ugly man, isn't he?" Brontë couldn't keep herself from scowling. "He looks a bit like a bespectacled, bloated elf."

"Or an obese leprechaun."

The man paid no attention to the young couple. His back was turned to them. He suddenly stuck his finger into the air and spoke loudly, "A-ha! You've done it again, Phipps! Even more brilliant than your last thought!" before moving swiftly away through the thick brush.

"He must be a lodger," Crockett said. "Why else would he be wandering through these woods."

"I hope the other guests are more aesthetically pleasing." Brontë stood up and dusted her trousers. "He looked as bad as my grandfather in his ridiculous Robert Edward disguise."[4]

---

[3] The author was just as surprised as you that the "for dummies" concept went all the way back to the early twentieth century.

[4] That was a spoiler for the first book, *Beatrice*. If I were a reader who had that spoiled, rather than being angry at the author, I would be mad at myself for not having purchased that book earlier. In fact, I would buy two copies to make things right.

Crockett slipped his hand into Brontë's. "I wouldn't say it was as bad as that! Robert did have a lovely beard, though. I wish I could grow one as exciting." The young lawyer patted his hairless face.

Brontë touched his cheek. "I think your face is lovely hairless. Hair is for bears and Russians if you ask me."

The two entered a moment of newlywed reverie. Crockett brushed a stray strand of Brontë's hair from her cheek, then traced his finger down her neck. His wife usually wore more comfortable, masculine-inspired clothing. Today, it was a checkered shirt with the top button undone.

Crockett was just leaning in for a rather romantic, woodsy, Austen-esque kiss, when a terrific, ghastly sound erupted from the man they thought had vanished into the brush. It sounded like the word *grock*.

The young lawyer jumped back. His wife gripped his hand and held him upright when he nearly toppled over.

"What was that?" he asked.

"It appears the little man—*Phipps* I believe he called himself earlier—is as repulsive aurally as he is physically."

Crockett cast a glance to the shrub from which the odd sound had come. While the Austen-esque passion had faded, he felt a more tepid, Collins-esque drive to place a kiss on his wife's cheek. He then extended his arm and the two walked together farther into the woods.

As they paced forward, the crunch of their footsteps the only sound, Crockett spoke. "What did you mean when you said, 'scientific analysis section' earlier?" he asked.

"Oh!" Brontë flushed. "I've been looking at the book Petrarch bought us."

"The detectivating one?"

"Yes." Brontë paused, unsure how Crockett would feel discussing the world of criminal investigation after their agreement to avoid conversations about murder.

Crockett, for his part, was elated at the joy that crossed Brontë's face when she mentioned the book. He gently prodded her further. "Well," he said, "what have you learned? The book is extremely heavy, so I hope it was worth carrying across Europe."

Brontë's eyes sparkled. "Oh, Crockett, it's fascinating!"

For the rest of the walk toward the inn, Brontë regaled Crockett with her learning. The chill in the air passed out of her mind as she discussed the most recent chapter, which focused on how footprints were the key to any respectable murder solution.[5]

Their conversation was so engrossing that they nearly crashed into the sign that marked the trail to the inn. They ceased speaking when their eyes fell on the dilapidated bit of wood and paint. Half of its words were faded or lost, so that they could just make out the letters *D-E...F-A-B* in pale red lettering.

"Oh my," Brontë said. Her eyes went up the hill to the main lodge. The building was poorly kept and covered in lichens. The wooden frame looked rotted in places, the windows partially covered in dust. One on the top floor was broken.

"Petrarch did say rustic," Crockett said softly.

"Hullo." The greeting came from a large bush nearby. Out of it emerged a young woman, her hair a snarled mess of dried leaves and twigs and her skirts covered in dirt.

Crockett and Brontë were both struck by how frail and sweet she looked. Everything about her had the appearance of a doll; she had long, delicate arms and legs that matched the straightness and thinness of her mousy brown hair. Her skin was startlingly pale, which had the dramatic effect of highlighting her large brown eyes.

"Who are you?" she asked, brushing a twig from her hair.

Crockett smiled. "We're the Cooks." Saying his and Brontë's new joint name made him shiver with pleasure.

The woman curtsied. "Very nice to meet you. I'm Sylvia Vindrikimmel, the maid at the Deutschefaber Inn."

Brontë, her detective faculties summoned during their discussion of the

---

5   In their original draft, Didiert and Earhart added an appendix with text from *Detectivating for the Dunce*. It included a rhyme about footprints to highlight their importance: "Don't freet, look for feet!" Judging from that one example, I hope the reader will understand why the rest of the appendix was cut.

book, noted that the young woman's eyes betrayed the smile on her lips. Something akin to fear twinkled behind the mask of welcoming propriety. "It's a lovely day," she said. She watched the maid's response closely.

"Indeed. I had a feeling it may rain this week, but I think it may turn out all right." Sylvia's eyes flitted about nervously, bouncing from Crockett to Brontë, then up to the lodge. She wiped some dirt from her skirt. "Can I help you go check in? Ursula, the innkeeper, will be waiting." As she said this, she tucked a strand of hair behind her ear, revealing a bruised spot on her forehead.

"Are you hurt?" Even Crockett, not feeling nearly as detectivey[6] as Brontë, saw the rather startling mark. "You've got a bruise on your head."

The girl's eyes went wide. She shook her hair down across her face. "It's nothing—nothing. I'm rather clumsy if we're to be honest. I often…get scrapes and bruises." A nervous, spasmodic laugh escaped her; its sound was so unnatural, Crockett and Brontë jumped.

"Are you quite all right, though?" Brontë looked to Crockett. She took his hand when she noted how worried his countenance had become. When she turned back to the maid, she studied her face with more perspicacity: the messed hair, twigs, dirt, and bruises on the young woman grew more menacing.

"Yes, I'm fine." Sylvia laughed again (trying very hard to make it sound less hysterical than her previous attempt). "Clumsy." She motioned to her messy garb. "Nothing to worry—OH NO!"

Something behind Crockett triggered this response. The young maid moved quickly, lunging forward and, in an incredible show of strength for the waifish girl, picked up both Brontë and Crockett's bags and started running up the hill.

"Follow me, then!" she called back. "We must not keep Ursula waiting!"

---

6   For some reason, Earhart and Didiert loved to tweak the word "detective" to fit different parts of speech. It is one of the more benign quirks of this text, so I chose to leave these choices in. It is far more reader-friendly than the French words I have omitted from the novel, which Didiert, in correspondence, said made the text sound "far more erudite and likely to be banned."

Crockett looked behind him and saw, a great distance away, the form of the ugly man that they had seen earlier. He was no longer distracted but looked toward them, deciding whether he was going to approach. Brontë waved halfheartedly to the figure.

Crockett turned his attention back to Sylvia who was nearly out of sight with their luggage.

"Odd girl," he said.

"Let's follow her," Brontë said. "Even with her maniacal laugh, she's more welcoming than the little man in the woods. It's no wonder she fled from him."

The two ran quickly behind the maid. Despite her small size and carrying the two bags, she sprinted ahead and entered the lodge well before them. When Brontë and Crockett caught up to her inside the main building, they found themselves sweatier and more out of breath than they would have liked.

Sylvia stood before them near the front desk. Her posture was rigid. She was looking upon the large, forbidding figure manning the check-in. The twinkling of fear in her eyes Brontë noticed earlier was now a strong glow. The cause for this change appeared to be the person behind the front desk.

And fear was a justified feeling to have in the presence of Ursula Deutschefaber. The woman stood with the erect precision of a commodore. She was large, perhaps huge, in fact, with piercing green eyes and an expression that made one think that someone near her had let out a terrific, odious fart. Her actual physique could generally be described with one simple adjective: square. Her head was a block that sat on the cube of her torso supported by the rectangular prisms of her legs. The pen in her hand looked infinitesimal in her massive fist. Crockett was sure it was going to crack under the pressure of her grip.

Although she was an intimidating figure, Brontë did appreciate that she wore no makeup and trousers instead of a dress.

"Can I help you?" The innkeeper's English was crisp and precise with only a faint trace of a German accent. "Sylvia," she said brusquely to the maid. "That will be all."

Sylvia, showing great relief, hustled past Brontë and Crockett and left the building.

"How do you all speak such marvelous English?" Crockett smiled brightly. "Everyone here is so good at it. I can only speak one language."

Ursula turned her gaze fully to Crockett. Her countenance registered a look of shock. "You," she said stiffly, "are very handsome."

Crockett blanched. In the entirety of his life, he had only been called handsome by maternal figures (even Brontë said he was more "striking"). The compliment coming from the massive square woman before him compounded his feeling of embarrassment and confusion.

"Thank you…" was all he could muster as a response.

"Yes, well, compliments where they are due." Her face flushed. She turned her gaze down and began scribbling in a large book that sat open in front of her. Then, remembering Crockett's earlier comment, said quickly, "I studied a correspondence course in English."

Brontë's lips pursed. She looked at the large innkeeper with narrowed eyes. "Well," she said emphatically, "my *husband* and I have a reservation."

"Yes." Ursula looked up from her scribbling and nodded. "And a very lucky woman you are." She looked back at the book and scanned the page quickly. She made a mark next to one of the entries. "I assume you are the Cooks. Let's hope you aren't like the other couple, the Gestahlts, who suddenly decided to bring their wild children and muck up my reservations. Poor planning." The large woman sniffed with judgment. She opened a small cash box next to her. "I'll need to collect payment."

Crockett nodded and reached into his suit to get the fee. Brontë, with more force than she intended, gripped the money from Crockett's hand and pushed him out of the way.

"I'll take care of this, Crockett," she said. "You look after the luggage."

Crockett, flabbergasted that the women were fighting over him, withdrew quickly.

Ursula, seeing him turn, looked at Brontë and sighed. "Even good from the backside."

"Madame!" Brontë flushed.

The two women began quibbling. Crockett's scalp grew hot from embarrassment, so he shifted his attention away from the front desk and toward the interior of the lodge.

It was cheerier than he would have thought from the dilapidated façade. The main room was large and open, with a huge chandelier made of elk horns filled with electric lights hanging from above. The furniture was in various states of disrepair, but was covered by cozy red and green blankets, adding an air of rustic comfort.

At the center of the room, above an imposing fireplace, was a portrait of a family. There was a young man and woman and three children. The husband and wife were beaming; the woman had a knot of blond hair on her head; in her arms was a beatific baby with bright blue eyes. Standing beside her were the two other children, a girl with a dour expression, her figure squarish, leading Crockett to the conclusion that this was a young Ursula, and, close to her was a boy whose eyes were so unfocused and distant that Crockett looked across the room to see if the child saw something in the direction of the billiard hall.

The women's voices grew softer. Crockett, feeling that the better part of their confrontation was over, drifted back to the main desk.

Ursula was speaking as he grew closer. "You will be in cabin number three," she said. She handed Brontë a small booklet. "This guide has all the information about the lodge and Praktisch. It is a very nice, cozy hamlet except for the large and very scary castle which was turned into a prison."

A drawing of the castle in question was on the front page of the booklet, which Ursula held up for Brontë. It did look truly terrifying. The stone structure was decaying, chunks of stone fallen from its ramparts. Torn banners rippled on its towers in an unseen breeze. For some reason, the artist even rendered the sky dark and menacing. Gray, swirling clouds decorated the image's background.

"In regard to the inn," Ursula continued, "we have a very small staff here. If you have any questions, they can be directed to me at the front desk or Sylvia, the maid. My name is Ursula Deutschefaber. You may see my brother, Bristol, at times, but he is not to be asked questions." Her eyes flicked between Crockett and Brontë, looking for confirmation of understanding. "Any questions?"

"No." Brontë grabbed the guide and moved toward the door.

"You will also need this." Ursula held up a bronze key. Brontë turned and ripped it from her hand, giving her a surly look before storming away.

"Excellent. Goodbye." The large woman politely bowed, taking one lingering look at Crockett before resuming her focus on the large leatherbound book before her.

Crockett followed Brontë to the door. Before stepping outside, he took one last glance at the main lodge space, his eyes falling on the portrait and the severed animal heads, which created a ring around the room's perimeter. It was when he looked upward to the second floor that he saw a small, mysterious figure partially concealed in the shadows where the upper hall met the grand staircase. He only had time to see a ghostly white hand and a pair of luminous eyes before the figure vanished from sight. When he turned to Ursula to ask who the figure was, his voice halted in his throat. The imposing innkeeper was looking in the same place, her face contorted into a frustrated scowl.

Crockett had little time to ponder this scene; Brontë gripped his hand and pulled him through the main entrance, back into the warm afternoon light.

3

The Less-Than-Delightful Mr. Phipps

The layout of the Deutschefaber Inn's grounds was a tad claustrophobic. The area consisted of five cabins situated along a single dirt path, which arched away from the main lodge. From each cabin's front porch, you could see clearly to the front stoop of your neighbors on either side; Brontë and Crockett both had hoped for a bit more privacy, especially on their honeymoon.

Their cabin was also a general disappointment. In selling the location to the young newlyweds, Petrarch told them it was warm, bright, and cheery. This may have been true in a preceding decade, but, in its current state, it looked as if it was an uncleaned bathtub; a dusty, gray film covered every surface. The cabin consisted of two small rooms—a sitting room and bedroom—with the kitchen partitioned from the sitting room by two walls of cabinets. Bathroom facilities consisted of a small outhouse to the back of the cabin and a large, claw-footed tub, which sat very near the bed. The décor was aged and cheap, a litany of animal heads placed on the wall along with scenic photographs of varying locations (including an odd one of the Eiffel Tower positioned above the fireplace in the sitting room). In sum, the feeling the cottage evoked was one of resigned, woodsy indifference. There was neither joy nor charm nor warmth in its interior. The atmosphere was further sullied by the anger of Brontë, which boiled over the moment they stepped across the threshold.

18

"The nerve!" she said pacing the floor in a frenzy. "To so overtly compliment you in my presence. It's lewd. It's disgusting. It's disrespectful—"

"It was a bit odd, wasn't it?" Crockett put down their baggage and embraced his wife. She rested her head on his shoulder, still perturbed. "Brontë, it's really nothing! She's a large, square woman—you know I hate Euclidean geometry."

Brontë resisted a smile. "She was very square, nearly cubular." [7] The restrained smile blossomed into an expression of joy. "I suppose it is much ado about nothing. She is an odd duck, isn't she?"

"The queerest of waterfowl!" Crockett affirmed.

Brontë squeezed Crockett tightly.

As they rested in silence, the image of the white hand at the top of the stair ran through Crockett's memory; a chill ran down his spine. He pictured Ursula's fierce gaze staring toward the second floor of the lodge. For a moment he thought he would tell Brontë, but then he remembered the strangeness of town, the murder, the policeman, and the man-fairy who warned them of the strange air of mystery and thought better of it.

"Are you still with me, love?" Brontë looked into Crockett's eyes. He had stopped stroking her hair; his gaze was distracted and distant. "It feels as if you've gone off somewhere."

Crockett started. "Oh, no. No, I..."

She followed his line of sight to a dusty, decapitated animal, mounted above the fireplace. It was an elk, but one of its horns was broken, and the nails did not fully hold it so that the dead beast's visage was askew. Its mouth hung open as if in the middle of asking the question, "May I disembowel you?"

"Oh dear," she said. "Well, if that animal caught your attention, I can see

---

[7] While cubular isn't really a word, I thought I'd leave it in as further evidence that Earhart was very into the experimental—art *and* prose. His and Didiert's love of cubism had a larger presence in the first draft; an entire character named Cubesy McGillicuddy had to be cut due to offensive Irish stereotyping and the fact that all his speech was written backward (e.g., "Olleh" was "Hello"). This is all to say that while this novel may not be perfect, it could be much worse.

how you were distracted."

Crockett, who had been lost in his own musings about the sad little town, regained focus; upon noticing the animal Brontë mentioned, he jumped.

"My word! Was this some kind of joke from Petrarch? This place is a mess."

Brontë pulled away from Crockett's embrace and walked closer to the elk head. She gently touched it, hoping it would slide into its original position; it instead twisted further on its hook. This movement was enough to trigger the mangled horn to pop off and fall to the floor. The ensuing crash caused both husband and wife to shriek.

Crockett was so taken aback that he fell backward over the coffee table in the sitting room, knocking over a vase of dying flowers.

It took a moment for them both to regain their composure, which was followed by a frantic fit of giggling. Brontë leaned over, extending her hand to help Crockett up.

"You know," he said, taking her hand to get back onto his feet, "we should see opportunity in this instead of despair! We can clean the cabin up a bit and make it our own. When I lived in the poorhouse in London, I made my small cot a livable space. We can make this a proper home for the next several days. By the time we see the fairy lights and have to return home, we won't want to leave."

"Mr. Cook, I do believe you have stumbled onto a marvelous idea. I'll prepare some tea."

But before Brontë could enter the tiny kitchen area, their cabin door flew open with a loud *thwack*.

The uninvited guest spoke immediately upon entering. "Is everything all right? I thought I heard a crash."

The intruder was the small, ugly gentleman they'd seen earlier in the woods. Brontë found that now that she was closer to him, the immediate feeling he inspired was annoyance (as well as the earlier disgust), not merely for his forced entry but also for the peevishness of his squat, know-it-all face.

"Hullo," Crockett said, keeping the edge from his voice. (He also felt a whirl of distaste upon the little man's entrance.) "May we help you?"

"Yes, of course, thank you so much." The man bowed slightly then clomped to the sofa and took a seat. "Thank you for inviting me in. I did wonder when you'd have me over. I'm Elsinore Phipps, your delightful American neighbor in cabin two. My friends call me 'Elsie,' but you may call me anything that calls up 'towering genius' to your mind." His eyes found Brontë near the threshold of the kitchen. "Oh, yes, and tea would be lovely. And something to eat. I'm rather peckish after so much thinking and geniusing in the woods. Do you have a ham?"

"No," Brontë said flatly. Even though Ursula had made advances toward her husband, Brontë found herself loathing Phipps almost equally just for his unbearable…well, everything.

Phipps, now seated, began to make the same loud, grating phlegm sounds that interrupted the newlyweds' romantic moment earlier. "GROCK! GROCK!" He pulled out a handkerchief and wiped his mouth. "Sorry, I always clear my voice when there's opportunity. You never know when one will be called to say something inspiring."

Crockett looked to Brontë. His wife, realizing preparing a cup of tea would keep her from entertaining the horrible little gentleman, fled into the kitchen.

Crockett watched her turn away with a feeling of abandonment. He looked back to Phipps, who was now…snorting? The exact word for the noises coming from his face was hard to describe. It was more out of a desire to end the grotesque vocal operetta than actual interest to the question's answer that led Crockett to inquire.

"Did you say your name was Mr. Phipps?"

"Yes, I'm working on my masterpiece. Thank you for asking."

"Did I ask?" Crockett was sincerely confused.

"It was implied." Phipps turned to Crockett and smiled. His teeth were too large for his small mouth. He sniffed again and let out a more tasteful grock.

Crockett didn't know what to say; however, he inferred after only a minute in Phipps's presence that the little man would have no trouble filling the silence. "Masterpiece, you said? That's a very strong word. Are you a painter? These woods would be a beautiful spot for inspiration."

"Ugh!" Phipps's nose went up in disgust. "Painters are the tablespoons of the art world,[8] mostly unnecessary now that we have photography. I, sir, am a writer."

Crockett's countenance fell. He vividly remembered the oppressive personality of Pip Hawsfeffer in their first mystery and quickly wondered, after so many encounters with such an obnoxious caste, if he would ever read again. "That…well, good for you," Crockett said half-heartedly.

As Crockett grew more and more desperate and disinterested with Phipps, Brontë was in the kitchen greatly enjoying herself. The staff had filled their cupboards with some lovely jam and biscuits. Fresh butter sat on the counter next to a small container of milk. She also found a box of a dark substance which could have been tea or dirt.[9] Since Phipps was both uninvited and obtrusive, she hoped for the latter; she also would not be sharing their jams with the vile man.

She took as long as she could to prepare the drinks, searching through the kitchen for the dirtiest cup she could find for Phipps. When she found one covered in dust, she stirred a few spoonfuls of the dark tea substance into it. For herself and Crockett, she prepped a safe cup of hot water.

She entered the sitting room with a serving tray. Phipps was in the middle of an ambling diatribe.

"So, you see," he droned, "that's really what *Walking in the Woods While Walking* is about at its core—the very nature of human existence as it fundamentally relates to the binary nature of our Anglo-Judeo Christian religious paradigm. Also, there are lots of birds because I rather like them.

---

[8] Being a "tablespoon" was very offensive in this era. Didiert and Earhart belonged to a literary society called The Forks which played on the cultural distinction their society placed on what kind of tableware you represented. (For the readers benefit: forks are good, spoons bad, tablespoons very bad, and being referred to as a ladle was tantamount to using a slur.)

[9] It's unclear, but I believe this to be a veiled insult from the very British Earhart about German tea.

But birds are very often like Jesus, the dove and all that at the baptism, so really it all functions together perfectly, dove-synecdoche and all."

Crockett stopped listening the moment Brontë entered, sighing with profound relief.

"Thank you so much, darling," he said.

"Took a while, didn't it?" Phipps asked, nearly wrenching the dirt water from Brontë's hand.

While he took a drought, there was a luscious three seconds of silence, which Crockett enjoyed immensely. He suddenly started, however, as Phipps primed himself for another tirade, letting out several more throat-clearing grocks.

Wanting to prolong the Phipps-free silence for a little longer, he spoke up, hoping to end the mystery of Sylvia's earlier behavior and disposition, her bruise, and the terrified response she had to the obnoxious man. "Mr. Phipps," he said, "we spoke to the maid earlier this morning. She seemed a bit scattered. Is that her normal character?"

Phipps's arrogance faded. He reached into his jacket pocket and pulled out his handkerchief. Crockett and Brontë exchanged a surprised look. The sudden transformation in the man was striking. His red face turned white. His hands trembled.

"Yes, yes." He took another drought of his dirt water and looked, for the first time, directly at Crockett. "I saw you and I…" He paused for a moment. "I wondered, you see, if she told you."

"Told us?" Brontë looked at Crockett. "What would she have told us?'

"Well," Phipps said, his voice softer, less pugnacious than it had been, "last night the maid, Miss Vindrikimmel, and I saw each other very late. Her family has a magic sense—a premonition that occurs in the face of danger—and this magic sense had awakened her, and I was out on my general walk cultivating my own genius."

Brontë moved to question the use of "genius," but Crockett motioned for her to stay quiet.

"We saw something horrible." Phipps looked between them. His beady eyes were filled with terror. "It was a large, hulking figure. Perhaps it was eight feet tall with the muzzle of a puma and the body of a bear. On its head it…well, it had a crown of large, terrifying elk horns."

Brontë leaned in eagerly. Crockett felt his heartbeat race. The ominous feeling he had upon their arrival resurged.

"It was devouring an animal. Blood was everywhere." Phipps again used his phlegm-covered handkerchief to dab his face. "We couldn't even scream in the dark; then it…it…" Phipps closed his eyes. Both Crockett and Brontë suddenly felt some compassion for the little man, his arrogance and ego vacated, primordial terror writ on his features. "It came at us, running and making this horrific sound…a wail, a scream…" Phipps shook his head. "I don't know how even to describe it—even with my deep and profound knowledge of the English language." A bit of color returned to his cheeks. "It passed us, thank God, and ran into the woods. Sylvia lost consciousness and fell, which is why she now has that unbecoming bruise. I was very strong, as I remember, seeming to swell in heroic fortitude in the aftermath."

Brontë couldn't refrain a loud "tsk" that escaped after this statement.

Phipps didn't notice this as he concluded his story. "I asked her what it was. I thought perhaps in the dark we had both imagined something…or fear transformed something mundane into a beast. But…" Phipps again lost his color. He sighed heavily. "She said it was very real. In these parts they have a name for it."

Brontë could not restrain her curiosity. "What is it? What do they call this creature?"

Phipps looked at them both, a cold sweat emerging on his brow. "*Dämonenbär des Waldes*," he said quietly. "The demon bear of the woods."

4

The Caddywampus

A profound, fear-filled silence followed. Brontë leaned back in her chair, her eyes instinctively going to the window, looking outside as if the *Dämonenbär* would appear with a "Good afternoon." Crockett had begun to perspire. It took a great deal of strength for him to keep himself upright.

Phipps, admiring his effect on the young couple, regained some of his old arrogance. "I told Sylvia that the tourists will have difficulty with that name—the funny *a*'s with the hats on them—so I suggested we call it the Caddywampus."

The fear in the room dissipated, as if absorbed by an emotional sponge.[10] It was replaced by a general air of superiority (for Phipps) and annoyance (for Brontë and Crockett).

Brontë shook her head. "That doesn't sound nearly as horrifying. I feel like it's a bit too...well, silly."

"Pleeeeease," Phipps drew out the syllable dramatically. "In the great United States, where I'm from, it means exactly what I'm saying it means: a terrifying creature of the woods."

"But why not call it the *Dämonenbär*, which hits it more correctly,"

---

[10] I feel it is better for me professionally to say that I did not write this simile. This was all Earhart.

Brontë continued to argue, driven only by her deep, inherent loathing of Phipps. Now that the little man's vulnerability was fully displaced by his priggishness, she was, once again, ready to toss him from their cabin.

Phipps crossed his arms and scrunched his face in petulant rage, his ample neck bulging. "Well, I suppose you tea-time-trash English people wouldn't appreciate the finer dialects of America, if we're going to get into it."

"Tea-time trash!" Crockett, now fully over his earlier fears, sat bolt upright. Never one to trumpet his Britishness, he became instantly patriotic. "I think that's quite unfair. We're the ones who started the whole English-speaking part of English!"

Phipps stood. He thrust his great belly out as if he were a cobra showing its hood.

The argument would have turned into a proper row, but the enraged party was interrupted by another *thwack* from the front door. Two individuals had entered and now stood in the threshold of the cabin. Sylvia, who was leading, turned a deep shade of crimson realizing she'd made an error.

"Oh, I'm so very sorry!" she gasped. "I must have the wrong cabin for the colonel!"

Phipps, his mercurial state in full display, walked forward and bowed to the maid. "Miss Vindrikimmel!" he roared. "We were just speaking of last night. What we saw!"

Sylvia opened her mouth to respond, but she was thrust aside by the second member of the party, a large, barrel-chested older man holding an armful of guns, maces, and other assorted weaponry. He was both impressively giant and friendly—like a grizzly-size teddy bear. Despite the heft of his arms and midsection, however, his legs were thin, almost feminine. They stuck out like the appendages of a stork from his khaki shorts. Atop his head was a long, beautiful shock of silver and black hair partially covered by a taupe slouch hat. His mustache perfectly matched his two-toned mane and was so full that it nearly covered his mouth.

"You saw it, too!" The man's accent struck all of them. It sounded neither American nor British; it was folksier and more congenial. Although Crockett and Brontë had never encountered a tone like it before, they believed it belonged somewhere in the Commonwealth. Perhaps the large man was from Canada or Australia.

"I did!" Phipps was slightly shocked by the appearance of the larger man. The weapons along with his sheer size appeared to intimidate the diminutive writer.

"Excellent!" The old man dropped his weapons and took off his hat. Once it was removed, he stood fully erect as if reporting for duty. This made him seem larger, which made even Crockett and Brontë slightly uncomfortable. "The name," he said in his accented English, "is Colonel Collin Collanhall!" He saluted. The rest of the party awkwardly returned the gesture. "I've come to hunt the creature!"

Sylvia looked out the window. Her eyes were filled with fear. "Should we discuss this a bit more quietly?"

"Ah yes!" Collanhall bowed politely to Sylvia. "I shall keep my part of the bargain."

Brontë turned to Crockett and mouthed the word "bargain?" Crockett shook his head. He also didn't understand the new wave of chaos that had crashed into their cabin.

Phipps was staring incredulously at Collanhall. "Hunt it! My dear man, that's insane! You haven't seen… It's…it's monstrous! Terrifying!"

"We barely escaped with our lives…" Sylvia's voice was nearly inaudible.

"Huh!" Collanhall laughed and took a large step into the room. "In my home country Australia, this creature wouldn't even be an appetizer to a hunting meal. Have you ever seen a bimbleburkey?"

The rest of the party could only return negative responses.

"Head of an alligator, face of a lion, body of a man with the hands of a walrus."

"Would those be flippers then?" Brontë asked.

"I suppose," Collanhall said loudly, "but they do have fingers on them."

Sylvia looked as if she was going to vomit. Collanhall noted this and let out another bark of a laugh. "If you can't handle the bimbleburkey then I won't begin discussing a trollyhopper."

"It seems…" Crockett scratched his head. He felt he was in a room with

Brontë's younger, dreamy, and incoherent sister, Kordelia. "It seems, dear Colonel, that this may be a task you're very much ready for." He looked at Brontë nervously. "We can all rest easier knowing you're staying here."

Collanhall nodded proudly. "It's why I came to this godforsaken continent," he said. "In Australia the *Dämonenbär* is one of the most prized monsters of Europe. Speaking of," he put his hat back on and lovingly began picking up the machetes and shotguns which had fallen to the floor, "I need to go prepare for the hunt. Miss Vindrikimmel, if you would please show me to my correct cabin."

"It will be cabin five," the young maid said, stepping back through the door.

Phipps gripped Sylvia before she could leave. "My dear, you've done enough. I can take him to his cabin. We'll be neighbors this week, so why not get to know each other? He hasn't yet heard about my book." Phipps, without waiting for a response, took the key from Sylvia and left.

Collanhall clicked his heels together and bowed slightly. "Tally-ho!" he said and marched out of the cabin.

Sylvia took in a deep breath and turned to Brontë and Crockett. She smiled slightly and turned to leave.

"Miss," Brontë said quickly, "would you like some tea?"

Brontë's detectivian instincts were alerted the moment Sylvia looked out the window when the *Dämonenbär* was mentioned. Beyond her awkward behavior in the morning, her abrupt entry with the colonel, and the fact that she had personally encountered the creature the night before, something else was off-kilter with the young maid.

Sylvia, misreading Brontë's shrewdness for concern, sighed pleasantly. After a night of the *Dämonenbär* and a morning of the blustering Collanhall, she was ready for a peaceful moment.

"I would love it," she said softly. "Thank you very much."

Crockett, his own detective instincts dulled by fear and confusion at the bizarre cast of characters filling the Deutschefaber Inn, believed his wife's invitation to be innocent rather than an interrogation. He motioned toward the sofa. "Please, take a seat Miss Vindrikimmel."

"I'll get the tea and some biscuits!" Brontë bowed as she went to the kitchen to look for something to drink which didn't have the look of soil.

Sylvia took a seat. "Thank you for the invitation," she said. "It's been a chaotic day here. We're not used to so many guests."

At that moment, the mangled elk head which hung over the fireplace followed its twisted horn and crashed to the floor. Sylvia shrieked; Crockett, as was his impulse in instances of shock, gasped and toppled over. Brontë reentered the room to check on the noise. Her alarm gave way to laughter; she was unable stop herself from giggling upon seeing Crockett tilted over like a possum.

"We had noticed," Brontë said between chuckles indicating the fallen trophy, "that the inn is in…well, it's in a state of disrepair."

"I apologize for that," Sylvia said. "There hasn't been time to fix anything. I've been here a few weeks. Ursula only hired me recently. She knew that they would need help with the festival."

Brontë, grateful for having read chapter three of *Detectivating for the Dunce* for its discussion of vocalizations of common criminals, noted that when Sylvia mentioned Ursula's name, the timbre and tone of her voice altered.

"How is Ursula?" She tried to keep her voice casual. "She seems to be a very stern mistress."

Sylvia looked downward. "She runs a tight ship…" She tried to hide a look of fear. When she believed it had passed, she turned her gaze upward. "*Tight ship?* Is that the correct term? That's one of the colloquial phrases they use in my correspondence course."

"Yes." Crockett pushed himself up. His face was still white, but color was returning. "That's correct."

"She very much wants to be sure this week goes well with the festival," Sylvia continued. "Both her and Bristol are on edge."

"Bristol?" Crockett asked.

"Her brother," Brontë responded. "She mentioned him earlier, when we checked in."

"Yes." Sylvia nodded. Her voice again altered, but Brontë was not sure what to make of this change. The young maid began wringing her hands. "Perhaps," she said standing, "I should go. I don't want to intrude."

"No!" Brontë said abruptly.

Sylvia's eyes went wide.

Brontë, realizing she had spoken too loudly, reduced the volume of her voice and made it sound high and sweet. "No, Miss Vindrikimmel. We'd love to have you for tea. I'll go finish preparing. I got distracted with the crash."

Brontë disappeared. Sylvia turned her attention to Crockett, who was staring at the fallen elk head. When he turned and looked back at her, his large eyebrows furrowed.

"It's not real, is it?" he asked quietly. He was embarrassed that he needed to ask it. Part of him hoped Brontë did not hear.

"What, sir?" Sylvia asked. With the elk head falling and the mention of her mistress and Bristol, the young girl had forgotten the earlier discussion of the *Dämonenbär.*

"The monster..." Crockett looked to the kitchen to see if Brontë was coming. "The thing you and Mr. Phipps saw last night."

Sylvia bit her lip.

Had it not been for the show of vulnerability from Crockett—his earnest, childlike desire to know—she might not have spoken. The unease which Brontë triggered in her fled now that it was only her and the sweet, young man.

"To be honest," she said after a prolonged pause, "nothing since I've arrived has been normal. It's all been odd." Crockett kept his steady gaze on Sylvia. He nodded reassuringly. The young woman had not seen such empathy, even from those she liked, since arriving in Praktisch. She found the words spilling out of her, "When I arrived about a fortnight ago, I felt that something was a bit off... It's hard to describe, my family refers to it as our *besonderer Sinn,* our special sense. Since I've arrived it's been—heightened." She began to play with her skirts nervously. "Then...this week...it's been madness."

"Madness?" Crockett couldn't help but draw a line between the young girl's *besonderer Sinn* and his own unease upon their arrival. "What has your bondage sheep told you?"

"My what?"

"Your…" Crockett, realizing he should himself enroll in a correspondence course before their next trip to the continent hesitated. "Your…bediggle sheen? Does it have an opinion on the beast in the woods?"

"Oh! My *besonderer Sinn?*"

"Yes, that," Crockett said quickly.

"Well, it…it's hard to say exactly—"

"Tea is ready!" Brontë entered the room with a manic energy. The news of more mayhem and mystery had ignited her passions. Although she was trying to keep them subdued, an impulse rose in her—a desire for action. Something about the young Miss Vindrikimmel was both sympathetic and troubling. Brontë knew the *Dämonenbär* was causing her anxiety, but there was something else…something just out of reach.

Brontë set down the tray of tea and biscuits and grew self-conscious. Both Crockett and the young maid looked troubled.

"Are you… Is everything all right?" Brontë smoothed her trousers during the ensuing awkward silence.

Crockett finally shook himself from the melancholy. "Yes, darling! Thank you. Miss Vindrikimmel and I were discussing the inn. We both have…a fear about this place."

Sylvia rose. "I'm sorry to trouble you. It's nothing." The young woman attempted a smile, but it only flashed briefly then vanished. Her countenance fell into an even graver state once it was gone. "I'll show myself out. There is much to do this evening. Thank you," she said quickly, "for the hospitality."

Brontë followed her to the door to show her out. As Sylvia opened the door with Brontë behind her, they both gasped. On the front stoop of their cabin Ursula stood with an unknown gentleman. From his menacing, stiff appearance, Brontë assumed it was another Deutschefaber—most likely Ursula's brother, Bristol. They appeared to have been listening to the conversation.

Ursula, with more force than necessary, gripped Sylvia's hand and pulled her away from the door. The giant innkeeper nodded at Brontë but said nothing. Acting quickly, Brontë waved at the little party and then shut the door. She then scurried behind the window dressing to watch them.

From her concealed position, she sized up Bristol, who was as blocklike as his sister. He, however, was shorter, thicker, and more muscular. His neck bulged under his shirt collar. The brown suit he wore strained to contain his powerful figure. His face matched the brutishness of his form: deep, gray eyes were set under a heavy brow.

Brontë was delighted to see that the trio hadn't gone far once they left the front stoop. Sylvia had pulled away from Ursula's grip and now stood apart from the innkeeper and her brother, causing them to pause on the path directly in front of the cabin.

Crockett rose to come after Brontë, but his wife waved him away. She held up a hand for him to be quiet.

She pushed against the window with the hope that it would open. She had to restrain herself as she nearly squealed with pleasure when it gave way and she could hear the low voices of the party outside.

"—fraternizing with the guests." Brontë caught the very end of Ursula's speech.

Sylvia looked at the ground. Bristol stared at the young woman with an uncomfortable intensity.

"I'm sorry, ma'am," the young maid said. "I only was trying to be welcoming and sociable."

"Too sociable," Ursula said shortly. "You're German after all, so what is all this talking and social butterflying?! The guests are already speaking about the events from last night."

"Ma'am, I didn't say anything. Mr. Phipps—"

"Mr. Phipps nothing! I told you we are to keep what is happening quiet. The incident in town, the creature, and the children—it must be..." Ursula went white. Bristol gripped her arm. His eyes went to the window curtain behind which Brontë stood.

"German," he rasped. "There are no guests present! Speak German!" This was followed by a burst of angry, German speech.

Brontë, who had been mostly concealed behind the curtain, felt a surge of terror run through her. She turned fully away from the window, her heart pounding.

Sylvia looked back to the cabin. As she did so, Bristol grabbed her—a less forceful grip than he had used with Ursula, but still very sharp and quick—and pulled her toward the main lodge.

"What was it?" Crockett asked. His neck felt hot. His wife looked alarmed.

"Something is going on. The Deutschefabers…" Brontë slowed her breathing. She closed her eyes and regained her calm. "They were talking about 'the incident in town' and 'children.' They also mentioned the 'creature.'"

"Caddywampus!" A voice called from outside the window at the back of the cabin.

Crockett jumped. He turned toward the voice and walked tentatively toward the window that faced the woods. When he threw open the shutters, he saw the spherical figure of Phipps scribbling in a notebook, which the little man promptly hid behind his back.

"Phipps!" Crockett was aghast. "What are you doing?"

"I was writing and walking. I can't write about walking in the woods while walking without doing a lot of it. Anyway, she's talking about the Caddywampus. I just wanted to clarify. She hasn't started using the proper nomenclature yet."

Brontë came beside Crockett and slammed closed the shutters. "Please," she said through them, "be kind enough not to listen to our private conversations, Mr. Phipps!"

"Well, try not to have them so loudly, Mrs. Cook!" Phipps snorted.

Brontë's cheeks flushed. She slapped the shutters in hopes of scaring Phipps. When she turned back to Crockett, she saw that he was deep in thought. Her husband locked eyes with her and shook his head.

"Bondage sheep," he said softly.

"I'm sorry?" Brontë asked.

"Sylvia told me she has a bondage sheep which indicated something nefarious is going on here at the inn."

"Well," Brontë said, still terribly confused, "I don't know if you need an imprisoned sheep to tell you that something mysterious is afoot. With the murder in town, the creature, and now something with children, I don't know if we should ever trust Petrarch to recommend a holiday destination again."

"It may be better to stay on our little island of Britain moving forward…at least until we get to the bottom of this string of coincidences which puts us in the middle of lethal events."

The two were silent for a moment. Crockett walked over to the fallen elk head and attempted to lift it back onto the wall. When it crashed a second time, he gently shoved it into the corner. He decided it best to leave the repair to Bristol or Sylvia.

After giving up on the cabin maintenance, he returned to the sofa and found Brontë staring toward the window, deep in thought.

"What's on your mind, darling?" he asked.

Brontë hesitated. "Crockett…what if…I mean, the events surrounding us are not what we wanted for our honeymoon, but we do have experience in this realm. We solved the murders with Beatrice and the Mayweathers…" She tried to keep the excitement from her tone, but she could not hide the soft glow in her cheeks. The joy of another possible adventure was difficult to suppress.

Crockett was torn. He felt the tug of his bondage sheep, but he was also moved by the sight of Brontë on the cusp of another mystery.

"Darling, we can offer help, if—"

But Crockett did not have time to finish. Brontë, upon hearing agreement from Crockett, leapt from her seat and ran to the bedroom. She returned in seconds holding *Detectivating for the Dunce*, her eyes sparkling.

5

The Manageable Pursuit of a Demon Bear

"Let's see," Brontë said flipping through the pages of the book. "I suppose I should catch you up on what I've read so far."

"Who knew there was so much to learn?" Crockett marveled, not for the first time, at the massive tome in Brontë's arms. "After us successfully stumbling blindly toward mystery solutions in the past, I didn't think there would be this complicated a method to learn."

"It's positively massive, but I took notes." Brontë flipped through pages. After a moment, she paused and handed the book to Crockett. "Come to think of it, those would be a better place for you to start. I'll go get them. I'll be right back."

Crockett opened to the first page and began to read aloud.

"*If one is to detect with the powerful insight and keen perspicacity of the greats such as Sherlock Holmes or the stable of calm, brilliant, and focused men of Scotland Yard, they must first begin with an inward journey—this is not a journey of carriages or motorcars, but a deep, physiological, spiritual endeavor...*'" Crockett's voice faded. "This is very impractical."

"Why are all writers so verbose?" Brontë called from the other room. "Between Phipps and my cousin, I really don't think I need to ever meet another writer."

"I think after Phipps, I don't need to meet another American."

Brontë emerged from the bedroom with her small notebook. She flipped it open and scanned the pages.

"Let's see," she said. "The first eleven chapters were actually about spirituality, God, the reign of Charlemagne, Sir Arthur Conan Doyle, and Queen Victoria and then somewhere in part two, they took on more recognizable themes."

"Charlemagne?" Crockett's eyebrows raised. "What could he have to do with it?"

"I wish I could tell you. I skimmed very quickly. I think there was a lot of crime in the Holy Roman Empire."

"Leave it to the Holy Romans."

"That is what they say."[11]

Brontë suddenly stopped flipping through the pages of her notebook. She let out a proud, "Aha!" before settling down onto the sofa next to Crockett.

"As I mentioned in the woods," she said, "footprints are very important. Before we get to the shape of a brogue, however, we really should focus on the high-level items—physical evidence being prime in monster business like this."

Crockett ran a hand through his hair. "I see. I just…perhaps we should take a step farther back."

"Farther?"

"Brontë, I—well, you know I have a kind of premonition of something bad in this place."

"Yes."

"Promise me that we'll assess the *danger* before we get too far into things. I just worry…"

Brontë reached out and took her husband's hand. "Crockett, I think that's exceptionally wise. I'm only talking about Phipps and Sylvia's monster. We

---

[11] I did try to find any reference to this phrasing. At first, I thought it was a play on "When in Rome…" but I could find no connection. The closest thing I could find to the phrase was a 70's rock cover band called Levi and the Holy Romans, which plays frequently at the Cincinnati Gallery of Fine and Less Than Fine Art.

don't have the purview to solve anything regarding the strangling murder in town. I have a very hard time believing this creature exists—body of a bear and the face of a puma. It's a bit ridiculous."

Crockett brightened. "Indeed! There's no sense in getting in over our heads—again. Let's see if we can uncover what this 'beast' is that is terrorizing Sylvia and Phipps. Collanhall hunting it doesn't exactly give the creature credence. He made up words left and right this afternoon. I'm sure he's just as capable of making up monsters."

"And it's just polite—we can't have the other guests suspended in terror of some fictional creature! And we are very good at our heads being *overed* and still persevering," Brontë added eagerly.

"We've been lucky, I should say. But," Crockett grew grave again, "luck runs out."

It was after this ominous observation that a knock thumped upon the door.

Crockett gasped and fell off the couch in surprise. Brontë helped her husband up, then, stifling laughter, went to the door. She was puzzled to see no one present. She then noticed the distant lurching form of Ursula stalking away; it took a moment for her to discover mail left on the front mat of their entry.

"We've received correspondence," Brontë said.

Crockett scratched his ear. "Who could possibly be corresponding with us?"

Brontë shook her head. With a bit of apprehension, she unfolded the first bit of parchment to find that it was an invitation:

Welcome to the Finnlicht Festival.

There is an air of carnival and fun. (A very small air.)

Join us for an event for

all guests of The Deutschefaber Inn this evening in the main lodge.

Time: 6-8pm

All guests are required to stay on the main floor in the main hall or billiard room.

DO NOT go upstairs.

Hors d'oeuvres will be served with wine and local beer.

Please do not anticipate enjoying yourself too much.

"I feel this must have been written by Ursula. Not a single exclamation point. And the promise of a reprimand for going upstairs."

Crockett gently reached over and took the letter from his wife. In doing so, he inadvertently knocked a second letter from her grasp. Both were so intrigued with the invitation to the party that they didn't pay attention and quickly forgot about the second note falling to the ground and sliding under the sofa.

"Should we go?" Crockett asked.

Brontë's eyes were glowing with excitement. Crockett did not need an audible response. "That's a yes, then?"

Brontë already had a plan in mind. The gears in her mind spun rapidly. "It will be a wonderful opportunity for us to dip our toes into the waters of the inn's monster mystery. I bet all the guests will be there."

Crockett felt something of his old self in this conspiratorial moment. His fears from the morning vanished like fog in the morning light. "We can find out more from Sylvia and Phipps about what they saw," he said. "Collanhall will have more information as well. The wine and beer provided will loosen tongues."

"Indeed!" Brontë clapped her hands together. "Crockett, this will be a lark! No murder or danger, as you mentioned. We can simply pose some questions and find out what this beast is. I'm sure it's an overgrown bear with some twigs around its head."

"A bear with a crown!" Crockett smiled broadly.

"Yes!" Brontë gently kissed his cheek. "We should dress and prepare!" Brontë picked up the tray of untouched tea and biscuits and headed to the kitchen.

Alone in the sitting room, Crockett turned his thoughts to the mysterious creature on the cabin grounds. From his perspective, something had to be very real and very feral to scare Phipps and Sylvia and draw Collanhall to this region to hunt. It was odd that Petrarch never mentioned anything to Crockett or Brontë about it when he was pitching the inn for their honeymoon. Ursula and Bristol would most likely have the best information about the creature since they owned the inn and were familiar with the grounds.

Crockett suddenly gasped. He remembered the white hand visible at the top of the stairs.

"Brontë," he called quickly.

His wife peered out from the kitchen. "What's going on, Crockett? It's not another bad premonition, is it? I'm beginning to worry about your oppressed sheep."

"No," Crockett shook his head. "But I forgot to tell you about what I saw in the main lodge."

"You saw something?"

"Yes." Crockett felt guilty he withheld the information initially. Now that they had discussed the importance of keeping out of danger, the thin hand at the door was less threatening; the bounds of the mystery took on very firm and decidedly manageable contours. "Before we left the lodge, I saw someone."

"Not Ursula? Or Bristol?"

"No," Crockett said. The thin hand had not belonged to either the stalwart innkeeper or her short, muscled brother. "I'm not sure who it was. My thought is that it's the younger brother."

"Younger brother?" Brontë's eyes narrowed in thought. "We haven't heard of a younger brother."

"We haven't," Crockett said, "but he is in the painting over the fireplace."

Brontë clapped her hands. "Well done, Crockett! You're exhibiting a true, detectivesque eye for detail."

Crockett blushed. "I was trying to distract myself from your feud with Ursula. But I'm glad the distraction bore fruit."

"Ursula…" Brontë scoffed. She adjusted her brassiere under her shirt. "I think I let my temper get away from me. I don't see you falling for such a stolid woman."

"It's not possible." Crockett smiled. "Not when I have you waiting."

Brontë flushed. She pulled a strand of hair behind her ear. The compliment further inspired her plan for the evening. "What about this?"

she asked. "We'll talk to the guests and find out if any of them know more about the *Dämonenbär*. This could be wrapped up quickly if Collanhall knows as much as…well, as *he* thinks he does."

"A very good plan."

"If there is a need for further insights, we can contemplate finding the youngest Deutschefaber. We know Bristol and Ursula won't speak of the creature. They nearly brained Sylvia for mentioning it to the other guests. If the other lodgers are as guarded or don't know anything, the younger brother may be able to shed light on the truth."

"Brilliant!" Crockett rushed forward and caught his wife in an embrace. "That book has done wonders. You're so methodical. I have no reason to fear with you on the case."

Brontë kissed him lightly on the cheek. "In that case, I shall go prepare for the fête."

Crockett bowed. "Milady."

When Brontë left the room, Crockett picked up the detectivating book. He flipped through its many pages, growing overwhelmed as he took in chapter titles like "Chemistry for the Detectivator" and "Phrenology: Why Large Foreheads Are to Be Feared." It was at the end of the massive tome that he came across an appendix of acronyms. What struck him wasn't their inclusion but their ridiculousness. Among "International Police Organizations" he saw CHOCLIT, BISKIT, and FART listed as regional monikers in central Europe.

At that moment, the elk head, which Crockett thought was adequately out of the way in the corner, toppled over onto its side with a loud thud. He started and turned toward the noise. In the fading light, the head took on a terrifying appearance. Red light from the setting sun caught its glossy eye, which shone from the growing shadows of their darkening cabin.

"Maybe," Crockett said recovering from the surprise, "we do have a reason or two to fear."

6

Everybody Inn

The fête at the main lodge carried the atmosphere of a funeral. Ursula Deutschefaber stood near the grand staircase, arms behind her back, resembling an aloof vulture. Her eyes roved, unemotionally, over all the guests. Should one approach her with a smile, she would mirror the action and say "Guten" and little else.[12]

Her brother, Bristol, added to the mournful air with his black suit and matching midnight-colored bowler. At the beginning of the party, he was more active than his sister, approaching guests and gruffly asking them about their stay. It was during this fit of sociability that he approached Sylvia and the two engaged in an intense discussion. After that exchange, Bristol grew withdrawn, standing to the side of the party and frequently checking his pocket watch. After a short time, he left. Sylvia soon drifted away as well, wiping her eyes as if she had been crying.

Phipps proved to be a more difficult individual to track. He flew from guest to guest like a gnat, zipping between them in the main hall and the billiard room. Crockett saw him grabbing an appetizer at the check-in desk and then, almost instantaneously, appearing at the elbow of the colonel,

---

[12] Didiert originally drafted this chapter for Earhart. He called it an "abstract collage of clues." In it, he listed pages of untagged dialogue for the reader to sort through and figure out their meaning. Cubesy McGillicuddy was especially chatty in this scene. Between his backward dialogue and Collanhall's raving, it was more than a chore to get through.

chatting about "the Caddywampus" and his preposterous book.

His campaign to rename the beast took root, which irritated Brontë and Crockett; they had no connection to the moniker but hated the priggish gentleman winning his rhetorical endeavor. The whisperings and mutterings that met their own ears referred to the beast by the American's new title. The positive side of this development was that people were already discussing the monster, so Brontë and Crockett did not need any elaborate talking points to draw out the other guests' thoughts.

Their line of inquiry started with the first set of lodgers they had not met. The Gestahlts were a quiet, Eastern European family who spoke very little English. The most jarring thing about them was their pitch-black hair. In and of itself the color was not odd, but that the exact shade of black was shared across the family showed an extreme hereditary propensity for this hair color. Father, mother, and both children tried eagerly to communicate with Brontë and Crockett, but the language barrier made it difficult.

"Hullo, you guest also?" Mr. Gestahlt appeared to be very young, likely the same age as Brontë and Crockett, and very boyish in appearance. The newlyweds were taken with his bright, warm smile. His skin was smooth and almost startlingly white. From under the unkempt sweep of his black hair, his eyes shone a deep, oceanic blue. "We come far from Sorbia to see lights. Beautiful! I am Viktor and this wife, Ambrosia. She love buggies with the shiny backside."

"Sorbia?" Crockett tapped his chin with his finger. "Serbia do you mean?"

"Sorbia," Mr. Gestahlt said quickly.

Mrs. Gestahlt nodded profusely and added a short, clipped, "Yes!" This was quickly followed by "Love buggies!" She appeared a bit older than Mr. Gestahlt but just as endearing in her bearing. She had high cheekbones and a bronze complexion, as if she had just come from Italy or Spain.

The children danced between their parents. They were a spirited pair, a boy and girl both about seven or eight years old. It appeared they could not remain still even if they were to be chained in place. After a moment at rest, they would resume activity at double the rate as when they stopped.

Crockett watched them scamper away toward the billiard room of the lodge then turned and spoke. "We are looking forward to the festival ourselves," he said.

Brontë saw the other unmet guest, an older, stately woman enter the party. With a small curtsey and a polite "Excuse me," she left Crockett and the Gestahlts and went to introduce herself.

Crockett tried to continue the discussion with the young couple. He learned very little except Mr. Gestahlt was a machinist and his two children were named Ava and Adon. Mrs. Gestahlt exhausted 50 percent of her own English vocabulary with her earlier "Yes!" and "Love buggies!" The other half consisted of "How do you do?" and "You don't say!"

When pleasantries were exhausted, Crockett did his best to address the creature in the woods. He ventured the question after a particularly long lull in conversation and Mrs. Gestahlt's third "How do you do?"

"Did you hear about the *Dämonenbär?*" he asked.

The question was no sooner out of his mouth than Phipps appeared at his elbow, the little man even more pugnacious than he'd been that afternoon. A small bit of mayonnaise from the sandwiches was stuck to his cheek and his breath reeked of gin.

"Caddywampus?" he asked loudly. "I do say, what do you know? You know I know I saw it. I did. Harrowing experience. I was quite heroic. You can ask the maid."

"You don't say!" Mrs. Gestahlt said fervently nodding.

Mr. Gestahlt's eyes went wide. "You see it?" he asked nervously. "Here?"

"Yes!" Phipps said. "Last night when I was brilliancing about, I encountered it with the maid, Miss..." he hesitated, "Miss Vinddybimmsel."

"Vindrikimmel." Crockett grunted.

"Yes, that." Phipps licked his lips. His eyes swept the room. "She's not here, but we saw it. It was huge and ghastly!"

"Ghastly!" Now it was Collanhall interjecting. The towering colonel stomped into their social circle. His eyes were narrowed as if ready to pounce on someone or something. "Phipps told me all about it. His description, more or less, matches what I have been researching."

"Half elk," Phipps said.

"Half bear," Collanhall added.

"And half puma." Phipps hiccupped after this was out.

Mrs. Gestahlt shook her head. "How do you do…" she said morosely.

"Quite well," Collanhall said with a short bow to the young mother. "But that creature won't be half as well when I get my hands on it."

"You fight it?" Mr. Gestahlt shook his head in disbelief. His black hair flopped from side to side. "It frightening—scary!"

"Ha ha! We'll see about that!" Collanhall puffed out his large chest to accentuate this statement.

He was so loud that Ursula took note of their discussion from her perch by the stairs. Her lips pursed and she stepped closer to hear their discourse.

"Well," Collanhall continued, "if you can take a mudslack down in a swamp, then you can take a Caddywampus down in a forest, am I right?"

"You don't say!" Mrs. Gestahlt responded.

"I do say, my dear!" Collanhall rolled up his sleeves. "Now if you want to catch a mudslack, then you've got to go for their—pardon the expression—sexual piping."[13]

"Sexual piping?" Crockett blushed doubly, once for the mention of the word *sexual* and secondly because, despite several recent, post-marital encounters with Brontë that he deemed successful, he had no idea what sexual piping was.

"Yes, one must always maneuver to the sexual piping. Have you never hunted mudslacks before?" Collanhall turned to Phipps and Mr. Gestahlt as if Crockett had exposed himself as a failure of masculinity. The other two men did not respond to his question. Gestahlt had lost comprehension at the word "mudslack," meanwhile Phipps, through the lens of several gins, saw the approach of Ursula Deutschefaber as an act of overt flirtation. He smiled and waved to the hulking innkeeper as she approached their small party.

"Hello," she said coldly.

---

[13] Earhart very clearly entered a love affair at some point in the construction of this novel. Amorous pursuits are referred to with frequency throughout the text.

Ursula's sudden appearance behind him made Collanhall jump. The colonel and innkeeper were nearly the same height, but Ursula had nearly twenty pounds on the ex-military man.

"I came to see that you are all doing well." She crossed her arms. The statement seemed more a threat than an inquiry into their well-being.

Phipps, still not sensing the menace behind Ursula's words said, "Much better now that you are here, my dear."

Ursula shuddered. "Mr. Phipps, please refrain from amorous intentions toward me. I have no interest in anyone in the present company, except Mr. Cook, but he is spoken for."

The entire party appraised Crockett, who had turned the color of a plum. "Yes," he said softly, "taken."

"Indeed." Ursula sniffed to show that the matter was fully resolved. "I also heard," her lips pursed slightly, "that you were discussing the *Dämonenbär*."

"Caddywampus." This was spoken by everyone, including Crockett, who grew angry with himself immediately after saying it.

"Yes." Ursula, for the first time, looked surprised. "Well, I can assure you it is nothing but a local rumor. After speaking with Miss Vindrikimmel today, she admits she was out of sorts. She has been known," Ursula put a hand to her mouth as if to divulge a secret but did not lower her voice, "to nip brandy before bed, so I can assure you the story she shared with you was quite exaggerated."

"Exaggerated!" Phipps pushed out his belly in indignation. His amorous interest in Ursula appeared to vaporize. "Madame Deutschefaber, your maid may be a lush, but I am a very lucid drunk and I know what I saw! It was a *creature*. I'm not sure of what making, but I am sure it was not a *natural* animal."

"And," Collanhall said quickly, "his description matches all of those from my guidebooks. A half elk, half bear, half puma."

Ursula clasped her hands in front of her. "You may believe what you want, but I can assure you, you are completely incorrect."

"Maybe," Mr. Gestahlt started, "you all right. Maybe a big bear. Maybe scary but not monster."

Phipps put a finger to his mouth in contemplation. "That," he said after some thought, "is a possibility I could entertain."

Ursula nodded. "That is what I'm saying. You can get mauled by a bear in these woods, but there is certainly nothing mythological."

No one quite knew if they were supposed to feel better about this prospect, but, regardless, the general air grew less tense.

Ursula's presence sucked the frivolity from the gathering. After her entry into the conversation, everyone scattered to different pursuits. Collanhall, Mr. Gestahlt, and Phipps attended the bar; Mrs. Gestahlt was forced to pursue her children, who had found the hors d'oeuvres and looked to be attacking them with all the politeness of two wild boars; and Crockett joined his wife and the elderly woman on the sofa.

This last guest was an ancient dame with a polished, regal air. She must have known of the funereal tone of German parties as she wore an all-black dress and hat. Her tightly pinned, silver hair was swept up under her headwear's large and ostentatious form. Perched atop the towering hat was a papier-mâché raven. Brontë had just returned from the bar with a glass of sherry for the old woman. She introduced the behatted septuagenarian to Crockett as Greta van der Raaf from the Netherlands.

"Thank you, Mrs. Cook," Greta said, her voice soft yet confident. Her dulcet tones were a far cry from the operatic crooning of Corinthiana Hawsfeffer, the other elder stateswoman in their lives, Brontë's grandmother. "It is so nice to find young people who keep respectful airs for their elders."

"Crockett and I are both very attached to the elders in our families. We tried to get our dear," Brontë hesitated, trying to find the right word to describe the close, yet non-familial relationship with Crockett's master, "*uncle*, Petrarch, to join us for this vacation, but he refrained."

At this, Madame van der Raaf's eyes glowed brightly. "Well, if you two are honeymooning, it's best to be alone. Then you can be free and wild.[14] I don't blame him for not joining you."

––––––––––––––––––

[14] As mentioned before, Earhart was clearly "getting some" as we'd say in the modern parlance.

Brontë flushed. Crockett, although flabbergasted himself, quickly spoke to help turn the direction of the conversation from yet more discourse on sexual piping. "Yes, well, what brings you to Praktisch, ma'am?"

"Ah!" Greta nodded. "As you can see, I'm very old." She paused and stared at the young couple. It took several moments before they realized it was polite to deny this.

"Oh, no!" Brontë said.

"I'd never say ancient," Crockett added.

"Ancient!" Madame van der Raaf hissed. "Who said ancient?"

"No one!" said Brontë.

"They'd be a lunatic to!" Crockett said.

This pleased Madame van der Raaf's vanity, so she continued with more warmth. "Since I am still able, I'm taking a few last adventures before my time on this earth ends. Most of my life has been…full of waiting with a bit of remorse. I'm trying to take advantage of the last of my golden years."

"Remorse?" Brontë's detective instincts flared. There was slim possibility this old woman was connected to a woodland monster, but any clue was an asset at this juncture.

"Yes, my dear." Madame van der Raaf put her hand on her heart in an earnest display of emotion. "Even though you both appear to be rather dull, you will find you can still do a great many things to regret."

"Dull?" Crockett asked.

Madame van der Raaf ignored the question. She was already speaking again. "I hope to…find someone," she said. "I'm not sure if we'll be to connect."

Brontë was on high alert now. She cleared her throat and was about to inquire into this certain *someone*, when Crockett interrupted.

"Madame, have you heard anything about a creature in the woods here?"

"Ha ha!" The old woman's laugh was shockingly precise, the *ha*'s each clipped to a staccato sound, nearly as short and reliable as the tick of a clock. "It's all poppycock and nonsense." She lifted the sherry to her lips and drained it in one gulp. "To be honest, it's all I've heard about since I've gotten here. That foul little man with the piggish face accosted me upon arrival to tell me about it."

Crockett and Brontë exchanged an amused look.

"What does *concern* me," Madame van der Raaf continued, "is the missing children. That is an odd coincidence."

"Missing children?" Crockett's face turned white. He wiped his brow with the back of his hand. He now understood Ursula's mention of "children" in her earlier diatribe in front of their cabin.

"Yes." The old dame's eyes flicked between the young couple. "You didn't hear? There were two children missing in town. They were charity cases, in the orphanage. Allegedly, they were beautiful little blond cherubs. Now, I don't care for children—needy, nasty things—but with the legends about the beast…you know, others may jump to conclusions"

As if the two Gestahlt children heard Madame van der Raaf speak ill of their kind, they launched onto the sofa at that exact moment, landing between Crockett and the old woman.

Mrs. Gestahlt came forward in a rush. She appeared more disheveled than she had upon her arrival at the party. Her pinned hair was loose. Perspiration decorated her brow from the pursuit of the children.

"Love buggies!" She tried to keep the matronly anger from her voice but was losing the battle.

Adon, the boy, grabbed Madame van der Raaf's sherry glass and hurled it against the wall. The old woman's neck bulged like a bullfrog. A white froth appeared at the edges of her mouth.

"Chiiilllddreeeeeennnn," she hissed.

Brontë and Crockett slipped away from the sofa and stood to the side of the room near the great fireplace. Crockett assessed the locations of the guests to be sure no one would overhear their conversation. There was no need for concern. Phipps, Collanhall, and Mr. Gestahlt were growing very drunk. Collanhall appeared to be fake wrestling Mr. Gestahlt, his arm gripping the young man's neck. Additionally, things continued to escalate with Madame van der Raaf and the children. The old woman was straddled on the sofa, both children trying to pull the papier-mâché raven from her hat. Even Ursula had let her guard down. The innkeeper was wiping dust from a table in the back corner of the room.

"Missing children—orphans," Brontë said softly. "Crockett... I..."

"I think perhaps a coincidence." Crockett tried to sound optimistic, but his stomach plummeted when the old woman mentioned the lost little ones. The dread he felt upon their arrival roared back with even greater force. "It couldn't...I mean...Madame van der Raaf mentioned a legend, I just think..."

Brontë turned her attention to the staircase at the back of the room. It was a grand wooden structure, clearly carved specifically for the inn. The spindles took the forms of twisted vines and jovial woodland creatures. The kind carvings, however, belied a menacing journey should one proceed upward. Although the bottom was bathed in the warm light of the horned chandelier, the further Brontë's eyes ascended, the deeper the shadows and mystery met her gaze. At the top, it was completely dark. From her position, it appeared one could choose to go right or left, taking them to an assortment of rooms on either side of the main, cavernous hall.

"Darling," she said, "we haven't learned much this evening. I think we pursue our final thread of interest: the youngest Deutschefaber."

Her husband looked at her intently. As before, Brontë looked alive and alert, whilst Crockett had the appearance of one who'd just eaten a basket of spoiled meat.

He took in a deep breath, trying not to give away the trepidation he had had about everything associated with their holiday since stepping off the train. "Ursula clearly was serious about her directive keeping us from the second floor." They both looked at the staircase blocked by the stalwart innkeeper. Despite her dusting, she remained alert, throwing intermittent glances over her shoulder to be sure no one approached the stair. After assessing the innkeeper, Crockett turned and looked intensely at Brontë. "What plan did you have for meeting this young man?"

7

The Search

Brontë scanned the room once more to be certain no one was focused on their conversation. To her relief, everyone remained occupied. She and Crockett were far from the center of attention, as the others had all escalated their mischief: Phipps stood on the hotel check-in desk reciting a poem, Greta had gotten on her feet and was being pursued by Mrs. Gestahlt with Adon and Ava, and Ursula had ceased dusting and was assessing a second table near the stairs which appeared a bit wobbly.

"Crockett," she said watching Ursula flip over the small table for further inspection, "perhaps we can use your masculine charms in our pursuits."

Crockett followed Brontë's gaze. "Oh…" he said. His face warmed. "Brontë, I thought you were angry about Ursula's overt interest in me."

Brontë smiled. "Crockett, I trust you. You said she's not a threat to our relationship. My confidence was further renewed when I saw her flip over that table. She also smells slightly of aged vermouth. And," Brontë winked, "I can offer you something, as Madame van der Raaf said, 'free and wild' for your efforts when this is all done."

Crockett's heart pounded in his chest. He nearly forgot his brewing dread as his thoughts focused on their future rendezvous in the cabin.

It was a stroke of luck that Phipps, still in the middle of his recitation, let out one of his disgusting grocks and shook Crockett from his stupor.

Despite his nerves, he felt that the quest to reach the second floor carried only limited stakes. The worst thing that could happen was Brontë's discovery and a scolding from Ursula.

He gripped Brontë's hand. "You promise you'll be careful. There's little threat here, but…just be safe, please."

"Of course," Brontë squeezed Crockett's hand. "We need to distract her… Do you…"

"Believe it or not, I have a plan." Crockett eyed a bottle of wine sitting on the front desk. "I'll be right back. When I have her pulled away, go do your sleuthing and see if the youngest Deutschefaber knows anything about the monster."

"I shall sleuth my heart out."

He readied himself, taking a deep breath and focusing his attention on his new mission. When he felt centered, he made his way to the front desk.

As he approached, Phipps—staying true to his gnat-like presence—leapt off the table and bounded into the billiard room, leaving what was left of the child-boar-eaten appetizers and wine unattended. Crockett was relieved he'd avoided another conversation with the disgusting author and merrily poured himself and Ursula glasses of spätburgunder.

While carrying the wine across the main hall, he peeked into the billiard room. Mr. Gestahlt, Phipps, and Collanhall were ferociously depleting the hard liquor stored there. Gestahlt appeared the least drunk but still very merry. Gripped by Collanhall, the group of three swayed merrily to some unknown song. It appeared that this bit of dancing was inspired by the presence of a piano which Crockett had not seen. It sat at the opposite end of the room from the billiard table. Despite no one playing the instrument, it moved the three men to use their own, woefully out-of-tune voices to accompany their movements.

Crockett could not help but laugh to himself as Phipps began making up lyrics and the entourage sped their swaying. This bit of mirth was interrupted when he turned away and Ursula Deutschefaber entered his direct line of sight. A shiver of panic rumbled down the young man's spine.

"My goodness," he whispered to himself, sweat forming on his palms. "I had a plan, but…."

Had Ursula not looked up from her work on the table and seen him, Crockett most likely would have diverted his course and abandoned the task altogether. As it was, however, he found himself sweating profusely, shaking slightly, and staring into the cloudy, green eyes of the matronly innkeeper.

"Hu-hu-hello…gruten! Gutenlo, mademoiselle." Crockett marveled at his own incompetence, having mangled three languages in one greeting.

Ursula stared at him blankly. "Can I inquire as to why you are approaching me, Mr. Cook? As I recall, your wife was very upset about my casual mention of your devastatingly good looks earlier this afternoon."

"*Devastatingly?*" Crockett blanched. Never one to earn any compliments, this one nearly knocked him off his feet. "Would one call my looks *devastating?*"

"A hot-blooded female would, I should say."

Brontë, watching this interaction from across the room, began to doubt sending Crockett on this mission. In the abstract, a mild flirtation with a woman who resembled a blocky shrub was a good idea. Seeing it play out, however, was making her scalp itch with jealousy.

"Well," Ursula looked at the two glasses of wine in Crockett's hands. "Is that second drink for your wife, me, or are you prone to excessive drunkenness?"

Crockett forgot he was carrying wine. He looked at it in surprise. "Oh! Yes, it's for you, I suppose. I saw you working and…well, I felt bad about the earlier altercation with Brontë." He extended the glass, his hand shaking from his nerves. A bit of wine leapt up in the glass and threatened to fall onto the wooden floor.

Ursula lunged forward and grabbed it from his hand. "Mr. Cook!" she shrieked. "Please, be careful with the wine. We want to avoid any spills in the main room."

"Terribly…terribly sorry."

"Yes, it is a magnet for spills and stains. Some lodgers have even imbibed too much and regurgitated in a number of places—the fireplace, the bathroom, the front stoop—one gentleman from Portugal excreted feces in the grand piano."

Crockett's face turned green. "Oh, well…yes, I'll be very careful." He paused, considering this deluge of information. "How," he asked finally, "does one clean an…excrement-filled piano?"

"Oh, Mr. Cook…" Ursula grew radiant. She took a drink of her wine; her eyes sparkled. "It is a time-consuming, laborious process." The word *laborious* brought a passionate flush to her cheeks on par with the one elicited by Crockett. "Would you like me to walk you through it? I'd be delighted. Very few individuals even ask after the nuance of cleaning excrement—it's both an art and a science. There's so much to it. Follow me, please!"

Ursula stormed away from him and toward the billiard room. Crockett, shocked by how quickly his non-plan succeeded, threw a glance at Brontë. His wife's expression when their eyes met was a mixture of awe, jealousy, and confusion. Having overheard the exchange, she was unsure how to feel.

"Mr. Cook!" Ursula bellowed from the billiard room. "Bring my wrench when you come. I'll require it for the de-excrementing."

"Yes!" Crockett tried to suppress the disgust in his voice. He turned to Brontë and mouthed the word *Go!*

Brontë hesitated a moment longer near Crockett. They were both fearful of the extent to which Ursula would take the cleaning simulation. Brontë was also not fully certain the burly maiden wouldn't charm her husband in some…odd way.

"AND THE HAMMER, MR. COOK!" Ursula yelled.

"Go! Now!" Crockett shooed Brontë away. He picked up an assortment of Ursula's tools and ran into the billiard room. "Coming, Ursula!"

Ursula's yelling drew the attention of those not in the billiard room. Adon and Ava ceased their irritation of Madame van der Raaf and sprinted after the innkeeper. Mrs. Gestahlt followed, as did Greta, who shook her empty sherry glass and muttered "I need another" as she tottered toward the bar.

Brontë found herself alone on the grand staircase, her hands wrapped around the soft wood of the banister. A thrum of excitement tremored from her heart and shivered through her body. She stilled her breathing then raced quickly up the stairs.

At the top, she assessed her choice of going to the right or left. The upstairs was a horseshoe shape with a small corridor at the top of the stair that led to a row of rooms on both sides of the main hall. Once she chose a direction, she could turn a corner and be obscured from any prying eyes below. Nervous someone would return to the main room before she could decide which way to go, she turned rapidly to the right.

Once she was around the corner and in the dark passage, she took a moment to breathe. She peeked back into the main hall to check that no one was in pursuit.

"What am I doing?" she muttered, pressing herself against the wall of the shadowed corridor. "What if I find the younger Deutschefaber? What do I say? 'Tell us about your monster?' I don't even have a lamp to get down these halls."

These thoughts and her lack of foresight to bring a candle made her feel ridiculous. She may have turned back, had it not been for her seeing a pale glow emanating from the farthest end of the corridor. It was the dim shine of a candle coming from a crack under the last door.

"Hello?" she whispered into the dark.

She looked over her shoulder again with the feeling that she was being pursued. After observing the emptiness of her surroundings, she assured herself she was still alone and crept toward the dim light. Each step she took felt as if it brought her no nearer to her goal. The hall extended forever. By the time she arrived at the end, her face was flushed and her palms were drenched with sweat.

She stood outside the door contemplating her next action. She was torn whether to knock or peer in. It would be rude to peek in on the other Deutschefaber if he were sleeping; however, a knock may make the young man raise an alarm.

But would the knocking alarm be more manageable than a peeking-in alarm?

"If only I'd read more of the detective book…"[15]

Choosing to peek in, she took a deep breath and placed her hand against the door. Slowly, she pushed it forward. As the portal drifted open, she sighed with relief. The room was empty. Lined with boxes of linens and amenities, it appeared to be a large storage closet. Looking around the small room, she took a moment to laugh at her trepidation.

"Linens and towels, nothing in the least bit terrifying."

She perused the folded sheets for a moment, running her fingers over the coarse fabric. When she'd traversed the tiny room, her eyes fell on the candle.

It was then she had a sudden, rational realization that sent a chill down her spine. The candle was freshly lit. A match next to it still emitted a sulfuric odor and a curling stream of smoke. Whether it was the mysterious other Deutschefaber or someone else, a human presence had been here moments before her.

She spun away from the candle and turned toward the door. Her breath came in ragged gasps as the full stupidity of her actions became clear.

No sleuthing was required to solve the mystery of who lit the candle. The figure appeared in the threshold.

It was Bristol Deutschefaber.

He stood in the dim light, a malevolent presence in the tiny room. In closer proximity, his appearance was more fearsome than he'd appeared earlier. He wore a white undershirt which clung to his body; his thick arms rippled with knotted cords of muscle. Around his left bicep was tied a vivid green and gold handkerchief.

Brontë tried to speak. "Hello, I—I—I—"

Bristol's jaw flexed. He stared at the young woman with beady, narrow eyes. "Guests are to stay downstairs," he said. His voice was a low, throaty growl.

---

[15] The book contains a chapter entitled "Practical Tips for Sleuthing in Murderous Manor Homes." Under the topic *What to do when encountering a door behind which may lie a mysterious stranger*, it recommends making the sound of a cat to draw out the unknown person.

"I was trying to find something." Brontë's voice quaked. "I saw the light…"

Bristol cracked his knuckles. In the dim light of the candle's flame, Brontë saw his tongue snake out of his mouth and lick his lips. "You were snooping. And around here," he snarled, "we don't care for snoops."

8

The Myth of the Demon Bear

Brontë closed her eyes in terror, expecting to feel the violent strike of Bristol's hand on her face. When several seconds passed and there was no act of aggression, she opened her eyes and looked at the squat, muscled man.

"Pathetic," he said through barred teeth. "You English fear everything."

"I… Mr. Deutschefaber, I can assure you it was an honest mistake—"

"Get out."

"I merely came up—"

"Go."

Brontë again closed her eyes in fear. This time Bristol's firm grasp closed on her wrist. He pulled her from the small room and pushed her into the hall.

"Don't let me catch you looking around this place again." He slammed his fist against the door frame of the storage closet.

Brontë retreated.

She tried her best to keep her wits about her, but each moment she attempted to restore her logical facilities, she felt the phantom grasp of Bristol's cold hand around her wrist or saw the glint of his menacing stare from the shadows. It was with a faster pace than she intended that she stormed down the stairs and returned to the main hall.

The rest of the party was preoccupied in the billiard room and bar. The only person who saw her descend from the second floor was the Gestahlt's little boy, Adon, whose hands were full of the last of the hors d'oeuvres.

He stared at her blankly. Their gazes remained locked on each other for some time. Mrs. Gestahlt finally broke the tension when she entered from the billiard room.

"How do you do!" she called.

Brontë jumped with surprise at these words. She muttered a response to Mrs. Gestahlt and feigned a smile.

The awkward moment left no impression on Mrs. Gestahlt, however. She was preoccupied with her son. She gently ushered Adon toward the front door. The irascible boy broke free from her, but she eventually corralled him through the entry. The door closed behind them with a flurry of Serbian (Sorbian?) reprimands.

Once they were gone, Brontë took a moment to calm herself. Her hands still trembled; her heart thudded at uneven intervals. The detective book left out the emotional side to detectivating. She could know everything about Charlemagne but nothing about being faced with a cruel, angry man in a dark closet.

It was in this state of shock and distress that Crockett and Ursula found her; Crockett returned to his wife with a much keener understanding of the effects of bowel movements on the workings of pianos.

"Hello, darling," he said warmly as they crossed the room.

When he caught sight of Brontë's face, however, he stopped. There were few times he had seen her look so tortured. "Brontë—"

But Brontë shook her head and smiled. Simply seeing his reassuring face made her countenance glow with relief. "Hello, Crockett. I've grown tired, could we go?"

Ursula assessed the young woman with interest. "Are you feeling ill, Mrs. Cook? You look as if you've seen a ghost."

"No, I need to use the lavatory cand—"

"Ahh!" Ursula nodded. "Travel constipation has turned you into a feces-filled apparition. It happens to many of our guests. I may have something in the medicine cabinet for you. Please, once it takes effect, stay away from the piano."

"No, no, no." Brontë had not felt ill before, but a feeling of sickness swelled after the innkeeper's monologue. "I will be fine. I think I'm exhausted from the travel."

Crockett gently took Brontë's hand. It trembled in his grip. Her skin felt cold. "Are you really all right, love?"

"Yes," Brontë forced a smile. "Yes, I'll be fine."

"Very good!" Ursula swept her arm to the exit. "It is best you are leaving, as it is approaching eight o'clock and we must end things before the men get too carried away with the liquor." Ursula turned and took a large step toward the billiard room. She suddenly stopped and spun again toward Brontë and Crockett. "Mrs. Cook, I believe you'll be delighted to hear that after an evening with your husband, I have lost my amorous interest in him. While he still has the look of a horse-faced angel, his skill with a hammer wilts my affectionate spirit."

"Yes." Brontë said, unsure of how to respond. Ursula was about to turn and leave, when Brontë suddenly had an idea. The fog of fear lifted under the presence of Crockett's gentle spirit; her logical faculties returned. "Ursula," she said quickly, "while I was waiting, I noticed the painting above the fireplace. I assume it's your family."

Ursula's mouth tightened into a thin line. Once again, it looked as if an event of toxic flatulence occurred near her. "Yes," she said softly.

Brontë grew nervous at the shift in her mood. "Well, I saw you and Bristol, but I was curious about the third child in the picture. Is it another brother?"

Ursula's eyes flicked to the painting. To Brontë's surprise, a hint of a smile pulled at the woman's taught mouth. "Yes," she said after a moment's pause. "That is our youngest brother, Klaude. A very kind boy." She said no more. Then, with a surge of urgency, she strode out of the sitting room and into the billiard room.

Once she was gone, Crockett lifted his wife's face and looked into her eyes. "Are you sure you're fine?"

"Yes, I'll tell you—"

"EVERYONE OUT!" Ursula's deep voice bellowed from the billiard room.

"IT'S EIGHT O'CLOCK AND THIS IS NOT AN IRISH PUB!"[16]

There was a clatter and surge of chatter as the guests began to leave.

"We should go quickly," Crockett said. "The Gestahlts and Collanhall left but Phipps is in a state, and I don't want to get caught walking home with him." He thought for a moment. "Or Madame van der Raaf. After a few sherries she's turned into quite the ladle."

Brontë nodded vigorously in agreement.

Sylvia had prepared lamps on the main desk to be used to guide their paths home. Crockett grabbed one in hopes to escape before Phipps, however, the little man miraculously was at his elbow before they were able to flee.

"I'll walk you home!" Phipps's speech was slurred, so that he sounded like an inebriated snake. His eyes were glassy. "I did wanna sssay sssorry for the earlier sssenophobic insultsss about your beautiful language. I get carried away you sssee. A writer isss prone to esssenitrisssity…essannysssissy…esssentrattiesss…" Having failed to successfully say "eccentricities," the little man ceased speaking and filled the silence with a pronounced "GROCK!" He then barreled on, "But I underssstand if you were offended by my intelligensss and critique of your languagessss."

Crockett had no idea how to respond to this non-apology. "I… suppose we were offended," he said.

"Ahhhhhhhh! Can't blame you. Little witsss have little toleransss for critique," Phipps said. This was punctuated by a hiccup.

The party of three exited the lodge and proceeded down the front steps. Phipps teetered as they walked. At one point, he caught himself nearly falling forward into a faceplant. When he successfully righted his balance, he took off his glasses and studied them as if they were the cause of his current state.

The obnoxious writer's tottering forced him to focus on his own walking rather than additional insults to the British, so Brontë and Crockett enjoyed

---

[16] Cubsey McGillicuddy had a rousing, romantic speech about Ireland here to counter Ursula's prejudice. Once again it was written backwards, so I'll leave you with the summary of its spirit: selur dnalerI!

a majority of their walk in silence.

Crockett used the lull in conversation to examine their surroundings.

The main room of cabin one, the Gestahlt's lodging, was already dark. Crockett imagined a family with two young children greatly enjoyed moments of peace when they were available. A shadow appeared in the window as they came close to the small building. Crockett waved. The shadowy form hesitated before waving back then rapidly pulled the curtains closed.

Both Brontë and Crockett were perturbed when Phipps passed his own cabin with the intent of walking them all the way back to theirs.

"We can manage the walk, Mr. Phipps," Brontë tried desperately to keep the rage from her voice. "With all that's going on, we don't want to expose you to undue risk."

"Nonssssense!" Phipps honked. "In fact, I ssshould take thisss opportunity to dessscribe the idea of my book, which I know you're desssperate to hear about. It'sss all right if you're embarasssed to assk, I'm not perturbed in interessst in my work, which isss quite exssseptional. My mother alwaysss mentionsss how my geniusss isss a *presssence* in the world..."

"Phippsy!" A thunderous voice rang out in front of them. "You owe me a nip of American whiskey!"

Phipps hiccupped and squinted into the dark. Colonel Collanhall bounded toward them. Other than his red cheeks, the military man betrayed no traits of drunkenness.

"Good evening!" he bellowed. "Ran back home for a private moment—all that talk of the piano got my own bowels moving. It appears the party has disbanded."

Crockett gently mimed for him to be quiet and pointed at the Gestahlt cabin.

"Ah, yes!" The colonel was a poor whisperer, his reduced volume barely differentiated from his standard bullhorn tone. "People asleep! I forget we're not alone out here. Usually when I'm out hunting, I'm in complete isolation."

Brontë could not help slapping her face in frustration as the colonel joined them on their walk. He and Phipps began talking over each other, both having conversations in which the other was not participating.

"You can't beat this night air!" the colonel proclaimed.

"Well, the core of my book, it'sss heart isss…" Phipps continued.

In the end it was almost pleasant, the competing conversations creating a nice harmony in the night with the colonel's dull roar of a voice underpinned by Phipps's nasally, drunken drone.

Crockett glanced to their neighboring cabin. No light shone from the windows. Madame van der Raaf may have taken a moment in the main lodge before returning home. Hopefully, Sylvia would be able to walk her back in the dark; the old woman was no doubt exhausted after her raucous evening being chased by the Gestahlt children. As he gazed down the row of cabins, he hoped the colonel and Phipps would retire to the colonel's cabin so that he and Brontë could have a quiet conversation about Brontë's discoveries in peace.

He was shocked, however, after his musings to refocus his attention and hear Phipps and the colonel having a conversation which interested him.

"I've seen nothing out here," the colonel said quietly (truly this time, his voice was nearly hushed). "Didn't want to mention it so close to the children's cabin—don't need to scare them."

"Nothing?" Phipps appeared disappointed. "Not even a bear or a big rabbit?"

"Indeed," the colonel nodded. "Since you and the maid saw it last night, I was hoping it had grown brazen, but I did a bit of searching this afternoon and this evening and found nothing."

"Hmmm…" Phipps puckered his lips in thought. The return to a focused conversation pulled some of the slur from his speech. "I don't think whatever it is will be out until much later. Misss Vindrikimmel and I didn't see it until very late, nearly two o'clock."

"It truly is a night creature then…" The colonel's eyes suspiciously flicked from side to side. He dug into his trousers and pulled out a small notebook which he jotted in quickly.

"The creature is real?" Brontë's annoyance at being unable to speak with

Crockett in private was displaced by her interest in the monster. "It's a trophy in your hunting circles, Colonel?"

"It is. As with most *rumored* creatures, a lot of what there is to know about it is passed on in hunting journals and digests; my interest was first caught when I saw an article in *Aussie Wine and Hunting* about a recent sighting."[17]

"How recent?" Phipps's eyebrows went up. "Extremely recent?"

"Indeed. Within the past year."

Phipps, Brontë, and Crockett exchanged quick glances. The darkness of the night and Collanhall's low voice, made them feel as if they were by a campfire telling ghost stories.

"What…did the article state?" Brontë asked.

Collanhall cleared his throat. "Nothing that we didn't already know. It lives in this forest. The report in *Aussie Wine and Hunting*, however, was about a daylight encounter."

"Daylight!" Crockett swallowed. "It…comes out in the day?"

"Or night." Collanhall glanced at Phipps.

"So," Brontë said growing more skeptical as the conversation continued. "You read about this creature in a hunting magazine. The bulk of the article's report was that the creature could be seen in the day."

Collanhall nodded. "Correct. Or night."

"That doesn't sound like it's enough information to plan a trip to the European continent to pursue the creature, Mr. Collanhall."

"Well," the colonel coughed. "I've studied the beast assiduously since I found that article. I would say I know nearly everything one can know."

"Which is?" Brontë crossed her arms and looked intently at the military man.

The older gentleman put his hands behind his back; his eyes grew glossy as he looked to the distance. "The Demon Bear…"

"Caddywampus," Phipps interjected. Despite regaining the faculties of his speech, he still tottered awkwardly from his many drinks. "I think we're

---

[17] The title of this article was "Tiggle Crapshaw Shares Demon Bear Encounter over Cabernet."

all using different names, so it's best to use the standard American name."

The colonel nodded appreciatively. "Yes, the Caddywampus is a mysterious creature. Half bear, half elk, and half puma, it stalks these woods looking for food."

"How can a creature be made up of three halves of something?" Brontë interjected. She was relieved to finally ask this.

The colonel's face reddened in the dim light. "My lady, I find your skepticism grating. A three-halved creature is common in my line of work."

"Couldn't it be thirds?" Crockett offered. "That would make more sense."

Phipps nodded in agreement (or what could have been a nod; with his staggering, it was a difficult gesture to identify).

The colonel scoffed. "You British, with all your arrogance of numbers and know-it-all-ness in terms of bestiaries! I have seen creatures consisting of three, four, and five halves of things. The Queensland Zurgxie is nearly seven halves of entirely different creatures."

Crockett exchanged a glance with Brontë but chose to back down from the argument.

"If I may continue…" The colonel gave a look of disdain at Brontë. The young woman threw up her hands in defeat. "Very well, then," the older man straightened his posture once more. "This creature is rarely seen; hardly anyone has recorded what it looks like. That article in *Aussie Wine and Hunting* was a breakthrough; it was as if the beast was calling to me across continents and oceans, finally revealing itself."

"Wouldn't he be calling to the entire readership of the magazine?" Phipps asked. "I mean, you included, of course, but it seems a very wide net he's casting. A bit of a vainglorious beast, isn't it?"

Collanhall's ears turned red. "Do you wish to hear about the beast or continue this line of inane questioning?"

Brontë, Crockett, and Phipps shrank back like scolded children. They mumbled a few *sorry*'s and *apologies* and *please, do continue*'s.

"Very well," Collanhall sniffed. "The first sighting of the beast was nearly two hundred years ago. A monastery not three miles from here recorded the encounter—a monk was out and about and saw the monster feeding near a body of water. After that, the story traveled through the country. Scores of people came into the woods searching for the creature."

"Why search when he comes up to your doorstep?" Phipps hissed. "It sounds like it's just local folklore and nonsense. I believe my brilliant, monstrous imagination did run away with me last night. This is ridiculous."

"Ridiculous or not, Mr. Phipps," the colonel spoke between gritted teeth to keep his temper, "over the next two hundred years there were numerous reports of a beast in the woods. Even if it's only a large bear, I intend to find it and make it a trophy on my wall. I always get my man."

"Man?" Crockett looked at the colonel quizzically.

"Beast. Man. Whatever it is, I get it."

The colonel stood erect and straightened his shirt. Standing at his full height in the dark, he was an imposing sight. Phipps took a step backward out of instinct.

"Colonel," Brontë said, "Madame van der Raaf mentioned something about a myth regarding children and the beast this evening. She said there were children missing from the town…"

"Yes," The colonel said. His mouth hung open as if he would say more, but he paused.

Phipps, still a step back from the others, spoke up. His voice shook slightly. "There is a connection between missing children and the beast?"

Crockett shivered. He remembered the anxious mother they'd seen when they came into town. Murder and kidnapping? How could any parent let their child out in the town with such chaos?

The colonel scratched the back of his neck. "That is…well, there is a story. The monastery where the beast was first found, they wrote a legend about it."

Phipps, Brontë, and Crockett leaned in closer.

Collanhall, seeing their interested faces, went on reticently. In the light of Phipps and Crockett's lamps, he looked older and tired—deep gashes of shadow lined his leathery face.

"They say the beast was once a man. He was a lonely sort, hidden deep in the woods. Well, one day, the devil, red as blood, eyes the color of deepest night, met him in a glen. The man had decided he no longer wanted to live his solitary life—he'd tragically lost his parents, his wife, and only child. That day he met the devil, he had a rope suspended from a tree, his feet on a stump; he was ready to jump. The cunning devil saw an opportunity and made him a deal. He offered the man a wife. He said that there was no longer a need to be lonely, that he could once again feel love."

"The man didn't want anything to do with the devil, but the devil, being well-versed in how shortsighted humans can be, showed the man a beautiful damsel. She was tall with long, blond hair and ruddy cheeks."

"Instantly, the man fell in love. So, the devil drew up the contract. The man didn't read its words but signed it in blood." The colonel looked up. He scanned the eyes of Phipps, Brontë, and Crockett. He attempted a halfhearted laugh to lighten the mood, but it caught in his throat. In the darkness, with the macabre glow of the lamps around him, the story regained its haunting, mythological power. The colonel's eyes fell downward as he continued. "Immediately the man was transformed—he became a cruel beast and the damsel, who had been suspended in the air by the devil, fell to the ground. She had no legs and no arms."

The colonel, at this moment in the story, to indicate the falling of the damsel, smashed his fist into his open palm. This caused Brontë, Crockett, and Phipps, who were all transfixed by the sad tale to gasp in horror.

Collanhall continued, the listeners quivering in fear. "The man, now a beast, took her back to his cabin and lay her on the bed. The woman immediately started crying. 'I'm hungry,' she cried. 'Feed me, my love!' The beast tried everything to satisfy his new wife, but she refused all. After a day of fasting, she made her cravings known. 'Young blood is what I crave, my love. Go and bring me back some taste of youth.'

'A young deer?' the beast asked.

'No, my love.'

'A young bird from the sky?'

'Indeed, no. I require the flesh of what you once were—the blood of young humans.'"

Brontë staggered back. She was both shocked at how very horrifying (and aptly German) the story was and how deeply it touched her.[18] Crockett stood still, his mouth agape. Phipps was enthralled, his doughy face staring intently.

"So," the colonel said sadly, "the beast hunts for his love. For despite him being a monster, he loves his wife."

The small group stayed silent for some time, the oppressive dark of the wood and the chilling tone of the colonel separating them all from the grounded reality of the inn.

"Children's stories…" Phipps broke the silence. He forced a laugh. "What they won't come up with to scare children about the devil and keep them from wandering off in the woods. In America we talk about a headless horseman. Ha ha!" The last *ha ha* came out sad and deflated. Phipps swallowed hard.

It was at that moment that they heard a rustling, a slow, labored gait in the depths of the woods. The party stopped speaking and listened intently. Unmistakably, they heard a low, throaty growl.

"Do you hear that?" The colonel asked quickly. "Do you?!"

The combination of the horror story and the sudden sounds caused Crockett to collapse in fear. A stiffness invaded his joints so that his back was firmly on the ground, but his feet shot straight up in the air. Brontë was quick enough to grab the lantern from his hands before he fell completely over.

"We should go look!" she whispered. Her voice trembled with excitement.

"I…well, I…" Phipps was white, his eyes pools of terror.

The colonel nodded at Brontë and opened his jacket to reveal a large knife. The young woman blew a kiss to Crockett, whose neck had also gone rigid, so he was staring straight up at the sky. Normally, she wouldn't leave her husband stiff and helpless in a dark wood, but as she was going toward the danger and Phipps was with him (who would be a much more tantalizing snack for a monster), she felt he was perfectly safe.

---

[18] This story makes even "Duck Man of the Old Hat" from *Beatrice* seem a light-hearted romp. Although he also stole children, he at least had all his appendages.

Together, she and Collanhall moved off the main trail and ran behind Crockett and Brontë's cabin into the deeper wood. After sprinting several yards, the old huntsman raised his hand and motioned for Brontë to slow her pace.

"We're coming to the ridge," he said softly. "There is a steep drop. Be careful."

At a slower pace, they treaded through the thick grasses and tall trees. The moon was bright, nearly half-full, casting a morose sheen on the green leaves and shoots on the path. Brontë's heart raced as she followed the colonel's practiced step. She felt clumsy and uneven behind him.

Collanhall threw out a hand, this time to fully halt her progress. Had he not, Brontë would have hurtled over the ledge and down the steep hillside that led into the ravine. She trembled at how close she could have come to an injury. The colonel stood silently, his eyes sweeping the hill below them.

His breath caught.

Brontë saw him raise his finger. It shook in the pale light of the moon and her lantern.

She held her breath as she followed its indicated direction, down the ravine and to a small opening halfway down the slope.

A creature stood on the hillside, its eyes dim stars in the shadows. Brontë only had time to see its curled, grotesque horns and the shape of its snout before it turned and rapidly vanished down the hillside.

9

A Calm in the Chaos

Brontë and the colonel were silent on their return to the cabins, both meditating on the beast seen in the moonlight. Brontë was in a state of deep reflection, trying to parse fantasy from reality; in each of the adventures she encountered with Crockett there had been some air of the supernatural, whether it was the macabre nursery rhyme during the investigation at her own house or the council of witches when they were assisting the Mayweathers.[19] But in both cases, it was only the appearance of these nefarious forces. When the curtain was peeled back, there was nothing truly horrible, merely her deranged grandfather and a group of eccentric women.

When they arrived at Crockett and Brontë's cabin, they found Phipps outside where they'd left him still struggling to overcome the goat-faint stiffness of Crockett's legs as he lay prone on the ground.

"What was it?" Phipps asked trying to straighten Crockett's left leg. "Was it…well, you know."

"Yes, it was," the colonel said. "I'm a bit embarrassed with my own reaction. I battled a dipgurdle in a treetop on the night of a new moon. I should have been able to chase the creature and finish it off tonight." He smoothed his

---

[19] This was one of the few places in Earhart's notebook that the events of the Mayweather Estate were given clearer form. It sounds as if the book was a bit of a *Macbeth* knock-off.

trousers. "I didn't have any weaponry, but my hands are certified as Class 5 Killing Bludgeons in Australia."[20]

"I also would have bested the beast." Phipps said this as he lost balance, rolling away from Crockett and falling on his back. His shirt rose so that the fleshy pink skin of his belly was exposed. "I'm just too empathetic, you know. I had to help this poor boy." He lurched forward and attempted to sit up.

The colonel, some of his bravado regained, leaned over and pulled Crockett up to his feet. The young man, once set upright, immediately keeled forward and landed on his face. It took the entire party, Brontë, Phipps, and the colonel, to drag him into the cabin.

When they attempted to get him onto the couch, chaos ensued. Crockett, despite his light frame, had a long, awkward form, so that once over the couch, he slipped from the colonel's grasp and hit the sofa, rolling off onto the floor. Brontë let them know she could take care of him from there, so the colonel (and Phipps, following Collanhall's lead) awkwardly saluted before leaving the cabin. Crockett, regaining some plasticity in his limbs, was able to wave as they shut the door behind them.

Once alone, Brontë pulled Crockett to a seated position and began exercising his joints to regain their function.

"Brontë, I'm so sorry. I should have been there to protect you. I've been rather good about keeping my composure, even this afternoon when the elk head kept crashing to the floor."

"It's all right, Crockett. I do wish you had seen it though." Brontë paused and looked deeply into her husband's eyes. "It was a huge creature—large, nasty horns." She mimed the twist of the monster's headpiece. "And it had a long, snout…" She ceased exercising Crockett and sat on the sofa beside him. "It was terrifying. And thrilling…"

Crockett's thick eyebrows knitted together. The feeling of dread he'd felt upon arrival in Praktisch (what he now knew as his bondage sheep, thanks

---

[20] It appears that until after the Second World War, one could register hands, feet, even large noses as weaponry in Australia.

to Sylvia) covered him like a thick blanket. When he closed his eyes, he couldn't help but see the image of the terrible beast pursuing Brontë, its giant claws reaching for her in a sea of darkness.

"It can't be real, though, can it?" Brontë asked. She was looking at the wall, deep in contemplation. "There are no such things as demon beasts transformed by devils who bring children as dinner to their wives. When we were returning from the forest, I thought of all the fake supernatural elements we've encountered recently…I can't imagine it's anything more than a malformed deer or bear."

"Did it *look* real?" Crockett asked.

Brontë hesitated. "Very. You could see it tremble in the moonlight as it breathed. Its eyes…" She shook her head. "But it can't be…can it?"

Crockett reached out and gripped Brontë's hand. "Brontë, I don't…you know when we arrived…Well, I felt…and it seemed…but now…"

Brontë fought a smile. "Crockett, you're a bit incoherent."

Crockett laughed. "I think even my brain stiffened when we heard the monster." The mirth quickly drained from his face. "I simply worry about you. When you ran into the dark and I couldn't go with you…What if something happened?"

Brontë squeezed Crockett's hand. The action suddenly shook her memory. She thought back to the lodge and Bristol's grip around her wrist. Instinctually, she trembled. Her hand pulled back from Crockett's.

"What's wrong, Brontë?" Crockett's eyes, the one green and one blue, were wild with concern.

Brontë smiled and shook her head. She extended her hand to retake Crockett's, but her husband did not see it. He was studying her face. Something other than the beast appeared to have caused this disruption in her mood. He suddenly remembered the plan and Brontë's excursion up the stairs—her terror when she returned.

"Brontë," he spoke gently, "you looked shattered when you returned from your excursion to find Klaude. Did something happen? Did you find him?"

"Oh! That!" Brontë searched for an excuse. It would do no good to alarm Crockett about the incident with Bristol, especially with his preoccupying concern with the monster. "I didn't find Klaude. So, I was disappointed."

Crockett did not look convinced.

"I was disappointed and…thinking…well, I simply…was thinking…sad thoughts."

"Sad thoughts?" Crockett let out a heavy sigh. "What kind, darling?"

"Just…well, you know, Klaude, the younger brother. I couldn't find him. So, maybe he's gone. Maybe lost, you know. Sad things like that."

Crockett's nose wrinkled with skepticism. "Are you sure that's all?"

"Quite so. It seems silly after the excitement with the beast." She cleared her throat. "Speaking of interesting things—"

"Were we speaking of interesting things?"

"There is a deep ridge behind the cabins."

"Really?" Crockett scratched his chin. "I didn't notice it at all."

"The colonel warned me of it during our pursuit." Relief flooded Brontë; she was thrilled Crockett followed her forced change of conversation. "Beyond the row of these cabins, the wood is deeper for a bit. It then comes to the edge of a steep hillside. Water must have used to run in the bottom of it, but it's all dried up now. The beast was meandering down the hill."

"Hmmm. That makes more sense than it being up by the cabins last night. I can't see a creature like that coming close to people."

"Perhaps it was hunting. Phipps and Sylvia said it had a carcass in its teeth."

The young couple sat in thought. Crockett, again, resumed his anxious musings about Brontë's pursuit of the beast.

Brontë pondered what to do next. With Crockett fearful about the monster, she did not know how to continue their pursuit for information about the beast. He did not even know about the disastrous encounter with Bristol which would surely cause him to abandon the adventure completely.

Both their thoughts were disrupted by Phipps and the colonel bantering loudly coming back toward their cabin. They passed and continued on the road back toward the lodge.

"Brontë," Crockett finally said, "perhaps we should let this all rest. I know we were going to keep things simple, leave the murder and the missing children to proper authorities and dally in trying to figure out if the beast were real, but…" He hesitated. "But after tonight…" He didn't finish his statement. Instead, he looked at Brontë pleadingly.

She, touched by his warmth, gently reached out and mussed his hair. "Crockett, if you're that concerned, we can 'let it rest,' as you said." She smiled. "I already said that you are my adventure, so we don't need to go looking into feral beasts or psychotic innkeepers."

Crockett's eyebrows raised. "Psychotic innkeepers?"

"Oh, no! I just…well, Ursula…" Brontë forced a laugh. She stood and went into the kitchen. "What do you say to a cup of tea and a snack before we go to bed?" She fled the room.

Crockett looked after her. He was about to inquire further when Brontë broke the silence.

"Tell me more about your time with Ursula," she called from the kitchen. "What did you learn about piano feces?"

This one question turned the mood completely. Crockett recounted his time with Ursula including observations about the drunken Phipps and Gestahlt.

"Gestahlt is an interesting sort. I don't know if there's any need to get to know either him or his wife since neither of them communicate very well."

"His wife only knows a few phrases. She must be mad for the bugs if she bothered learning 'Love buggies' along with 'How do you do?' But they do seem rather quaint and quotidian." After a night of threats and beasts, Brontë luxuriated in the casual conversation.

"The children less so," Crockett laughed. "Did you see them eating everything in sight? And chasing around Greta? The poor woman couldn't get a moment's rest."

"I don't know if I enjoyed Greta's company either." Brontë reentered the sitting room with some jam and biscuits and two cups of warm water. (She was still unsure about the dark maybe-tea substance in the cupboard.) "I don't know whether she was horrible or just old and a bit curmudgeonly."

"She's Dutch as well. They always have a bit of a…you know…a Dutch feeling about them."[21] Crockett turned up his nose at this—it was unclear whether the cause was a prejudice towards the Dutch or his discovery that there was no tea, only water.

"I *don't* know, Crockett," Brontë set down her coffee cup and stared at her husband. "Please elucidate on this Dutch feeling."

"Well, you know, it's a general queerness." Crockett set down his cup and pushed it away. "Petrarch and I had a client from the Netherlands, and we never did know what he wanted; nothing was ever correct in his eyes, but nothing was wrong, either. In the end he paid us for a half-completed will."

"Well, perhaps he was middle-aged and so only half-dead; he had only the need for part of one."

Crockett laughed. "Well, when you put it that way, I suppose the Dutch are simply more reasonable than any other group of people."

Brontë set down her warm water. A glow flushed her cheeks. "Well, Crockett, let's find out! Tomorrow we shall forget about the monster and Klaude Deutschefaber and the murder…and the missing orphans." It suddenly struck Brontë how macabre their arrival to Praktisch had been. "Anyway," she gathered herself, "we'll go take tea with Madame van der Raaf and then go into town. It will be a true holiday."

Crockett nodded. "I think the mystery of the Dutch is one I can get behind this week. Even the monster proved to be too much."

"Well, in the spirit of too much, then," Brontë said rising and coyly blowing out their lamp. "Perhaps it is time we act on Madame van der Raaf's advice and enjoy a moment of being free and wild."

Crockett, now fully mobile, rose and strode to his wife. He placed an emphatic kiss on her before escorting her into their bedroom.

Outside their cabin, the colonel and Phipps were still discussing the events of the evening. They heard a tremble and slight shake coming from inside the Cooks' cabin. Phipps leapt up into the colonel's arms, sweat pouring down his brow. The colonel also lost his composure for a moment

---

[21] This information about the Dutch was a wink to Didiert from Earhart. Didiert was half Dutch, half British, and in his diaries proudly referred to himself as Brititch.

before recognizing the timbre and intent behind the light ruckus.

"My dear Phipps," he said, trying his best not to laugh. "I think perhaps we're now being scared by a beast with two backs. If I can set you down, it may be best for us both to retire before we overhear something indecorous."

10

A Morning with Madame van der Raaf

The next morning a refreshing rain fell on the grounds of the Deutschefaber Inn. Brontë and Crockett, lulled by the soft pattering and the exhaustion of their activities the night before, slept later than they planned and awoke to the screaming of the two Gestahlt children.

Brontë leapt from bed and flew to the window terrified some act of horror was being enacted upon the children. When she parted the curtains, however, she saw the young boy and girl laughing and playing with odd contraptions on their feet. They appeared to be toys that left silly designs in the mud. Mr. Gestahlt was with them and waved to the open window.

"It fun a little play in wet!" he called happily. He motioned to the children, who giggled and began to run frantically behind the cabin. Their coal-black hair glistened, covered in the morning rain.

Brontë turned to Crockett and snorted. "Serbians are so odd. They're running around in this."

Crockett joined his wife at the window. "Hmmm." He looked toward the neighboring cabin and saw Phipps smoking a cigarette on his porch. "It looks like both Serbians and Americans enjoy the rain."

No sooner had he said this that Collanhall joined Phipps on the front porch. The military man was wearing rain gear, rivulets of water pouring down the fabric as he gesticulated to the tiny, fat writer.

"I wonder what they're doing," Brontë said.

"We will find out, my dear. Something tells me Phipps will tell us whether we want to know or not."

When the rain lightened, the young couple dressed and exited their cabin. The ground was riddled with muddy footprints, the Gestahlts having torn down the path in their game. The children were now running up and down the edge of the ravine and through the woods.

By the time they approached Phipps on his porch, he was alone. Collanhall had traipsed off on some errand. Brontë and Crockett, out of sheer curiosity about the strong bond that had arisen between the American and the Australian, approached him to discover what brought the two of them together so early in the morning.

"Hello," Crockett said tentatively. Upon drawing closer to Phipps, he saw that the writer's face wore the signs of his drinking the night before. His pink skin was now gray and large, black shadows sagged under his eyes.

"Hallo, Crumpet."

"Crockett," Brontë said, already sure they'd made a mistake in approaching Phipps voluntarily.

"I see you pulled yourself together," he said eyeing Crockett. This was punctuated by a thunderous "GROCK!"

Crockett blushed. "Thank you for your help last evening." Desiring to hurry through the conversation, he continued quickly, "You and Collanhall were out late and again early this morning."

"Yes." For the first time since they'd met him, the American did not add any color to his thought.

Brontë and Crockett waited in an uncomfortable silence. When he volunteered nothing else, Brontë probed further.

"Were you discussing the monster?"

Phipps pursed his lips. He thought for a moment, tapping ash from his cigarette. "We were. Collanhall has some theories about it. I'm not sure whether they are very *sound*."

Brontë grew overwhelmingly curious at this judgment of Phipps paired with his silence. The gears in her detective brain whirred. She engaged her powers of observation and swept her gaze around the porch. There were few clues of value. An ashtray filled with cigarette butts sat atop an American pulp novel titled *Duke Derring and the Cave of Gold* by Phillip Ellsworth. Above Phipps's doorframe, some naughty children had etched the word "POOP," which Brontë subtly pointed out to Crockett. Aside from that, the only other point of interest was Phipps's coat, which was laid over a chair.

"In the light of day, none of it seems sound, does it?" Crockett offered. He was trying desperately not to laugh at the word "POOP" on Phipps's stoop. "A demon, missing children—I feel we were all overcome by a midnight madness."

"A kookaburra morning to you!" The colonel appeared from behind Phipps's cabin. He marched toward them, his knees rising high into the air. When he was nearer, he greeted them with one of his salutes.

Brontë and Crockett returned the gesture uncomfortably.

"I was trying to do some tracking," he said loudly. "It occurred to me that if the beast was close last night, there may be some traces of him." He leaned toward the party conspiratorially. "I've found something quite interesting over this way."

Phipps rolled his eyes. "Yes, well, I'll let you all go busy yourself in the muck. I'm going to rest my eyes a bit before breakfast. My intellect is fatigued."

Phipps tapped the last of his cigarette and then turned to enter the cabin, picking up his ashtray and book as he went. The colonel was already marching in double time toward the path. Brontë and Crockett exchanged a look before following. As they kept pace behind the energetic Collanhall, Brontë reprimanded herself for not thinking of the tracking herself. The detective guide was adamant about searching for footprints.

Collanhall led them to the edge of the ravine. While most of the ground was illegible in terms of footprint reading, Collanhall indicated several large, circular footprints with claws just over the ridge. They were under the covering of a large shrub and had survived the morning rain.

"The rain washed away a good bit of the creature's tracks, but it looks like the footprints begin here."

It was too slick to attempt to climb down the slope of the ravine, but they were able to see a few of the circular prints trail down the hill. Once out of the shade of the bush, however, they vanished.

"They stop just there," the colonel said defeatedly. "But look here."

He led them further into the woods. The Gestahlts had made a mess of the pathway. Aside from the stomp of their feet, the children appeared to have also tussled along the path. Brontë looked on in horror as she saw them scamper between trees, covered in a thick layer of mud.

"Were it not fully light, I'd believe the Gestahlt children were woodland monsters as well. I can't believe their parents let them run wild without supervision."

It was at this moment Mr. Gestahlt appeared. He was also covered in a layer of mud. He waved jovially and then disappeared into the trees.

Collanhall snorted. "Like father, like children, I suppose. Serbians are an odd bunch."

"We were saying the same of the Dutch last night," Crockett said.

"Honestly, anyone out of the British commonwealth is suspect." Collanhall stopped walking and pointed down the ravine. "There!" he said indicating a spot on the hill. "Do you see it?"

Brontë followed his gesture and let out an audible "Hmmm."

"What is it?" Crockett squinted as if this would help him surmise what was so obvious to Brontë and Collanhall.

"It looks like…I don't know. It appears the beast was…" Brontë searched for how to describe her observation.

"Yes, my dear," Collanhall said beaming. "In Australia the trolleyhopper dances to attract a mate."

"Dances?" Crockett looked incredulous. "You're saying the *Dämonen-bär*—"

"Caddywampus," Collanhall and Brontë said together.

Brontë let out an audible "Ohhh…" when she realized what she'd done.

Crockett groaned. "The creature dances?" He refused to give Phipps a monster-naming victory.

"That's what would explain the mess of footprints down there," Collanhall said. "It danced then took off down the hill."

"I don't know about dancing…" Brontë spoke slowly, "but the creature did move around quickly, then marched out of sight."

"Could it have been the children?" Crockett could not get the ridiculous image of an elk-bear-puma doing a jig before gamboling down the hillside to devour a deer.

"It's too slick to go down this morning." Collanhall put his hands behind his back. "This is an interesting insight. I never thought a German creature would dance. They've no rhythm, you know." He turned abruptly and went back down the ridge, his eyes searching for more evidence of the creature. "Tally-ho, then!" he called as he disappeared into the thick foliage.

Crockett looked at Brontë defeatedly. "You know, I was beginning to think he was the one guest at the inn who made sense."

"Well, so far, I would say he's at the top of the heap." Brontë's eye caught a glow coming from a window in Madame van der Raaf's cabin. From their position on the ridge, they could just see her lodging through the mess of tree limbs. "But," she said, "we may as well find out if our dear Dutchwoman thinks the beast was doing a waltz or a reel. Let's pursue last night's plan and go speak with her."

Crockett extended his arm to Brontë. "Shall we dance ourselves? If a Caddywampus can do it, so can we."

The two skipped, danced, and joked all the way to Madame van der Raaf's cabin. They barely noticed the rain picking up again. When they arrived on the old woman's doorstep, they were red-cheeked and wet.

They had not even knocked when the old woman opened the door a crack. She looked at them suspiciously.

"Hmph," she grumbled. "I thought you were those awful children coming to annoy me once more. They nearly destroyed the raven on my hat last evening. *Hoedvogel*[22]—that is the raven's name—may never be the same."

Brontë and Crockett grew self-conscious. They dropped each other's

---

[22] This actually means "hat bird" in Dutch. Very fitting.

hands to look more grown up and less joyful.

Madame van der Raaf pulled open the door a bit further. Once more, she was dressed all in black, this time in less formal a manner, with a black housedress and a less ostentatious hat.

"May we join you for a cup of tea, madame?" Brontë asked. She had thought that the little woman would open the door and invite them in with warmth and candor. The suspicious, shifty character behind the door was not what she foresaw.

Madame van der Raaf threw glances down the path. Her gaze then flicked back to the young couple. She sniffed haughtily and then opened the door further.

"I suppose it wouldn't hurt," she said. "You two appear less terrible than the children and more intelligent than the American and the Australian."

She tottered inside, heading straight towards the kitchen. Brontë scurried after, hoping to increase the old woman's esteem for them.

"Let me help, madame," she said. She turned to Crockett and motioned for him to step inside the cabin.

Crockett was unsure of what to do once across the threshold. Having not been welcomed, he chose to stay in the front entry, apprising his surroundings. Unlike their own cabin, Madame van der Raaf's was immaculate. She'd tidied away the dust and gray film and doused the space in her lavender perfume; she'd even taken time to put up sketches to add to the homey atmosphere. Many of them were clearly old, depicting the work of an artist's deft hand that rendered a younger Greta with a man beside her. Hearing the clatter in the kitchen and the chatter of Brontë and the Dutchwoman made Crockett feel more comfortable. He moved closer to the pictures to get a better view. The man in them was handsome but slightly wily, his hair uncombed and his expression a mix of normal

Victorian photo seriousness[23] and alarm.

"Is this your husband, Madame van der Raaf?" Crockett called into the kitchen. The uniqueness of them being so young confounded the young lawyer. Why would she hang such old pictures about?

Hearing no response, Crockett turned toward the kitchen and let out a terrific scream when he saw that Madame van der Raaf was at his elbow.

The old woman, instinctively, covered her ears with one hand and began to slap Crockett with the other.

"What are you doing?" Crockett asked.

"What are *you* doing?" The old woman roared, continuing to bat him with her knotted, arthritic fingers.

Brontë entered into the chaotic and confusing scene, nearly dropping the teapot when she saw her husband being accosted by the old dame.

"What—what is going on?" she asked.

"Your nosey, prying husband is getting into my things!" the old woman yelled.

Crockett, unsure of how to rectify the situation, merely backed away from the Dutchwoman. This made matters worse, however, as he tripped backward and fell onto the sofa. A terrific crunch followed the impact of his backside onto the cushion.

"Oh no," he whispered.

"And now my hat!" Greta's mouth frothed with rage.

Brontë intercepted her before she could accost Crockett further.

"Madame, this is terrible! We are so sorry." Brontë looked at Crockett with wide, panic-stricken eyes. With a horrifying elk monster, a terrifying innkeeper, and a jingoistic Australian on the grounds, she had not assessed the greatest threat to be an old woman with a battered hat.

"I'm very sorry, ma'am! How can we make this up to you?" Crockett had

---

[23] Most contemporary readers think Victorians and Edwardians were stuffy and had, as a Gen X'er may say, "a stick up their butt"; however, it was common for individuals in early portraits and photographs to want to portray seriousness due to the formality of pictures. Stick-Up-the-Butt Syndrome didn't have its formal outbreak in Europe until 1937, far after this period.

pulled his legs onto the sofa and formed into a ball to protect himself from the old woman's flying fists. He had his hands raised in surrender.

But then, just as suddenly as the rage had overtaken her, it subsided. Madame van der Raaf's face softened. She took out a black handkerchief and dabbed her forehead.

"I apologize," she said. She tottered to the sofa and awkwardly plopped onto it. "I'm a bit on edge, and I didn't mean to be such a foul hostess."

"No, I'm at fault—" Crockett began. Before he could finish, however, Madame van der Raaf raised her hand to silence him.

"You do owe me a new hat. I believe there is a millinery in town. Make sure the new headpiece is sensible and demure. Nothing over three feet tall. Only birds or rodents as decorations, no reptiles and definitely no elephants."

"Yes," Crockett said. He still watched the old woman as one would a pacing, feral tiger.

"We will be sure to get you something, madame," Brontë said.

Madame van der Raaf nodded and then turned her attention to the fireplace. She said nothing, falling under the spell of the fire's dying embers.

In the ensuing silence, they could hear the soft patter of the continuing rain. Crockett turned his gaze to the fireplace where Greta's attention was so absorbed. Above the mantle there was a map of the grounds of the inn. It was an artistic rendering, the cabins drawn too large. Icons were placed around the portrait conveying the location of the ravine and a gazebo they had not yet encountered in the deeper wood. An image of a wild animal drawn near the ravine made Crockett remember the previous evening and the odd horror they had witnessed. In the daylight, it now appeared the more terrifying beast was the Dutchwoman in cabin four.

Crockett nearly screamed again when Madame van der Raaf's neck spun with alarming speed, her focus fixing on Brontë.

"Aren't you going to serve the tea and biscuits, dear? The younger, poorer folks should rise to their station."

Brontë nearly fell over herself rushing forward to serve the old woman. As she poured her a cup of the brew, the mercurial dame riddled her with commentary, "Not too fast. Does one not put in the milk and sugar first? Your pouring arm is weak. Did I say stop? We Dutch like our tea to the brim."[24]

Sweat was running down Brontë's face by the time she set the pot down and took a seat on the couch. Crockett was also still on edge, having not yet unballed himself from his defensive posture.

Greta took a long, dramatic drink of her tea, then set it down. Her steely eyes scanned the young couple. Both Brontë and Crockett felt as if they were bad children being appraised by a surly headmistress. When the old woman was satisfied, she posed a question.

"How did you meet then?" she asked dryly.

Brontë looked at Crockett, who gave her a pleading response with his eyebrows in return. She swallowed and spoke for them.

"We met at my grandparents' home. Crockett was assisting our lawyer, and we found a connection."

"I was once in love," Greta retorted, as if the conversation had become a competition.

"That's…lovely," Brontë said. She turned to Crockett and pursed her lips.

Crockett, understanding his wife's desire for him to enter the conversation yet also wanting to flee the cabin, bumbled into the fray with the only thing he could think of to say.

"We saw the monster, madame. You voiced your skepticism at the party, but Brontë saw it clear as day on the hill."

"Ha!" Madame van der Raaf let out one of her short, staccato laughs. "Poppycock! You saw nothing. Perhaps an overgrown squirrel. There is no monster." She took another long draught of tea, this time slamming the cup down with violence when she finished. "I know people in this town, and they have had rumors for years about it. I can assure you it is the most spurious, nonsensical wives' tale to ever be spun." To punctuate this the old

---

[24] The phrase "give me a Dutch pour" came from this stereotype which began when a Dutch king demanded all his cups of wine be filled to the brim. The author suggests not using it in a bar today as it now applies to an acrylic technique in painting.

woman let out a loud snort. The sound was so unexpected that Crockett scrunched further into his ball.

Brontë, however, became wildly interested in the old woman. She never suspected she would have ties to the hamlet of Praktisch.

"You know people here, ma'am?" she asked. "Have you often come to Praktisch?"

The old woman's brow furrowed in thought. She licked her lips and spoke slowly. "Not often, no. I used to have connections here but not anymore. I'm growing old, and I wanted to see it one last time before I pass on to the highest circle of heaven."

"Highest?" Crockett could not refrain from asking this of the violent, bad-tempered woman.

Her response was only to glare directly at him while picking up a biscuit from the serving tray.

Brontë's mind worked quickly. While Greta would not speak directly of her ties to the town, there was, perhaps, a way around it.

"My husband and I are going into town today," she said. "Having been here before, do you recommend any sights?"

Greta scoffed. "Ha! Sights? In Praktisch?" She motioned to the map on the wall suspended over the fireplace.

Brontë, seeing it for the first time, felt something was off about it. The iconography was too large, and it appeared different from the image she held of the grounds in her mind.

Greta continued, "Perhaps years ago, you'd find those who went to Praktisch for a holiday outside of the Finnlicht festival…" She stopped short, then abruptly her expression softened. Her eyes flicked back to the wall and the assortment of sketches there. Again, one emotion gave way to another in quick succession and her scowl turned on Brontë in a flash. "I would suggest staying on the high street. With the festival, there are pickpockets and nefarious folks about. That's also where you'll find the millinery in which to purchase me a new hat."

Brontë was disappointed. She thought for certain she would glean some insight into the old woman through an indirect line of questioning—a phrase she learned from her book. With a sigh, she prepared to rise from the couch to exit, when Greta, to her great shock, spoke again.

"And don't tell your story about the creature around the local folks," she barked. "They'll tell you the outlandish story of mad Dr. Gutermord."

"Dr. Gutermord?" Crockett, his interest piqued, rolled out of his ball and sat on the edge of the sofa.

"Yes." Greta looked at Crockett as if he were a cockroach. "I will not waste your time with details, but the belief is that a malevolent doctor of the wood created a creature of which he lost control."

"It sounds like the locals were a bit too enthralled with Mrs. Shelley's *Frankenstein*," Crockett said.

Greta rose. "Indeed," she said, "fairy stories from the ignorant British."

Crockett turned red. Had Madame van der Raaf been closer, he would have returned to his ball shape.

Brontë spoke to steer the conversation to something more pro-British. "We heard last night that the monster came from a deal with the devil. It was a very old tale from a monastery. That's what Collanhall said."

Greta rolled her eyes. "There is a tale about the beast from everyone in Praktisch. It's a crazed doctor, or a devil, or one farmer told me it was monster from the moon. I can assure you both that it is all stuff and nonsense." The old dame's eyes flitted up and she assessed the clock hanging above her mantle. "I suppose you should be going anyway," she said striding toward the bedroom. She did not turn back to them as she said her farewell, "Show yourselves out then."

The bedroom door slammed behind her.

Crockett and Brontë sat in an incredulous silence for some time before they were able to shake off the odd stupor of Madame van der Raaf's inhospitality.

When they were certain she was truly not coming back, Crockett took the remaining biscuits from the tray and stuffed them into his pockets. Brontë motioned toward the door; they said nothing as they rose and exited the cabin.

Outside, things were more welcoming. The clouds parted and shafts of white-gold sunlight sliced through the tree branches and threw clusters of ivory and green light onto the forest pathway. The inn grounds were full of life—the Gestahlt children were still playing, Mrs. Gestahlt was sewing and doing laundry in a basin while Mr. Gestahlt tinkered with an invention beside her, Phipps meandered through the trees scribbling in a notebook, and the colonel spoke and laughed with Sylvia as he shined what appeared to be a large, hooked Turkish sword.

The day and mood were lightening with rapidity.

"What an odd morning," Crockett said. He extended his neck so that his face was fully turned upward toward the sun. "But I feel this dash of sun bodes well for our trip into town."

"It does." Brontë leaned in close to Crockett, setting her head on his shoulder.

Crockett let out a contented sigh. "I think it's good we're focusing on our own journey this week rather than the Caddywampus mystery. I feel we can close the case on the van der Raaf affair as well. I don't know if it's a Dutch feeling, but it is a general feeling of hostility and eccentricity which exudes from the elderly woman."

"After battling my deranged grandfather and witches, I didn't think that little old woman would be such a formidable threat."

They both laughed at this and then continued toward the village. Crockett took out two of Madame van der Raaf's biscuits from his jacket and offered one to Brontë. His wife took it and put it to her lips, in hopes it would conceal the look of deep concern expressing itself on her features.

It was not Madame van der Raaf herself that caused the disquiet in her mind but rather the image of the inn grounds which hung above the fireplace. There was some oddity about it that she could not quite place. As the young couple started on the path toward town, she turned the image over in her mind. She traced the map over, finding it alarming that it looked both familiar and startlingly alien.

11

Bunce & Bosch

Brontë's anxiousness faded as Crockett prattled on about the beauty of the Praktisch woods on their walk into town. Just as her husband admired her excited energy about mystery and intrigue, Brontë couldn't help but be charmed by her husband's guileless wonder of the natural world.

"I've never seen anything like this!" He ran toward a tree covered in thick moss. His fingers traced over the soft and slimy substance. "The dread of the past day is gone. My bondage sheep, as Miss Vindrikimmel may say, has reached equilibrium. There's room in my mind to enjoy all this."

"You mean you didn't have any of these natural wonders in your workhouse in London."

Crockett continued to caress the tree moss. "You'd only find a substance like this after my cot neighbor Granny Pedigree[25] spent a night out drinking."

"Crockett!" Brontë playfully elbowed him in the ribs.

Her husband winked at her.

As they continued on the trail, all fears, apprehensions, and misgivings of the previous night faded. There was only a slight hiccup in the joy of

---

[25] There are not many additional records regarding Granny Pedigree, but she does sound like a very good time.

their stroll when they left the wooded trail to the inn and reentered town. Coming south, they, for the first time, were given a glimpse of the rickety tower of Praktisch Penitentiary, the "large and very scary castle which was turned into a prison." The crumbling, dark stone of the building cast a momentary shadow on their spirits. Verily, it was large and very scary. Brontë thought to raise the question of its use in the past, but when she saw her husband's attention diverted by a group of happy children, she thought it best to not distract him with questions of something alarming and unsettling.

On the high street, the town was alive with the sights and sounds of the festival. The young husband and wife marveled at the hubbub. There was a rush of voices, the sound of horses, the beeps of motor cars, and the lively squeals of gleeful children. On the air was the scent of crumbling leaves and roasting meat.

"This is much closer to what I had in mind for our honeymoon, Brontë," Crocket said as he saw a child scamper by holding a balloon. "I don't think one can plan for rabid elk monsters terrorizing one's place of lodging, but it wasn't on my imagined itinerary."

"What do you say we restart, then!" Brontë grabbed Crockett's hand and pulled him up the street. "Let's return to the candy shop and get something we enjoy. We'll pretend like there was no murder, monsters, missing orphans, or mayhem. Just a trip to get some sweets."

Crockett smiled. "Chocolate is always more appetizing without a side of homicide."

"Oh!" Brontë pointed across the street. The large, green man-fairy from the previous morning was handing out maps. "Crockett, even the fates want us to begin again. It's the same man who greeted us yesterday!"

The man-fairy noticed Brontë pointing and waved. They then saw him reach into his pocket and pull out a flask.

"Glad to see the events of the town and the inn haven't interrupted his drinking," Crockett said.

"Or they may be the cause of it," Brontë laughed.

In high spirits, they clambered up the wooden porch to the chocolate shop and frolicked through the front door. The chime on the door tinkled happily; it was an odd accompaniment to the red-eyed, sobbing mess of a woman who sat behind the counter.

"Oh, no…" Crockett couldn't suppress his disappointment.

The woman, however, put her handkerchief away and did her best to smile. Her teeth flickered brightly for a moment before fading and being replaced by scrunched cheeks and a pathetic, prolonged wail. "WAAAHHHHHH!"

"Right, then!" Crockett said quickly. "We'll be going. We thought this was the bank."

The young man spun to leave; however, Brontë caught him and pulled him around completely so that he lost his balance and fell forward, just missing a case of sour candies. Agitated that he tried to flee in a moment of need, she lightly kicked him in the stomach while he laid on the ground.

She then turned her attention to the shopkeeper and politely inquired after her. "Are you all right, ma'am?"

The woman, who spoke no English, feigned a smile. This lasted the duration of a second, before it was followed by another long, doleful "WAAHHHHHH."

Crockett pulled himself up to his knees and attempted to be friendly. "Can we help with anything? You seem upset."

The woman could only continue crying and point to a sign above her cash register. In block lettering it said "I didn't take a correspondence course. No English."

The realization that she could not interact with her customers only fueled her despair. She doubled over and continued to sob.

Crockett and Brontë looked at each other fearfully. It was Brontë who decided the best support they could offer was a commercial transaction. She piled the counter with candies and extended a wad of marks at the shopkeeper. This did seem to help a bit. She was able to wipe her eyes and get out a gargled *"Danke!"*

When they left the store, the joyous feeling that had accompanied them into town was all but gone. Crockett, in attempt to make up for his failure of Good Samaritanism inside the store, offered the bag of candy to a passing group of children. They took it happily and skipped ahead.

Brontë and Crockett watched them saunter away, a bit of joy sparking back inside of them.

This was promptly squashed by the appearance of two policemen and a dapper gentleman who approached the candy shop.

"Oh no…" Crockett said for the second time that morning.

The dapper gentleman bowed slightly and then entered the candy shop. Brontë and Crockett heard a joyful scream from inside. When they peered through the front glass, they were able to make out the woman who owned the shop leaping over the counter and meeting the gentleman with an embrace.

Their admiration of the happy reunion was cut short by a short, polite cough coming from one of the police officers.

"*Guten*," the man said with sharp authority.

This police officer who spoke was one they had not encountered. The other was the small, red-cheeked man they met the previous morning. While the new man stared at them with a perspicacious gaze, the man from the day before bounced back and forth on his heels as if waiting for a ride at a carnival.

In terms of looks, the two men could not have been more unalike. The bouncy man was short, fat, and red-cheeked with a thick nest of unruly straw-colored hair on his head. His partner was tall and thin with a thick mustache, black eyes, and carefully pomaded hair the color of ink. While they were both young, the shorter man appeared nearly childlike. His bright blue eyes twinkled as he addressed the young couple.

"Rainy morning becomes very good, yes?" he said.

The other police officer continued to appraise them. His searing stare made them both uncomfortable.

"What brings you to Praktisch?" he finally spoke again. His English was perfect.

"We came for the festival." Crockett, despite being unaccused and responsible for no wrong, felt his face flush and sweat appear along his brow. "We're only in the village for a few days."

The officer nodded. He turned to Brontë. "Newlyweds?"

Brontë's eyes went wide with wonder. "How…did you know?"

"You reek of it." The officer said this with no humor. He threw a glance at his partner, who was waving jovially at a family passing by. "This is Officer Bunce. I am Bosch. We are investigating the appalling events in town: the murder and the missing children. Also, the events of this morning."

"This morning?" Both Brontë and Crockett said this together, although their tones were on two dramatically different ends of the same scale—Brontë sounded as if someone had given her a new puppy, Crockett as if the offer of an adorable canine was rescinded.

"The recording house!" the red-cheeked officer, Bunce, spoke up. "The window—boom-crashed! Something purloined, thinks us."

"Purloined?" Brontë said impressed. "That's a wonderful word."

"I just start correspondence course." Bunce smiled.

"The same I took for my police officer training—wonderful program." Bosch looked between Brontë and Crockett. "When did you two enter town this morning?"

"We just arrived." Crockett's throat felt dry.

"We stopped at the candy shop, but that is all we've done," Brontë added.

Bosch nodded to Bunce. Bunce did not acknowledge this gesture; he merely smiled at Brontë and Crockett.

"Bunce," Bosch said, an edge creeping into his voice. "Could you please write this down?"

"Oh!" Bunce laughed merrily. "My job! Junior police. We write the things! Scribble-scrabble them down." Bunce dug into his pocket and pulled out a notebook in a state of total disarray. Pages jutted out, some of which fell to the ground. Bunce picked up the fallen pages and shoved them into his pocket. Bosch winced at his partner's casual incompetence.

"Now!" Bunce opened his notebook to a fresh page and licked the tip of his pencil. "Names, please!"

"Crockett and Brontë Cook," Brontë said. Normally radiant when she said her new name, in this instance she was terrified to be under interrogation by the humorless Bosch. The result was a flat, emotionless response.

"Bopitt and Crunte Book," Bunce repeated.

"No, Bunce." Bosch's face grew red. "Crockett and Brontë Cook."

"Kirkett and Brunty Crooks!" Bunce began to write again.

Bosch tore the notebook from his hand. His nostrils flared with rage. "We'll take notes later."

Bunce was unfazed by any of this. He resumed rocking back and forth on his heels.

Brontë looked at Crockett and saw he was flushed and sweating profusely. She spoke again to try to get them out of the stressful situation and her husband a glass of water. "We came down from the Deutschefaber Inn this morning—"

"Wowy zowy!" Bunce's mouth dropped open. "The inn? That was purloined thing!" Bunce gesticulated wildly at Brontë and Crockett.

Crockett went from eggshell white to ghostly pale. Even Brontë lost her composure.

"The inn was stolen?" Crockett said this with the tone of a screeching seabird.

"No. No. No." Bosch closed his eyes. He took a deep breath and slapped Bunce hard across the back of the head. "The records were stolen. Someone broke into the record house near the town hall and stole some documentation tied to the Deutschefaber Inn."

Brontë looked to Crockett.

"What does that look mean?" Bosch no longer sounded accusatory, merely interested. "Do you know something?"

"No," Crockett said quickly. "We just…we are staying there and it's a…well, it's an odd place."

"How so?" Bosch leaned in.

"The people staying there…the staff…it's oddity stacked upon oddity."

Bunce nodded. "Very strange! Fifteen years ago, it maybe nicest place."

"Really?" Brontë's brow furrowed in thought. "We wondered…our friend suggested we come to this festival and stay there, but it's not the place it used to be, I think."

"Hmmm…" Bosch sounded thoughtful. He looked between Brontë and

Crockett as if surmising if he could trust them. "It's true. Fifteen years ago, it was a destination. Now, it is not."

"What...happened?" Crockett asked.

"I say this to assuage your fears about the oddities," Bosch said. "You're correct, it is a place with a tragic, recent past. The youngest son, Klaude, was horribly injured. His father went mad and was put into prison. The mother did her best to keep it running, but she soon succumbed to the stress of it all. In the end, it was the girl, Ursula, who took control. She took a correspondence course on hoteling and has been mildly successful. The other son, Bristol, has been in and out of trouble with the law." Bosch stopped there. He put his hands behind his back. "So, yes. There is an air of sadness about the place, but it's nothing to be afraid of. I am interested to hear who is staying there—"

Bosch did not have time to finish his line of inquiry.

A woman screamed and ran toward him and Bunce. She accosted Bunce speaking in quick, frantic German. The two officers listened intently; she mimed across the street to a large crowd of people and indicated that they should follow her.

"We must go," Bosch said turning to Brontë and Crockett. He nodded politely. "Mothers are a top priority with rumors of missing children about. Thank you for your time."

"Goodbye, Brunty and Cocktail!" Bunce cried happily. He bounded after the woman as if she had asked him to play a game of cards.

The young couple watched them disappear into the crowd.

Brontë turned to Crockett and spoke, "What a sad history...I didn't...I mean, I never thought that something so awful happened to that poor family."

"It explains much, I suppose," Crockett said. "Not the least of which is Ursula's interest in intensely scrubbing excrement from musical instruments. She's trying to prove she can run the inn like her parents."

"Hmmm..." Brontë's thoughts came in frantic bursts. There was much to ponder: the Caddywampus, the mysterious Klaude, the murders in the town, the missing orphan children, and now the theft at the record house.

"I wonder what caused the injury that made the Deutschefaber patriarch go mad? What happened to Klaude?"

"I don't know…" Crockett looked to his wife. "I feel…" He paused. The sense of dread that met him upon their arrival shook his bones. "Brontë, how did we end up in the middle of all this?"

Brontë did not hear him, however. Her eyes were following a figure through the crowd. Had it not been for the incident the previous night, she would not have recognized him. But now, his gleaming, furtive eyes were burned into her memory.

"Crockett," she whispered. "There's Bristol…"

Crockett scanned the crowd. "I don't see him." He jumped to see over the rows of people. Brontë grabbed his suit sleeve and pulled him to the ground. She realized that in not confiding in Crockett about their encounter the previous evening, he was unaware of the danger the eldest Deutschefaber posed.

"Crockett! He'll see you!"

"Ah," Crockett felt his face begin to turn red. "Subtlety…it's perhaps in *Detectivating for the Dunce.* I should have read that chapter on Charlemagne…" Crockett looked at Brontë's face and realized there was more on her mind than bad detective work. "Brontë…what's the matter?"

"Nothing," she said quickly.

"But you look just like you did last night at the inn after…" Crockett's mouth fell open. "Bristol…what happened? Are you…he didn't hurt you last night, did he?" Crockett gripped Brontë's shoulders.

"Crockett, I'm fine. It was nothing, but…" Brontë's eyes followed Bristol through the crowd. "Will you trust me? I think we should pursue him."

"Pursue?!" Crockett's thick, caterpillar-like eyebrows nearly leapt off his forehead.

"There's something going on, and I think he may be at the center of it."

"But we weren't going to pursue this mystery…" Crockett's voice took on a pleading lilt.

Brontë lifted her hand. She gently touched Crockett's cheek. "I think we must, Crockett. We've been put here for a reason, I think." Her eyes flicked toward Bristol who was nearly out of sight. Brontë raised her other hand so that she was holding Crockett's face. She locked eyes with him and kissed him. "Trust me," she said breathlessly. "Follow me."

She then slipped away from her husband and moved through the crowd.

Crockett's heart raced—from fear, from the kiss, from the knowledge that Bristol had some contentious encounter with his wife the night before. It was in this maelstrom of emotions that he lunged forward to take his wife's hand.

She looked at him with a questioning glance.

Crockett did his best to smile. "I trust, and I'll follow," he said. "Let's go."

12

A Threat

With Crockett's blessing, Brontë ran after Bristol. Crockett scuttled behind, keeping a hold of her hand as they weaved in and out of the bodies of locals and tourists. The young lawyer was grateful it wasn't a challenging pursuit; the eldest Deutschefaber, solely focused on his destination, proved to be an easy mark. Not once did he look back or even throw a stray glance to any passers-by. His anxious, angry gait led him toward the farthest end of the high street.

At the very end of the road, he turned into a small tavern. Brontë and Crockett waited in a small crowd of people, keeping out of view.

Brontë assessed their position. After a few moments of thought, she took a resolute step towards the door of the tavern.

Crockett moved in front of her.

"Darling, no," he said. "I'm going in."

"You?" Brontë could only think of Crockett prone on the trail the night before, his arms and legs extended into the air. "But Crockett…you…"

"I'm aware." Crockett's joints tingled. "But I can't let you go in alone. Bristol will *know* you after the encounter last night. He and I have barely spoken two words, so I don't think he'd recognize me immediately. And…I can't put you in danger again. I wish I'd been there last night."

Brontë's expression softened. "Crockett, it was a fright, but he didn't do anything harmful. He reprimanded me for sneaking around. He does cut a terrible figure—his brooding eyes and thick musculature…"

Crockett pulled at his shirt collar.

Seeing her husband's fears, she gripped his hand and smiled. "Crockett, I can go in. There is a crowd, and you'll be waiting here. You don't need to be afraid."

But Crockett fixed his gaze on the door of the pub, then turned to Brontë and squeezed her hand back. "You took the danger last night—twice, if we include your pursuit of the Caddywampus in addition to the Bristol encounter. It's my turn." With a gentle kiss on her hand, he pulled away and marched toward the tavern.

Brontë watched with both admiration and fear as her husband crept up the steps of the building and peered into the window. From a distance, she couldn't help but compare his thin, stick-like build to the squat, muscular block of Bristol Deutschefaber.

"Be careful…" she whispered.

Dirt and grime obscured Crockett's view through the tavern's windows. He saw that the pub had a decent gathering of festival goers all having a drink or enjoying lunch. He turned to Brontë and gave her a nod.

They both took a moment to reflect on the situation and the best way forward. Brontë pondered the detective book's instructions. Despite its length and specificity, there was not a single chapter on following strangers into dimly lit and menacing pubs. She remembered a bit about entering a dinner party when one is unwelcome, but before she could practically apply it to their current situation, she heard the pub's door shut and saw Crockett disappear inside.

Crockett, upon entry, scanned the room and did his best to remain undetected. The dust on the window was an apt introduction to the place. It held the dark, musty air of a location which had not often seen the sweep of a broom. Cobwebs decorated light fixtures, and the tables and chairs were a cheap, dark wood which bore the marks of early onset rotting.

At the bar, an elderly gentleman quietly sipped on beer. The bartender was reading a newspaper. The full tables were occupied by jovial tourists, just starting lunch. They were attended by a heavy, ruddy-faced barmaid with a sour expression.

Crockett did two full visual sweeps of the room before he found Bristol. The eldest Deutschefaber was in the far back corner at a table hidden from the sparse light coming from the windows. He faced someone Crockett was unable to see, although he could tell Bristol's companion wore a top hat, which was visible over the back of the seat. Far from the maniacal and threatening figure Crockett imagined from Brontë's encounter, Bristol looked penitent and terrified. He rubbed his hands together and spoke quietly to the person across from him.

"*Guten,*" the barmaid approached Crockett. She was about to offer him a table; however, Crockett gesticulated wildly and ran to the bar.

He made his way to the side nearest Bristol's table in hopes of overhearing part of the conversation. To keep from being seen, he ran in a sideways, nearly backward fashion. The two elder gentlemen and the bartender looked at him with confusion and alarm when he fell onto a bar stool hip first, nearly tumbling over and collapsing into the wall.

Had Bristol not been fully occupied by the figure across from him, Crockett would have been discovered immediately; however, as it was, everyone *but* Bristol and his top-hatted friend noticed his chaotic arrival and stared curiously at the tall, thin foreigner.

Things did not get better once Crockett righted himself on the stool. He remembered he knew no German and needed to make a request of the bartender.

"Uhhhh…" he said, looking into the German man's confused face. "Beer… en? Drinken?"

The two old men grunted and then resumed their conversation. The bartender continued to look at Crockett with an expression of confusion so profound it could have been mistaken for horror.

"Beer…endrinken?" Crockett asked again.

The bartender was about to respond when there was a thunderous crash from behind them.

Whatever civil discourse occurred between Bristol and the mystery man was over. All eyes in the pub focused on the back corner. Crockett turned slightly, using his jacket to cover his face. Although he couldn't see everything happening, he could make out most of the frightening exchange.

Bristol cowered in his chair as the man across from him stood, towering over him. Crockett trembled seeing the man's full form. He looked like a shadow come to life. Atop his head was the large, black top hat that matched the midnight shade of his long cloak. The combined height of his form and hat made him nearly reach the pub's ceiling. His mouth and nose were obscured by a gold and green scarf. Visible over the top of this colorful accessory, piercing from the depths of his gaunt face, were two stark, black eyes. They quivered with a pale glow that paradoxically conveyed both malice and tranquility. The most striking feature of the man, however, was his thinness; Crockett appeared portly next to his gangly, spider-like frame. One of the man's long, arachnidian appendages extended across the table and held Bristol's coat.

"No, I… Kreuz, I promise that I didn't…" Bristol stuttered. His voice shook with terror.

The tension and terrifying figure of Kreuz aside, Crockett was relieved the two men were speaking English and he could overhear their conversation successfully. If Petrarch had been wrong about most of the circumstances around the Finnlicht Festival, the use of English was something of which he was absolutely correct.

Crockett had little time to delight in this fact before he had to duck. Kreuz, despite his alarming thinness, had found the strength to hurl his and Bristol's table towards the bar.

Bristol took the moment, free of Kreuz's grasp, to bolt from the pub and run into the street.

Outside, Brontë saw him bound out of the door. He slipped on the front stoop and fell into the dirt. She took a step back and did her best to hide herself in the crowd in the street. The ability to vanish grew more and more probable as the shouts and the slam of the pub's door drew curious onlookers. Even the green man-fairy sidled up behind her, sipping his flask and letting out the occasional belch.

The public attention was well earned. The scene grew more and more chaotic with each passing moment. The barmaid ran out of the tavern screaming. Many of the patrons scrambled from the main entrance and fled down the dusty road. Bristol tried frantically to get up and escape, but Kreuz was in hot pursuit. Brontë let out an audible gasp when she saw the gaunt man stalk from the bar, down the front steps, and stand over Bristol.

As Kreuz hovered over the innkeeper, the world stopped. Bristol held his hands over his face whispering pleas of mercy. The gathered crowd held a collective breath, both terrified and intrigued by the scene unfurling before them.

In the silence, Brontë looked back at the pub entrance and saw Crockett emerge onto the stoop. Although pale, he looked no worse for the wear. She smiled at him. Crockett could not muster the joy for a smile, but he saluted back (an awkward tic he picked up from Collanhall).

"I…" Bristol finally spoke up. He was scrabbling to get to his feet, swirls of dust surrounding him. "I told you…I didn't…it's not…"

"It would be a very big mistake." The handkerchief covering Kreuz's face whipped in the wind. His voice was deep and calm. "If you didn't tell us, Deutschefaber, that would be tantamount to treason."

"But I didn't! I…well, I…"

"No excuses."

Bristol appeared to give up after that statement. He slumped back to the ground and closed his eyes tightly. It looked as if he expected the sharp drop of a guillotine. The mysterious man stood over him; his long, dark cloak flapped in the wind.

"How did they know?" Kreuz spoke quietly, but it was just audible at the near edges of the crowd. Both Crockett and Brontë risked their safety to take steps forward. "Was it you?"

Bristol shook his head. Tears moistened his eyes. "I swear. I would never. Never!"

Silence enveloped them. The banners along the street rippled in the wind. Dust swirled through the air as Kreuz loomed over Bristol.

Brontë glanced to the pub. She saw the faces of the patrons pressed against the dirty glass, wiping away grime to get a better look. The bartender stood in the doorframe. He acted as if this happened all the time. He whistled a tune as he polished a beer stein.

Kreuz said something more, but it was inaudible. Bristol choked out a sob and turned his head away.

Slowly, the towering figure withdrew a blade from his pocket; he held it up for a moment. A collective gasp escaped from all those watching. Then, without flinching, the man ran the blade over his palm. A line of red blood appeared, which he held up and presented to Bristol. Deutschefaber, tears falling from his eyes, sighed with relief. He extended his hand and took Kreuz's blood-soaked palm. Once upright, he took the blade and ran it along his own palm. The two men then shook hands, their blood mingling together.

"If I find out you were lying," Kreuz said coldly, "this blade finds your heart."

He and Bristol embraced. As they were pulled into each other's arms, Bristol's gaze flicked over to Brontë. His steely eyes locked on her.

Brontë's heart raced. Terror kept her from moving. She then heard a slight rustle and commotion. When her eyes regained focused, they locked on Crockett who had pushed through the crowd and run to her.

"I think we've worn out our welcome," he said quickly.

Crockett pulled her away from the threatening scene. They began to run, pushing their way through the crowd. She turned back as they fled and saw Bristol's face. A look of dark resolution was writ on his countenance; his gray eyes sparkled with a vengeful glow. As they took flight, she felt his gaze follow them; on her wrist she felt the phantom clasp of his strong hand.

13

The Crossroads

Locals and tourists blurred as the couple raced to safety. Brontë's breath was coming in fits and starts. Crockett eyes were obscured by the sweat flowing from his brow. He gave Brontë's hand a squeeze and gazed back at her. She did her best to portray fearless, stiff-upper-lippedness, but visions of the tall man's skeletal frame and Bristol's cold stare jolted through her imagination causing her to tremble.

When they came to the center of town, Crockett assessed their surroundings. Brontë noted a passage between two houses which would offer an escape. They ran down it and then jumped over a small fence that protected the lawns of one of the cottages. They concealed themselves in the garden, taking refuge behind a wall of tall plants.

Brontë clasped her hands together and tried to force the images of Bristol and Kreuz from her mind. "What did we see?" she asked, her eyes wide. "What…was that?"

"I…don't…I don't know!" Crockett's face was pale. He wiped away the accumulating perspiration. "I didn't hear any of their conversation in the bar. By the time I attempted to order a drink, the conflict exploded."

Brontë released her clasped hands and flexed her fingers. She mentally reviewed the detective procedure from the book. "Let's be methodical," she said slowly. "What did we observe?"

"We saw a confrontation between Bristol and a tall, scary man." Crockett massaged his temples as he reviewed the scene in his head. "They discussed some sort of betrayal—*treason*, the man said. Bristol was terrified. And…" Crockett scrunched up his face in thought, "the man wore all black with a top hat and that rather garish green and gold scarf on his face."

Brontë froze. She'd seen that scarf before. "Crockett! Bristol had a similar scarf on his arm when I saw him last night."

"So, the green and gold scarf could be important?"

"Perhaps. I wonder what it means. Is it some fraternal affiliation? There is gold and green everywhere with the festival. Those appear to be the thematic colors."

Crockett tried his best to recall each detail of the encounter. Everything could be a clue if looked at through the right lens. "They weren't speaking German," he said after a moment. "Very convenient for us, but why English?"

Brontë pondered this. "Perhaps the top-hat man is not from Germany."

"Kreuz," Crockett said quickly. "I learned that in the pub. His name is Kreuz." Crockett let out a long, low breath. "You know we are on the border of three countries…maybe he's from Switzerland or France and English is Bristol and his common language."

"Why would the man be here, though? And why is he threatening Bristol?"

"Well, they share the scarves. Perhaps they're both part of some… international…" Crockett faltered. After a moment of confused thought, he finished awkwardly, "…gold-and-green-scarf-embroidering organization?"

"A very serious one," Brontë could not help but laugh. "If you betray the head embroiderer, there appear to be serious consequences."

Crockett shrugged his shoulders. "It wouldn't be the oddest thing we've run into."

The two exchanged a smile. There was a brief lull in the conversation filled by the breeze flowing through the garden and the distant voices of exuberant festival goers.

"You know," Brontë said after a moment's thought, "the policeman, Bosch, mentioned that Bristol has gotten into trouble with the law."

"Ah!" Crockett's face lit up. "Could this be the common link then? Maybe there was some kind of criminal enterprise that went poorly and Bristol was in the middle."

"What was the betrayal? Someone told someone something…" Brontë steepled her fingers. "Kreuz threatened Bristol with the knife. He said, 'Next time this blade finds your heart.'"

Crockett shivered. "That is definitely a warning—not in the least bit subtle." He sighed. The feeling of portending doom he'd harbored since their arrival writhed in his stomach. "Brontë, this…this doesn't seem like an issue we should get into the middle of. The Caddywampus is one thing. That's more of a lark at the inn, but a tall spider-like man threatening people with murder…I think that escapes the purview of our little adventure."

Brontë turned to her husband. "It is a mess, isn't it? Now in addition to missing children, a murder, and a monster, we have an international embroidery syndicate threatening Bristol."

The two remained silent for a moment. Then Crockett chortled. It started as one awkward laugh but soon transformed into a fit of giggles. The absurdity of the situation—a quiet honeymoon turned into a murderous, horror-filled adventure—terrified him so much that he could either weep or laugh. His impulse went to laughter.

Brontë turned to him, disconcerted. "Crockett, perhaps we should put jokes aside and focus. We're possibly being pursued by a madman and in the midst of an international criminal kerfuffle."

This only made Crockett laugh harder, the giggling going from quiet and coquettish to raucous guffawing. Brontë grew alarmed, peering over the edge of the shrubbery in the garden to be sure there was no one in pursuit. When she was satisfied they were safe, she gently pushed Crockett, who fell over amidst a new wave of laughter. In spite of herself, Brontë began to laugh as well while managing to ask, "What are you laughing at?!"

Crockett, between chuckles, said, "I don't know! I'm terrified! But now I'm imagining the embroidery syndicate full of little old ladies with knitting needles hunting us down.[26] When you tried to be serious, I lost it further! It's ridiculous! Brontë, we have become Ms. Fletcher! Wherever we go there is some disastrous event. Our morning stroll to reset our vacation turned into a robbery and a wild fight scene in front of a tavern. It's hardly the 'bucolic getaway' Petrarch promised us!"

Brontë then lost her composure and joined Crockett in his fit of laughter. The jolly moment lasted for nearly five minutes before they both collapsed backward, holding hands and wiping tears from their eyes.

Once the mirth passed, Crockett took a deep breath and sighed. "Brontë, I think…" he hesitated. "We appear to be at the crossroads now. As much as I hate to admit it, there is some force of fateful gravity which keeps pulling us into the mysteries of this town. My bondage sheep knows it and so do I. I hate it, but…well, should we do something? Is it our obligation? Should we address it or step aside? Keep detectivating by ourselves or confide in Bunce and Bosch everything we know and leave it to them?"

Brontë looked skyward from their position on the ground. The rain clouds of the morning had fled, the sky was a deep azure. It did feel like they were at an inflection point—a point between storms—in which to ponder their next course of action. "Crockett, I know you have reservations about this place and this adventure. I can't blame you. As you said earlier, while our previous encounters were confined to houses and estates, this feels boundaryless. There are many disparate pieces in play."

"It's like playing chess with Kordelia," Crockett said with a forced laugh. Brontë's sister was infamously difficult to engage with due to her bizarre manipulations of logic. "She always made us add in the hairbrush piece."[27] His mirth from moments before now gave way completely to the

---

[26] In our present day and political climate, I feel the need to apologize for the triggering effect this may have on those with family caught in the Little Old Lady Embroidery Massacre in Duluth, Minnesota, in 1823.

[27] In Earhart's notebook from *Beatrice*, he confirmed that Kordelia Winterbourne, when playing chess, forced her opponents to use random items from around the house as pieces. This included hairbrushes, crystals, clocks, and, in very odd circumstances, a cat. (A feline which *had not* been set aflame, for those fan(s) of the first book who may wonder.)

overwhelming fear and dread he first felt stepping off the train. He sat up and looked into Brontë's eyes. "Darling, as much as my senses are telling me to run, I also feel it is our duty to help if we can. Sylvia, the poor candy shopkeeper, the missing children…we could be of assistance."

Brontë nodded enthusiastically. She waited for her husband to continue.

"But," Crockett squeezed Brontë's hand tightly, "I also think we need to both commit to safety above all else. I know I am the one prone to hurtle into disaster without thinking, but I want us both to detective smarter."

Brontë sat up and put her arm around her husband. "I think that is a very wise commitment. We should take small steps to assist, no illogical head-first runs into danger."

They smiled at each other and then kissed. They both felt better; their extremities had ceased shaking and the tension between them regarding their role in investigating the mystery at the Deutschefaber Inn was resolved.

Crockett stood up so he was no longer protected by the shrubbery along the edge of the garden. It was at an inopportune moment, as the owner of the house had come out to fertilize her garden. As Crockett stood, he received a pail full of excrement and compost on his clothes.

"Agh!" The woman began screaming in German, "*Geh raus!*"

Brontë stood and pulled Crockett away. The young man was shocked to have become a human outhouse and lost his faculties of thought. They ran out of the yard, the woman screaming horrible words in German and shaking her fist. A few children saw the approach of the muck-covered Crockett, screamed, and fled.

They eventually scurried through the back roads of the town and found a quiet place outside of a small church to catch their breath.

"Brontë, this… seems foreboding considering our decision to move forward. I'm now covered in feces and children think I'm the Caddywampus. Perhaps we should rethink our offer to help solve the mystery. We could seclude ourselves in the cabin until the festival on Saturday evening. It may be best for everyone."

Brontë laughed. She pulled out a red handkerchief monogrammed with her initials from her trouser pocket. It was another wedding gift from Petrarch after their hurried nuptials weeks before. She used it to gently wipe the grime from Crockett's face. "Darling, I feel it's not a supernatural omen, merely a friendly reminder that rough times are ahead. It's nothing we haven't faced before, though. You've almost died a number of times. This, honestly, is not bad in comparison."

Once Crockett was cleaned (as best as they could get under the circumstances), they proceeded back to the high street. The excitement around the festival continued to grow. Jugglers, street performers, and hawkers now filled the scene. Children ran through strangers' legs, while their parents watched with anxiousness. Although it was still early in the day, groups of revelers filled with drink sang songs and tottered between the street acts.

The young couple barely noticed any of it, however, as their thoughts were focused on the intricate web weaving around them. Somehow Bristol was involved with a nefarious organization—the green and gold scarf its troubling emblem. But what, if anything, did that have to do with the Caddywampus? The dead man in the town? And the missing children or the records-office break-in from that morning? And what was the "treason" that the tall man said Bristol committed?

They walked in silence off the high street and onto the wooded path which led up to the inn. Crockett noted that the turning leaves and crisper air he admired on their way to the inn now took on an ominous tone; rather than representing the joys of autumn, they symbolized the coming cruelty of winter.

The young man was so lost in thought that he didn't see Ursula and Sylvia's approach until they were nearly upon them. Both women's faces registered shock when their noses caught the scent radiating from Crockett; Sylvia politely took a step back, while Ursula sniffed sharply and leaned closer.

"Is that a new cologne, Mr. Cook?" she asked, her face betraying no emotion.

"Feces...actually," Crockett said, red with embarrassment. "There was an incident in town. It's been a rather difficult morning."

Ursula nodded, her face stoic. "It suits you. The brown of excrement goes well with your two-colored eyes. If you'd like, I can clean you like I did that piano."

Brontë was both incensed and confused by this statement. While the innkeeper said she abandoned her amorous interest in Crockett the night before, it now appeared that the light of day and the odor of feces were rekindling her interests.

Sylvia was the one who broke through the moment of tension. "We are heading to town to get some supplies," she said. "We underestimated the food and drink we'd need with so many guests."

"Yes," Ursula said, as she continued to look at Crockett, her stare an off-putting combination of indifference and flirtation. "We need some additional food and beverages. We will be holding another social gathering this evening to kick off the celebrations that begin in town tomorrow. It will, of course, be muted. Some fun will be had."

"What a delight." Brontë's nostrils flared. Rage swelled in her breast, even though Crockett affirmed he had no interest in the rhomboidal Ursula. "We'll be there, of course. Husband and wife. Together. There and forever."

The thick innkeeper did not notice the threat in this. She nodded disinterestedly. "Marriages are wonderful until they aren't." She glanced back to the lodge. "Hopefully yours will stay intact through the weekend. We have no need for feuds or excitement."

"Yes, Miss Deutschefaber." Crockett flashed a gaze to Brontë. "In line with that, we heard this morning from a police officer about your parents. We were sorry to hear about the tragedy."

"What did you hear?" The woman's normally deep voice lifted several octaves.

"We heard about your father's imprisonment, mother's passing, and your brother's injury." Crockett tried to keep this vague in hopes the secretive Ursula might accidentally add color.

The square woman cleared her throat. "It was—is—isn't—it's all nothing. The source of it—the fount of all family tragedies—was a misunderstanding. It's nothing of importance. All of it is long in the past."

Crockett knew better than to press. He was pondering how to probe the matter further when Brontë spoke up.

"Speaking of startling occurrences," she said, "is there any news on the demon bear? We sighted it last night."

Ursula glowered. "Mrs. Cook, I have to say I find your inquisitiveness this morning quite obnoxious. As I have mentioned before, there is no demon bear, no Caddywampus, no Australian trollyhoppers or diggidongs! There may be a bear, but that is all there is! Please stop spreading such pernicious rumors!" Ursula turned dramatically to Sylvia. "Miss Vindrikimmel, please follow me. We have much to do and do not need to waste further time with silly stories for children."

She stomped off with the momentum and pomp of a grenadier. She paid little attention to Sylvia, who whirled around to address Brontë and Crockett.

"Be careful today," she said softly. "I feel that something is coming."

"Your bondage sheep…" Crocket whispered. "I wish we'd received the warning a bit earlier," Crockett motioned to his soiled clothes.

Sylvia looked slightly confused at the term "bondage sheep" but she soon remembered Crockett's inability to say anything functional in German. "I'm sorry to hear that. Praktisch is normally a quiet place. This week has been very difficult."

"Sylvia," Brontë's voice was low. She looked at Ursula, who had now realized Sylvia wasn't with her. The large woman stood further down the path tapping her foot. "Do you know anything about Bristol? Is he—"

But Brontë did not need to say anything further. Sylvia's face went white. "Nothing," she said, her voice trembling. "I don't know…He and I—it's nothing."

"Sylvia! Are the Cooks paying you or am I?!" Ursula boomed.

Sylvia looked at Brontë and Crockett as if they were ghosts. She attempted a polite nod but then fled toward Ursula. As she trudged down the path, she threw one more fearful look at the young couple before catching up to her mistress.

Brontë looked at Crockett. "What an odd encounter."

"It appears there are many secrets," Crockett said. "The Deutschefabers... Bristol...What does Sylvia know?"

"Or what is she afraid to tell?" Brontë asked.

They watched the young maid and the lumbering innkeeper disappear down the trail.

When they were out of sight, Brontë spun around and looked at Crockett. Her eyes sparkled. "Crockett!" she whispered. "Ursula has just left."

"Yes."

"Bristol was caught up in town. I'm sure whatever business he had with that Kreuz gentleman wasn't resolved when we left them."

"I would imagine not. I'd assume they had other crime and mischief to discuss."

Brontë gripped Crockett's hands tightly. "And Sylvia has gone to attend to Ursula's whims."

Crockett pursed his lips in contemplation. "Is this listing of obvious facts a chapter of the detective book?"

"Darling, the lodge will be empty."

"Yes," Crockett said. After a moment of thought, however, he caught his wife's inference, "Oh!"

"We can talk to Klaude! There will be no interruptions, death threats, or other acts of impediment by the Deutschefabers."

Crockett's scalp grew hot. "What if he's...? Well, we don't know what state he is in after the 'accident.'"

"If he's incapacitated, I'll leave immediately. But you saw him upon our arrival; he appears to be able to get out and about."

"What if he's...?" Crockett felt uncomfortable. "You know, a bit..."

"What?"

Crockett pursed his lips and thought for a moment. He finally found the character that best conveyed his discomfort, "Quasimodo."

"Oh..." Brontë flinched slightly. The thought that the man upstairs would be hard to look upon never crossed her mind. "Well, remember my grandfather's makeup and theatrical dress during the Beatrice incident? I don't think it could be worse than that."

Crockett allowed himself to smile, but then intensified his gaze on Brontë. "Darling, I'm just afraid. What if the Deutschefabers return? Bristol…"

Brontë nodded. "That's why, Crockett, you will serve as lookout."

"Lookout?" Crockett jumped.

Brontë began to pace. "Klaude may be the lynchpin that pulls this all together. He may know Bristol's business. We could get him to tell us the whole sordid history of the Deutschefabers." She grew so excited she leapt up and down. "He may even know what the creature is!"

Crockett sighed. Despite their decision to aid in the mystery, he couldn't force away his dread. "Okay. You will investigate, but I will be right there in case something goes awry." He drew closer to Brontë and kissed her hand; he pressed his forehead against hers. As gingerly and lovingly as possible, Brontë shoved him away, the scent of his clothes was nearly unbearable.

As they made their way to the main lodge, they continued to discuss the plan.

Brontë would ascend to the second floor of the lodge to search for the mysterious Klaude Deutschefaber. Crockett would stay in the main room, reading a book and looking out for the approach of Bristol and Ursula. Should either of the elder siblings arrive, Crockett was to yell "Diggleshroot!" loudly to signal she was to flee.

They felt both eager and fearful when they came to the main entrance of the lodge. The mixed feelings caused them to stand outside the door for a moment collecting themselves. Crockett may have waited outside the doors all day, but Brontë was anxious to remove the mystery around the youngest Deutschefaber. It was she who pressed forward and opened the door.

Upon entering, they were met with a profound silence. A clock ticked from the billiard room; the rest of the building was silent except for Brontë and Crockett's nervous breaths. Light fell through the windows of the main room, illuminating the animal heads littered around the walls. They looked startlingly lifelike, gazing on the young couple with curiosity. Crockett felt the skin on the back of his neck prickle with fearful anticipation.

"Diggleshroot," Brontë whispered, breaking the silence. She kissed

Crockett on the cheek, avoiding prolonged contact due to his earlier adventure with refuse.

As Crockett watched her run up the staircase, his heart slammed in his chest. She was barely out of sight when he heard a click behind him.

Turning slowly, he saw the main door of the lodge open. A small hand gripped the handle; a whirl of masculine voices filled the silence and echoed in the hall. Crockett held his breath with anticipation.

Already the plot was going awry.

14

Crockett Distracts

The voices revealed their masters immediately. Phipps charged through the door first, followed by Collanhall, with Mr. Gestahlt bringing up the rear. To Crockett's surprise, they carried a jovial air about them. It took only a moment for Phipps to draw close and Crockett to smell the telltale reek of whiskey on his breath. He quickly understood the source of their amusement.[28]

"Hullo, horsssse-boy," Phipps said with a loud hiccup. His drunken *s*'s had returned to his speech. "How wasss the walkabout town?"

"Horse boy?" Crockett asked. "I'm not sure I know what you mean."

"You look lika horsssse," Phipps said. This was followed by a loud, whiskey-fueled grock. "You know you gotta long, ssskinny facsssse—I bet you like carrotsss." He staggered toward the large sofa in the center of the room. "I dunno why the room isss ssso drunk right now. It canna even keep issself ssstraight." He collapsed forward, narrowly missing the couch and falling onto the floor. The little man was dressed even more garishly than normal. He wore a plum-colored suit with a bright red lapel pin circled in feathers.

Collanhall was inebriated in an entirely different manner. His senses and

---

[28] Earhart and Didiert originally designed this and the next chapter to be synchronously read. It was a daring (if brutally misguided) idea which had the text from both chapters written in columns on each page so that you could read them at the same time. Sometimes creativity is a hindrance, which is why I have split them into two, distinct chapters.

personality grew sharper, more piercing, from the spirits. He stayed by the front door for a long moment, assessing the room as if some looming threat awaited them.

"Mr. Cook," he said, far too loudly, saluting to the sky. He left his post by the door and came toward the center of the room. "How are you?"

"I'm well, Colonel. Could you..." Crockett saw Gestahlt sway as he watched a fly circle his head, "Could you tell me what you all have been doing this afternoon?"

"It was Colonel who drink. He fun." Mr. Gestahlt kept his eyes on the fly.

Phipps had gathered himself and risen from the floor. With an awkward, erratic gait, he began skulking toward the staircase.

"Oh dear," Crockett muttered.

He had thought the Deutschefabers would be the biggest threat to their subterfuge, not a carnival of drunks. While the inn guests were less threatening than the Germans, they could interrupt the plot with Klaude and would likely ask so many *questions*. There was no doubt Phipps would insert himself in the investigation.

As the writer drew close to the stairs, Crockett rushed toward him to divert his attention. As he spun Phipps around, Crockett's eyes flicked up and he saw Brontë peer around the corner on the second floor. Her face conveyed both humor and confusion.

"What is this?" she mouthed.

Crockett shrugged, then shooed her away. He next put his arms around Phipps and dragged him back toward the sofa.

"Mr. Phipps, perhaps we should keep you seated. I think the climb would be too much for you in the present moment."

"Nonssssenssse!" Phipps said this as if he would rise to the occasion, but he only slackened in Crockett's grasp, leading the young man to fall backwards, the spherical writer atop him.

"Oh, my," he said. "Wasssa that sssmell?"

Crockett had forgotten his current malodorous state. "I...fell into some mud in town," he said, realizing that Phipps had now come close enough to have received a transfer of the excrement. "It's nothing to worry about..."

Collanhall approached and lifted Phipps easily off Crockett. He held him under one arm and extended his other hand to help Crockett back to his feet.

"Right as a wallaby," he said gruffly. The colonel tossed Phipps back onto the sofa. The writer was surprisingly springy and bounced from the couch back onto the floor. As Phipps writhed on the ground trying to get his footing, Collanhall assessed him with indifference. "He'll be all right," he said. "Mr. Gestahlt, let's go into the billiard room and look for the whiskey! There has to be some left over from the party."

Phipps's collision with the floor made a crash seemingly incongruous with the action. Crockett's eyes lifted to the second floor, wondering if the noise was from upstairs and Brontë needed assistance. There was little time to contemplate this, however, as the colonel squeezed Crockett's shoulder and pulled him close. Years of military training made his grip like an iron vise. Crockett grunted.

"Ah, civilian constitution," the colonel said with an air of disappointment in his voice. "I thought you London folk would have a hardier makeup."

"I believe I've grown soft," Crockett said massaging his shoulder. "I used to be a child of the streets, but that was a very long time ago."

"Is true?!" Mr. Gestahlt peered in from the billiard room. He twitched slightly and began itching the back of his neck.

"Yes, I…" Crockett looked between the colonel and Mr. Gestahlt. He felt a sudden, odd rush of emotions.

The young lawyer never had friends in the proper sense. It was his inability to connect with his peers that led to his meeting his master, Petrarch, and taking his role as a junior solicitor. His childhood and young adulthood were solitary times in his life. But now, with the two men looking at him—one a spry, athletic father (a position he soon hoped to take) and the other a masculine paragon of military might—Crockett felt the need to impress them and win their esteem. He'd had this same desire before—a keen wish to be accepted, trusted, and supported—but hardly ever with his peers. It most often occurred in the presence of patriarchal or avuncular individuals. Now, however, he very much wanted to be included in the jolly coterie of the men from the lodge (Phipps, of course, definitely and completely excluded).

He continued, "Yes. I grew up in a rough part of London. There was a lot of fighting…there were many groups of nefarious boys about. Roughhousing was the sport of those days."

Mr. Gestahlt lost his interest in his search for alcohol entirely. Still scratching his neck, he came back into the main room. "Interesting! Did you be in a group, like a gang?"

"Almost…" Crocket said. "I…used to be a thief." He did not need to mention that he attempted thieving exactly once before Petrarch took him off the streets and gave him an apprenticeship in law. His attention also shifted, as Gestahlt was causing him concern. The Serbian's neck was turning red from the scratching. "Mr. Gestahlt, are you quite all right? That's quite an itch you have there."

"Ah!" the Serbian grimaced. "It the buggies in the bedsies!"

Crockett took a step back. His eyes were wide with disgust.

There was no time to dwell on this horror, however, as Collanhall grabbed Crockett by the collar again and dragged him toward the billiard room. "A thief, my man! Now, that is interesting! I took you for a pasty, but you may be a full rump roast."

Phipps, not wanting to be left behind, pulled himself up and dazedly followed the small party.

"Gestahlt!" Collanhall roared. "Did you find the whiskey?"

"I think yes!" Gestahlt scurried back to the bar. He pulled a small contraption from his pocket and approached a large wooden cabinet. With a flick of his hand, he inserted his device into the lock, and the door of the cabinet flew open.

Crockett could not help but stare at the man's red neck as he did his work. Ursula hopefully had some emollient to soothe his rash.

"Ha ha!" Collanhall was immensely pleased with the opening of the liquor cabinet. He punched Crockett in the shoulder causing him to wince. "It appears Mr. Gestahlt and I share an interest in tinkering and tunkering."

"Tunkering?" Crockett asked.

"Australian tinkering. Do you learn nothing culturally in London?"

"I suppose not…" Crockett responded.

"Well, being a member of the Australian Regional Society of Engineers, I tunkered for most of my youth. They called me Tunker Tom!"

"But your name isss Collin," Phipps slurred.

"Exactly!" Collanhall gave Crockett a light shove, which caused the young man, who was already in a precarious state of balance, to fall to the floor.

Gestahlt was now out of the way of the cabinet. Collanhall looked upon the rows of liquor with a zealous gleam in his eye. This joyful countenance caused a sudden surge of nervousness in Crockett. The colonel was an expert drinker, and no doubt expected all the gathered party to join him in his attack upon sobriety.

His instinct proved correct. Collanhall lurched forward and grabbed the largest bottle from the cabinet. The military man ripped out its cork with his teeth and took a long, exaggerated draught.

"Now that's koala-ty," he said.[29]

He handed the bottle to Crockett, who lifted himself from the floor and took a feigned sip. "Very nice," he said.

"Ah! Take a man's drink! Don't tell me you're afraid of a tankard of liquor having grown up on the streets!" He grabbed the bottle and forced it to Crockett's lips. The young man's eyes went wide as he unwillingly swallowed several gulps of whiskey. He coughed and reached for his throat, which had the feeling of being consumed by fire.

"Gestahlt!" The colonel pulled the bottle from Crockett and pointed it at the young Serbian. "Where are you from again? I hope they raise stronger drinking stock than this London picayune."

"I from Soborbia," Gestahlt said, his eyes looking fearfully at Collanhall.

"Serbia you mean?" Crockett asked.

"Serbia, Soborbia, Sherbet Land, what does it matter?" Collanhall asked. "Open up, Gestahlt."

---

[29] While this Australian pun is a crime against humanity (and was most likely never uttered by the colonel), I felt it necessary to keep as much of Earhart in the text as possible.

Before the young father could protest, he received a steady stream of whiskey in his gullet.

The afternoon of light drinks was quickly turning into an alcohol-tainted free-for-all. Collanhall's sheer size and presence made it difficult to maneuver out of the situation. Even Phipps was forced to take another sip of the bottle whilst he lay on the ground intermittently hiccupping.

The spirits quickly attacked Crockett's senses. Very rarely would he have too much to drink; when he did it was in the security and safety of Petrarch's office after a long week of work. This drunkenness was much more lion than the lamb-like imbibing he did with his master. As the world began to wobble on its axis, he recognized he had to pull them all back to the main room so that he could still serve as lookout for Brontë. He took a deep breath and prepared to direct them away from the liquor cabinet.

"Let's go have a seat," he said with as much authority as he could muster. "We can do…" he struggled, "a game…"

Collanhall sloshed the bottle in his hand, an act of approval. "I can show you all how to play Dingo Dip Dip!"

The group of men went into the next room. Crockett soon regretted the decision to suggest a game, as the next thirty minutes passed by like a train without brakes. Collanhall's game of Dingo Dip Dip was little more than an advanced game for drunks. It involved substituting the words "dingo" or "dip" for numbers as you counted from one to twenty-seven. The rules continually changed and transformed as light does in a prism. If you said "dip" or "dingo" at the incorrect moment, you were forced to take a Colonel-sized drink from the bottle of spirits.

"So," Collanhall said at one point, "you said 'dip' on seven, however, it was two dips after the last dingo was called. This means it's five dips before a dingo unless someone calls tillywiggles, in which case we all reverse."[30]

It was Phipps who caused the game to end. He stood up and indecorously

---

[30] Dingo Dip Dip was brought to the text by Didiert, who sailed as a young man and met a group of Australians at a pub off the coast of Italy. Earhart and he would often play before the ballet, a perfect "pre-game" to the event, as they hated ballet but felt compelled to go to appear cultured. They both much preferred bouts of Greco-Roman wrestling.

loosed his stomach contents into a large decorative vase on the center table. After retching, he stood and examined himself. He removed some of the regurgatory refuse from his shirt and lapel pin. Crockett felt slightly better now that he wasn't the only one covered in filth.

"Maybe," Gestahlt said itching his neck, "we take break."

"If you need it." Collanhall pulled the bottle close to him as if it were a baby.

Crockett desperately tried to keep his wits about him. As the dingo game progressed, the colonel eased off his pressure so that Crockett began to take non-sips of the liquor. Although he was in better shape than either Phipps or Gestahlt, his head was filled with a thick, whiskey-laden fog. He knew he must keep the gathered party in the sitting room so that he could watch the door for the return of the Deutschefabers. He closed his eyes and took stabilizing breaths.

"Wanna hear a sssecret?" Phipps, post sickness, had returned to a position on the floor.

"Always," Crockett said quickly. His heart quickened.

"I'm not writin' the book you think I am." With this out, he started chuckling like an old turtle. "Heh, heh, heh."

"Well, mate," Collanhall said taking a sip of the whiskey. "What is it about then?"

Phipps's turtle laugh ceased. "It'sss a hissstoricul book. That'sss all I'll sssay!" He paused for an infinitesimal moment before droning on, "The old woman knowsss more than ssshe sssaysss. Ssshe's not helping with it at all."

"Madame van der Raaf?" Crockett asked.

"Yesss! Veeerrry uncoopertive. Uncoopertave. Uncooperatin." He began to turtle laugh again. "Heh, hehe—you know whatta mean."

"What's the historical subject?" Crockett hadn't found Phipps interesting until this moment.

Rather than answer, the writer just continued to chortle. He rolled onto his side, sleep starting to saturate his voice, "It'sss about none of yur busssinesss, horssse-boy." This slight was immediately followed by Phipps's snores echoing in the open hall.

"That's very interesting," Crockett said. He warily turned to Gestahlt, who was still dealing with the "buggies" on his neck. "Do you know what it's about?"

The young father said nothing. His eyes were cloudy. "No," he said abruptly. "Don't know it."

"I would imagine this place," Collanhall said loudly. "He probably is writing about the tragedy."

Crockett turned to Collanhall. "You know about it?"

"Of course! Leapin' emus, mate, how do you go to the Deutschefaber Inn and *not* know?"

"Did you know, Mr. Gestahlt?" Crockett turned to the Serbian (Sorbian? Soborbian?).

The young father looked ill. He shook his head.

"Hard to believe, that," Collanhall continued. "Everyone knows about the tragedy. The father found out about his son helping the doctor, but it was too late. He had already been injured in the experiment. The Deutschefaber patriarch went crazy, killed the doctor, and then went to prison."

Crockett's mouth dropped open. "What?! Doctor? Experiment?"

"Sorry, I would have said something sooner." Collanhall took another sip of whiskey. "I assumed it was common knowledge."

Gestahlt rose. His face was now green. His hands were shaking. "I go," he said quickly.

"Do you need help?" Crockett asked. "We can walk you..."

"No! I be fine." The Serbian's eyes rolled back in his head slightly. He staggered and nearly fell.

Crockett desperately wanted to find out more from Collanhall about the sudden revelation of the doctor, Klaude's injury, and murder. "Collanhall..." Crockett moved to ask a question, but, before he could speak, Gestahlt staggered again and toppled to the floor. The crash caused Phipps to jolt awake.

"Such weak constitutions!" Collanhall shook his head. He looked at Crockett with approval. "You appear hardier! I did expect more from the American and Soborbian, though. I'll get these gentlemen back home."

The colonel lifted Gestahlt off the floor. The Serbian, dangling over Collanhall's back, called out to Crockett, "Your thief group in London. It have name?"

Crockett shook his head. "It was unorganized, just a bunch of rough children trying to impress each other."

The Serbian itched his neck in response.

Phipps rose slowly. His eyes were glassy. Both his hair and the feathers of his red lapel pin were mussed. Sensing his own intoxication and the movement toward the exit, he plodded past Crockett with a nod and joined Collanhall at the door of the lodge.

"Cheerio, my boy!" Collanhall waved as he pushed Gestahlt and Phipps outside and followed behind them.

Crockett breathed a sigh of relief when the door slammed shut. The Deutschefabers were still absent; he now could solely focus on his mission to protect Brontë as she searched for Klaude.

With the copious amounts of alcohol in his system, the events surrounding the Deutschefaber Inn began to coalesce in interesting ways. It appeared that the threads of the guests at the Deutschefaber Inn were more interwoven than he and Brontë believed. Greta had some past connection to the town. Phipps was writing a history novel about the inn, if Collanhall was correct, and he was trying to source Greta's input for it. Collanhall was presumably at the inn to hunt the beast but was also aware of the many secrets the Deutschefabers were hiding. But were they actually secrets if Collanhall was aware of them? Did Collanhall have a reason for being at the inn aside from hunting the beast? He seemed to know the most. Could he be in alignment with the mysterious Kreuz and know about the green and gold handkerchief? And what of Gestahlt? Was he truly the benign father figure he appeared to be? What was the itching, and why was he so interested in Crockett's thievery?

And, most importantly, what were the details of the events regarding the murder of the doctor and Klaude's accident?

Crockett's musings were interrupted by footsteps on the stairs. He turned toward the approaching sound with a broad smile, anticipating seeing

Brontë's charming face coming toward him.

But it was not his new bride who drew near. He took in a sharp breath as he saw both Ursula and Bristol pounding down the stairs. Their faces were contorted into looks of rage. Sweat poured from Crockett's brow as he recognized a small item hanging limply in Bristol's hand.

It was the red monogrammed handkerchief Brontë used to wipe the muck from his face earlier that day.

15

Brontë Sleuths

At the beginning of her mission, Brontë hurried up the steps to the second floor of the inn. Guaranteed no intrusions, she knew she could find Klaude and learn more about the tangled, tragic history of the Deutschefabers. With his perspective, she hoped to be able to draw real connections between the events of the week. He could even successfully put the Caddywampus rumors to rest if he knew something of the local wildlife.

This time at the top of the stairs, she turned left, knowing that the right passage led to at least one storage closet.

As she turned the corner into the hallway, she imagined what the youngest Deutschefaber would look like. She figured he had to be close to twenty; in the family portrait, he was a small child, but it appeared from Ursula's age that at least fifteen or more years had passed since then. Based on the picture, she also assumed he'd have blue eyes, and, if physiques were consistent in the family, he would be either square or muscular or, likely, a combination of those qualities. There was a chance the infamous accident may have affected the young man's physical appearance. It was Brontë's hope that Crockett had been wrong about him having a frightful, Quasimodo-like deformity.

This thought about the mysterious accident forced more questions into her consciousness: What if he couldn't speak? What if he was so disfigured that he must be hidden away? What if the accident left him bitter and cruel?

These musings were interrupted by the arrival of Gestahlt, Collanhall, and Phipps in the main hall. She went back to the main passage and peered around the corner. When she saw that it was not a Deutschefaber causing the ruckus but the arrival of the other lodgers, she expressed her relief in a beaming smile. Crockett looked up to her from the main room and shooed her on.

Her full attention turned back to her quest. She reentered the second corridor and assessed her surroundings.

It was the mirror image of the other side. Three closed doors flanked a dimly lit hall. Brontë was prepared to do a thorough investigation of each room, putting her numerous (if abridged) detective skills to work. She hoped there may even be a portrait of Charlemagne to guide her investigation.

It was with a hint of disappointment, then, that as she knelt to the floor to begin looking for footprints, her eyes flitted up to see an obvious clue. The middle door in the hall had a clear sign on it which read "Klaude."

She stood and dusted off her trousers. With a few tentative steps, she arrived at the door. While she hoped the young man knew something of the current mystery, she also feared the individual who awaited her on the other side of the portal. What was the accident that affected him and the family so deeply?

She rapped softly on the door and took a deep breath. When no one responded, she knocked with more volume. It appeared no one was in the chamber.

Her fears subsiding, she pushed open the door.

"Hullo," she said, entering the room quietly. "Is anyone here?"

The room was a delightful contrast to the dim hallway; the overall impression was of a bright, tidy quarters. A large window overlooked the deep woods behind the lodge and illuminated the room in warm, autumn light. The bed was made, and although there were hundreds of books in the room, only one was out of place and off the shelf, laid open on a table in the center of the room. The rest of the volumes were neatly stored and aligned in four large bookcases pushed against the walls. On the table, next to the open book, was a small journal. Bound in leather, its brown pages fluttered lightly from a breeze flowing through the open window.

Brontë approached the journal curiously. She had just pressed her hand to the page, her eyes beginning to scan it, when there was a click.

Her eyes lifted. They tracked up toward a small closet that she had not noticed before. As the door pushed open, her heart shuddered and then stopped. A figure emerged from the hidden space. She shook with horror as its vile form came into the full light of the room.

It sat in a chair. Its face was inhuman. The eyes were large, dark, and ghastly, lined with red. Around the perimeter of the face were an erratic collection of hair and feathers. Had Brontë been asked in that moment to name the creature, she would have suggested it was the floating offspring of the Caddywampus.

She toppled backward as the grotesque figure glided rapidly toward her in the chair, its hair and feathers that lined its frightening face quivering in the rush.

In her desperation to get away from the monster, she tripped backwards and fell over the small table on which the journal and the book were laid. The form suddenly stopped upon seeing her fall. Brontë held up her hands to her face and tried to flee by crawling to the window. She heard the odd creature respirate loudly as its wild eyes sized her up. Its face turned slightly. A low, odd hiss escaped its mouth, after which two human hands gripped the terrifying face and lifted it. The mask (for that's what it was) having been removed, Brontë now found herself looking upon the very human face of Klaude Deutschefaber.

The nervous, innocent countenance looking back at her was not what she expected. The young man had bright blue eyes and was very thin. Instead of inheriting the bulky, square build of his sister and brother, he appeared to be more of a short 5line segment—thin and short. The result of the accident that had affected him so deeply appeared to be the wheelchair he traveled in, along with a long, purple scar that ran down the left side of his face. His small hands were raised high into the air, as though he were surrendering.

"*Wer bist du?*" the small man asked. His eyes were neutral, his voice soft.

Brontë shook her head indicating she didn't understand. He continued to stare at her as one would examine a bug under a microscope.

"English?" she asked finally.

He said nothing.

"I came up—"

"You shouldn't be here," he said quickly. Despite sounding resolute, his hand twitched slightly. When Brontë did not respond, he continued, "My sister will not like you coming up here."

Brontë did not want to be turned away so quickly. Now that Klaude Deutschefaber was revealed and confirmed as staunchly not horrifying, she wanted to ask if he knew something about the present circumstances. Moreover, his twitching hand and a slight sparkle in the young man's eyes belied his resolve; she hoped to capitalize upon these hints of friendly ambivalence. She kept her eyes on him and stood from her collapsed position on the floor. "I like your mask," she said. "Where did you get it?"

Klaude appeared to have forgotten about the mask. He looked at the object in his hand then set it in his lap. After a moment of examination, his eyes flicked to the door. He hesitated briefly, then spoke, "It was a gift."

"It's lovely." Brontë pressed on to encourage conversation. "Who was it from?"

"A friend." Klaude looked torn. His mouth opened to speak again but then closed abruptly. Instead, he turned his gaze down and looked at the mask once more.

Brontë was unsure what to do. She bemoaned not having dug further into the detective book. When she and Crockett hatched their plan, she imagined Klaude as an accomplice to the chaos around them, but seeing his small form in his wheeled chair made her unsure about his knowing anything. His speaking was labored and uncertain, as if it had been a long while since he used his voice.

"Which friend—" she began to ask.

She was cut off by Klaude, "You shouldn't be here." This time he said it with an edge of fear to his voice. "My sister doesn't like when…" He paused, thought for a moment, "Well, she doesn't like when things are disrupted. She's very protective."

Quickly, Klaude turned his chair and wheeled away from Brontë. It appeared he was going to leave the room completely.

In an act of desperation, she called after him, "I'm sorry! It's just strange things are happening around this place!" She sounded more hysterical than she would have liked. "I hoped you could shed light on some questions I had about your family."

Klaude's chair stopped. Slowly, he turned towards her. This time she was certain she saw fear in his blue eyes.

"It's best not to ask questions. Everything you think you know happened a long time ago."

"It's more recent, actually," Brontë said. She knew the wrong word would send Klaude skittering back into the shadows. Her mind worked rapidly to find some point of interest that would keep him talking. Having heard Klaude speak about Ursula with fear, she wondered what he thought of his older brother. "Your brother appears to be in some kind of trouble."

Klaude's face fell. "Trouble? Is he safe? Healthy?"

"Yes…well, for now." Brontë's heart pounded. "Today in town we saw someone threaten him."

The young man wheeled back toward Brontë. He took a moment before he spoke again, "Threaten?" His voice wavered. "But he's okay?"

"Yes, he's fine. He and the attacker left on good terms, but do you know why someone would be after him?" She looked intently at Klaude. The young man sat in silent reflection. Brontë again felt desperate; a chill down her spine told her there was not much time. She hurriedly asked, "Have you ever noticed him wearing a green and gold handkerchief?"

Klaude scratched his head. "A handkerchief?" He thought for a moment. "No…I don't recall him wearing anything like that."

"What about monsters? A monster in the woods?" Brontë imagined the author of the detective book groaning at this disastrous line of questioning.[31]

For the first time, Klaude showed a semblance of a smile. The edges of his mouth turned up slightly. "A monster?" he asked. "What kind of monster?"

"The Caddywampus."

"Caddy-what?"

Brontë cringed, realizing Phipps's moniker was now the more common. "The *Dämonenbär*. It's...well, we've heard it's a monster."

Klaude laughed slightly. His blue eyes sparkled. "The *Dämonenbär*? Where did you hear about that?"

Brontë felt horribly stupid. "Well, it's...we've seen it. It's in the woods."

Klaude's light giggles turned to a loud guffaw. "You've seen it?!"

"Yes, it's...well, Collanhall, Phipps, and Sylvia saw it, too. It's big! Half puma, half bear, half elk. It's...well, it's terrifying...really..." Brontë watched Klaude grow more and more amused. She couldn't help but start to laugh herself. "It's not...I mean, it's not funny. We saw it!"

"The mythical *Dämonenbär*?" Klaude, in an attempt at politeness, covered his mouth with his hands to hide his laughter, but it was becoming harder to conceal. Brontë was losing control of her own fit of giggles.

"It is! It's out there!"

Before long they were both laughing hysterically. They recognized they shouldn't be enjoying themselves this much—Brontë was meant to be in the middle of a heated investigation, and Klaude would be threatened by his sister if he were discovered. But they could not stop themselves. As soon as they'd be on the verge of regaining composure, they'd immediately break into renewed fits of mirth.

It was a full minute before they both calmed down enough to converse. Klaude, relaxing from his fearful state, was the first to speak.

---

[31] Speaking of questioning, in the initial draft, Didiert and Earhart titled this chapter "The Interrogation." It was written in an obnoxious question/answer style, i.e., "Q: Was the mysterious figure who emerged from the closet seated or standing? A: He was seated, his hands pressed against two, metallic wheels suspended from the sides of his chair." It was over seventy-five pages long. It wasn't too unbearable until they got into questions about carpet fibers and parchment coloring.

"I don't know anything about handkerchiefs or my brother's attacker, but I can assure you that the monster is a myth. Bristol and I used to camp out in the woods and look for it. It's still a bit of a joke." Klaude indicated the mask in his hands. "He was going to come up this afternoon, which is why I put on the mask…to surprise him." He seemed to be delighted by these memories. He continued with more energy. "We'd camp in the woods. With our lanterns lit, we'd lay awake listening for strange sounds. My father would dress up and scare us…" The young man stopped abruptly. He choked down emotion. The joyous feeling evaporated. "It's…it's not real," he said with finality.

Brontë reached out. She was unsure the best way to offer some condolence. Having heard the story of his father, she could only imagine the pain even a happy memory would bring upon the young man.

"Klaude, I'm sorry—"

"You really should go," he said. "I can't—Ursula wouldn't approve, and I truly have nothing to say. I stay up here nearly every day. Ursula demands it…and, to be honest, I acquiesce a bit too readily." The earlier look of fear returned to the young man's eyes. "If you're looking for information, I'm afraid you've come to the wrong place. I don't know anything about Bristol or handkerchiefs or…" in spite of himself, he giggled once more, "or monsters."

Brontë felt sheepish. The young man was confined to the upstairs. She had stormed into his private quarters and forced him to converse with her. It was both rude and uncouth—a mad, desperate attempt to give light to a mystery which she and Crockett shouldn't have been pursuing at all.

She wrung her hands and sighed. "I'm sorry for bringing this up and bothering you this afternoon, Klaude," she said. She looked at the mask which still rested in the young man's lap. "You said this was a gift?" She hoped to at least leave on a happier, friendlier note.

"Yes," Klaude said. "Dr. Gutermord used to live on the grounds. My parents bought the land for the inn from him. He traveled the world when he was young…this was one of the things he collected."

"Dr. Gutermord?" Brontë remembered the name from their earlier exchange with Madame van der Raaf. "Does he still live on the grounds?"

Klaude shook his head. "No, he…" Klaude looked toward the wall. Above it was a large map of the grounds. "There," he said pointing to it. "He used to live in the ravine, in a small home away from the main lodge and the other cabins."

Brontë remembered the map above Greta's fireplace. "There is a sixth cabin…" she said softly. That's what had struck her as odd about the image in the old dame's sitting room. There was an additional cabin below the ridge. She counted six instead of five and it confused her.

"I believe it's abandoned now," Klaude said. "After everything…it…" He stopped speaking and turned toward the door. He glanced between it and Brontë. His eyes lit up for a brief moment before he sighed and drooped his head. He spoke, a resigned tone in his soft voice, "You should go."

Brontë hoped he would say more. Instead, he nervously bit his lip and tapped his skinny fingers on the mask, which was still in his lap. She looked into his sad, blue eyes and felt another wave of overwhelming regret for her actions; she was both ashamed regarding her poor detective work—the reckless certainty that had empowered her to accost Klaude—and horrified she had destroyed the peace of the poor, diffident man on the second floor.

"I'm sorry to have disturbed you," she said standing up and heading toward the exit. "I don't know why I thought…" She shook her head. "My husband and I are amateur detectives, and we thought you could provide some insight into the odd coincidences going on around us. It was rude to interfere, come up here, enter unbidden, and make you uncomfortable. I'm very sorry."

A spark returned to Klaude's eyes. "Detectives?"

"Detective adjacent, may be more apt."

Klaude moved his chair forward. He picked up the book which had been on the small table before Brontë toppled it to the ground. "Detectives," he said with a smile. "Bristol finished it—it's in German. He said it was quite good."

Brontë examined the book. The cover had a woman tied up on a cliff being attacked by a shark with wings.[32] "That…looks very interesting."

"I have yet to start it. It looks like an adventure story Bristol and I would have liked when we were young." He picked up the book and flipped through the pages. Another smile appeared on his lips. "If you are a detective, you would like the mystery of Dr. Gutermord's cabin."

"There is a mystery about it?" Brontë felt her stomach twist with anticipation.

"Long disproven, but for many years people would come out to the inn looking for a treasure."

Brontë's eyes widened. "A treasure?"

"It was a rumor from a long time ago. No one found anything."

There was a bang in the distance.

The color from Klaude's face drained. "My brother and sister…," he whispered.

"Oh," Brontë said. "But…my husband was watching the lodge entrance."

"There's a back stair," Klaude said quickly. "They use it often when they come visit. They don't want…well, Ursula tries to protect me in her own way. She doesn't want to draw attention to my presence."

Footsteps grew louder in the hall. Brontë looked at Klaude for an indication of how worrisome the current predicament was. Judging by his waxen complexion and shaking hands, it was dire.

"No… you…" Voices could be heard in the hall. Klaude's gesturing grew frantic. "Go to the closet, please. You need to hide. As I said…well, she does not like disruption."

Brontë did not want to tempt upsetting the innkeeper. She leapt toward the closet. Just as the door shut behind her, she heard Klaude's chamber open and Ursula's voice ring out. She spoke a warm, German greeting to her little brother.

---

[32] This was another shameless plug for one of Didiert's books. After *The Murderer Is the Son* was translated into German, the Germans loved it so much that Didiert gained some fame. His next book didn't do as well, primarily because Didiert did the translation himself, mistranslating the title from *The Woman and the Mythic Shark* to *Female Shark and Dead Shrub*.

Shaking, Brontë reached into her pocket to withdraw her handkerchief to wipe away perspiration. She hoped there was a small, untarnished corner that escaped the mess of Crockett's earlier adventure. It was then, however, that she realized it was gone. Her hands flew to her mouth to suppress an exclamation. The handkerchief had her monogrammed initials. It may have fallen from her pocket when she stumbled to the ground. If it were seen…

Ursula continued to speak to Klaude in German. Her voice was full of joy, much different from the cold, terse tones she used in her role as the innkeeper. Brontë pressed her ear against the door. While Ursula's voice was loud and boisterous, Klaude's was soft and barely audible. She hoped that her handkerchief had fallen out of her pocket and drifted out of sight. Klaude and Ursula exchanged a few more words and then a third voice joined.

Brontë cringed; she recognized it as Bristol's. The eldest Deutschefaber sounded more businesslike than his sister. Although she could not understand what they said, she knew Bristol was asking Klaude sharp, direct questions.

There was then a sudden gasp.

Brontë heard footsteps pound across the room. Ursula's voice roared out, now filled with a pulsing rage.

"Handkerchief." Brontë could not help but whisper the word out loud. Her hands trembled. She shut her eyes and rubbed her temples.

The voices grew louder and more frantic. Someone struck something out of frustration. There was a flurry of footsteps and then the sound of a slamming door.

Brontë pressed her eye to the door. Although nothing was visible, she strained in the hopes of catching a glimpse of what was happening. She trembled, wondering if Bristol would find her. What would he do if he discovered her nosing about twice in a day?

There was no time to ponder this question. Klaude quickly threw open the door. His face was red.

"You have to go," he said quickly.

"What is going on?"

"Bristol…He said someone was searching around last night. They found your handkerchief." Klaude shook his head. "It reeks of excrement."

Brontë blanched.

Klaude, so frantic that he was incurious about the odorous handkerchief, searched around the room. It was then that his eyes rested on a trunk pressed against the wall beneath the window. "You'll need to trust me," he said.

Brontë nodded excitedly. "As another quasi-detective, I trust you completely."

The two locked eyes, an exuberant energy passing between them—Brontë felt the warmth and pride of a teacher for her student as Klaude, in their short exchange, had transformed from a shy, diffident shut-in to a brazen co-conspirator. Klaude himself felt the joy and excitement of comradeship, something he'd sorely missed in the years since his accident. His whole family chose to distance themselves, Bristol treating him as fragile and weak and Ursula becoming his overprotective nursemaid rather than his sister.

It's rare for seeds of friendship to bloom so thick and lustrously, but in the quiet of Klaude's chamber, the autumn breeze passing through the curtains, both Klaude and Brontë felt they had been friends for life.

Klaude, smiling, wheeled his chair to the trunk and opened it with a flourish. His hands vanished for a moment before they were again visible, gripping a long, white sheet.

16

The Next Steps

As Klaude assisted Brontë's escape, Crockett found himself face-to-face with an infuriated Bristol. The stocky gentleman's breath smelled of gin. "Where is your wife, Mr. Cook?" he bellowed. "Is she snooping around the lodge?"

Crockett, still decently intoxicated himself, tried to handle the situation with confidence.

"She is…not…She is not." His legs shook. Bristol's eyes were red with rage. His hands clenched. Crockett was grateful for the alcohol. Had his brain not been lubricated, there was the very real possibility he would have fainted under the crazed questioning of the maybe-gangster.

"Then, Mr. Cook…" Bristol's teeth gnashed together. He held up the excrement-covered handkerchief. "What is this? Why was her handkerchief in my brother's room?" With a pugnacious snort, he indicated Brontë's initials on the small piece of cloth.

Crockett's lips punched out a like fish. "I…well, you know…I know…we know…"

Ursula felt pity looking on the drunk, young man. "Bristol, perhaps he doesn't know."

"I saw his wife snooping around the lodge last night! Then, I see him and his wife following me this afternoon when I was at—" Bristol paused abruptly. It appeared he did not want his sister to know specifics about the

135

incident at the pub. "Well, they followed me! And now this is mysteriously in Klaude's bedroom! What is your game, Cook?"

Bristol took a step closer to Crockett. Their noses were nearly touching.

"That question…" Crockett started slowly, "is one… which…I would say…is an excellent question. But," the young lawyer swallowed hard, "if I were to pick…a game, I would say my game is whist."

Bristol looked on the verge of lunging at the throat of Crockett when Brontë appeared at the front door.

The young woman looked disheveled; she was limping, and her hair was full of twigs. Her blouse was torn, and she winced with pain as she held her left arm. She tried her best to not sound frantic. "Hello!" she said in a high, strained voice. "Oh, my handkerchief!"

Bristol turned his enmity on Brontë. His face's color changed from red to purple.

"You!"

He shoved Crockett down on the sofa and stormed over to Brontë. The young woman tried to remain calm as the menacing gentleman stomped toward her.

"Good afternoon," she said with as casual an air as she could muster. "You look well!"

Bristol forced the handkerchief up to Brontë's nose. Some of the smell of waste had evaporated, but it was not a pleasant experience. "Why," he said through gritted teeth, "Was. This. In. My. Brother's. Room?"

It should be noted that Klaude tried his best to aid Brontë's escape. The young man created a ladder from the bed dressings in his trunk. He thought this would help Brontë gently drop from the second-floor window. The makeshift escape device, however, proved to be only half-reliable. As she descended, the bed sheets unraveled, and she plummeted into a large, flowering bush. Her sole focus had been getting to Crockett, so she took no time to fix her appearance. She was standing on the threshold of the inn looking like a madwoman. The sudden realization she had not concocted an actual reason for the handkerchief to be where it was found hit her like a stomach cramp.

"It waaassss?" She said this and looked at Bristol with both confusion and anxiety.

Bristol was so taken aback by her appearance and the general confusion everyone appeared to have upon the handkerchief's discovery that he merely said, "Yes. It was."

There was an uncomfortable pause as Brontë worked to fabricate an excuse for the handkerchief. Ursula turned her attention to the upstairs, hoping her youngest brother was all right. Bristol's temper, which dropped slightly upon Brontë's response to his question, was beginning to soar once again.

It was Crockett, responding as best he could, who interjected. "It flew!" he said standing up from the couch. "It was…must have been the easterly up from the west—the wind here—my word, it's nothing like in London!"

Brontë stared at him, as did Bristol.

"Yes," the young lawyer said gaining momentum, the alcohol working to its full effect. "We were on our way up to the lodge, and Brontë took out her handkerchief…to do handkerchiefly things…"

"Clean excrement!" she added, trying her best to help her prattling husband.

"Yes! I was covered, because I smelled it. I like…the smell…and it got all over." Crockett cringed, horrified by his own inept cover story.

"You…" Bristol's emotional balance shifted from rage to confoundment. "You enjoy the smell of excrement?"

"Most definitely!" Crockett nodded enthusiastically. "Ask Ursula! I was overjoyed by the tale of droppings being in the piano."

Ursula turned to Crockett. Her eyebrows raised. "This is true," she said, a look of admiration on her face.

"So…" Crockett planned to continue; however, Brontë was growing very concerned about the direction he would take the conversation, so she interrupted.

"I took it out to wipe Crockett off, and then it got caught in the western-easterly-southerly and shot up into the air!"

Bristol turned to her. Brontë hoped he would ask a follow-up question, but when none came, she added more clarity out of nervousness, "It flew up and then it sort of danced…and then it swooped…"

"There was a lot of swooping," Crockett added.

"So much that it flew around the outside of the lodge and into a room, which I gather happened to be Klaude's."

"Yes!" Crockett exclaimed. "Brontë was planning on climbing the lodge to get it," he indicated Brontë's state of mess, "while I thought it best to come inside and use the stairs."

"He likes smelling excrement, but he is very logical when it comes to finding the second floor of things," Brontë added with immediate regrets.

Crockett nodded, finding himself completely confused as to what their explanation had become.

Ursula and Bristol had no desire to probe further into the incident. Bristol was horrified by Crockett's odd interests and Ursula by Brontë's lack of logical faculties preventing her from climbing the side of the building. The brother and sister looked at each other, shrugged, and returned the handkerchief.

Brontë took it and immediately wiped her face, which was cause for a swift look of revulsion. She did her best to conceal her horror.

"Oh! So glad to have it back," she said through gritted teeth.

Crockett sensing the conversation could transform into something even worse at any moment, reached forward and grabbed his wife's arm.

"Thank you so much for your help!" he said quickly guiding Brontë to the door. "This was such fantastic service."

"It really was!" Brontë added, throwing back a smile before she was led out.

The door to the lodge slammed shut, leaving Bristol and Ursula standing in a state of bewilderment.

"I suppose," Ursula said, smoothing her blouse, "we can attribute it to their Englishness."

This satisfied Bristol, who gave a "harrumph" in response and stalked off toward his quarters.

Outside, Brontë and Crockett walked back to their cabin in silence. Both were taking time to process their acute sense of shame about what had happened—their feelings of awkwardness and incompetence outweighing their ability to appreciate the success they had in collecting new information at the inn.

Brontë finally spoke as they came to their cabin and Crockett held the door open for her to enter.

"We'll laugh about this later, right, Crockett?"

The young man thought for a moment, unable to commit to a reassuring answer. Finally, he said, "Or cry. I feel the memory may conjure a mix of emotions."

#

The couple spent the next few hours pondering their humiliation. They boiled water and took baths in the tub, then treated themselves to some biscuits and jam. The afternoon was a welcome respite from each other and the mystery; they came back together refreshed and less ashamed. Crockett sat on the sofa and drank a cup of tea (Sylvia had replaced the dirt substance with something that looked closer to Earl Grey); he was starting to feel less intoxicated and more like his old self. He was grateful he avoided the full fury of the colonel's whiskey binge earlier. It was a distinct possibility Phipps and Mr. Gestahlt would be incapacitated until morning.

"Well, I don't know what to make of it, Crockett," Brontë said sighing. "We keep learning more, but it doesn't appear to lead anywhere." She exercised her arm which had been injured in her fall from the window. To her great relief, after the rest, it was feeling as good as new.

Crockett put down his tea. "I fully agree. What did you learn about Klaude?"

"He was very pleasant, a bit sad. He's confined to a chair due to his injuries; it was not the Quasimodo situation we feared, however." She sat down on the couch next to Crockett. "Did you find out anything from the gentlemen?"

"Many odd things."

"How so?" Brontë clasped her hands and tucked them between her legs. The excitement of Crockett having new clues made her jittery.

"Well, Phipps isn't writing the novel we think he is. He said it's a historical book."

"It's not surprising Phipps would be up to something. But does it connect to the mystery?"

Crockett smiled. "Which one? There are several to parse through. We can hardly keep track."

"To be sure, we'll start broadly. Does it apply to any of the open investigations we have started?"

"I'm unsure. But he did state that Greta has been 'uncooperative.'"

"Greta? Uncooperative?"

"Collanhall is the one who suggested he's writing about the Deutschefabers and the tragedy surrounding them."

"My word." Brontë shook her head. "Phipps as a sensationalist novelist; that's not surprising."

"Not in the least, especially considering his penchant for listening at our window."

This comment caused both Brontë and Crockett to turn to the window. With a deft movement, Brontë leapt toward it and threw open the curtain with a triumphant "Aha!"

To the relief of both, Phipps was not present. They saw only a large, fat bird, which looked gravely upset at being disturbed.

"Sorry…" The anthropomorphic features of the bird[33] compelled Brontë to apologize.

As she stepped away from the window and pondered this new information, Crockett continued, "But it still doesn't clarify why Phipps would be talking to Greta…or trying to talk to her."

"She does have some history with the town…" Brontë began to pace the room. "Is Phipps writing about all of Praktisch?"

---

[33] The bird in question was well known for making locals feel uneasy and apologetic. Its piercing eyes and high, blond crest made it look as if it wanted to speak to your manager.

"It's a possibility."

Brontë rounded the couch as she continued to contemplate the new facts of the case. She once again glanced uneasily at the window, somewhat worried the bird was going to fly in and give her a stern lecture.[34]

"Did you find anything else?" she asked. "The Phipps bit is interesting, but I don't see how it applies to the Caddywampus, the murder, Bristol, the missing children, or the break-in at the public records office."

"Hmmm..." Crockett nodded. "The other interesting thing was Collanhall. He knows the full history of the Deutschefabers. Apparently, Klaude was involved in some experiment with a local doctor. It went awry and led to the 'accident' that Bosch told us about in town. The madness he referred to must have been the father's murder of the doctor."

"A doctor?" Brontë stopped pacing. Her neck swiveled and she stared at Crockett. "Was it Dr. Gutermord?"

"Gutermord?" A flicker of recognition flitted through Crockett's mind.

"Greta mentioned him earlier. Klaude did, too. He didn't elucidate much, but he did say that the doctor used to live on the grounds. There's a sixth cabin that used to be his home."

"Really?" Crockett's eyebrows furrowed. "Where is it?"

"It's down the ravine."

"The same ravine into which we saw the Caddywampus abscond..."

Brontë and Crockett looked at each other. The unspoken question of whether to venture to the sixth cabin hung between them. Crockett abstained from speaking. The same tickle of fear that had troubled him since stepping off the train made him wary of any further investigation into the Caddywampus. Brontë also had her doubts. While she and Crockett undeniably appeared to still be in the center of a great many mysteries, she was not altogether confident that they had the genius or the resolve to be able to connect the many disparate threads they'd found. Brontë wanted to

---

[34] Sorry about the meditation on the bird. In the initial draft (as part of his continued experimentation with prose), Earhart wrote this chapter from the bird's perspective. The first-person bird voice was written in lofty, poetic English.

probe into her husband's possible interest in pursuing the adventure.

"I'm not sure of our next steps," Brontë said, breaking the building tension. "Klaude was very amused about the rumors of the monster on the grounds. He clearly doesn't believe it exists."

"Really?" Crockett asked.

"Yes." Brontë could not help but smile remembering her and Klaude's fit of laughter. "He also knew nothing of the trouble with Bristol; he had never seen him with a green and gold handkerchief."

"I suppose he also had no further context regarding the missing children, the murder, and the robbery at the records office?"

Brontë shook her head. "I didn't ask, to be honest. He was so sweet and charming. It appeared he didn't know much of anything. I don't know if they ever let him leave his room."

"That seems cruel. The grounds would be a wonderful place to explore, even in a chair. There are a number of beautiful spots he could enjoy on his own or with a little help."

"It's odd…It may be embarrassment at his condition. I'm unsure." Brontë sighed. She suddenly twitched with a stray thought from her conversation with Klaude.

Crockett's thick eyebrows rose. "Darling, is there something else?"

"It's just…" Brontë took a seat next to Crockett on the sofa once more. "Klaude spoke fondly of the past, especially Bristol…and the doctor."

"Really? But Collanhall said the doctor…"

"I know," Brontë interjected. "It's odd. If the doctor maimed Klaude and then was killed by his father, there would have to be something other than fondness there, some sort of charged feeling."

"Did he say anything else? Did anything else provide insight into the family?"

Brontë closed her eyes and attempted to relive the entire conversation in her mind. "He did say that it all happened a long time ago. He thought I wanted to talk to him about his family drama. He said, 'Everything you think you know' when I brought it up."

Crockett pursed his lips. "That's curious. What did he think that you thought you knew?"

"I'm unsure." Brontë then laughed. "To add a cherry on this bizarre cake, he also said that people believed the doctor had a treasure hidden in the sixth cabin." When she saw Crockett's eyes widen, she shook her head. "There is no treasure. People have searched for years and have found nothing. It's an old wives' tale."

After the last bit of information about their adventures in the lodge, the couple drifted into an intense bout of thinking. It appeared the more they discovered, the more questions arose. Now they had nothing definitive about the happenings in the town or the inn, but what they did have led directly to the sixth cabin at the bottom of the ravine.

Crockett tsked. "Did he say anything about Ursula?"

Brontë, still in her contemplative reverie, sounded distant. "He appeared to be very fearful of her…The poor man flinched every time he spoke of her."

At that moment there was a knock on the door. Brontë jumped, coming out of her churning thoughts. Crockett went stiff with surprise.

Once Crockett shook off his fears, he approached the door with small, nervous steps. His hand rested on the knob for several moments before he gained the courage to throw it open. To his great relief there was no one present. In the distance, he saw Sylvia marching to the cabin next door. When Crockett looked down, he saw a note written in a childlike hand.

"It's another invitation," Crockett said closing the door. "They do have a large number of parties here."

Brontë, regaining her nerves, said, "Ursula mentioned there would be an event tonight when we saw them on the road to town."

Crockett handed her the note:

*The Finnlicht Festival Opening Night Event**

Time: 8-10pm

Hors d'oeuvres will be served with wine

And local beer.

**Note it is not a party – please refrain from too joyous*

an attitude

Then, written in hurried, frantic script, in all capitals:

NO PEOPLE OR HANDKERCHIEFS ALLOWED ON THE SECOND FLOOR!

Crockett laughed. "It seems we caused an alteration in the invitation, and, well, hopefully Collanhall gets this note. I did not realize how very much he enjoys spirits. He definitely may get 'too joyous.'"

"Hmm…" Brontë looked out of the cabin and saw that evening was approaching. The sky was yet to turn to its palette of twilight colors, but they only had an hour before dusk was upon them.

Although they were indoors, Crockett knew her gaze was directed through the wall and to the edge of the ravine.

"What is it, Brontë?" He asked the question certain of what the response would be.

"We discussed the crossroads, correct?" Her mouth tightened with resolve. "We said it was our responsibility to pursue a course of action that would help the largest number of people."

"Yes." Crockett nodded. Now that the idea was being broached, he knew the only way forward. "The sixth cabin," he said softly.

"If you're willing. Although we drift further from resolution, we dive deeper into mystery."

"Which calls you." Crockett smiled at her. "We do this together, safely. What do you suggest?"

The young woman's qualms vanished. A tranquil feeling overtook her. Crockett's multicolored eyes were a link to the infinite, a reassuring ocean into which she could throw herself.

"We journey to the sixth cabin and see what we find," she said.

Crockett nodded. "I can't say I feel less dread about what is ahead, but I'm confident we can face it together."

They prepared quickly for the journey. Crockett fetched a lamp and Brontë scouted the front of their cabin to be sure no one would see their exit toward the ravine. When she was sure it was clear, they ran into the deeper woods.

Crockett did his best to play the supportive, brave husband, but as the trees closed in around them, all of the misgivings from the past few days swelled and threatened to overtake him. Goosepimples formed on his arms. He took a deep breath and closed his eyes. He spoke to himself with a calm assurance, "Nothing can happen. You'll be safe. The monster isn't real. You are safe together."

This worked nicely until they came to the lip of the ravine. Evening was coming, the azure sky of the afternoon turning lighter blue. Shadows grew longer in the dense foliage of the forest. Down the hill, Crockett's attention went to the spot where Brontë had seen the Caddywampus the previous night. He hesitated at the edge of the steep incline. He tried to catch his breath and restore his calm.

Brontë noted his face and its rising apprehension and gently gripped his hand.

"Nothing to worry about, Crockett." She smiled brightly in an effort to calm her own fears; they had surged when she saw the spot where the monster danced the night before. Around them, chirruping bugs sang a melancholy, dirge-like song. She squeezed Crockett's hand and tried her best to suppress a tremble in her own voice, "There's nothing to fear when we're together," she said. "Let's carry on."

17

The Sixth Cabin

The journey down the ravine was treacherous. The path was rocky and root-covered, most of it concealed under dense shrubbery. Crockett was only about one-third of the way down the hill before he tripped and tumbled into a ball. He descended the rest of the hill rolling like a hedgehog before colliding with a massive tree at the bottom of the slope. Brontë took the path with a more feminine grace, stepping lightly and avoiding any rapid modes of descent. They were both grateful she had been put in charge of the lantern so that it had not shattered due to Crockett's clumsiness.

When she arrived at the bottom and they confirmed Crockett's appendages were unbroken, they turned their attention to their surroundings.

In the coming twilight, it was a beautiful space. Crockett landed in a clearing surrounded with trees, their leaves slowly turning a cornucopia of fall colors. The fading sunlight cascaded through the greenery in shafts of warm, golden light that rippled across the forest floor. The wind swept lightly through the trees, their leaves shivering out a quiet song.

Brontë closed her eyes and breathed in the scent of leaves and sun and forest.

"It's lovely, isn't it?" she asked.

Crockett scoffed. He felt his fall was a direct attack by the flora and fauna. He half-believed a tree maliciously tripped him on his climb down the slope.

"It's fine, I suppose," he said indifferently.

Brontë chose to continue savoring the air and to ignore Crockett's peevishness. "After this we should take a vacation to somewhere without a murder. We deserve a respite."

"If that's possible," Crockett said dubiously. "I hope our current luck isn't permanent. I don't know if we will ever be able to escape murder moving forward."

Brontë's eyes fluttered open; her face, in the receding August light, shone with a glow of serenity.

Crockett, upon seeing her tranquil state and the sun shining through her hair, grew calmer. He smiled, remembering the first time they met. She had entered the grand foyer of Hawsfeffer Manor and left him utterly breathless. Her chestnut hair had waved in the summer breeze; she had looked at him with her hazel eyes and sent a shock of elation to his heart.

"If that's the case," Brontë said, a smile on her lips, "then we'll have to get better at solving them."

"I suppose we can always plan five days of holiday and keep two reserved for murder and investigation."

"That is what the book suggests."

They both laughed, a joyful eruption that echoed in the quiet wood.

Their happy outburst seemed to cause another sudden noise in the brush. Crockett gasped. Brontë instinctively threw herself in front of him. Whether from the sun shifting behind clouds or altered psychology, the newlyweds felt the forest grow darker and more menacing.

When Crockett recovered from the slight shock, he pressed his back to Brontë's and suggested they rotate and scan the trees. Brontë used the lamp to throw light into the darkening woods, but nothing was revealed in their maneuver.

Crockett, again, spoke softly to himself, muttering, "There is no monster," over and over.

Brontë heard his whispers and squeezed his hand. "It's nothing, darling," she said warmly. "That was most likely a bird or rodent scurrying for cover after seeing us in the clearing. I told you Klaude laughed me out of the room when I suggested there was an actual *Dämonenbär*. We've most likely been scared by a bear wearing an elk-inspired hat. Perhaps he borrowed it from Madame van der Raaf."

"Yes." Crockett tried to keep the squeak of fear from his voice. "It's all…well, I'm fine."

After another rotation and scan of the forest, they both relaxed. During their search, Brontë found a small, untended path which looked as if it may have been a proper trail at a point in the past.

"Let's follow this trail and look for the cabin," she said.

Crockett nodded enthusiastically. "The sooner we get out of here the better. I think we failed to consider the denseness of the forest below the ridge. It will get darker sooner than we thought."

Brontë responded by moving with swiftness down the path.

Although both were on high alert, nothing caused them alarm on the lower trail. A few sounds were emitted from the brush, but the appearance of a live bird and squirrel made them realize their imaginations were simply overreacting.

They walked nearly a quarter of an hour before the cabin appeared before them. Its sudden manifestation in the wilderness came as a surprise. The building was so covered with roots, vines, and leaves, they nearly walked past it.

"I'd say calling it dilapidated would be a compliment," Crockett said nervously.

Brontë did not respond. She did not want to alarm Crockett, but, from somewhere around them, she thought she heard low voices.

"There is no monster," she said quietly to herself.

Crockett furrowed his eyebrows. "What's that?" he asked.

Brontë feigned a smile and indicated the cabin door. "Let's go in."

It was upon opening the door that Crockett plummeted to the ground in horror.

A cloud of screeching bats blasted from the entrance of the house with such force that the young lawyer was sure it would be the end of them. He screamed shrilly, nearly matching the high-pitched tone of the bats. While

Brontë was also frightened, she stood stiffly upright, thus retaining her sense of dignity.

When the winged creatures cleared, Brontë turned to Crockett, trying her best to resist collapsing with laughter. "Are you all right?"

Crockett's jaw was locked, so he could not answer. He indicated he was alive by waving in confirmation.

Brontë helped her husband stand and then pressed forward into the cabin. She stifled her giggles by pressing her fist to her mouth.

With the quickening dark and the shadows of the deeper wood, Brontë had to use the lamp to inspect the small abode. After an initial search of the main room, she discovered it was completely empty. Floorboards were ripped up and windows shattered. She was doing a second scan of the premises when Crockett entered the cabin, shaking slightly but no worse for the wear.

"Sorry about that," he said, his face still waxen. "Surprised by those little creatures."

Brontë chuckled. "As was I! It's okay that you have a more sensitive spirit, darling."[35]

Crockett turned red. "I was on edge before, but those feral, flying rodents nearly pushed me to madness. My sensitivity may kill me in this place."

It took little time for them to investigate the other rooms of the cabin. The kitchen and the sitting room were together in one large space. There was only one additional room which was much smaller and looked identical in terms of its condition: it was gray, dusty, and half-destroyed.

"This is a bit of a disappointment," Brontë said. She waved the light one more time around the room; this final search revealed only shadows and cobwebs. She laughed remembering Klaude's story about the treasure. "Klaude's story about the treasure seems even more ridiculous after seeing this place."

"Well," Crockett removed a spiderweb that clung to his hair, "to some this

---

[35] Fan(s) of the first book will appreciate that according to *What Colour Is Your Spirit?* by Divina Q. Wellesly, Crockett's spirit is Grasshopper-Leg Green.

may be a treasure. It needs repair, but it's not altogether a terrible spot for a cabin."

"I did hope there would be something." Brontë turned around and walked back into the main room. She once again raised the lamp and shed light into the dark corners.

"Brontë," Crockett smirked, quite impressed with himself, "a wise woman once told me that we should always be looking for footprints."

Brontë's face lit up. She lowered the lamp, illuminating the ripped floorboards. The joy in her countenance quickly gave way to confusion. "It's freshly swept," she said looking at Crockett. "There's dust everywhere along the windows and walls, but the floor is clean."

Crockett closed his eyes to aid his concentration. "Why would someone sweep the floor?"

"I would guess to cover tracks." Brontë shone the lamp on the floor and circled the room. Her heart began to race. There *was* something happening in this cabin.

As she investigated the interior, Crockett exited the cabin and examined the earth around the entrance.

The ground was smooth, nearly untrodden. He kept his eyes downward as he circled around the shack. His heart nearly stopped when, near the back of the old home, he saw large, claw-like footprints.

His bondage sheep nearly exploded with ominous premonitions.

"Brontë…" A shiver went down his spine. His voice came as a rasp.

He lifted his gaze. It was both a trick of the light, the stark golden beams cutting through the lower part of the forest, as well as Crockett's heightened senses that made him aware of something distant and nearly invisible in the shadows. The object was tiny. Were it not for all the looks of disgust that Crockett sent in the general direction of Phipps that afternoon, he wouldn't have recognized it. But the trace of the small, piggish man was there: a tiny, red feather from his odd lapel pin. It quivered in the tangled branches of an ancient, dense bush.

The shock of seeing an article from the writer overrode Crockett's fear. He went closer to inspect the feather.

At first, he saw nothing. He plucked Phipps's molting and examined the large shrub. After prodding the twigs, it became clear that there was a pathway through the brush. It was not obvious, but a figure could slide through the brambles, squatting, then crawling, to get through the heavy shrubbery. The intrigue of this new discovery pushed the monstrous paw print out of his mind. He leaned over and forced his way through the dense branches.

The farther he moved into the shrub, the more he doubted himself; not only the decision to pursue the pathway but also his choice to leave Brontë in the small shack despite discovering the beastly footprint. His sense of regret grew as the short, narrow trail became a winding tunnel. The thought crossed his mind to return to Brontë, but the sun, almost as if sensing a discovery approaching, appeared to be sinking more quickly below the horizon. His intuition told him to press onward before it grew fully dark.

Eventually, he emerged into a small clearing surrounded by brambles. On the side farthest from him there was a huge, gnarled tree. When he turned to look back at the shrub, he could barely see the cabin. What he did see sent a wave of relief over him. Brontë's light shone out of the rear window.

"She's all right then," he said softly.

The anxiety about Brontë's safety assuaged, he turned his attention back to the clearing and the large tree. "Why would Phipps crawl through here?" He clicked his tongue. From every angle, aside from his point of entry, he appeared trapped by the ring of brambles.

Approaching the tree, Crockett squinted in the dim light to look for a sign or indication that there was a route forward. Out of frustration, he placed his hand on the tree's lower branch; he intended to shake it out of angst; however, it gave way. A tiny, metallic click sounded, and the base of the tree slid open.[36]

Crockett stood dumbfounded, looking into the darkness of the compartment. A cacophony of questions erupted in his mind: Should he go get Brontë? Explore on his own? What if Phipps was down there? What *was* down there?

There was a sudden sound from inside the portal, less like a movement in the forest and more akin to a voice. His whole body shook; his pulse raced.

He remembered the conversation with Brontë—the crossroads. Something told him that he must move forward, that the discovery ahead of them was more valuable, in this moment, than anything behind. Terror and curiosity mixed in his blood. The fine balance bolstered his nerves so that he found the courage to approach the hole and enter the tree.

With a single step forward, he found himself plummeting. He fell, suspended in air for a moment, before landing with a loud thud on rocky ground. Looking above him at the last light of day shining through the portal of the tree, he realized that the entry had opened directly into a hole. One more acquainted with the nature of the portal would have scaled down into the chamber using the rope that was hung from the entrance.

"If I'm not dead tomorrow," he said softly to himself, "I will be very sore."

Ahead of him a lamp glowed ominously in a small, cool room. The resolve which swelled in Crockett outside the chamber diminished. Realizing he was in a confined space where someone (by indication of the lamp) had been recently, he grew nervous.

He stood at the entrance to the room, his legs shaking. His eyes roamed over its contents.

It was very cave-like. The walls were a ragged, gray stone. The sound of dripping water came from someplace in the distance. Whatever voice he heard before entering had ceased.

---

[36] The author realizes this is oddly convenient. Didiert and Earhart originally put in an odd maze/puzzle at this point of the novel so that the reader could simulate Crockett's figuring out the path forward. It was not altogether a bad idea; however, the publisher of this book said the colored ink required of the image would be too expensive. So, you get the simplified version.

His eyes adjusted to the gloom, and he began to make out wooden bookcases shoved to the sides of the room. To Crockett's surprise, not only the bookcases, but the walls, corners, and every empty space in the cave were filled with books.

Still unsure if there was another presence in the small, dank hole, he looked around furtively before crawling slowly toward the closest bookcase. At random, he picked out one of the books and looked at it.

He opened to a page in the middle and found an intricate diagram of a machine. Everything was labeled neatly in fine, German script. On the next page, a long entry appeared to detail more information about the nature of the mechanism and its construction.

"Next time someone is murdered, I hope it is in an English-speaking country," Crockett said flipping through the worn pages.

Growing more confident that he was alone, the owner of the lamp making no sounds and the room itself not large enough to hide within, Crockett was emboldened to open more books. Most all of them followed the same format as the first: pictures of inventions and machines accompanied by long entries detailing how to build them.

After several books with the same content, Crockett closed the one he was looking at and contemplated his discovery. Perhaps this secret room was the "treasure" Klaude spoke of; maybe the nature of it wasn't gold and rubies but ideas. But how had Phipps found it? And was his real book something to do with the doctor? Or perhaps his inventions?

His train of thought was derailed by the sound of a loud, panicked scream.

Crockett jumped up and scrambled to the rope. The only thing that could supersede his goat-fainting cowardice was the thought that Brontë could be in danger. Should the problem be anything but another colony of bats, he would have the fortitude to help.

Despite the brambles, he was able to fight his way out and to the front of the cabin in a much shorter time than it took him to enter. He was panting heavily, his eyes wild as he came upon the scene of terror.

For her part, Brontë was doing an incredible job holding her ground. She stood with a feral grimace on her face, her lamp extended. With large swipes of the lantern, she attempted to drive back the beast that confronted her.

If Crockett thought that the monster did not exist, this belief crumbled with the vision before him. The Caddywampus stood in all its wild glory at the entry of the cabin. Its teeth were bared. Its huge, destructive paws were raised in a warlike posture. With a thunderous lunge, it took a step forward, creating a huge print in the dirt. It staggered slightly, the force of its attack knocking it off balance.

"Crockett!" Brontë's face was flushed with fear. "You're back!"

"Yes! How are you?" he asked, not fully understanding why. Things were clearly in a very, very bad state.

Brontë swung her lamp again. "A bit distracted…"

The beast turned and growled, an odd, mangled sound of both a bear's roar and a bird's scream. It echoed through the deep ravine; birds shot up from their rest in the trees and into the twilit sky. The beast's claw slashed through the air, causing Brontë to slip back and fall to the ground. Her lamp crashed; its flame extinguished.

In the dark, Crockett ran forward. Full of adrenaline, he extended his hand and pulled Brontë up with a quick, uncharacteristically strong tug. She came into his arms. As she regained her balance, Crockett shoved her forward along the trail.

"Run!" he called.

Crockett refused to look at the beast, afraid he would lose his composure and collapse. Instead, he kept his face down and kicked up a spray of dirt from the path. His dire hope was that it might blind the creature and aid their escape. With the dirt flying, he sprinted after Brontë.

The monster let out another terrifying wail as they scurried into the darkness. The forest echoed with the beast's feral cry.

As Brontë ran forward, she looked back to be certain Crockett was behind her. He was pale and terrified, but he was there. Beyond him, was the beast. In the shadows of the forest, she could still see its blood-red eyes shining in the dark.

The two continued to race away from the monster along the trail. They flew down it, coming quickly to the bottom of the ravine. They steeled themselves for the journey back up, an endeavor which proved to be a frantic, terrifying ordeal. While the steep trail had been difficult on the way down (especially for Crockett), the journey back up found them scrambling with effort up the dirt path, gasping for breath. Their panic was only increased by the roar of the Caddywampus, which, though it grew more distant, echoed around them.

With great heaving breaths, they emerged on the top of the ridge. Brontë collapsed from the effort. Crockett fell to his knees beside her. He pressed his hand to hers.

"Darling, can you continue? We will be safer in our cabin." He looked into the dark. He was fearful the creature was scaling the ravine behind them, but the forest had grown quiet. The path was untouched by the grotesque presence of the monster.

Brontë's eyes were wide and frightened. She could not get out a word, but she nodded and tried to stand up. Crockett extended his hand.

Together, Brontë leaning against Crockett and Crockett shoring her up, they walked slowly back to the cabin.

It was jarring to come back to the main path. After an encounter with a massive beast in the dark, they both expected the world to be changed in some way. However, the lamps outside the cabins burned merrily. Insects and frogs were in the throes of their evening song, and Greta was out in front of her cabin in her usual, black-toned best, speaking with Phipps.

When Crockett and Brontë appeared on the path, both Phipps and Greta paused their conversation, assessing the young couple's weary state.

"Hullo…" Greta studied Brontë's gray coloring. "My dear, you look awful. Well, that is to say, more than usual. What has happened?"

Phipps appeared to be struggling from the afternoon libations. His fat cheeks were colorless and his eyes watery. "Were you in the woods?" Saying the words seemed to require a great deal of effort.

Crockett felt a small shock go through him seeing Phipps in the flesh after having just found traces of him in the cave. His eyes instinctively went to the red-feathered pin on his lapel. It took a moment for him to compose himself and answer.

"We've been on a walk," he said, still winded.

Greta and Phipps both looked suspicious.

"It must have been a very vigorous walk," Greta said, her eyes narrowed.

"Yes," Brontë said. She hoped to add more, but she was still unable to form coherent thoughts.

"It was very, very vigorous," Crockett added. He kept staring at Phipps, looking for any sign of him being in the woods. "In fact," he continued, "we should go prepare for tonight's fête."

Crockett bowed slightly then dragged Brontë toward the cabin.

On their way back home, they were cut off by the Gestahlt children sprinting rapidly from the depths of the forest. They nearly caused Crockett to trip, toppling with his precious cargo.

"Wild ones, aren't they?" Brontë asked, relieved Crockett kept his balance.

Crockett watched the boy and girl run toward the lodge. He tsked. "Mr. Gestahlt is a very inept father. He was so drunk this afternoon I'm sure he hasn't had an eye on them all day. He probably hasn't even been able to accompany Mrs. Gestahlt to the festival she came all this way to see."

"I hope they tell them to stay away from the ravine…" Brontë grew pale, imagining them running into the Caddywampus. "Oh, Crockett…this is…"

"I know," Crockett said softly. "Let's talk inside."

Brontë walked with stability up the steps. Her strength was returning by degrees. If a recommendation for physical exercise was not included in the detective book, she would be sure to write and suggest it be added.

Crockett opened the door for them to enter. Now that he finally had some time to speak about his discovery, he could not wait to divulge the cave, books, and the mysterious lamp.

"Brontë, you would not believe what—"

He stopped when he saw his wife's face register a look of euphoric surprise. His eyes followed her gaze, which led straight across the room to the far wall. Once he saw the object of their focus, he felt a storm of emotions: surprise, joy, and relief. In truth, it was the one appearance that could shock the Caddywampus from his thoughts.

It was the figure of their dear friend and Crockett's master, Petrarch Bluster.

There was a tremendous thump as they both fainted with exhaustion and surprise. Petrarch, who had been doing jumping jacks, paused and patted his belly with intrigue.

"Well," he said stroking his beard, "not the welcome I expected."

18

The Unexpected Visitor

It took Petrarch a moment to revive the young couple. He, at first, tried to shake them, but the stupor was so intense that this failed. Eventually, he resorted to water, tossing a teacupful on each of them to jolt them awake.

They came to on the sofa, wet, pale, and dumb, intensely confused by everything that had occurred.

Petrarch, disoriented by their surprise at his arrival and their general states of terror, tried to make idle prattle as he fetched towels for the two newlyweds. He hoped his benign chatter could help draw out clues to their current mental distress.

"The cabin isn't as nice as I remember," he said.

Crockett turned to him with a glazed expression. He opened his mouth to speak, but then turned away, his brow furrowing. He absently wiped his forehead with the towel Petrarch provided.

It was Brontë who finally broke the silence. She rose and poked Petrarch softly with her index finger. "You're really here," she said softly. She turned to Crockett and nodded, confirming she jabbed real flesh.

"I am, my dear..." Petrarch was growing frightened by this welcome. "I hope I'm not imposing."

"No!" Crockett said this quickly. He attempted a smile, but it faded. "We're terribly sorry, Petrarch, it's just...we didn't...well, it's been an odd few days."

"To say the least." Brontë returned to her seat on the sofa.

"Can I ask," the old solicitor went on warily, "if my letter reached you?"

"Letter?" Crockett shook his head. He pondered a moment and then recalled their arrival at the cabin. "Oh!" He moved off the couch and crouched down to gain a vantage point below the sofa. It took only a moment for him to find the letter that had fallen from their grasp upon arrival. "We were distracted and missed it!"

"Oh dear." Petrarch shook his head. "I am sorry about that. You two were so kind to invite me. You had just left with your goodbyes, and I changed my mind about coming. I didn't want to impose, but I thought the vacation would be nice. There is travel in Praktisch that I haven't done; they give tours of the large and very scary castle that has been converted into a prison, which I would be interested in seeing. Regardless, it seemed like a good idea, so I posted the letter and packed my luggage. I am sorry it came as such a surprise."

"It is—but a wonderful one." Brontë rose and went to the small kitchen. She began preparing a cup of tea but stopped and turned to Petrarch. "You didn't, by chance, bring any gin, did you Petrarch? I think some spirits may be required to catch you up on the madness of this week."

The old man winked. "Several bottles! It was a long journey."

Once glasses of liquor were poured, Brontë and Crockett told the tale of the Deutschefaber Inn. Petrarch listened with keen interest. The points that elicited the most excitement from him were the mysterious Klaude, the story of Kreuz and Bristol's encounter at the pub, and their recent, narrow escape from the Caddywampus. After they recounted all of this, Crockett turned to Brontë.

"Brontë, you won't believe what I discovered when I ventured away from you."

Both his wife and Petrarch listened with awe as he recounted the story of Phipps's feather and the hidden cave full of mysterious books.

When Crockett finished his tale, Brontë filled in the gap of her time in the cabin. She had taken pains to review every inch of the place, reviewing the crevices and cracks in the broken-up floor.

"I did find this," she said, taking out a small pin, shaped like a kangaroo. Below the little animal were four large letters: ARSE. "I think it's obvious who it belongs to."

"The blustering Aussie colonel you mentioned." Petrarch dabbed his forehead with a handkerchief.

Crockett stared at the pin. "But what does 'ARSE' mean?"

"I've no idea…" Brontë turned the pin over in her hand.

"My word…" Petrarch set down his glass of gin. "This is not how I expected my arrival to be."

"We apologize again for collapsing, Petrarch," Crockett said. "We'd just seen," he shivered, "the monster, and your arrival came at the end of a general day of chases, mysteries, and, of course, far too much excrement."

"Any excrement is far too much," Petrarch said seriously. He steepled his fingers and stared intently out the dark windows.

"It seems we can't outrun this mystery," Crockett said. "Everywhere we've been the past two days has some wild, bizarre tie back to the inn. Petrarch…" the young man hesitated, "since the moment we stepped off the train in Praktisch, I've felt an overwhelming fear…I can't quite describe it."

Petrarch nodded. "My boy, fear is very natural. It's how you tame it and use it that makes the man."

Crockett did not feel comforted by this.

"The book you bought us is helping, though," Brontë said. "It has aided us in focusing our search." She set the kangaroo pin on the table. "There is still nothing to do with Charlemagne, but I assume that will come in later."

"There never is," Petrarch said matter-of-factly. "In law school we had to take an entire course called Charlemagne and Torts, but there is far less Charlemagne in law than we were led to believe."

Crockett stood and went into their bedroom. When he returned, he carried with him the detective tome. "Charles the Great aside, I think we should be turning to our logical faculties to sort through the chaos surrounding us."

"An excellent idea!" Petrarch finished his glass of gin in one go.

Crockett opened to the table of contents and reviewed the chapters. He grew irritated immediately. "I don't know if this will help. We still don't even know what we're investigating. There is a monster. There is a murder and a crime spree happening in town—"

"And then we have the odd guests…the Gestahlts, Collanhall, Greta, and Phipps," said Brontë.

"Don't forget Sylvia, Bristol, Ursula, and Klaude."

Brontë and Crockett exchanged confounded, exasperated looks.

"Perhaps we take this one step at a time." Petrarch refilled his gin glass.

"Indeed." Crockett returned to the bedroom and reentered with a small notebook and a pen. "One step at a time."

"Well," Brontë said, "we have our list of persons of interest. Everyone we mentioned."

"My dear," Petrarch said, his voice becoming thick from the two successive drinks, "I think we need to look one step higher. Let's examine the larger events."

Brontë nodded.

"Let's start then," Crockett said. He scribbled in his notebook as he vocalized the details of the mystery. "First and foremost is the Caddywampus. It was sighted the night before we arrived, last night, and then," Crockett turned pale reflexively, "tonight, of course."

"Excellent!" Petrarch, his logical, lawyer mind churning, grew merry. "What should we ask next?"

"If it means anything," Brontë said, "Klaude says there is no monster, so I think it may just be an overgrown bear…or…" She remembered the sight of the beast in the forest, its large claws raised and its feral scream in her ear. She hugged herself. "Although it appears to be very real."

Petrarch's eyes twinkled. "But, my dear, from what you have told me, the current mythical beast only began appearing this week."

"Oh," Brontë said. She was unsure of what this fact should mean to her.

"Crockett?" Petrarch asked.

The young lawyer's brow furrowed. "Well, if the beast only started appearing this week, then it may be tied to the events of this week."

Brontë's cheeks reddened with excitement. "Crockett, we both thought it odd the beast is relegated to the ravine or, at the very least, the ravine is the only place it has been seen entering and exiting."

"We saw it at the cabin…" Crockett's eyes widened. "Is it…protecting something?"

"Ah ah!" Petrarch shook his head. "Do not overreach, my boy. In the Beatrice[37] affair, you had a knack for

taking the most imaginative course of action." Crockett blushed slightly as Petrarch continued, "Let's record this line of logic: the beast appeared this week along with other strange occurrences, and it appears to have an inclination for venturing in and out of the ravine."

"Yes," Crockett said.

"And what else?" Petrarch picked up his cup and took another draught of gin. "Is there anything else which may be related?"

"It does not tie directly to the beast or the other mysteries, but we do know that Phipps and Collanhall were in the sixth cabin; Collanhall left the pin and Phipps left a feather."

"Zeibnaughts!"[38] Petrarch nodded so enthusiastically he spilled some of his gin. "We can't connect them to anything, but those pieces of information are critical to keep in mind."

"Also," Brontë said, "just like the pin and feather, it's *possibly* related, but, running parallel to the beast and its appearance, there is the matter of Bristol."

"At the very least, he appears to be involved in something nefarious." Crockett thought of the gaunt man and his green and gold handkerchief. "But it appears to be broader than Praktisch. The gaunt man, Kreuz, spoke English."

"With an odd accent," added Brontë. "Not German or British or

---

[37] The author still doesn't know how it got solved. That is the real mystery of Brontë and Crockett's first adventure.

[38] I don't know whether Didiert or Earhart was responsible for Petrarch's bizarre exclamations. The author does conject that "Zeibnaughts!" may have turned into our present day, youthful retort "Deez nuts!"

Australian—we've heard them all this week, but his is unique."

Petrarch clicked his tongue. "It's all very interesting, isn't it?"

"Terrifying, I would say." Crockett absently tapped his pen on his chin. "Does it do us any good to keep delving further? We came to this place for a quiet, relaxing honeymoon. I don't know if we have the skill or tools to get to a solution in this situation."

Brontë also felt that the boundaries of the mystery were now far beyond their expertise. She could not get the image of the Caddywampus out of her mind. The moment she closed her eyes, she saw its horrible claws reaching toward her.

"That's always the question, isn't it?" Petrarch asked. "When do we interfere and when do we step back? In both the Beatrice and Mayweather affairs, the murders were intertwined with our own goals, but this is far different. You have a very real choice to ignore the incidents and enjoy the Finnlicht Festival."

"Crossroads," Crockett said softly. "Brontë and I have had this discussion before, Petrarch. We thought Klaude would be the key to resolving all the mysteries storming around us, but he has only confounded them. Now we have a mysterious cabin, a room full of books, and an encounter with a forest monster to grapple with."

"Don't forget the ARSE," Petrarch said.

"Indeed…our Australian ARSE," Crockett said. "Brontë reached into that crevice and pulled it out. Despite its shiny exterior, it's a dark hole filled with mystery."

Brontë moved to speak, but Petrarch waved her off and leaned in closer to her. "It's best not to draw attention to the double entendre, my dear," he whispered.

Crockett, who still did not realize he was inadvertently making bum puns, continued, "But, as you said, Petrarch, the question remains as to whether we insert ourselves into the mysteries of the ARSE."

Brontë and Petrarch remained silent for a moment, uncertain how to move forward without further enticing Crockett to make accidental inappropriate comments.

"Perhaps," Petrarch said, "we put aside the pin."

"That may be a good idea," Crockett said. "We can cover it up, the cheeky little thing."

Brontë turned to the front window, both exasperated by Crockett's cluelessness and thoughtful about what their course of action should be. She heard muffled voices outside, which triggered a thought.

"Crockett," she turned to her husband, "what if we repeat our plan from the first night?"

"What do you mean?"

"During the party we investigated the guests to see what we could learn. Tonight, we can passively see what people know and then go from there. If we don't learn anything, we agree to continue our holiday and enjoy the festival. If we get some bit of crucial information, then we can proceed with our investigation."

Petrarch, feeling the full effects of his gin, stood up. "And what if we took the investigation one step further?"

"How so?" Brontë asked.

"Well," Petrarch leaned in conspiratorially, "if everyone will be at the party and no one knows that I am here, we could run a physical investigation. I could nose about the cabins and see if there are any items of interest."

"Collanhall may have another ARSE you can get your hands on!" Crockett said. "Imagine—"

"Crockett," Brontë looked warily at her husband, "don't focus so intently on the pin."

"It has rather sat—"

Petrarch cleared his throat to cut off Crockett. He then continued quickly, "I think we have a good plan of action. You two shall go to the party and listen and inquire. I will make my way around the cabins and see if there is anything which would tell us more about our present situation. There may be something incriminating, which would blow the entire investigation open."

"I—"

Certain Crockett would follow the word "blow" with another mention of Collanhall's pin, Brontë interjected, "Crockett, I think it may be most helpful for us to focus our investigation on Collanhall and Phipps. We know they were in the cabin below the ravine, so they may know something more than they're letting on."

"Good idea, my love. We know Phipps is writing a history book and Collanhall has a great deal of knowledge regarding the events that happened to the Deutschefabers. Perhaps there is some connection there. Either way, they both are interested in the sixth cabin."

"It sounds like we have much to learn and not much time to prepare," Petrarch said scratching his belly.

The three investigators leaned in closely to discuss their plan for the evening. Crockett opened his notebook to a new page and took furious notes.

None of them noted the figure outside the window or the light flutter of the curtains as the shadow turned and sprinted into the darkness of the wood.

19

Thwarted Subterfuge

Crockett and Brontë bid adieu to Petrarch and ventured to the main lodge.[39]

Petrarch prepared for his covert mission by doing a handful of pushups and jumping jacks. Once he was sufficiently winded, he poured himself another cup of gin. He wanted to give enough time for all the guests to get to the fête before beginning his investigation. He expected to find nothing of interest, but he very much enjoyed assisting Brontë and Crockett in their efforts.

After a quarter hour, he put on his hat and went to the window. The main pathway through the cabins was clear. The din from the main lodge was growing louder, a good sign that no one would be leaving the party for quite a long time.

When he stepped out into the night, he marked it was cool and pleasant. Had he not been tasked with spying on the other lodgers, he would have enjoyed a walk around the grounds. In London he did not get to see skies like this—jeweled blankets of infinite stars. The path was lighted with

---

[39] *Sigh* The author again asks for the reader's patience as this chapter and the next were meant to be read simultaneously. They have been broken up to offer a more seamless reading experience. Be grateful you aren't reading Didiert's *The Woman and the Mythic Shark* aka *Female Shark and Dead Shrub.* In that book *every* chapter was written from the perspective of both the shark and the woman.

glowing kerosene lamps placed on the front stoop of each cabin. It gave the entire scene the look of a fairytale village.

It was agreed that Crockett and Brontë would spend the thrust of their effort on finding out more from Phipps and Collanhall, as they were now directly linked to the sixth cabin. Petrarch would direct his investigation into nosing about the cabins of the Gestahlts and the Dutch dame, Madame van der Raaf.

He had barely gotten away from Brontë and Crockett's cabin when he heard two very distinct sounds: the sniffle and slight gasps that come from crying and a low, growly feminine voice. The mystery was soon set straight as two women stepped out of the darkness of the path near cabin one. Petrarch guessed their identities based on the information from Brontë and Crockett's account of their time at the inn; it appeared to be the stately Madame van der Raaf comforting the young maid, Sylvia.

Madame van der Raaf heard his approach and turned with a suspicious glance. Sylvia did not look up.

"And who are you?" Madame van der Raaf asked sharply.

"Oh!" Petrarch smiled broadly. He had prepared for the possibility of being discovered in his mission and already prepared a story. "I'm Crockett's uncle, Petrarch Bluster. How do you do?"

Now that Petrarch was fully in the pool of light created from the cabin, Greta's expression changed. The hard lines around her mouth softened. "I did not think the boy would have such a handsome uncle. I expected something more pinched and equine."

Petrarch's eyebrows went up. "Oh, why Madame, thank you. It's not a blood relation."

"Clearly." Greta slightly adjusted her hat. That evening's headpiece was a massive, towering construction of black lace which could have been a vampire's birthday pastry.

There was a moment of silence. Sylvia continued to look downward. In the soft light, Petrarch saw silver tears loose from her eyes and splash onto the dirt path. "If I may ask," the old man said, "is the young lady all right?"

Greta hesitated. "I'm not sure…"

"I'm awful," the young woman said softly. "I have an overwhelming feeling something horrible will happen tonight."

"Oh," Petrarch used his most avuncular tone, "my dear, we often have feelings like that. It could simply be that you ate a bad walnut."[40]

"Mr. Bluster," Greta said shaking her head, "the young girl *knows* when things are about to happen."

"*Knows?*"

"The women in my family have premonitions, sir. We can see danger coming."

Petrarch remembered Crockett's description of Miss Vindrikimmel's "boobie feet," which allowed her to know the future.

Sylvia, distracted by her own preternatural fears, took a step backwards and, when her foot encountered a small hole, toppled over.

Greta and Petrarch immediately assisted her. Once they helped her regain her balance, Greta explained what brought them there, "When I arrived at the party, I found her crying in the billiard room. She politely asked if I might go for a walk with her."

"Is there something else wrong, my dear?" Petrarch scanned the visages of the old woman and the maid for any indication of the trouble. "Aside from the family magic?"

Greta and Sylvia exchanged a look. After a tense moment, Sylvia nodded, what appeared to be a sign of acquiescence.

"I found her because I heard her fighting in the billiard room," Greta said.

"Fighting?" Petrarch leaned in closer to the two women.

"With Mr. Deutschefaber. Bristol." Greta said this with a note of disgust in her voice.

"What were you fighting about?" Petrarch turned his attention to Sylvia, who was facing cabin one.

"It was nothing. I…well…" She wrung her small hands. "I told him that I

---

[40] This turn of phrase isn't really a turn of phrase, but it was included as an homage to Didiert and Earhart. Based on their diaries, Earhart saved Didiert's life when he choked on a bad walnut during a particularly raucous dinner party at the estate of a Greco-Roman wrestler.

was worried something was going to happen tonight."

"He called her a *dummes Mädchen* and shoved her down." Greta's face turned red. "I helped her up and, after a brief explanation, we were on our way here, to the Gestahlt cabin."

Petrarch's ears perked up. "And why the Gestahlt cabin?"

"I needed to scrub out their bathtub," Sylvia said sadly. "The family has made a mess of it. There is an inky black substance covering the whole thing. At first I thought it was blood."

Both Greta and Petrarch gasped.

"No! No! It is not; I'm not sure the cause of it, but it will come out with a bit more scrubbing. I needed to get more materials this afternoon, but then I got distracted..." The young girl trailed off. Although she no longer sniffled and gasped, tears flowed more steadily from her eyes. Petrarch now noted that there was a bucket of cleaning materials and a lamp near her feet.

The old man thought quickly. "Well, my dear, why don't I help you into the cabin? I can assist you with the cleaning supplies and make sure you're settled."

Sylvia sighed. "That would be kind. Thank you."

Greta stepped out of their path as Petrarch helped the young woman into the cabin. Once inside the lodging, Sylvia turned up the kerosene in the lamp, showering the ground in golden light. Petrarch followed her carrying the cleaning substances and rags into the bedroom, which contained the large, porcelain tub. When they entered the small room, he took the time to scan the space and make note of the odd substance that stained the bath. Before he left, he saw that Sylvia appeared even paler than she did in the dim lamplight outdoors. Her hair stood on end, and her eyes held a deep melancholy. Petrarch felt the compunction to hold her as he would a small child.

"My dear," he said softly, "are you sure you're quite all right?"

Sylvia smiled dolefully. "Yes, sir. Thank you. I just hope you are right, that this premonition is nothing more than a walnut."

With that, she gently closed the door to the bedroom. He heard the rattle of the bottles and the continued sound of her sniffling. There was a moment when he thought he might go back in and assist with all the cleaning, but he had work to do.

He reentered the main room of the cabin to take stock of its contents. He was shocked when he saw the figure of Madame van der Raaf standing in the threshold.

"How is she, Mr. Bluster?"

Petrarch, so surprised by her appearance, forgot his purpose for entering the cabin initially. "How is who?"

"Sylvia," Greta said.

"Ah! Yes!" The old man adjusted his suit coat in embarrassment. "She is in a state of dire melancholy. I wonder—"

Before he could finish, Greta motioned for him to be silent. She signaled for them to leave the cabin. Petrarch looked around confusedly, unsure of what was happening. When it was clear Petrarch was fully confounded, she spoke quickly, "Outside, Mr. Bluster. There are ears everywhere in this place."

Petrarch's face fell. The old woman turned with a whirl of her skirts and disappeared out the front door.

The old solicitor took out a handkerchief from his pocket and dabbed his forehead. He was entirely unsure of how exactly he had lost control of his mission for the evening. With as much perspicacity as he could muster, he scanned the interior of the Gestahlt cabin to look for anything out of the ordinary beyond the stains in the tub. He had only taken inventory of half the room when Greta hissed at him from outside the cabin.

"Mr. Bluster, time is of the essence!"

Petrarch assessed what little more he could before exiting the cabin and meeting Greta in the dim lamplight.

The old woman tapped her foot in agitation. She looked anxiously up and down the forest path as Petrarch drew closer to her.

"Madame, I—"

"Mr. Bluster," she drew closer to him. Her voice was hushed. "There may be something nefarious going on between the housekeeper and Master

Deutschefaber." Her eyes flew to the cabin to make sure Sylvia had not reappeared.

Petrarch's face paled. "Nefarious?"

"Miss Vindrikimmel didn't know that I heard more than what I told her."

"What else was said?"

"The two…" The old woman took a deep breath. "If you'll pardon the indecorous way I must say this…" She opened her mouth to speak but closed it immediately. "I don't know if I can say it out loud!" With the quickness of a stoat, the old lady grabbed Petrarch's wrist. She looked deeply into his eyes. "The two are having some sort of…" She paused once more; her eyes grew wide and wild. "Well, I'll just say it! They're having some sort of affair!"

With the revelation out, Madame van der Raaf nearly fainted. Petrarch reached out and gripped the old woman's boney shoulders to keep her upright.

"An affair?!"

Greta fanned herself and continued with labored speech. "Master Deutschefaber said something to the effect that their 'secret must not be known.' There was then…well, I heard the…It was outrageous!"

"What did you hear, Madame?"

"I heard…oh my, my old heart…It was the telltale sucking sound of lips pressing against each other."

Petrarch started. "My word! But then how did the conversation take such a violent turn?"

"Miss Vindrikimmel then said he 'must not do it.'"

"'Must not do it'?!"

"'Must not!'"

"But what?!"

Greta was hysterical. Her pale face matched the color of the moon. "I don't know, Master Bluster. But 'it' mustn't not be done."

Petrarch let go of Madame van der Raaf to reach into his pockets. Whenever problematic events aroused his nerves, he was wont to find his thinking pipe and relax into a deeply concentrated stupor. This was an inopportune moment to let go of the old Dutchwoman, however; with the support of Petrarch's hands gone, the old woman toppled to the ground.

"Oh, my!" The old woman then hollered something in Dutch, which, to Petrarch, sounded a bit like "Jeep oodi toot toot!"

With the old woman down, Petrarch responded chivalrously. He knelt beside her on the dirt path and wrapped his hand around hers.

"My dear Madame van der Raaf, I apologize for letting you go."

The old lady looked into Petrarch's eyes. She was about to reprimand him, to send a volley of Dutch curse words in his direction that would make a criminal blush, when something happened. The dim lamplight reflected in Petrarch's warm eyes. The illumination also struck his bald head so that it shone regally in the darkness. The smell of gin mixed with his natural, masculine musk also found its way to the old woman's nostrils.[41] She found her breath stolen and her curmudgeonly heart beating faster.

"Oh," she said finally. "It's…well, I suppose…" She could not take her eyes off the old solicitor.

Petrarch also came to a sudden realization that he was struck by the looks of the old Dutchwoman. Beneath her bulbous neck, she had a very regal chin. Her erratic black hair, freed from the vampire pastry hat during her stumble, caught the light of the moon so that its intermittent silver threads shone majestically in the dark.

The dramatic pause continued for some time. It was eventually Petrarch who broke the spell.

"I believe, Madame, that you have dropped your hat."

He rose, helping Greta get to her feet. He then walked several paces to retrieve the oversized headpiece. Greta felt a flush come to her cheeks, a feeling so foreign to the old dame that she wondered if she'd contracted a terminal illness.

Petrarch handed her the lost hat and politely bowed.

---

[41] The author has tried to find historical information regarding whether the combined smells of gin and musk were attractive in this era. It may, however, be a fetish belonging specifically to Madame van der Raaf.

"I'm sorry again for letting you fall," he said.

Greta nodded. "Yes, well, I suppose it happens even to the best of us. What…what were we talking about?"

"The affair, I believe," said Petrarch, unable to help himself. His flirtatious side, long buried, emerged from the deep sea of his heart like Botticelli's Venus.[42]

Greta's cheeks became so hot that she was sure her face had combusted. "Oh! Oh!" She searched for something else to say but could only exclaim once more, "Oh!"

Another silence enveloped them. It was a great relief to Greta that Sylvia exited the Gestahlt's cabin and clambered down the front steps.

"Clean as I can get it," she said softly. She looked between the old couple; her eyes went wide. "Am I interrupting something?"

"No!" Greta squawked.

"Nothing at all." Petrarch's voice rose much higher than usual.

Sylvia suddenly understood the emotional charge surrounding them. A smile came to her lips. "Can I get you two anything, then?" she asked. Her eyes flicked between the two elderly guests. She was especially charmed to see Madame van der Raaf's alabaster skin taking on a (tepid) red glow. It brought her a brief reprieve from her own emotional turmoil.

"I think we are fine, Miss Vindrikimmel," Petrarch said. He cleared his throat.

Greta nodded in agreement, unable to speak.

"Well, I shall leave you two. Have a pleasant evening."

"Are you all right, though?" Petrarch added quickly. "You seemed very upset earlier."

Sylvia hesitated. She looked toward the main lodge, her eyes, again growing damp. "I will be fine," she said. "It's—"

"Have a cup of tea with us." Greta nodded enthusiastically. Her disdain for the young woman's impropriety was outweighed by the possibility of

---

[42] This simile is actually quite nice. I assume Didiert and Earhart plagiarized it from somewhere.

using her as an excuse to spend more time with Petrarch.

Sylvia's eyebrows went up. "A cup of tea? With you?"

"Yes," Greta said. She had already approached Sylvia and linked their arms together. "Master Bluster and I were just saying that we weren't in the mood for a party this evening."

Petrarch thudded his belly. "It's a delightful night for quiet conversation."

Sylvia, given an opportunity, would have rejected the offer, but Greta had already dragged her partway back to cabin four. Petrarch followed them, a joyful spring in his step. The three soon began to speak to each other about the lodge, the other guests, and the mysterious substance in the Gestahlt's bath. It was not long before even Sylvia forgot her earlier anguish.

They disappeared into Greta's cabin. The door shut behind them just as the whole little party erupted into a fit of laughter.

With the door closed, the cabin grounds grew peaceful. Only a keen eye would have seen Bristol Deutschefaber emerge from the main lodge, his stout form casting a long shadow as he slipped from the inn's back exit.

His head swiveled between the lodge and the cabins. He had to be certain that his egress was secret. When he was satisfied there was no one near, he stepped quickly and resolutely forward. His swift steps took him down the pathway and away from his guests. The eldest Deutschefaber had important business in the crowded center of Praktisch.

20

Encroaching Horror

Crockett and Brontë found the mood at the second soiree of the Deutschefaber Inn more austere than that of the first.

Ursula, after the events with Klaude and the handkerchief, barricaded the main staircase with a line of chairs to be sure no one could ascend. She stood in front of this makeshift wall, arms crossed, scowling. Bristol was beside her. He shook the chair structure to confirm the obstruction was secure. When he saw Brontë and Crockett arrive, he gave them both searing looks before disappearing into a room near the foot of the stair.

Mr. and Mrs. Gestahlt were present with the two children. Present may be the only way to describe their contributions to the party. Mr. Gestahlt, although considerably less intoxicated than the last time Crockett saw him, was seated with his head bent over his knees. His wife stared fixedly at the wall, rubbing Adon's dark mess of hair. Her hands were red and cracked from what Crockett could only assume was her work on the day's washing. It was a shock to see the rambunctious children subdued. Ava's eyes fluttered open and closed, resisting sleep.

Although their primary task was getting more information from Collanhall and Phipps, Brontë and Crockett were so concerned about the married couple, they approached them first.

"Hello," Crockett said. "How are you both?"

Mr. Gestahlt lifted his head and attempted a smile. Mrs. Gestahlt gave a halfhearted "How do you do?"

"Tired this evening?" Crockett asked. "It's been an exciting day around the inn. Mr. Gestahlt, did you continue your drinking adventure with the colonel and Mr. Phipps?"

Mr. Gestahlt itched his neck. "No," he said absently. "No more party for me. We come tonight for children."

Brontë looked at the two children who were now both fast asleep.

"You don't say," added Mrs. Gestahlt, motioning to the sleeping babes.

"Yes," Brontë said. The family's lethargy was only increasing her alarm about their well-being. "Well, we hope you all get some more rest this evening."

Mrs. Gestahlt put all her effort into a polite smile and then resumed her dazed activity of staring at the wall.

Crockett and Brontë paused a moment, uncertain if their interaction was at an end. A combination of Mrs. Gestahlt putting her head on her husband's shoulder and Adon letting out a slight, airy sleeping fart confirmed that they were free to withdraw.

They turned their attention to Phipps and Collanhall, who were both in the billiard room. When the young couple entered the salon, they found that the colonel and the writer appeared to have bounced back from their previous intoxication. Phipps looked a bit waxen, but no worse for the wear. The two of them were near the liquor cabinet, whispering in secret. With everyone preoccupied, Brontë spoke to Crockett in a hushed voice.

"What is wrong with the Gestahlts, do you think?"

"I don't know. I assume traveling with those energetic children would wear on anyone, though. Mr. Gestahlt is hungover, and Mrs. Gestahlt was probably stuck with the burden of the children this afternoon."

Brontë did not look convinced. She remembered Mr. Gestahlt sprinting through the woods earlier in the morning. "I don't know, Crockett." She dropped her voice further. "I believe your sense of dread is contagious. I have a feeling something is not right this evening."

Crockett, having felt consumed by fear since their Caddywampus encounter, had not noticed a marked change in Brontë's level of Deutschefaber Inn anxiousness. "Really? What do you think—?"

Before he could continue, Phipps and Collanhall approached. They both held fresh drinks.

"Good evening, Cooks!" Collanhall, like the Gestahlts, appeared fatigued despite his best efforts to conceal it. "How are we?"

"We both are feeling well, thank you," Brontë said.

"Have you both recovered from Dingo Dip Dip?" Crockett asked.

Collanhall laughed. He slapped Phipps on the back. "Of course! Fresh air returned us to our senses."

"Mr. Gestahlt appears to have suffered the worst," Brontë said.

"I don't think it was from the drink." Phipps arched his tiny eyebrows. "When I awoke from a brief respite in my cabin, I noticed the whole family was gone."

"I imagine they went into town." Collanhall finished his drink with one, quick draught. "I can only imagine the exhaustion of taking those little demons around. They're worse than a pack of biggoggins."

Crockett opened his mouth to inquire what a biggoggin was, but Brontë stopped him. She was fearful of another long, meandering tangent, so she continued a line of polite, controlled discourse, which would hopefully give some hint at their presence in the sixth cabin, "And what did you two gentlemen get up to this afternoon?"

Phipps sniffed. "I wrote for a bit after my post-drinking nap then sought out Madame van der Raaf for a chat. I was bored with Collanhall gone."

"I went tracking." The colonel winked at Crockett for an undetermined reason. "You can't catch a Caddywampus if you don't put in the work."

Brontë focused her attention on Phipps. The little man, despite having his usual pompous demeanor, looked anxious. His beady eyes scanned from side to side throughout the conversation. Occasionally, his glance would flit to the window and remain there, filled with concern. "Was Madame van der Raaf more talkative this evening when we saw you speaking?" Brontë asked. "Crockett mentioned you said she was 'uncooperative.'"

Phipps's mouth fell open. He assessed Brontë's face, trying to understand the root of the question. "I don't know what you mean." His voice wavered.

Crockett shared Phipps's shock in Brontë's boldness. He assumed their line of questioning would be less direct. "While we were chatting this afternoon," he added trying to smooth the exchange, "you said she was 'uncooperative' when you tried to speak to her about your book."

The writer's face paled. He resembled a fat, elvish rat trapped in a cage. Collanhall, not noticing his associate's terror, inserted himself.

"Ha!" he bellowed. "'Uncooperative' is the kindest thing you can say about that old bat. I ran into her this evening, and she called me 'the Australian Cro-Magnon.'"

Phipps attached himself to this, avoiding Brontë's questions. "Exactly, my dear Collanhall! An old bat! Uncooperative! You can be sure a hostile old Dutchwoman will appear in one of my next novels."

Brontë's eyes lit up. "Novels, Mr. Phipps? I thought you only wrote long, rambling literary works full of incoherent and labored descriptions. I didn't know there were characters and plots."

Phipps withdrew his handkerchief from his pocket. His face grew shiny with perspiration. "Well, my dear, she has inspired me to write something new, a book titled *A Novel is a Novel*.[43] A writer cannot be beholden to one form. The imagination is boundless." With this out, he waved his full glass of whiskey. "I believe I need another drink."

Collanhall caught him before he walked away. "Another for me also, while you're up!"

Phipps took Collanhall's glass and stormed away. Crockett felt uncomfortable about the encounter, but Brontë wore an expression of self-satisfaction.

"Interesting, wasn't it?" Brontë asked. "Phipps appears to be out of sorts this evening."

"I don't know if he's the kind of man who gets *in sorts*, if you catch my meaning." Collanhall stood erect, his hands behind his back. "Loves to talk

---

[43] This was actually the title of Didiert's last book before he passed away. The full title was *A Novel Is a Novel Is a Novel Is a Novel: A Novel*. It was lost to time (thank gawd).

about himself. He's much more tolerable with a drink in hand."

"Is that why you've consumed so much the last few days, Colonel?" Crockett asked. He hoped to circle back to an explanation of why he and Phipps were in the remote cabin.

Collanhall, watching Phipps, said nothing. When he returned his gaze to Brontë and Crockett, he was surprised to find them staring at him.

"I'm sorry?" he asked.

"Is your camaraderie with Mr. Phipps the reason for your…spirit of celebration this week?" Brontë reiterated Crockett's question.

The colonel paused for a moment. A look of consternation passed briefly over his countenance but vanished quickly. He smiled. "I am always one to have a drink if it's available. But Mr. Phipps does make it even easier to say yes."

Brontë steeled herself for her next question. It was both a question and a lie, something to get the colonel talking about the pin from the cabin. She also felt Phipps's agitation indicated that the free flow of information would soon be cut off.

"Colonel, could I ask you something?" She leaned in toward Collanhall and lilted her voice to add an unthreatening note of silliness. Her hope was to avoid appearing confrontational in the light, conversational moment. "I had a friend in Australia, and he often mentioned his involvement with something called ARSE. Do you have any idea what that is?"

Collanhall blinked. His confidence wavered for only an infinitesimal moment at the surprising question. "My dear, you never mentioned you knew an Australian!"

Brontë, as evidenced earlier in her encounter with the Deutschefabers, was not gifted with the power of extemporaneous speech. She faltered.

Crockett (also, as evidenced earlier, equally as terrible at extemporaneous speech) jumped in, "Well, we forgot him."

"Forgot him?" Collanhall scoffed. "It's difficult to forget an Australian!"

"This man is very forgettable," Brontë said. "In fact, I nearly forgot what we were discussing as we brought him up."

Collanhall, Brontë, and Crockett shared forced laughter as Phipps reentered the conversation.

"What is so humorous?" He eyed them all nervously.

"We were discussing an Australian friend of mine," Brontë said. "I was asking Collanhall for insights."

Phipps took a sip of his drink. "Insights into what?"

"ARSE," Crockett said.

Phipps's countenance resumed its caged-rat expression. "I…what? How…?"

Collanhall slapped Phipps on the back. "Australian Regional Society of Engineers. That is what ARSE is. I was involved myself."

Phipps handed Collanhall his drink, then withdrew his handkerchief and wiped his face once more. Collanhall stood solidly still, a smile frozen on his lips. There was an uneasy silence between the four individuals. It was finally broken by a near-desperate interjection from Phipps.

"I should go home!" He consumed his full glass and then nodded to the gathered party. "I…well, I'm not feeling well."

He tottered over to the bar and set down his empty drink.

Collanhall saluted Brontë and Crockett and went after him. He also finished his drink at the bar and then walked with Phipps towards the exit of the billiard room. The pair was near to the main hall when Collanhall turned around, returned to the bar, and grabbed a bottle of whiskey, which he tucked under his jacket.

"Take the party home!" he said. "I want to make sure our Phipps gets to his cabin safely. Leave no man behind!"

Crockett and Brontë pursued them into the main sitting room. Collanhall waved one final time to the newlyweds and called to Ursula.

"Another excellent party, Miss Deutschefaber!"

"Better than some parties I've been to in Ohio," Phipps added, just as he crossed the threshold to exit.

Ursula snorted in response.

Collanhall paused at the door. He clicked his heels and bowed before turning abruptly and following Phipps outside.

An eerie silence settled in the main hall once the door clicked shut. Brontë and Crockett were the only guests left. The Gestahlts appeared to have given up on the party as well.

Ursula, satisfied the stairs were secure, left her post and approached Brontë and Crockett.

"Hullo," she said. "I trust you've tamed your problematic handkerchief."

With the chaos of the afternoon—the sixth cabin, the monster encounter, and the arrival of Petrarch—it took some time for them to realize what the innkeeper was speaking of.

"I'm sorry," Brontë said. "Problematic handkerchief?"

"Yes." Ursula's eyes narrowed. "This afternoon it flew out of your grasp and into Klaude's room."

"Oh! Of course!" Crockett nodded enthusiastically. "We burned it. The last thing anyone needs is a reckless handkerchief. Especially with your treacherous easterly-southerlies out here in Germany."

"Good." Ursula's voice warmed with satisfaction. "Well, since everyone is gone, I hope you two will also be leaving the premises. It's been a rather long day and I could use beauty rest."

"Much more than one night, I'm sure," Brontë said. This personal barb was said in direct response to Ursula's flirtatious gaze directed at Crockett. The square woman did not even hear the insult as she was anticipating her next question for the young lawyer.

"Although," the large woman's cheeks flushed slightly, "before you go, Mr. Cook, with your interests in all things fecal, I do have something you may wish to see. An outhouse toilet is having an issue—"

"No!" Brontë and Crockett screamed simultaneously.

Ursula's face drooped. "Oh, I suppose you must be going."

"Very going," said Crockett. "The most going. We also need loads of beauty rest."

"Loads!" Brontë reiterated.

Ursula bowed slightly. "I shall show you to the door then."

With the conversation ceased, the small party noted sounds outside the door. There was a faint rustling and a light bumping. Suddenly, they were punctuated by the sound of a voice; it was a loud, urgent shout.

"Do you hear that?" Ursula's lips pursed. "What is it?"

They listened carefully. Each passing instant, the din grew. More voices joined, swelling into a jumble of unintelligible shouts. This was followed by the sound of pounding footsteps on the gravel. Crockett gripped Brontë's hand.

"The Caddywampus," he whispered.

Suddenly, there was a crash. The door of the main lodge slammed open. Crockett's heart pounded. He pulled his wife closer to him.

Standing in the threshold was Sylvia. The young maid was gripped by terror. Her mouth was agape, her hands extended outward covered in a thick, red substance; she tried to utter something, but no sound escaped her trembling lips.

"Miss Vindrikimmel…" Crockett ran towards her.

Sylvia stumbled forward. She made a brief, throaty rasp before collapsing into Crockett's arms.

Ursula moved toward the door to see the cause of Sylvia's distress. When she peered outside, her shoulders rose. While the bulging, serious woman was incapable of a scream, she was able to make a loud, sharp bark. Brontë rushed to her side just in time to try to support her as her legs gave out. Brontë could do little to fight the innkeeper's mass, but she did slow her descent to the floor.

With Ursula out of his line of sight, Crockett finally saw the cause of Sylvia's anguish. Holding Sylvia, he looked through the threshold and saw a shadow swinging in the air. Suspended from the beams of the front stoop was a body, covered in blood. It was riddled with cuts and gashes. The corpse was dismembered, one arm and a foot removed completely.

It appeared to be the work of some large, feral animal, what Crockett could only conjecture was the Caddywampus.

<h1 style="text-align:center">21</h1>

Beyond Mischief

Brontë was the first to recognize the body. She was the only one in control of her senses after the discovery of the murder. Realizing the significance of the swinging shadow, Crockett had collapsed holding Sylvia. Brontë kneeled beside their fallen forms. She absentmindedly tried to shake them awake as she pondered the meaning of this new atrocity.

Crockett awoke from his faint first. He immediately reached out and gripped his wife in an embrace. Sylvia remained knocked out cold, her head, which was resting on Crockett's stomach, got mashed between his and Brontë's pressing bodies. When Crockett noted this, he gently shifted her of him and laid her out on the floor of the lodge.

Crockett and Brontë stood, assessing the carnage.

"Your bondage sheep was right, Crockett," Brontë said. "Things have fully gone beyond mischief." Emotion choked her voice. "The body is Bristol."

"Bristol?" He cast a quick glance at the mutilated corpse before he felt queasy. "Do you think it was the creature?"

Brontë did not have time to respond. Phipps appeared at the door, his face the color of chalk.

"My my," he said. He reached into his pocket and pulled out a small flask. He made quick work of it, sucking its contents with a few large gulps. Once it was depleted, he opened his mouth again; Brontë and Crockett expected a quip, an insult, or a tirade about his novel, but the little man could only muster a refrain of his earlier thoughts, "My my."

A groan came from the other side of the room. Ursula was stirring.

"Unnghhhhh…" She sat on her knees and looked out the door. She shook her head with what appeared to be disappointment. "Bristol…" she said coolly.

"Miss Deutschefaber," Brontë said, "I'm so sorry. You should—"

The innkeeper cast an annoyed look at the fainted maid. "Someone wake up Sylvia," she said with her old bark, "and tell her to retrieve the *large* mop. This is going to be a taxing clean-up effort."

Even Phipps was taken aback by this response to her brother's death.

"Miss Deutschefaber, perhaps you should—" Crockett began.

"Terribly sorry about this," Ursula ignored Crockett. "It's always something. If it's not excrement in a piano, it's a murder on the stoop."[44]

Ursula stood and went to the staircase. "When Sylvia awakes, put her to work with the mop. It would also be helpful if you made sure no guests were killed in this incident. It would be bad for business." She removed one of the chairs used to barricade the stairs and stomped to the second floor without another word.

"Well," Phipps said, "I think it would be best if I stayed here and supervised while you two go out and see if there are any more corpses."

"Supervise what?" Brontë gritted her teeth.

"Everything!" Phipps motioned all around the empty room. "This hall can't supervise itself. Look!" He motioned to Sylvia who was showing signs of life. "I must be here for her! I'm very sensitive and supportive, you know."

Crockett choked down a knot of anger. "Fine," he said. "Brontë and I will go see to the guests. Phipps, stay here and 'supervise.'" Crockett took Brontë's hand and led her to the door. As they crossed the threshold into the darkness he whispered, "I hope the beast returns and makes him dessert."

---

[44] This was an actual colloquial phrase used by innkeepers during the early 20th century. Wild times.

The couple sprinted past the suspended body of Bristol. Crockett felt his knees go weak at the sight of the gore, but Brontë held him tightly and helped him stay erect.

"Strength, Crockett. We need to be sure everyone else is all right."

It did not take long for them to round up the rest of the guests. The Gestahlts heard the scream and were roused. Mrs. Gestahlt stood in the doorway looking toward the main lodge.

"Yes?" she asked fearfully.

Mr. Gestahlt appeared behind her. Brontë was about to begin the explanation of events when Greta and Petrarch emerged from the darkness of the path.

"Ho!" Petrarch called. "What is going on? We heard noises in the dark then a scream. The colonel blazed past our cabin and ran into the night."

"It's very unsettling," Greta said. Crockett barely recognized the old woman; she looked…less consternated in some way. "I hope whatever it is that happened has happened and we can go on with our business." She turned and caught Petrarch's gaze. She smiled coyly.

Brontë's eyes flicked between the older couple. The murder fled her mind as she pondered what emotional connection was burgeoning between the two most senior folks at the inn.

There was little time to consider this, however, as Greta's eyes caught the figure swinging on the lodge's front stoop. She took several steps forward and then turned back to look at Brontë and Crockett.

"Who?" she asked.

But before anyone could respond, a loud, doleful wail burst from the lodge.

"I think Sylvia is awake," Brontë said sadly. "I should go to her. Phipps will be of no use." She bowed slightly and ran toward the lodge.

"What is going on?!" Greta took several steps back as she watched the body swinging. "Who?"

"Bristol," Crockett said. "We don't…we were the only ones in the lodge with Ursula when we heard a commotion. When we opened the door…well, he was there."

"Who did it?" Petrarch was aghast. "Why?"

"We don't know," Crockett said.

"Mr. Bluster, Sylvia, and I didn't see anything," Greta said. "We were in my cabin having tea. Sylvia left to see if there were more spirits in the lodge that we could use to add a bit of bite to our drinks. She left just moments ago."

"We no see!" Mr. Gestahlt shook his head. "We all sleepy time."

Crockett nodded. He had some doubts about the alibi of Mr. Gestahlt. His wife was in her night dress, but he was fully clothed, his hair slightly disheveled.

Petrarch's eyes lingered on the body. "We should go see what we can do to help."

They turned toward the cabin just as the sound of hooves echoed from the direction of Praktisch. Emerging from the path toward the town, a pair of horses galloped out of the darkness and toward the lodge. On the back of one, gripping its rider, was the large frame of Collanhall.

"Tally-ho!" he called. "Brace yourselves, gentlemen!"

It was hard to tell in the darkness, but Crockett thought he made out the figures of the police offers Bunce and Bosch as the riders of the horses.

"I believe Collanhall got the police," Crockett said. "I should go tell them what occurred."

"We should all go," Petrarch said. "Except for Mrs. Gestahlt. She should see to the children. We wouldn't want them to come across this scene."

Mr. Gestahlt nodded his head. He told this to his wife in Serbian. The woman looked uncertainly at him for a moment, to which Mr. Gestahlt responded in a short, clipped foreign phrase. Mrs. Gestahlt still appeared unsure, but she bowed politely to the group and gave them a final "Love buggies!" before disappearing into the cabin.

When they arrived at the main lodge, they found Bunce and Bosch were indeed the riders. They quickly took charge of the investigation. Bunce was smiling as he took out his messy notebook and began scribbling. Bosch immediately forced everyone into the billiard room so he could begin interviews. Only Collanhall refused to be herded. He tried to interject himself in the proceedings with a long diatribe about his résumé.

"I'm sure I could be of assistance," he said. He stood fully upright, his chest thrust outward. "You know in the military I conducted a number of interviews for the general. Many were to find a better line cook, but experience is experience. I also, of course, have my experience being interviewed by *Aussie Wine and Hunting*."

"Oh!" Bunce gasped. "So famous! Bosch, maybe he help."

Bosch slapped Bunce lightly on the back of the head. "Please, Mr. Collanhall, join the others in the billiard room."

"I'm quite good at joining others in billiard rooms as well, but I think my real talent—even art, if I may be bold—is in interview techniques."

This discussion kept going for an uncomfortably long time. Bosch finally ended it by unceremoniously gripping Collanhall and shoving him into the billiard room.

Collanhall stumbled through the doorway and was met by Ursula, who dragged him toward the bar.

"Get out of their way, Master Collanhall," she said coldly. "The sooner this is over the better."

The innkeeper continued to be unfazed by the murder. Her attention was solely focused on getting through the investigation and cleaning the front stoop.

After a quarter hour, Bosch entered the billiard room and called the first witness. Ursula jumped at the opportunity to speed things along. As they exited the room, she said something to him in rushed German. Bosch looked slightly taken aback by whatever was said. His mouth hung open as he pulled the door to the main hall closed behind them.

Left alone, the rest of the lodgers were unsure what to do. Brontë and Crockett sat on the piano bench, pondering this crime's place in the general mystery. Petrarch focused out the windows on the front stoop. Although Bunce and Bosch pulled down the body, the rope still wavered gloomily in the wind. Gestahlt and Greta stood by the entry of the room, both looking rather forlorn and uncomfortable. Sylvia had placed herself away from everyone else. She looked overwhelmed with melancholy, her shiny tears falling onto the carpet. Only Collanhall appeared to be in his element. He was conversing with Phipps at the bar.

"This is a fine mess." Phipps turned his attention to the liquor cabinet and took out a bottle of whiskey. "As if there wasn't enough going on, now we have a body."

"*Another* body," Collanhall added. "There was one in town the day we all arrived."

Brontë, as she had all evening, took the direct route. "Does anyone know what is going on?"

Collanhall, Gestahlt, Greta, and Phipps shook their heads vehemently.

"Nothing about this," Greta clucked. "I came into town on a sentimental journey."

Brontë was tired of subterfuge and games. "Who was the 'someone' you wanted to find in Praktisch, Madame van der Raaf?" she asked. She stood from her seat at the piano and paced the room.

"The 'someone' is a very old friend," Greta said. "We had a falling out and I'm unsure if I should seek to make amends."

"What was the falling out about?" Brontë asked.

Greta grew ruffled. "What do women fight about? It was all stuff and nonsense from the past. Can I ask what you are doing here, Mrs. Cook? You seem eager to cast an incriminating light on the rest of us!"

Brontë raised her hands. "No, Madame, I'm sorry if it sounds confrontational. I only wondered what brought you here. Something very odd is going on. And now Bristol has been mauled by the creature…"

"Ho ho!" Collanhall let out a loud, pronounced snort. "My dear, that is not the work of a wild animal."

"It's not?" Brontë bit her nail.

"No, someone *did* that to Mr. Deutschefaber. You could tell by the wounds. It wasn't reckless like an animal but very precise. And the hand dexterity required to suspend the poor man on the stoop—no. Someone tried to make it look like an animal, but the gashes were too clean. There were no tooth or bite marks. I didn't need to gaze on his suspended body for long to assess that. The only animal who could make wounds anything close to that and have the rope skills to tie him up would be a Western Phylido—"

"Yes, yes!" Crockett did not have the energy to hear another entry in Collanhall's fantastic bestiary. "If it wasn't an animal…what kind of cruel person would do that?"

"That is the question, Mr. Cook." Collanhall took a glass and poured himself more whiskey.

Petrarch cleared his throat and walked to the center of the room. "Very curious," he said. "If it is indeed a person, then I think we may take a very direct route to figure out if there is a threat among us."

Everyone in the room grew extraordinarily tense. Greta reached to straighten a hat that was not there. Mr. Gestahlt rubbed his hands on his trousers. Phipps and Collanhall scanned the party. Even Sylvia lifted her tear-filled eyes and focused her attention on the group.

Petrarch continued, "In the present case, we need only to know the location of all of you at the time of the murder. I can vouch that myself, Miss Vindrikimmel, and Madame van der Raaf were together in cabin number four. Sylvia left but…well, it was her discovery of the body that precipitated this gathering."

"Hmph!" Greta threw a contemptuous look at Brontë. "A secure alibi, my dear."

Crockett responded quickly to ease the tension. "I can also say that I was with both Brontë and Ursula at the time of the incident. We were in the main hall of the lodge."

"And I sleep with family," Mr. Gestahlt said.

Brontë pursed her lips. "Can you then tell us why you are still fully dressed, Mr. Gestahlt? Shouldn't you be in your night clothes?"

Gestahlt shook his head. He rubbed a hand through his thick, black hair. "No, no, no. I…" He looked around, his cheeks turning red. "I…drink too much. I not make to night clothes."

Brontë continued to look at him suspiciously.

"And, his clothes are clean, my dear," Collanhall spoke up. "His rumpled shirt is much less suspicious than a clean costume. If he were freshly dressed,

I'd be suspicious that he removed them to hide his bloody mess."

Crockett and Brontë looked at Collanhall with growing admiration.

"Well observed!" Petrarch thrust his hands into his pockets. "And where were you, Colonel?"

"Phipps and I went into his cabin for a nightcap."

"Then we heard it," Phipps interjected. "I was in the middle of a delightful anecdote about my dear friend Simon Pettifizz…" Phipps stopped speaking and looked around to see if anyone recognized the name. When no one showed interest, he continued, "a delightful anecdote about Simon Pettifizz, the acclaimed author." He once again paused for admiration, which never came.

"Yes," Collanhall jumped in. "Well, he was going on and on and then we heard the slightest noise. To be sure, if it weren't for my keen tracking sense, it would have gone unrecognized. I went out and saw the ne'er-do-wells hanging the body. I pursued of course. Although they had a good lead, I'd faced much longer odds the time I chased a quippie down the Cartillon Mudflats." He paused here to wait for general admiration or incredulity. But, just as with Phipps and his Pettifizz anecdote, Collanhall was met with blank stares. He rambled on, "I lost them. They vanished into the woods and the crowds of the festival, but it was with a bit of luck that I encountered our two police friends right on the high street. They were on patrol. We hopped on their horses and rushed back."

"I also heard the slight noise." Phipps appeared upset he lost the spotlight. "I have very delicate and precise writer's hearing. Simon Pettifizz was always talking about my 'ethereal auditory sense.'"

"Is that the same skill you use to listen at people's windows, Mr. Phipps?" Greta glared at the portly author.

Phipps's face turned purple. "I don't know what you mean, Madame!"

"I saw your fat figure snooping around my cabin just yesterday."

"We have seen him at our window as well," Brontë said.

Phipps let out one of his terrific grocks from sheer consternation. When he had cleared his throat sufficiently, he began speaking with extreme rapidity, "I…I…well, I'm not eavesdropping, if that's what you're implying.

I'm walking in the woods while walking—it's the title of my book, you know. I've told you all about it!"

"You said that it's not what you're writing about, though, Mr. Phipps." Crockett's eyebrows furrowed. "You said you were working on a historical book."

"It is hysterical—historical—it is that. One book can be many things and does not need to be confined to your narrow, British, tea-doily thinking!"

"And what does it have to do with Madame van der Raaf?" Brontë felt she was moving into checkmate. While Phipps was not a murderer, he was sufficiently up to something. They would at least get to the bottom of the odd charade about his book. "This afternoon you spoke of her being 'uncooperative.'"

Phipps began making sounds like a stuck motor car.

"I can say," Collanhall entered the conversation speaking with a calm authority, "that Mr. Phipps is only interested in Madame van der Raaf's history in this area. *Walking in the Woods While Walking* is a book with a historical angle to it. Because Madame van der Raaf has been in Praktisch, he is interested in her insights."

Madame van der Raaf looked greatly disturbed. "Is *that* why you kept trying to speak with me, Mr. Phipps?"

A sheet of perspiration formed on Phipps's brow. He wiped at it with the sleeve of his coat. "Yes," he said. Everyone waited for him to add a rhetorical flourish, backhanded insult, or statement of self-aggrandizement, but the little man said no more.

After a lengthy pause, Petrarch thudded his belly. "Well, that seems to be a very simple mystery with an exquisitely tight solution."

The room grew quiet. Brontë returned to the piano bench and sat next to Crockett.

"One thing explained," Crockett whispered to her. "Phipps is a bad writer, writing a bad book, with a historical bend. It's all very believable."

Brontë did not respond. She looked past Crockett at Phipps, who was still perspiring. Collanhall was speaking to him in low, soothing tones.

"I just don't know, Crockett..."

But she had no time to elucidate. Bosch appeared at the door, his mustache twitching and his countenance like one who had eaten a very bad walnut.

"Mr. and Mrs. Cook," he said with solemnity, "we will speak to you next."

22

The Interrogation

Crockett and Brontë took a seat on the sofa in the main hall. They sat far apart, believing that creating a distance between them would make them look more chaste and trustworthy. Bosch precipitated this need to look innocent, as the moment they entered the room, he glared at them with searing disdain in his black eyes. After they were seated, he said nothing. He took out a notebook and flipped through it tediously, stopping every few pages and making small "tsk" or "hmmm" vocalizations.

Bunce broke the tension with a short laugh. His red cheeks were even rosier than usual. "Bosch! They no do it! Why you looking like sad bird? It our friends Brumpy and Cookie."

"Brontë and Crockett," Brontë said quickly.

"Our *friends*?" Bosch's neck flared. (Crockett then understood Bunce's 'sad bird' description.) "Hardly friends. The fact that we have run into them both near the events of the missing records and this murder is very suspicious, my dear Bunce. No one is innocent until we know *all the facts*."

"You know it's not—it wasn't the creature that did it, then?" Brontë thought this fact may have escaped the two police offers. She thought Collanhall's observation was commendable.

"What creature?" Bosch's mustache twitched. "What are you talking about? If a man is stabbed and maimed with physical weapons, then we

193

can be sure there was a crime."

"You found weapons?" Crockett leaned forward.

Bosch scoffed. "I believe Bunce and I are running this investigation. Bunce, will you please start recording the conversation?"

Bunce nodded enthusiastically. He then jumped onto the couch next to Crockett and landed with a satisfying plop. "Good for me see you, Craggy," he whispered to Crockett as he withdrew a notebook and a pencil. It was the same notebook they saw him with earlier in town—it was just as unkempt and full of loose papers. The pages flew about the chubby, little man as he flipped to a clean sheet.

"Bunce." Bosch was rubbing his temples in frustration. "We do not fraternize with the suspects!"

"Who fratergize?! I say hello!"

"Did you say *suspects*?" Brontë asked. "You think it was someone here?"

"We think it is everyone until we know *all the facts*, Mrs. Cook."

Brontë winced.

A smirk appeared on Bosch's lips. He was delighted he had put Brontë on her guard. "Now," he said, "let us return to the creature you mentioned. What are you talking about? And why would you think it was an animal?"

Crockett felt self-conscious about the stories regarding the Caddywampus and its reign of terror over him. Despite having stared into the beast's eyes, there was something still unbelievable about the half bear, half elk, half puma. He hoped Brontë would tell the tale of the beast and their multiple encounters.

Brontë also felt slightly ridiculous believing that someone clearly murdered with knives was the victim of a mythological creature. She finally spoke up, "We've seen an odd creature in the woods around the inn. There is lore about the monster in the local community."

"*Der Dämonenbär!*" Bunce laughed. "We look for him as childs. We sleep in woods, bring guns, kill frogs—"

Bosch waved for Bunce to be quiet. "But…you thought it killed someone? A creature?"

"We saw it, Mr. Bosch," Brontë said. "It's real… we didn't think…"

Bosch looked to Bunce, who was now occupied with collecting the loose papers that escaped when he opened his notebook.

"Bunce!" Both Bosch's neck, and a vein upon it, bulged. "What are they talking about?"

"Ah!" Bunce ceased his effort at collecting the pages and clapped his hands. "*Der Dämonenbär* is a creature that appear in woods. Some say it evil spirit, like crazy devil. Others say it science project. But it not been seen for long time. A few when I was childs, like I say. But not for long time."

Bosch stroked his mustache. "That's very interesting."

"Oh, is it?" Brontë asked. She was sure the policeman thought she was incompetent for bringing it up.

Bosch glared at her. "It may be interesting. When we have *all the facts.*"

Crockett took a breath and spoke. Bosch's methods of investigation disoriented him so that he was unsure what anything meant anymore. Was it a murder? Why was a creature interesting? "Officer Bosch," he said, "if you'll excuse me…It's…We spoke to the other guests, and everyone is accounted for during the events tonight. I hardly think there is a suspect among us."

Bosch snorted. "Do go on, Mr. Cook. I am very curious how you would have any expertise in the matter."

Brontë spoke up to support her husband. "We have done some detective work, Mr. Bosch. We are hardly amateurs."

"Well, darling," Crockett said, "I would say we are very much amateurs. Perhaps not entirely incompetent, but I would not say experienced."

Brontë could not argue that point. In two days of their own investigation, they found little more than continued confusion and dead ends.

"So, please," Bosch, for the first time since they had met him, smiled, "tell me your theories, Mr. and Mrs. Cook."

"Speak clear!" Bunce said, his eyes sparkling. "I write down."

Crockett continued to feel small and unsure of himself. He cleared his throat and began, "Ursula, myself, and Brontë were here in the main lodge."

"Yes." Bosch's smile grew larger.

"Mr. and Mrs. Gestahlt were at home with their family. Greta, Petrarch, and Sylvia were in Greta's cabin, and Phipps and Collanhall were together. All were accounted for."

There was a long silence. Bosch clasped his hands and leaned forward. "That is your evidence," he said.

Brontë and Crockett both shrank back into the sofa.

"Yes," Crockett said softly.

"So, you are relying on three," he held up his fingers to emphasize the point, "groups of people with varying alibis and trusting their testimony?"

"Yes," Crockett was speaking in a whisper.

"And you didn't even mention Klaude Deutschefaber, who is also on the premises tonight."

"But he's not able—!" Brontë felt protective of the young man after he saved her. Bosch cut her off with a "tsk."

"Let me give you a bit of advice," Bosch said. "Never infer truth without evidence. In my opinion, you two and Mrs. Deutschefaber are the *least* likely to have committed the act, but I still have reservations. I will trust no one until I have examined and cross-examined their compatriots. Ursula has refused to let me see Klaude, but I will wear her down, even if it takes a fortnight. I trust no one."

"We…that is—" Crockett started to speak but then ceased. He felt thoroughly defeated.

Bunce tucked his notebook into his pocket. "I junior police and also bad at this." He patted Crockett on the back. "Do not worry, Bippy and Coocoo!"

Bosch's eyes darted between the newlyweds. He seemed enthusiastic about their awkward defeat at his hands.

"I will go call another suspect," he said. "I may also treat myself to a glass of whiskey. Please," he gave a sardonic smile, "feel free to return to your cabin."

He stood and walked briskly away. Crockett and Brontë, both deflated, continued to sit, gathering their senses.

Bunce stood and stuck out his belly. "It okay! He kind of a…" the pudgy policeman thought for a moment, "in German we say, 'man with head made of garbage and vomit.'"[45]

"That's exactly what he is." As Brontë thought about the encounter, her temper rose. "To be so cruel! We were trying to help!"

"There many thing," Bunce said. "He know more than you know, so he act like intelligentsia."

"What else does he know?" Crockett asked.

"Man who garrgged," here Bunce made a dramatic choking motion, "in town square was from far. They think Bristol know him from crimes. Bristol also die, because he family with him."

"Family?" Brontë's brow furrowed.

"Oh!" Bunce giggled. "Maybe not word. He…in group. Like bad people group."

"Like a mob?" Brontë asked.

"From the Danube?" Crockett hoped the kindly gentlemen who helped them in the Beatrice episode were not responsible for the present murder and mayhem.[46]

"Yes!" Bunce clapped his hands. "Yes, yes! Mob! Not Danube, I think." Bunce noted a few papers which escaped his previous effort to be collected. He reached down to grab one. "Yes. Bristol's *family* is Ursula, Klaude, and father."

Brontë's eyes narrowed. "Father?"

"Yes! I tell him about you seeing *der Dämonenbär.* He think funny!"

"How will you tell him?" Brontë's voice became shrill.

"He in prison. Long time. Because he kill the doctor. Tomorrow I see him and tell him."

Brontë and Crockett looked at each other. They both felt incredibly idiotic.

---

[45] Germans always have the best, most efficient words. I could not find the translation of this word; it may have been colloquial slang that fell out of fashion after WWI.

[46] Fan(s) of the previous book will be happy to know the Danube Mob is a pacifist group of reformed organized criminals. They are more Santa Claus than mafia.

"Why did we think he was dead?" Brontë asked. "We thought…I don't know why we thought that."

"Not dead!" Bunce smiled, collecting the last of his papers. "Unless he die tonight. Then he dead. He live in the large and very scary castle which has been change into prison."

Before Brontë and Crockett could say more, Bosch reentered wearing a much less smug expression. At his elbow was Phipps, prattling about his book.

"It's brilliant," the obnoxious writer said. "'A work of genius, my mother says. And she's only read the title page…"

Crockett and Brontë took this as their excuse to leave. They politely nodded to both Bunce and Bosch (and reluctantly to Phipps) and headed for the door.

Bunce called after them as they left, "Goodbye, Bizzy and Coolio!"

They waved once more and then exited into the night.

Neither wanted to be close to the scene of the murder, so they rushed down the front steps of the lodge and toward their cabin. Once out of earshot of the lodge, they spoke in hushed voices.

"Master Deutschefaber isn't dead…" Brontë was still reeling from this revelation. "Why did we assume he was?"

"I'm not sure." Crockett ran a hand through his thick hair. "Bosch was very insulting, but I believe he is correct about our lack of experience. We need to spend more time with Petrarch's book."

"We should really read all of it."

"It's almost negligence at this point…"

The two stood in contemplation on the dark path. While Brontë mused on the events of the evening—the murder, the chaos, and clues that swarmed around them like a maelstrom—Crockett focused on the churning feeling in his stomach. His bondage sheep felt especially tortured.

"Crockett—"

"Brontë—"

The husband and wife spoke at the same moment. They both laughed at the exactitude of the timing. Crockett extended his hand and put it on

Brontë's shoulder.

"You go ahead, Brontë. What were you thinking?"

Brontë's smile faded. She shook her head. "No, you speak first, darling. To be honest, I'm not sure what I think."

Crockett dropped his hand from her shoulder and crossed his arms. He focused his gaze on the façade of the lodge. From outside, the body removed and no blood visible, it revealed none of the terror that plagued its guests that week. The warm light in the windows made it seem almost welcoming.

"Brontë, I feel we have come to another crossroads. At first this mystery was a kind of…lark…as it's been previously with your family and the Mayweathers. There was no immediate threat, and we both felt compelled to help." Crockett looked to Brontë. His wife was also staring at the front of the lodge. Her hazel eyes revealed no emotion. "Now…the fear I felt when we arrived, it's been given a clear shape. It's the creature that scared us in the woods, and it's also the body on the stoop."

"Not to mention the gaunt form of Kreuz on the steps of that tavern…" Brontë sighed. "From what Bunce told us, Bristol's dealings with him and others lead to this bloody night. It's not a creature or a treasure or a mystery but cold-blooded murder at the hands of criminals."

Crockett nodded enthusiastically. He reached out and gripped Brontë's hand. "I just think it would be best," he said, "if we put this to bed, so to speak. It's spiraled far out of our control. The suspicions we discussed with the others—Phipps's silly book, the kangaroo pin at the cabin, Greta's past here—none of it adds up. And things have grown far too dangerous."

Brontë squeezed Crockett's hand. "You're right, Crockett."

Crockett felt his heart lighten. "I am?"

"Yes!" Brontë laughed. "It's very dangerous. We have an active mob murdering people in town! It's not my lunatic grandfather or the incompetent conspirators at the Mayweathers.[47] You're right to want to

---

[47] The author does apologize for the vagaries around the Mayweather events. With the text of that adventure lost, there is no way to add shape to the matter without vast amounts of conjecture. Also, a description of a character as "incompetent" in these texts applies almost unilaterally.

withdraw. It's the safe, intelligent thing to do."

Crockett drew Brontë in for an embrace.

Brontë, however, slackened under his contact. The young man felt this shift in her body. He pulled back and looked deeply into her eyes.

"Brontë…"

His wife hesitated. She brushed a strand of hair out of her eyes; she could not hold Crockett's gaze. "But…"

"But?"

"There is one last course of inquiry." She forced herself to look at Crockett.

The young man's face went pale. He knew exactly what she meant, "Master Deutschefaber," he said.

"Yes."

Crockett exhaled. He shoved his hands in his pockets and gazed at the inn. Shadows flickered by the light pouring through the windows. He pictured the towering, decaying prison in his mind's eye.

"Crockett, it's simply to tie up the loose ends. If he won't speak to us, we resign. He will know about the inn and Klaude. It has nothing to do with Bristol or the danger of the mob."

Crockett nodded. "It is safe," he said softly. "Master Deutschefaber is locked away. There can be no murder or monsters lurking around the old castle." A smile flickered on his face. "I will accompany you," he said, "under the condition that it is our last inquiry. After this, we withdraw, and we enjoy our honeymoon and the festival."

Brontë's eyes shone. She stuck out her hand. "Mr. Cook, I believe we have an agreement."

Crockett took her hand and shook it with vigor. "Mrs. Cook, I look forward to this business agreement."

The two laughed. Crockett pulled Brontë close to him and kissed her lightly on the lips.

"Why, Mr. Cook! One should not mix business and pleasure."

"Not even under the most extenuating of circumstances?" Crockett's thick eyebrows raised.

Their banter, however, was broken up by the emergence of Phipps and

Collanhall on the front stoop of the lodge.

Collanhall was whistling a jaunty tune. As they came down the front steps, he closely examined the rope which had held Bristol's body. He knelt and examined the dried blood spilled on the porch. Phipps walked ahead smoking a cigarette. When he saw Brontë and Crockett, he picked up his pace to meet them.

"Hullo," he said. "Mess, isn't it? How did your interview go?"

Both Crockett and Brontë were taken aback by Phipps asking a direct question to them. It was as if he cared for something other than the sound of his own voice.

"Bosch was very direct. He thinks we're all suspects," Crockett said.

Phipps grocked loudly. He then wiped his nose with his hand. When this abhorrent task was done, he said, "He said the same to me. As if I would have the gauche inclination for murder. My hands must be kept pristine, clear of blood and dirt, so that they may be holy conduits to my—"

"Genius." This was spoken by Brontë, Crockett, and Collanhall. The colonel had completed his exploration of the crime scene and joined them.

"Exactly!" Phipps excitedly took a puff from his cigarette. "I can tell you one thing; I shan't return here. It's far too much for my constitution."

"The murder and the beast." Collanhall crossed his arms over his large chest. He was so much larger than the rest of them, they all had to look upward to see his expression. "They're doing shoddy policework. I've seen Tasmanian devils with more sense." He paused and relaxed his posture slightly. "But I am glad they're looking into it. I can continue to focus on my hunt for the Caddywampus."

"You two are staying on much longer here then?" Crockett asked. "Brontë and I only have two days left. We don't foresee any more horrors befalling us in that time."

There was a pregnant pause. Collanhall and Phipps exchanged a look—Brontë and Crockett were unsure if it was layered with meaning or simple contemplation.

"Yes," Phipps bumbled quickly. "Well, I came to work on my book, so I won't let this distract me. I will keep working!"

"With that in mind," Collanhall let out a terrific yawn, "I think we all need rest. Tomorrow things will be brighter. The festival will be on and our cares will be whisked away."

Collanhall turned abruptly and walked away. Phipps jumped slightly at his exit; he rushed quickly to catch up with him. "I'll walk with you home, Colonel," he said. "Goodnight!"

Once they were down the path, Brontë spoke, "Odd, aren't they? I have no doubt they are up to something, but it's hardly murder."

"I agree," Crockett said. He watched the moonlight shine through Phipps's cigarette smoke as he trailed away from them. "We have let our imaginations run wild. The murders, the record house break-in, and anything else fueled by criminal intent must be the responsibility of Kreuz, Bristol, and their handkerchief crime syndicate."

"And tomorrow," Brontë wrapped her arm around Crockett, "we shall pursue our *final* line of inquiry and put it all to rest."

"Yes," Crockett smiled.

"But for tonight, my little didi,"[48] Brontë gently tapped Crockett's nose, "I say we avoid rest for a bit, especially before Petrarch returns to the cabin."

Crockett laughed. Brontë ran ahead of him on the trail. She clambered up the front steps of the cabin and threw open the door.

Despite the intense excitement for the impending romp with Brontë,[49] Crockett felt the same constriction press around his heart as he had the previous several days. The dread was palpable in the air, even more dramatically now that he was alone on the darkened path. The lamp

---

[48] Reader, you may be surprised or not surprised, but it appears that Didiert and Earhart were not simply friends and colleagues. It wasn't until this line in the original book that I realized "didi" was not a well-known term of affection for this period but an allusion and celebration of Earhart's affair with Didiert "Didi" Piedmont. It does clarify their close connection and the blindness to each other's lack of writing talent. All I can say is that it's rather lovely and I'm glad Earhart found someone to share his bathtub gin with.

[49] Yes, now that the gay cat is out of the proverbial bag, it's clear the more amorously charged nature of some of this text was influenced by Earhart's affair with Didi. I won't touch the constant allusions to ARSE—even for this second-rate author, that is a fruit that hangs too low.

suspended outside their cabin wavered in a slight breeze, scattering shadows through the rails of the banister on the porch. A cloud flitted across the moon like a bird's wing. He shuddered remembering the black birds that covered the forest path upon their arrival.

He hoped that it was a passing dread, the emergence of a childhood fear in the deep, natural darkness. Regardless, he felt as if the night were alive, as if in the depths of the shadows, eyes, whether beast or man's, held him in their furtive stare.

23

A Storm on the Horizon

Crockett slept little.

Part of this was the incomplete nature of his and Brontë's wild and free activities. Petrarch arrived at the cabin just minutes after them, not even offering enough time for Crockett to remove his jacket completely. Still slightly drunk with both alcohol and his emerging fascination with Madame van der Raaf, Petrarch did not say much. He was soon asleep on the couch, snoring with the intensity and enthusiasm of a wild boar.

The disrupted tryst and Petrarch's snores contributed to his lack of rest, but the principal reason behind his sleeplessness was the vividness of his first dreams that evening. Out of the darkness of his subconscious he had visions of the towering, decrepit Praktisch prison looking larger and much scarier in his nightmares than in real life. This merged with images of the Caddywampus, claws and red eyes roving through the darkness.

He lay awake for hours, waiting anxiously for dawn. When he could bear it no longer, he rose before the sun. Rather than wake Brontë or Petrarch, he used the time to take a turn around the grounds.

It was very close to sunrise. The air carried the first notes of birdsong, and the grass was cool and damp, shimmering in the last light of the moon and stars. Crockett discovered that he could remove the lamp suspended above his door. He found a match in his pocket and lit the last of the lamp's kerosene to aid his perambulation.

For the first time since their arrival, the atmosphere around the Deutschefaber Inn was calm. Phipps's voice could not be heard blathering about his new book, and there was not a shriek or call from the Gestahlt children. He felt light, as if the dread and portent of ominous things he'd felt upon their arrival was the dream, and he was waking to a welcoming inn at the edge of a German town. He smiled to himself and proceeded down the pathway.

If only this peaceful feeling would last, he thought to himself, looking up into the sky. It was rapidly changing from black to purple to whitish blue.

He went down the pathway and found himself outside Greta's cabin. To his surprise, a light was shining through the windows.

He thought the elder woman might be an early riser. For a moment, he pondered visiting her but then recollected their last encounter in her cabin—her hollering and the smashed hat—and the young lawyer decided it best to keep walking.

It was as he was heading toward Collanhall's cabin that he heard a rush of sounds to his right: the rustle of leaves, the snaps of twigs, a hushed sound which could be voices or wind. The noises rose from beyond the Dutch dame's cabin, in the woods near the edge of the ravine. In his half-awake state, just before the world entered morning, he was unsure if what he heard was real or a dream.

His nightmares re-emerged into his mind's eye. The possibility of the Caddywampus lumbering over the ridge, fangs bared and claws raised, haunted his imagination. This thought was enough to send the young man staggering backward.

"It can't be…" he muttered to himself. "But no. There is no need for me to get involved." He turned around and retraced his steps back down the path.

Although it had grown quiet again, he felt surrounded, as if the one Caddywampus brought an entire brood to attack the lodgers. This swarmed feeling made his chest tighten. His walk back to the cabin turned into a run. The gangly man nearly tripped as he picked up speed.

But he abruptly stopped as he approached his cabin.

His eyes locked on Phipps's lodging. Something in his brain clicked. His memory recalled the previous morning when he'd seen the little man and Collanhall on his stoop. He remembered the book, Phipps's pile of cigarettes, and the etched word "POOP." This moment flashed through his brain and then vanished. He could not fully contemplate the odd spark these memories caused; they were interrupted by the return of unsettling sounds in the forest. They rippled around him, a disturbing auditory hallucination.

Crockett ran up the steps to their cabin and entered. Once inside, he closed the door and leaned against it, his mind a flurry of vague, vaporous thoughts. His breath came in quick gasps.

"It's nothing," he whispered to himself. "Nothing."

There was another rush of sounds: shaking trees, soft voices, and crunching steps. He was certain the Caddywampus brood was swarming around the cabin. The sound built in intensity and then broke, as if the sonic wave hit the house and then receded. When it was again quiet, Crockett slid down the door. He sat on the floor for some time, his heart beating rapidly. His hands trembling.

He shut his eyes and forced the fear to fade. He felt startlingly uncertain about whether the morning walk had been a dream or reality. The forest sounds continued their ghostly echo in his imagination. The memories of Phipps's cabin shimmered in his mind like the pale sun on the surface of a small pool.

#

Brontë awoke to find Crockett in the chair next to Petrarch's sleeping sofa, cup of tea in hand, staring into the empty fireplace. Beside him, Petrarch snored loudly. The old solicitor mumbled something about "torts." She mimed for Crockett to enter the bedroom.

Crockett set down his tea and followed his wife. They entered the next room and both took a seat on the bed.

"Did you sleep?" she asked.

Crockett shook his head. "No. I—well, I tried to, but it didn't take." The young lawyer closed his eyes.

Before Brontë awoke, he'd risen from his position by the door and gotten his cup of tea. This calmed his nerves and allowed him to more lucidly ponder what had happened since they'd arrived. In the pre-dawn hour after his walk, it all felt unreal, as if he'd been in a vague dream. But now that a little time had passed, the puzzle box in his brain—the little wheel that turned when he confronted their previous mysteries—creaked and churned to life. The box had been closed tightly when they arrived, sealed by his own fear, but now something…something thin and vaporous was taking shape.

"Crockett?" Brontë gingerly caressed Crockett's face with her hand. "Whatever is the matter?'

"Oh?" Crockett's eyes, the green and the blue, flew open. "Yes, sorry…I awoke early and thought I heard something."

"What was it?"

"Sounds. It was as if the forest was creeping around me."

"You're sure it wasn't a nightmare?"

"It wasn't." Crockett laughed joylessly. "I had plenty of those last night. I kept seeing images of the prison and the Caddywampus." He then paused. "But it might have been…Oh, Brontë, I don't know!"

There was a rustle outside their bedroom window. Brontë started. She rose and went to look outside. The sun was nearly up, but it was hard to tell what caused the disturbance. A thick layer of clouds was moving swiftly across the sky, a storm drawing near. Looking around, she saw Phipps going down the trail in the dim, dawn light. The Gestahlt children weren't far behind. The grayness of the day matched the children's mood. They moved haphazardly in a zig-zag pattern down the trail. The little girl said something in a foreign tongue, to which the boy responded with a shove. Soon the children were on top of each other screaming and crying. Mrs. Gestahlt appeared behind them. She reached down and gripped the boy's neck with a strength Brontë had not seen from the small woman.

Brontë turned away from the window. "I think the stormy weather is affecting everyone. I didn't even hear Phipps talking to himself."

Crockett did not respond to Brontë; he was lost in thought.

"Crockett?" Brontë waved at her husband to catch his attention. "Perhaps you should get rest this morning. You appear as if you are traveling to another planet in your thoughts."

"POOP," Crockett said abruptly.

Brontë traversed the room and sat on the bed once more. "Poop? Darling, no more excrement, please. After the incident with the handkerchief, no more ever."

"This morning, all these pieces began shaking around in my head in odd ways," Crockett said. "Last night with the chaos of the murder and Petrarch's arrival, we didn't even discuss the Caddywampus encounter or the odd, secret room, or the proof that Phipps and Collanhall were in the sixth cabin…"

At that moment, Petrarch appeared at the door. He was still lightly affected by the alcohol from the previous night, his eyes a bit glassy.

"Hullo," he said. "What are you two doing up so early? It's barely six."

Crockett sighed. "I couldn't sleep last night. I don't know what to make of any of this Petrarch. None of it adds up."

The old man yawned, then spoke, "Well, my boy, after last night, I should say a great deal doesn't make sense. That detective was an ogre! And the cast of characters at this establishment…Aside from the gorgeous and ethereal Madame van der Raaf, they all could be in a Punch and Judy show." Petrarch bent backwards, which was accompanied by a loud pop from his vertebrae. This transitioned into the old man doing toe touches in his nightshirt. "Quick morning exercises, if you both don't mind."

"Not at all." Brontë had seen her husband look like this before. It was as if he were in a logic-seeking, detectivian trance. "Crockett, what do you think of all of it?"

Crockett turned to his wife. In the gray light of the stormy morning, she looked angelic, her loose hair catching the light as if she wore a crown. He reached out and pulled a hair back from her face. When she smiled at him, her eyes squinting warmly, he remembered himself. The puzzle box ceased creaking; he shook his head.

"It's nothing, I think," he said. He forced a smile. "It may be the little sleep I had and the general drowsiness of this grim morning."

"Very grim!" Petrarch popped his back again. "If you ask my opinion," he cleared his throat, "I believe you should let the police handle the malfeasance around this place."

"You think so, Petrarch?" Brontë asked.

"Indeed. It's your honeymoon and things have gone a bit awry. The clues and small suspicions you harbored earlier have taken on a gruesome appearance in light of Bristol's murder. The reason I told you to take this escape was to get away from murder, mayhem, and nonsense."

"We appear very good at attracting it," Crockett said. "We're as bad as Ms. Fletcher. Everywhere we go there is some catastrophe."

Brontë bit her lip. "There are so many disparate threads: the Caddywampus, Collanhall and Phipps at the sixth cabin, missing orphans, two murders, the green and gold handkerchiefs…" She crossed her arms. "Maybe we shouldn't go to the prison, Crockett. Last night I was energized by the mystery—this morning, with the gray sky and threat of rain…"

"It doesn't portend something pleasant." Crockett reached out and took Brontë's hand. He put it to his lips and gave it a small kiss. "Whatever you would like, darling. We could forgo the large, very scary prison and enjoy the festival. We have yet to go to the field and see the insects."

A loud blast of thunder shook the windows. Crockett tumbled backward, dropping Brontë's hand, and falling off the bed.

"Crockett, my boy!" Petrarch lurched forward and extended his hand. The young lawyer took the support and stood, his cheeks red.

"My goodness," Crockett said, "even the weather is threatening us." He moved to sit on the bed again, but then gave a wary eye to the window. He decided to stay standing. "I kept such good composure last night in the face of all that blood and murder and now a storm has frazzled me."

"Well, you've had little sleep." Brontë rose. "I'll fetch us all something from the kitchen. Perhaps we could all use a restful day—without prisons, murder, or excrement."

Brontë exited the room.

Petrarch began doing sit ups in the corner. Crockett kept his gaze out the window. Despite his fears and the foreboding storm, he couldn't stop his mind from attempting to put the puzzle pieces together. What about the memory of Phipps's cabin jolted him so? As he contemplated this, he looked up and saw Petrarch mid-sit-up gazing at him fondly.

The old man smiled. "You've grown up so much, Crockett. Six months ago, if someone said you'd be married and staying upright in the face of a gruesome murder, I would have called them quite mad."

Crockett itched his neck in embarrassment. "Well," he said warmly, "I give all credit to my very good teacher, and…" he looked to the kitchen, "a very good partner."

Petrarch winked at him.

A delightful silence blossomed between the two men. The soft clatter of dishes and cups drifted in from the other room. While luxuriating in the calm, Crockett's eyes fell on *Detectivating for the Dunce*. Lightening flashed in the window, accompanied by a blast of thunder. Crockett's jaw fell open.

"Oh my," he said. "Oh my, oh my, oh my."

"Crockett?"

The young man went to the book and flipped through its pages. He found the appendix of Very Important Acronyms for the Detectivator to Know.

"POOP, Petrarch. Well…" He paused. "And ARSE, too, I suppose."

"Crockett, I have to say your fixation is becoming a bit—"

"No, Petrarch, I saw it in this book. POOP is an acronym for an Australian police force, The Police Officers of Perth."

"What does that have to do with anything?"

"It is carved onto the threshold of Phipps's cabin. But…It would have to be Collanhall who did it. No one else could be from Perth…"

Petrarch's eyebrows raised. "Crockett, any child able to speak English would get a lark out of carving P-O-O-P on a stoop. It's very clever, actually—a poop stoop!"

Crockett was not listening. His eyes glowed. He charged into the living room. Brontë had completed making tea and preparing a light breakfast of jam and biscuits. She set the serving tray on the small table in the center of the room.

"Brontë, something…Well, I don't know if it's anything, but I think we should talk to Collanhall."

"Why?" Brontë trembled with excitement. "Crockett, what did you find out?"

"It may be nothing, but I think we should investigate this small thread. It could help us unravel quite a bit." Crockett began pacing. "What if—just please, humor me for a moment—what if Collanhall and Phipps are in collusion? Collanhall may be POOP."

"POOP?"

"A Police Officer of Perth."

"Oh!" Brontë remembered the letters carved on the stoop. "The word on Phipps's cabin!"

"Yes! What if they are…Oh my, I don't know!" Crockett ceased pacing. He ran a hand through his coarse, brown hair. "Are they both Australian?"

"You think Phipps isn't who he says he is?" Petrarch was fully sucked into the conjecture, seeing the enthusiasm of Crockett and Brontë. "One moment!" He ran to his bag and pulled out his thinking pipe. "Continue, my boy!"

"What if…!" Crockett, in a burst of enthusiasm, jumped onto the table in the center of the room. It was not made for the weight of even a spry and light lawyer, and so it collapsed. There was a monumental crash, the aftermath of which was Crockett, sprawled on his back covered in the shards of third-rate china, hot tea, and crushed biscuits.

"Oh dear," he said.

Brontë and Petrarch moved to help him, but he waved them off. Rising from the wreckage, he tried to keep his balance, swaying back and forth whilst shaking his finger at them in joyful triumph.

"What if they are aligned and they are…searching for the green and gold gang!" Crockett finished. His head began to throb.

"So they were after Bristol, possibly?" Brontë said wide-eyed. "But why?!"

"I…don't know," the young lawyer, after the unleashing of his revelation and his dramatic fall, collapsed in a chair, his head spinning. "I don't know."

Petrarch shook his pipe at Crockett. "My boy, that is why they were both at the other cabin. They are looking for something!"

"But what?" Brontë asked.

"The books?" Crockett scratched his chin.

"Who would want those old books?" Brontë began picking up the smashed tea set. "Crockett, you said it was a lot of old sketches in German."

Crockett gasped. At the exact same moment, Brontë dropped the china pieces she'd collected.

"Treasure," they said together.

"Not necessarily the books," Crockett said, "but something hidden near the sixth cabin. They must believe there is something down there still."

Petrarch took a moment to catch on, but then joined them in their reverie. "Treasure…" he mumbled seconds later. "The mythic treasure that Klaude said was in the doctor's cabin?"

The three sat in a stupefied silence. Rain began to pelt the windows. There was a short calm before there came a light tap at the door.

Brontë bore a wide, beaming smile when she went to open it. When she did, she was met with not one but two guests: Madame van der Raaf and Sylvia. They did not look as if they traveled together. Madame van der Raaf appeared incensed that Sylvia was in her presence. The young maid's face was white as a sheet. The redness around her eyes made Brontë believe she had spent the night weeping.

"Good morning," Brontë said. "Would you…like to come in?"

"I came to see Mr. Bluster," Madame van der Raaf said coldly. "We had an appointment for breakfast." The old dame nearly shoved Brontë over as she pushed her way into the cabin.

Petrarch, realizing he was still in his nightshirt, grabbed his suit from the front chair and ran into Brontë and Crockett's bedroom. Brontë did her best to discreetly remove the wreckage of the tea service.

Sylvia shook her head. When she spoke, it sounded as if it took all her effort, "I came merely to say that there is to be a torrential storm this morning. Ursula wanted me to warn you all. The pathways and the road to town may grow very wet and treacherous. The hope is that it will clear by mid-morning." The young woman never lifted her eyes as she spoke. When she finished, she curtsied slightly and turned to walk away.

Crockett sped after her. His head was still paining. He staggered slightly, catching himself on the doorframe.

"Miss Vindrikimmel!" he called out the door.

The young maid turned. For the first time her eyes lifted. She looked at Crockett.

"If you've been around the cabins this morning, have you by chance seen the colonel?" As Crockett said this, Brontë appeared by his side.

Sylvia sighed. "I did. I warned him not to go."

"Go?" Brontë exclaimed. She and Crockett exchanged a shocked glance.

"Where would he go?" Crockett asked. "It's very ominous out this morning. And very early."

Sylvia turned away from the couple and looked down the path that led to town. "I'm not sure why," she said, "but he told me he was going to Praktisch Castle."

Brontë and Crockett looked out the doorway. Although obscured by distance and the dense trees of the forest, their imaginations saw something looming on the horizon: the ruined, shadowy form of the town's prison.

24

A Brief Meeting in the Rain

Brontë and Crockett took little time to decide the next course of action. As Sylvia departed to warn the other cabins of the storm, they spoke in hurried voices.

"Praktisch Castle…" Crockett whispered.

"Why is he going there?" Brontë shook her head. "It's so odd—"

"That was to be our course of action—"

"But what does he hope to find?"

"I don't think he'd be hoping to interview Master Deutschefaber."

Brontë stepped outside the cabin. She gently pulled Crockett out with her. "Crockett, we find ourselves at a crossroads again."

A great peal of thunder echoed overhead. The light rain grew heavier, drumming steadily on the cabin roof.

"Should we pursue the colonel?" Crockett's eyebrows furrowed. "With the coming storm…"

"We could interrogate Phipps," Brontë said. "He may know something which could be useful. That may last long enough for Collanhall to return and us to find out more. And we'd be safe in the cabins."

The young couple let this alternate option hang between them. With the rain growing stronger and the wind beginning to rock the tree branches above them, they wanted to believe it was the wisest course of action. Their contemplation was interrupted by a small branch that was dislodged by the strong winds; it sailed through the air and slapped Crockett across the face.

"Ouch!" Crockett fell forward and stumbled down the steps of the cabin, landing in a growing puddle of mud.

Brontë hesitated to assist her husband. Although she wanted to ascertain if he was all right, she also did not want to get soaked in the process.

Crockett sat up from his tumble. Rain pelted his face; his hair blew in the wind.

"Perhaps even nature knows what we should do," he said.

The wind had risen to a gale so that the only thing Brontë heard was "Nat no do!" She nodded politely and hoped her husband would elucidate and give her additional context clues.

When Crockett heard no response, he yelled, "The prison!" over the growing storm.

Brontë heard this clearly. Her heart leapt, both with the excitement of pursuing Collanhall and the uncertainty of going into the village in the middle of a torrential storm. She started forward but stopped short.

"Parasol!" she screamed above the sound of the storm. With haste, she reentered the cabin. She gave a polite nod to Madame van der Raaf, who had helped herself to biscuits as she waited for Petrarch to dress.

Outside, Crockett, now thoroughly soaked, turned his attention heavenward. Although above them the sky was a menacing black, there was already the appearance of a calmer gray over the town.

"A large and very scary castle," Crockett said to himself. "Let's hope it divulges some of its secrets."

As he said this, Brontë appeared at the door, parasol in hand. She bounded down the stairs and took Crockett's elbow. Heads down, their hearts racing, they fought the wind and headed down the trail into town.

#

The trek proved to be worse than expected. Before leaving the grounds of the inn, Brontë's parasol caught a gust of wind, turned inside out, and then soared out of her hand and into the sky. In light of this development, they hurried their steps to get through the rain and closer to the castle, but the deepening, thickening mud on the pathway hindered their progress.

By the time they arrived in town, their trousers were covered in mud and their clothes were fully saturated with the rain. The sky, however, was continuing to lighten and the rain went from thrashing to dousing, so that they could at least see the path ahead of them.

Praktisch itself was abandoned. All the revelers and festivalgoers stayed indoors to wait out the tempest. The only person within sight of the couple was the green man-fairy, who was smoking a cigarette on the covered stoop of the candy shop.

"What do you think brings him out in this storm?" Crockett asked.

Brontë, covered in mud and rain, cared little. "Perhaps he wanted to watch the storm and have a cigarette."

The green man-fairy saw them standing in contemplation and gave a wave. "Oi!" he called. "Why you out in this mess? Come and rest under the stoop."

Crockett and Brontë acquiesced. They sprinted over the muddy earth and huddled under the awning next to the man-fairy.

"Much better, yes?" he asked. His eyes assessed the young couple, who resembled two kittens who'd been dipped in a mud puddle.

They nodded in confirmation.

"We can only stop for a minute," Crockett said, rubbing his hands together. "We needed a brief respite before carrying on."

The man-fairy took a drag from his cigarette before speaking again. "And what has you in such a hurry this stormy morning?"

A bolt of lightning cut a jagged line through the sky. The flash was much less ominous in the graying clouds than it had been in the black sky of earlier.

"We are headed toward the castle," Brontë said.

"Seems like a tourist location that could wait for the rain to stop," the man-fairy observed.

"Our friend went ahead of us," Crockett added. "We wanted to catch up with him."

The man-fairy said nothing else. All three of them watched the curtains of rain sweep through the high street.

"What, er, brings you out?" Crockett asked. Despite being outside in the thrashing rain, the man-fairy appeared to be dry.

He took some time to respond. His lagging speech gave Brontë and Crockett enough time to exchange a questioning glance. After another long drag from his cigarette, he spoke, "Came to see my friend at the candy shop. We got to jabbering and before I knew it the storm was coming."

"And why are you outside now?" Brontë asked.

"To watch." The man said this and then stubbed out his cigarette.

Another pause followed this response.

During the silence, Brontë remembered their first encounter with him; he was the one who told them about the murder in the square prior to their arrival.

"We saw you at the train station when we arrived," she said. "You spoke of someone being murdered."

"Ay," the man-fairy said. "Another dead as well. Bristol Deutschefaber died up at the inn."

"That's made its way around then?" Crockett asked. "We are staying up there."

"Ha!" The man laughed loudly, but it was mirthless and quite unpleasant. "Try to hide something in this town for more than an hour and see what happens. We all knew before Deutschefaber was cut down from the stoop."

The rain lightened further, the downpour replaced by a drizzle.

"I see," Brontë said. "Do you—the people in the town—have any idea who may have done it?"

The man-fairy looked back into the candy shop as if searching for an answer. When he turned back, his expression was altered. He appeared to be jolly, an abrupt transformation from the stoic indifference with which he'd met them.

"Depends on who you talk to," he said. "There is a different theory for everybody in this town: the milkman, the butcher, the candy shop owner." He laughed again, this time with more earnestness. "If you ask me, it could be anyone."

Brontë and Crockett could find nothing to say. The oddness of the man-fairy's behavior, his abrupt shift in tone, confounded them.

Crockett held his hand out from under the awning of the candy shop. Light rain tapped his fingers; the change in weather could provide them with an excuse to leave.

"Well," he said quickly, "the storm is fading a bit. We should be off."

The man-fairy nodded politely. "Be careful up at the castle. Don't venture into the dungeons. That's where the real danger is—it's not up here. Oh, and…" he reached to remove a handkerchief tied to his wrist, "take this and remove some of that filth. You look like you just dug out of a diamond mine."

Crockett cleared his throat, again uncertain what to say in response to the odd man-fairy.

Brontë reached out and took the handkerchief. "Thank you!" she said. "We certainly will do our best to avoid dungeons."

The young lawyer stepped out into the rain. He was several paces from the candy shop before he realized Brontë had not followed. When he turned toward his wife, he saw her staring at the man-fairy. She opened her mouth as if to speak but then closed it quickly. Her eyes flicked over to Crockett and then her expression changed as if she were waking from a dream. A smile came to her lips, and she bowed politely to the strange fellow. Crockett could not hear what she said, but the man-fairy said something in return. She then came out from under the awning and approached Crockett. As she drew near, she turned back and waved at the man-fairy. When this was done, she linked her arm in Crockett's and pulled him with her at a harried pace.

"Darling," Crockett said. "Did you notice something?"

Brontë faked a laugh. She turned back to the man-fairy and spoke in a whisper.

"Crockett, the man he—"

"Yes?"

She looked back again. Her pace quickened. "The handkerchief he gave us is green and gold!"

Crockett's eyebrows went up. "Like the one Bristol wore?"

"The very same."

Crockett glanced back at the man-fairy. Brontë lightly slapped his wrist.

"Ow!"

"Sorry, darling, but I think it's best not to draw attention."

"Why would he have that handkerchief?"

"I don't know."

"If he's in the same sort of gang as Bristol, is he in danger?"

"I don't know."

"Do you think he would know something? We asked him, but he avoided the question. He said it could be anyone."

"All excellent questions, Crockett. If there is a link, what could it be? And why was he out this morning? I don't think it was a trip to the candy shop."

"That's unfair, Brontë. Even criminals enjoy a sweet every now and then."

Brontë was about to respond to this when she caught sight of their destination. They had come to the bottom of the hill on which Praktisch Castle rested. The far-off vistas of its scarred, horrible form did not do it justice. As they looked up at the crumbling gatehouse, a large, black crow flitted onto a sign that directed visitors toward the castle. The couple rushed past the bird, feeling a sense of doom as it cawed menacingly after them. At the same time, a brick from one of the towers, loosened by the winds of the storm, fell and crashed to the earth below.

The sight of the bird, mixed with the sounds of the falling brick and a blast of thunder, scared Crockett stupendously. He leapt into Brontë's arms. His spry wife, used to such acts of cowardice, caught him.

"Thank you," he said quickly, hopping back onto the ground. "I wasn't ready for the collision of these macabre sights."

"Your fear is warranted, Crockett. The moniker 'large and very scary' is understated."

The crow jeered at them again then took flight.

"We perhaps should set aside the mystery of the fairy and focus on the task ahead," Brontë said quietly. "I feel we need all of our wits and resolve for venturing into this place."

"All and more."

Brontë reached out for Crockett's hand. He gripped it tightly. Without a glance or an exchange of words, they moved tentatively up the hill and toward the gate of the castle. Once they arrived at the large, wooden portal, Crockett raised his hand. Before he could knock, the door was pulled open. From the darkness within, the rotund, smiling figure of Bunce stepped into the gray light.

"Boozy and Coldy!" he exclaimed. "Welcome to Praktisch Castle! We expecting you!"

He then turned and walked down the passage. His small, flouncing footsteps echoed behind him. Crockett hesitated for a moment, but Brontë forged ahead. As she disappeared into the darkness, Crockett took a deep breath and followed behind.

25

In the Dungeons

The passage through the front gate led them into a large, muddy courtyard, surrounded by many odd, misshapen buildings. Up close, the whole complex did not look like a storybook castle, but neither did it appear to be a fortress. It was made up of a plethora of broken, dilapidated buildings, which could have been stately had they been built with matching pieces. The resemblance to Brontë's family home, Hawsfeffer Manor, was striking. The buildings were varied and included barns, shacks, thatched buildings, and brick houses that all looked undersized next to the large, moldering castle tower that rose sixty feet into the air.

Bunce led them through the courtyard, humming a tune as he went. The rain had slackened further. With the break in precipitation, the air cooled. Brontë and Crockett shivered as they followed the officer into one of the barns.

The inside of the barn was startlingly cozy. Bunce took a seat at a tiny wooden desk surrounded by glowing lamps. Other officers meandered insouciantly around the building, stopping to chat at other desks scattered throughout the room.

Bunce, once seated, patted his belly and smiled at them. Both Brontë and Crockett expected him to say something by way of introduction, but the joyful man stayed silent. His rosy cheeks shone in the light of his lanterns. He opened his mouth as if to speak, causing both newlyweds to lean forward

221

in expectation. Their eagerness, however, was unwarranted. Bunce merely yawned and then sniffed dramatically. When this was concluded, he clasped his hands together and put them on the desk.

"Well—" Crockett began, but he was immediately interrupted by another loud, pronounced yawn from Bunce. Once he had finished, he waved for Crockett to continue.

Crockett took this invitation with alacrity, but he had barely opened his mouth before Bunce broke into a startling, fitful cough.

Brontë and Crockett looked around at the other officers as the coughing spell continued. The rosy-cheeked officer began turning the shade of a ripe plum. The other men soon took notice of his distress and rushed to his aid; one, a mustached gentleman, thumped his back while another fetched a cup of water. Brontë grew more and more perturbed as the scene continued. They had little time to find Collanhall…if he was still even at the prison. The task he came to complete may have been accomplished already.

After a frantic shuffling of many policemen and the exchange of several German words, Bunce's coughing spell terminated. He laughed and sent the other officers back to their desks. The little officer let out a soft sigh and then turned his attention back to Brontë and Crockett.

"Bunce—" Brontë began, but she was cut short by Bunce himself.

"Maybe I speak first," he interjected.

Crockett nodded politely, but Brontë's patience failed her, "Bunce, where is Collanhall?"

The policeman pursed his thick lips. "Collyhollow?" he asked.

"Collanhall," Crocket said.

"I don't…" Bunce looked toward the ceiling in deep contemplation. He breathed deeply and crossed his arms over his chest. "I don't know a Collyhollow."

"He's the large gentleman who fetched you both last night!" Brontë's fingers gripped the edge of the desk. After spending only two minutes alone with Bunce, she now understood Bosch's unique frustration with his partner. "He came to get you; he largely interfered with the interrogation last night."

"Oh!" Bunce's face contorted into a broad grin. "COOOOLLYHOLLOW! Yes, I know him. Very talk a lot."

Crockett laughed. "Yes, he does have—"

"Have you seen him this morning?" Brontë had no more time for polite conversation. "We were told he was coming to the castle."

"Which castle?" Bunce asked.

"This one!" Brontë's knuckles turned white as her grip on the table tightened.

"Oh, this castle? I don't know. Let me question." Bunce shouted across the room to a young officer with blond hair. They exchanged a few words in German. The other officer shook his head and called to another officer. That officer came closer to his blond colleague and the exchange continued. This policeman (the one with the mustache) began talking very earnestly. Brontë and Crockett leaned in closely trying to gather what they could from the German-language discussion. The mustache man nodded with fervent enthusiasm and then pointed out the door. Brontë and Crockett followed his finger and looked out into the courtyard. Mustache continued speaking quickly, growing almost frantic. Bunce shook his head in disbelief. At long last, the mustache man gave one last, prolonged shake of his head and then walked away.

Bunce turned to Brontë and Crockett.

"I don't believe!" he said softly.

"What?!" Brontë and Crockett leaned in together.

"He see wolf outside this morning! I never see one this close! Gone now, unfortunately. I show you if—"

"Bunce." Brontë's eyes took on a crazed glow. "Have they seen Collanhall?"

"Ah!" Bunce smiled warmly. "Collyhollow come in this morning, but he gone now."

Brontë withered. "He's gone?"

"Yes! He ask speak to prisoner."

"Who?" Crockett asked.

Bunce shrugged. "Normal criminal. He a thief we pick up in town this week."

Brontë leaned back in her seat. Crockett turned his gaze on her.

"What do you think, Brontë?" he asked.

His wife shook her head. "I don't know. What would Collanhall want with a random criminal?"

Crockett turned to Bunce. "Could we speak with the same prisoner?" he asked.

Bunce nodded happily. "Yes! I show you him." The police officer stood up and grabbed one of the lamps from his desk. "He up here, not in the dungeon." As he turned up the oil on his lamp, he laughed lightly to himself. "It funny," he said. "Bosch said he sure you come to talk to old Deutschefaber man, not other criminal."

Brontë froze. "Bosch said that?"

"Yes! He say, 'Snoopy people at lodge…'" he said, pointing to Brontë and Crockett, "that mean you, Bricky and Crisket. He say, 'Snoopy people at lodge will want speak to Stefan Deutschefaber.' That why I say we expect you." Bunce, finished preparing the lamp, pointed outside. "Now we go!"

Brontë, however, reached out and stopped the little man. "What if we do want to speak to Stefan Deutschefaber?"

"Then I take you there!" Bunce looked unfazed by this change of plan. "Bosch always right! I think maybe wrong this time."

Brontë turned to Crockett. "What do you think?" she asked. "I think we have more questions for Mr. Deutschefaber. We can do the unknown thief afterwards."

"Excellent," Crockett said. "I agree completely."

Bunce shook his lantern in approval. "Then let's go away!" The policeman turned and rushed out of the barn.

Crockett and Brontë followed. They journeyed back into the storm. The rain had ceased, but thunder bellowed in the distance. A bolt of lightning split the sky on the western horizon.

"Oh!" Bunce turned around. In doing so, he spun the lamp and hit Crockett in the chest.

"Ow!" the young lawyer squealed.

"Sorry Crispy!" Bunce said. He gently patted Crockett's chest. "You okay." For the first time since they had met the odd policeman, his face grew serious. The rosiness in his cheeks dwindled. "Dungeon scary. Prisoners also very scary. Rats even most scariest. It all very scary."

At the conclusion of this, he spun back around and headed into the crumbling tower. A large door was cut into the stone. It led to a spiral staircase that twisted down into the darkness.

Staring into the black void behind the door, Crockett felt his legs grow weak.

Brontë squeezed his elbow and spoke softly into his ear, "I'm right here. We'll be safe. Master Deutschefaber is behind bars. Nothing can scare us."

Her husband nodded his head, but his face only grew paler. Brontë very nearly had to drag him into the stairwell.

The trip into the castle's depths did nothing to assuage Crockett's fears and only increased Brontë's. Bunce led them into the earth via a long, winding stone staircase. Torches were set in the stone walls, which gave an ominous, demonic light to the masonry. By the time they came to the bottom of the stair, Crockett and Brontë needed to support each other—had either of them let go of their grip, they both would have collapsed onto the floor. This would have been an even more unsettling experience, as the floor was littered with large, portly, most-scariest rats, who hissed and skittered through the shadows. In the dim light of the lamps, Brontë made out many of their furry corpses as well as their droppings which were littered across the earthen floor. Bunce indicated a particularly menacing and fat rat and pointed at it.

"His name Gregor! Hullo, Gregor!"[50] The rat screeched and leapt toward Bunce. Bunce did not appear at all upset by this. He giggled happily and stepped out of the rabid animal's way.

As they continued down the corridor, Brontë and Crockett noted that

---

[50] This little aside was kept in the novel for Earhart. In the original, experimental draft, Bunce gave the young couple opium before their descent into the dungeon. Having taken the drug, Brontë and Crockett entered a fever dream state and the rat, Gregor, told them the history of the Deutschefaber family. It was altered for the sake of general readability.

along the sides of the narrow hall were several cells. Most of them were empty. Two held prisoners: one was a young street urchin and the other was a sad-looking woman. The woman did not look up from her suffering, but the man stood and ran toward them. When he drew closer, his thin hands gripped the bars of his cell.

He spoke in rapid German. While Brontë and Crockett had no idea what he said, he seemed pleasant enough. He was very thin but smiled from the dark as he spoke. Bunce tsked at the boy and shook his head. The boy grew incensed and stormed away from them, taking a seat in the back of the cell.

"What did he want?" Crockett whispered.

"Oh, he say he eat you." Bunce said this as if he were simply recounting the weather.

Brontë leaned forward and gripped Crockett's arm.

They passed several additional empty cells before coming to the end of the corridor. In the faint light they had not noticed that Bosch was standing outside the final cell. He looked to be infuriated as they approached him.

"Bunce!" His voice was a low hiss—he sounded very much like Gregor the rat, "*Was machst du?*"

Bunce saluted his superior officer. "What am I doing?" He winked at Brontë and Crockett. "English for you," he whispered. He turned back to Bosch. "You say 'Whatever you do, bring the couple down to the dungeon.'"

Bosch's mouth fell open. "Bunce, I said 'Whatever you do, DO NOT bring the couple down to the dungeon.'"

"Oh!" Bunce looked up at the ceiling in deep reflection. After a second of silence, he shrugged his shoulders. "I know it one of those...do or do not do."

Bunce and Bosch squabbled over this misunderstanding. As they bickered in German, Brontë's eyes flicked over and she saw the man behind the bars of the cell lean in closer. The light of Bunce's lamp cast an eerie glow on his features. When he looked up and made eye contact with her, she was surprised that his eyes betrayed not a feral, violent murderer, but a defeated, melancholy old man.

Brontë felt a compulsion to reach out and take the prisoner's hand. This was interrupted by Bosch beginning to scream at Bunce, growing so enraged that he lunged at his associate, which knocked both Bunce and Crockett down. The three of them rolled on the floor for several moments before Brontë intervened, pulling Bosch from Bunce.

Crockett escaped and went to curl up in the corner of the corridor. He crawled away so quickly that he put his hand on a rat, causing both the rat and Crockett to squeal. This set off a chain reaction of shrieks as Brontë followed Crockett's lead, screaming when she saw the rat on the floor. Bunce found the hysterics to be quite fun and joined the screaming out of a sense of camaraderie.

By the end of it, Bosch was standing over them, a vein in his neck the size of a python throbbing with rage. Stefan Deutschefaber's eyes sparkled. He began to grunt jovially, what sounded like a dry, spirited laugh.

"Fine!" Bosch nearly screamed. "Fine! You obviously are following your inept detective instincts. Interrogate! Why would I interfere? What are facts when you can bungle around playacting?! Ask him your questions! Show him true English idiocy at work!"

Bosch stormed away from them down the corridor. He went so quickly, he stepped on another rat, which set off another chain of shrieks from the rat, Crockett, Brontë, and Bunce.

When things settled down again, Bunce indicated the cell. Brontë and Crockett drew near, looking into the dark cove and at the hunched form of Stefan Deutschefaber.

"I will translate," Bunce said. "Deutschefaber no know much English."

But Stefan Deutschefaber waved him off.

"I know some from prison correspondence course," he said softly. His shining eyes stared at the young couple. A smile appeared on his face. "If they want know Deutschefaber story, they hear it from Deutschefaber." He indicated a stool in the corner, which was concealed in shadow. "Sit lady." He pointed at Brontë. "Tell me what you want know."

26

Icarus

Brontë took her seat. Crockett stood behind her and placed his hand on her shoulder.

She was about to speak when Bunce interrupted. "I have question, Master Deutschefaber," he said. "Your wife very tiny but your daughter very large. Why that happen?"

Deutschefaber stared at Bunce; the junior detective looked very pleased with his question.

Bronté and Crockett expected Deutschefaber to offer no response, but the old man took a moment of contemplation before answering. "My aunt very large," he said. "Maybe she get bigness from her?"

"Ah!" Bunce dug into his trousers and pulled a notebook out. He began scribbling. "My mama and papa are very slim and I very regally plump. It also from my aunt."

The two began a rather pleasant exchange slipping into German and discussing Tante Sourbach (Bunce's aunt) and Tante Masslebaum (Deutschefaber's).[51]

Bronté looked to Crockett. He shrugged his shoulders.

---

[51] This was a nod to Earhart's own Aunt Masslebaum, who supported his and Didiert's homosexual lifestyle. She allowed them to stay as a couple—in the barn of her third country house. (She was both accepting and also not. It was the 1920s, if you'll recall.)

"I'm terribly sorry," she said interrupting them. "We are…on a rather tight timeline." She was picturing Collanhall, his inquisition at the prison closed, sprinting back toward the inn. "Would it be all right if we asked a few questions, Master Deutschefaber?"

"Ah ha!" Bunce reached between the cell bars and nudged Deutschefaber. "English no like to wait." He winked at Brontë. "It okay Boopy, you ask questions!"

Brontë nodded at Bunce (whom she was nearly on the verge of strangling) and focused her attention on Deutschefaber.

Now, with time to focus, she assessed his features. It was true what Bunce said; he was nowhere near the height or imposing girth of his daughter. The old man was slim, much more Klaude in appearance than either Bristol or Ursula. His eyes were kind, sunken into his wrinkled face. A sparse, wild beard of black and gray hung from his chin, matching the few remaining salt-and-pepper wisps of hair on his shining head. He did not look like a murderer, but a kind, old man stuck in a dank cell.

Brontë felt a compassionate warmth in her breast. While she intended to begin an interrogation, the empathy exuding from Deutschefaber's twinkling eyes brought a more human question to the fore.

"Mr. Deutschefaber, did Detective Bosch tell you about your son? Bristol?"

Deutschefaber sighed. "Son is dead," he said matter-of-factly. "I know this."

Crockett wondered, again, at the peculiar Deutschefaber tendency to care little about the demise and evisceration of their nuclear family members.

As if sensing the confusion he was causing Crockett, he continued, "He do some bad thing. Once he in prison with me. It was…" He scrunched his eyes in thought, "Sorry I forget English phrase from correspondence course. It inevtivitabbly."

"Inevitable?" Crockett offered.

"Yes," Deutschefaber confirmed. "Sad. No surprise."

With domestic matters resolved, Brontë moved to more direct questioning. She improvised a little—*Detectivating for the Dunce* often suggested interrogating suspects with a baton to bludgeon them for "faster coopera-tion."[52]

"Mr. Deutschefaber," she said, "we hoped you could add some context to odd things occurring around the inn. Not just your son's death, but there has been a creature lurking about."

Deutschefaber pursed his lips. "Creature?"

"Yes," Crockett added himself to the conversation. "The creature of the woods—the one rumored to lurk about and steal children."

"Klaude said that he and Bristol used to sleep outside and wait for it to appear," Brontë said. "It's called the *Dämonenbär*? One of the guests at the inn told us it was a creature created by an evil doctor."

With the speaking of the word "doctor," the old man's demeanor shifted. His eyes glinted with rage, and he turned away from the young couple.

A long silence elapsed. No one spoke. Brontë and Crockett looked to Bunce, but the jovial policeman was not following the conversation. Gregor the rat had returned and was distracting his attention.

Left to their own resources, Brontë gently lifted Crockett's hand from her shoulder. She stood and stepped closer to the cell. "Mr. Deutschefaber—" she began.

But the old man growled and cut her off. "Huh!" His voice shook. "Only monster in woods is that man! That the monster, not animal!" He turned back toward them. As he approached, spittle flew from his mouth. "I not kill him! He…" The old man suddenly grew consumed with sadness. Tears traced down his face; he wailed and stumbled into the corner of the cell.

Brontë and Crockett had not been speaking of the doctor of the sixth cabin, so Deutschefaber's response took them both by surprise. A moment passed before they remembered Klaude's story and the rumors Bosch told them in the street.

Brontë leaned into Crockett's ear. "The doctor in the sixth cabin…I don't

---

[52] The author eventually found a copy of this famous book and can confirm this is all accurate. The book was difficult to procure, as both red and blue states in the U.S.A. had finally agreed on something, which was that this was one book they preferred to ban, mainly due to the consensus that Charlemagne has no place in modern investigatory frameworks.

know…"

Crockett gently touched his wife's back. "Let's let him speak. A circuitous route may lead us to answers," he said softly.

The young man then leaned forward, placing his hands on the bars of the cell. "Mr. Deutschefaber," he said, "are you all right?"

The man, however, would not move. He remained huddled in his cell. Intermittent sobs caused his whole body to shake.

The cry out of outrage and grief pulled Bunce from his visit with Gregor. He sidled up next to the young couple "Perhaps," he said watching Deutschefaber shake with heavy sobs, "we go. I no think—"

But, in another sudden shift, the old man was back up; he frantically wiped the tears from his face. "No! No!" he yelled. "Please! No!"

All three of the visitors staggered back from the cell as the old man rushed toward them. His eyes were full of tears. He pressed his hands to the bars.

"It been long, long time since I have visit. I…" He wiped his eyes. Taking a deep breath, he fought through a sob. "No one visit. No one help. It that woman! She do this!"

Brontë and Crockett exchanged curious glances. "What woman?" they asked together.

"The baroness," Stefan said. His voice, again, had a feral, vengeful rasp. "She pay—she pay to do this to me!"

"The baroness?" Crockett drew closer to the bars. "Who is she?"

Even Bunce grew interested, pressing his face closer to the cell.

"She wife of doctor."

"But why would she do this to you?" Brontë asked.

The old man sighed. He pressed his hands to his face. "No one believe me. No one believe truth!"

"We will!" Brontë stepped forward. She reached through the bars and gripped the old man's hands.

Deutschefaber, touched by Brontë's show of affection, gently kissed her hand. "It been long time since I see friendly people," he said squeezing her fingers. "Ursula keep Klaude from me. She lock him up, scared he get hurt again. She like vulture over him!" The old man dropped Brontë's hand and slapped the bars of the cell in frustration. "She scared of me. She believe *that* woman. She not let Klaude come. No one come."

Crockett stepped forward next to Brontë. "Mr. Deutschefaber, perhaps you could start at the beginning. Who is the baroness? And how did she make you end up here?"

Deutschefaber, eyes shining, looked between Crockett and Brontë. As he glanced between them, his face relaxed. Years melted off his withered visage; he grew sad and vulnerable.

"At first, it okay," the old man began. "The doctor live in woods; he very friendly man. We buy land from him. Klaude, my boy, love him. He love science; he love machines; he love the doctor ideas. But the doctor go too far. His machine…the flight—it make person like bird. He say you move arms like bird and move through sky."[53]

"Oh no…" Brontë foresaw the conclusion.

The old man sighed. "It not work. Doctor too proud and my son test machine. He fall from sky and…" Deutschefaber's voice broke. Tears, again, poured from his eyes. "He lose legs. Doctor…" The prisoner coughed. His voice grew cold. "Doctor do that. He hurt, my son. My boy…"

There was a loud sniffle and both Brontë and Crockett turned. To their surprise, Bunce was overcome with emotion.

"Of course I anger!" Deutschefaber's face flushed as he continued. "He hurt my boy! What he do? He smart! But very hard in that chair. It so difficult…" The old man's face contorted between grief and rage. "But I no kill! He do himself! I find him…I going to make him leave, but he already go…"

"The doctor killed himself?" Crockett asked quickly. "He wasn't murdered?"

"No!" Deutschefaber bellowed. "But I anger! In town before I at bar. I drink. I say—maybe I not smart—but at bar I say I kill him. But I just anger!

---

[53] Inspired by this, Didiert and Earhart booked a flight with the North Joyfuncharmington da Vinci Society. It was an inaugural excursion on a replica of da Vinci's famous flying machine. Although it could not take flight, bored city folks could pedal the contraption around in a field full of sheep.

I not do it!"

"But what that have do with baroness?!" Bunce, fully invested in the story, was leaning forward, nearly pressed against Brontë.

The young woman looked at him and then back to Deutschefaber. "It's a good question," she said with a nod.

"Agh!" The prisoner spun away from the bars. He stomped in a circle around his cell as he went on. "The baroness and doctor—they marry but no work out. I no know why. But she go—But!—she very rich. She leave spies to watch doctor. They tell her gossip; they say I kill him."

"Oh no…" Crockett sighed.

"Baroness pay much money to police. They take me—they lock me here. But…" Deutschefaber's voice shook. "Worst is family. It confuse them. My wife…she get sick. She think I evil! Daughter blame me for both doctor and her mother. But…Klaude…" The old man let out a prolonged, piteous sob. "Klaude…I never see Klaude again. He keep away. Ursula not want him remember the accident or that father a murderer! But I want him know! It not me!"

The old man finally broke down completely. He crawled into the corner of the cell, overcome with emotion.

Crockett embraced Brontë.

Bunce joined them, wrapping his pudgy arms around the young couple. "Such tragedy," he said.

Brontë and Crockett, not wanting to ruin the emotional force of the moment, did nothing to shake him off.

As Crockett pondered the story, he realized it had nothing to do with any of their present lines of inquiry. The puzzle box in his mind whirred, the gears nearly smoking with effort. Who was the baroness? What did she have to do with the present appearance of the Caddywampus, the mob, and POOP?

"Mr. Deutschefaber," Crockett started softly, "I'm sorry to keep probing, but would there be something that ties Bristol's death to any of this?"

The old man sniffed. "Bristol die by mob. Once I go and mother die, he use them to help pay monies for inn. For while people call it 'death inn' from all mess with doctor. They find way to keep open…deal with devil, you ask me."

"Oh dear," Brontë said, both from the revelation of the "death inn" moniker and the fact that Bunce was still embracing her. She gently shook him off. "So, Bristol used the mob to keep the inn open."

"And something went sour, and he was killed," Crockett said.

"Would the mob be behind the appearance of the Caddywampus?" Brontë asked Crockett. "Was it an elaborate plot to extricate themselves from blame? If the monster was in the woods, it could share the blame for the death of Bristol."

"The what?" Deutschefaber asked.

"The forest creature…" Brontë started.

"An American named it—it's…" Crockett added.

Deutschefaber continued to stare at them in confusion.

"You know what," Brontë said quickly, "it doesn't matter. It's…well, the mob did it. Bristol isn't the source of some mystery. That case is very much closed."

Crockett sighed. "Now we just have to figure out POOP, Collanhall, and the treasure."

Upon hearing the word "treasure" the old man snorted.

Brontë and Crockett leaned forward. Bunce, who had been distracted by more rats, regained his focus and pushed between them to hear, not fully knowing why he should be interested.

"Why did you make that sound?" Brontë asked.

The old prisoner shook his head. "Doctor say there treasure. He leave notes when he die. I find them with him."

"Oh!" Bunce cried, realizing the topic of their inquiry. "Treasure fun!"

"The doctor said there was a treasure?" Brontë could not contain herself. She gently pushed Bunce behind them to get closer to Deutschefaber. "What did the note say?"

The old man snorted again. "It all nonsense. I go to cabin and there nothing! Note say two keys open up 'the treasure of his heart.'"

"Two keys?" Crockett's mind whirred.

"One key to baroness. One key to my son."

"Why wouldn't Klaude mention it?" Brontë asked. She turned to Crockett. She was electrified by this new revelation. "He mentioned the sixth cabin, why not the key?"

"You said he was very disparaging about the treasure," Crockett said. "He is probably also convinced it is a myth."

"It is!" Deutschefaber scoffed.

"Yes!" Bunce joined him. "Even I look for it. Nothing there!"

"No treasure! I search when doctor die. There not even keys! Just two notes, one for Klaude and the other for baroness. I give baroness letter to police and Klaude his letter. I no find anything."

Crockett leaned forward, pressing his face against the bars of the cell. "But did you know about the secret room. The cave?"

Bunce looked surprised by this.

Deutschefaber crossed his arms. "Of course! Klaude in cave every day before accident, helping with machines."

"What cave?" Bunce asked. A glow crept into his eyes.

"But why would he say it…" Brontë began pacing in front of the cell.

Crockett still had his face pressed against the bars. He closed his eyes in thought.

"What cave?" Bunce asked again.

Deutschefaber watched the young couple strain to make sense of this new information. His head sagged slightly, his voice filling with pity for the young couple's excitement. "Many search for treasure. No one find it! After I tell police, whole town search. There nothing." Deutschefaber cleared his throat. "Before he die, doctor…he a little crazy. When we first meet, nice man. But…" He took a step back, his hands balled into fists. His eyebrows furrowed. "He take risks, like with Klaude! The boy could be dead!" Heavy sobs seized the old man. He turned away and sulked to the corner of his cell.

Brontë and Crockett stepped away from him to converse quietly. Bunce, unsure whether to console the old man or join the conspiratorial gathering, hesitated between the two. As Brontë and Crockett spoke in excited, hushed whispers, the policeman leaned in closer to Deutschefaber, whispering kind words to him in German.

"There may be a treasure," Crockett said.

"Klaude has a key." Brontë quivered with excitement. "But the other…"

"What does it have to do with Bristol's death and the Caddywampus?"

"I don't know."

"And where is it? If people have been searching for years…"

"I don't know."

They paused, nearly breathless. Deutschefaber shook with emotion in his cell. Bunce continued his half-listening, half-emotional-supporting.

Brontë and Crockett looked deeply into each other's eyes. At the same moment, they spoke their next course of action, "We have to speak to Klaude again."

They both smiled; for the first time since their arrival, the rapture of the mystery equally consumed them.

"Thank you, Master Deutschefaber," Brontë said. "We know this has been a difficult conversation."

The old man turned his head slightly. In the dim glow of the dungeon's lamps, a tear sparkled on his cheek. "Can you do thing? For me?"

Crockett and Brontë leaned in closely. "Of course," Crockett said.

"If you talk Klaude…ask him if he come. I know Ursula not let him, but I—" He broke off. He sniffed and faced the corner of the cell.

"Master Deutschefaber," Brontë spoke, her voice trembling with emotion, "we will do all that we can to get him here."

Deutschefaber turned toward them. He smiled slightly and gave a wave. "Okay," he said. It appeared he wanted to say more, but tears returned to his eyes, causing him to turn away.

"Aw!" Bunce walked forward and put his arms around Crockett and Brontë. "This very nice. It like sentimental book."

The young couple, exhausted by the prattling Bunce, bid him a quick farewell and headed toward the exit. They were much quicker than the chubby officer and gained ground quickly. Bunce, who hoped to debrief the conversation, called after them.

"I just have question about cave! It secret but where it at?"

"In the wood!" Crockett called back, doing his best to appear polite.

When they emerged from the dungeon, they were disconcerted to find that the waning storm had regained strength. The earlier lull appeared to have been a prelude to something larger. The sky grew darker; the wind gained force, whipping through the open courtyard with growing menace.

They passed Bosch in the courtyard. The officer glared at them as they rushed toward the castle gate.

"Did you find anything?" he asked mockingly. "Are Mr. and Mrs. Detective now hot on the trail?"

Crockett, again, out of politeness, gave a wave and said, "Nothing extraordinary!"

They rushed past him and out of the prison. Bosch snorted when he saw them disappear. He grumbled under his breath in German. This irritated soliloquy was interrupted by Bunce, who finally emerged from the dungeon and ran toward him.

"Bunce!" he spoke in German.

The junior detective gasped for air. "Oh-hello-you-see-them-pass?"

"Yes. What transpired?"

Bunce (between heaving breaths) grew emotional recounting the story of the keys, the doctor, the baroness, and the cave. Due to his physical exhaustion and the slight blubbering from his tears, the monologue was completely incomprehensible. The little man had also drawn close to Bosch and threw his arm around him, attempting to fully portray the emotional depth and intimacy of the dungeon encounter.

Bosch, annoyed but intrigued by the pieces he gleaned from Bunce's garbled retelling, encouraged him to continue. "Facts only, Bunce. None of this ridiculous emotion. Start at the beginning, and, if you please, get your arm off me."

27

Odd Encounters and Consternation

nce outside the prison, Brontë and Crockett gathered their thoughts. With the new information and revelations from Master Deutschefaber, they needed to reassess their strategy.

"This is all very interesting," Crockett said. "I feel pieces are beginning to fall into place."

"I agree." Brontë looked toward the sky. Her hair swept across her face. "My question is if the treasure is perhaps the lynchpin. Is that what has brought these events to transpire? It's the only motive which could make sense."

"There are too many unknowns. Perhaps Klaude could provide some insight."

"At the very least, we should see if he still has the key."

"Whatever it is, Master Deutschefaber said there wasn't a key with the letter." Away from the dungeon and the steady excitement from Stefan Deutschefaber's story, Crockett's heart grew heavy. He remembered the body of Bristol suspended from the lodge, the terror of Kreuz in the street, and the chilling roar of the Caddywampus. He shivered. "Brontë, we do need to exercise caution."

Brontë also had a rising fear. "There are truly malevolent forces at work." A peal of thunder rumbled in the distance.

"I can't tell if the storm is coming or going," Brontë said. She looked skyward and a drop of rain fell on her nose. This answered her question. "We should walk and talk, Crockett. We may be caught in another downpour on the way home."

The two moved quickly down the muddy path away from the castle. Their voices tremored with excitement as they discussed the new facts of the mystery.

"If we keep to our line of thinking from this morning," Crockett said, "then Collanhall and Phipps may be aligned in some way."

"In pursuit of…something…"

"And we now know that there are two keys of some kind."

"One is held by Klaude and the other by the baroness."

"Another character. Who could she be? And what—" Crockett's gasped with a revelation. "Oh…"

Brontë nodded. She also had followed the line of logic.

They both recollected their morning in cabin four: the images on the wall, the old pictures of her and a man, the story of her mysterious friend, and her ties to Praktisch. "Madame van der Raaf…"

"She must be the baroness. But why is she here?" Brontë walked around a puddle. "Why bring the key now? What force has drawn everyone to Praktisch for *this* festival?"

This question was posed as the two newlyweds reentered the town. Some of the festival goers were trying to take advantage of the break in the rain and return to joyous activities. The man-fairy had a crowd of bawdy men around him scrambling for moonshine. Children frolicked in the street, splashing through puddles. A little girl did not pay attention to her course and nearly collided with Brontë and Crockett. When she realized her error, she looked up and let out a short, staccato scream.

The young couple tried to calm her, but she could not be consoled. She ran back toward her friends. Soon her arms were waving in the air, and she pointed backward to indicate the young couple. The other children turned and also exhibited signs of terror. They ran off quickly.

"What frightened them so?" Brontë asked.

But Crockett understood. He began to laugh uncontrollably.

"Crockett, what's so funny?" She lightly slapped her husband out of annoyance.

He shook with laughter. "Brontë, we've been so enthralled by our mystery, we haven't noticed our own appearances."

Brontë's eyes went wide. She attempted to find a looking glass. The closest option was the windows of the candy shop where they had encountered the man-fairy. She ran up to the porch and assessed herself. She first gasped then joined Crockett in his mirth. He came up behind her, putting his hand on her shoulder.

The children were right to be frightened. The couple resembled shorter, less menacing Caddywampuses. Brontë's hair was askew, her face covered in splotches of mud. Her shirt and trousers were splattered with grime from the dungeon's depths. Crockett was her horrifying equal. His skin was so caked with rust-colored mud, he looked like he a bronze statue in a forgotten corner of Hyde Park. His soaked hair hung limply over his forehead.

"It's too bad we couldn't get a picture," Crockett said. "This is certainly a good representation of our honeymoon thus far."

They laughed again. It was disrupted, however, when the shopkeeper appeared in the window and let out a terrific shriek. Crockett jumped and staggered backward. Brontë turned and caught him just before he tumbled over the railing of the porch and into a puddle.

The door of the shop pushed open and the shopkeeper appeared. She waved them inside speaking very concerned German. Another shock quickly followed when they entered: Madame van der Raaf was inside the store perusing a shelf of candied apples. Today, she again wore all black, other than her headpiece, which was a collection of white and black flowers soaring nearly as high as the ceiling.

"Oh!" she squawked upon seeing them. "I see you've decided to dress to match your intellect."

Brontë and Crockett were so flabbergasted by the Dutchwoman's presence that they couldn't think quickly enough to ask her about the new information from Master Deutschefaber. The shopkeeper also distracted them with her continuous clucking. She went to the back of her shop and returned with a few towels and a small basin of water. Before Brontë could protest, she was under attack by the woman scrubbing her face with a wet towel.

As she scrubbed, she threw Crockett the other towel and turned to Madame van der Raaf. The shopkeeper spoke hurriedly.

"Would you mind translating, Madame?" Crockett asked. "Dull, dirty intellect, you know."

Madame van der Raaf snorted. "Ha! Well, you're lucky I'm feeling generous. You dolts still haven't replaced the hat you destroyed!" She leveled a menacing stare at the young couple. Crockett swallowed and started to apologize, but the old woman carried on, "She's saying it's imperative to get you clean as the children will be frightened."

"Why?" Brontë was able to get this question out before the shopkeeper took the young woman fully by the ears and dunked her head into the washbasin.

There was frantic gurgling from Brontë as Madame van der Raaf spoke, "It's gossip among the youth that the two children who were taken were stolen by a pair of 'mud people.'"

"Mud people?" Crockett asked.

Brontë would have also responded, but her head was freshly removed from the basin, and she was gasping for breath.

"Petrarch's faith in your detectivery[54] must be misplaced! You obviously haven't been doing a competent investigation into the goings-on if you don't know that!" Madame van der Raaf's neck bloated like a bullfrog with this chastisement. "The children say that the two who were taken were stolen by a man and a woman who were covered in grime and came from the woods. They were convinced to follow them with bribes of candy. Orphans are easily seduced, you know."

"That's true," Crockett said remembering his own parentless childhood

---

[54] It's honestly growing impressive how many ways Earhart and Didiert were able to butcher the word detective.

when he had been convinced to rub Granny Pedigree's bunions for a rather shiny piece of string.[55] "But still…what an odd story."

The newlyweds were in such a state of mental chaos that they had no idea what to ask or do next. The description of the mud people was confounding, as was the unexpected encounter with the Dutchwoman, who they had just realized was the secret baroness/wife of the old doctor of the woods.

Brontë was formulating a question when Madame van der Raaf adjusted her hat and bowed.

"I must be off," she said haughtily. "Petrarch and I have a tea appointment this afternoon." For the first time in the afternoon's encounter, the woman's voice lost its condescending edge. Her pale cheeks filled with color. "Excuse me!"

She bustled out of the shop before they could say another word. When the door closed, the shopkeeper rambled to them in German. While they could not understand a word, they gleaned that Madame van der Raaf was someone the shopkeeper esteemed highly. She spoke in warm tones and motioned toward the door through which Greta had exited.

By the end of the shopkeeper's bathing work, Crockett and Brontë had clean faces. Brontë's hair was drier and pulled back, and Crockett's jacket had been dusted and his hair pomaded. While they did not look entirely pleasant, they would no longer horrify children.

They exited the shop with their fresh faces and handfuls of treats from the shopkeeper. She walked them out the door and waved.

In the street, Brontë and Crockett stared at each other, dazed by the previous quarter hour.

The atmosphere of earlier had shifted. Peeking from behind a curtain of silver clouds, the sun signaled that the storm had altered course. With this change in weather, the celebrations stepped up; children sang, adults carried tankers of lager, and policemen kept a nervous watch over all the proceedings.

A drunken Englishman nearly collided with them as they contemplated

---

[55] The author is thrilled there is more of Granny P. included here.

their new information. Realizing they were in the way of the swirling crowd, Crockett gently pulled Brontë back toward the porch of the sweet shop.

When they were out of the way, Brontë lowered her voice and spoke, "I have to steal a line from Alice, Crockett: 'Curiouser and curiouser.'"

Crockett ran a hand through his hair, accidentally mussing it and pulling out a hand slick with pomade. He cleaned the sticky substance off on his trousers. He could do nothing but sigh in exasperation. "Brontë, I'm nearly exhausted from the new developments. I don't know where we should begin."

"The mud people information was certainly a shock. Who could the man and woman be? If it's related to the Caddywampus and the inn, is it people we know?"

"The Gestahlts?" Crockett asked. "They do have children."

"But you've seen their hair. Madame van der Raaf said the missing children are blond cherubs. The Gestahlt children have their shocks of black hair and act more like devils."

"Could it have been Bristol and Ursula?"

"But why?"

Crockett couldn't help but laugh. "Why anything? Why is Greta here? What is the treasure? Is it even real? The couple could have been Phipps and Collanhall for all we know."

"Phipps does have a rather effeminate bearing."

"True. Maybe even Sylvia and Ursula."

Brontë laughed. "Well, I would say the only way is forward. Shall we go back to the inn and check on Klaude and Collanhall? I feel that will be a direct course—" She stopped herself when Crockett's face registered such a shocking change in expression that the words caught in her throat. "Crockett, what is the matter?"

The young lawyer's blue and green eyes formed into round pools. His face turned such a shade of white as to resemble new-fallen snow. Brontë followed his gaze and gasped when she saw the subject of Crockett's consternation; yards ahead of them, looping through the growing crowd was Kreuz. He looked even more menacing than in their previous encounter—his tall, ghastly figure was a stark juxtaposition to the ruddy-faced revelers. His long legs pulled him forward at a blazingly fast pace. Brontë whirled and faced Crockett.

"Should we...?"

Crockett turned. To his left, he saw an opening in the crowd beyond which their path back to the Deutschefaber Inn was clear; the sun shone on the dusty trail, as if inviting them to return safely.

To his right, in the direction of Kreuz, the scene was much different. The passing storm's wake of black clouds glowered in the distance. Revelers who lined that path were more intoxicated and menacing; their whoops, jeers, and laughter filled the pauses between cracks of thunder.

"Crockett?" Brontë saw her husband's pale complexion and readied herself to catch him in case a fainting spell came on.

She was shocked, however, when he turned to her and gripped her wrists. Her heart fluttered.

"Brontë, go back to the inn. Find out what you can from Klaude and Collanhall."

Brontë watched Crockett's eyes flick after Kreuz. "Crockett, we should go together."

He shook his head. "From the beginning I said your safety is my chief concern. I couldn't live with putting you in the kind of danger Kreuz may portend."

"Crockett..." Brontë felt a collage of feeling: pride in Crockett's courage, disappointment that she would not pursue Kreuz, and elation that the mystery was now revealing itself and they had definite lines of inquiry to follow.

She had no time to protest. Crockett gripped her face and planted a kiss on her lips. A passing dame croaked in disgust. The man-fairy across the street whistled.

"If I don't return," he said breathlessly, "I'm most likely collapsed outside the tavern." He winked at her. "You'll find me there."

He squeezed her hand and bounded off. She saw his shining, pomaded head disappear into the crowd.

245

28

What Happened at the Pub

Despite the swirling army of festivalgoers, Crockett had little fear he would lose Kreuz. He was certain the gaunt man's path led directly to the tavern. Not just the tavern, but the same small corner table at which he'd been seated the previous day. Subterfuge was also simplified amid the sloppy celebrants; the roar of their cries and the rapidity of their drunken movements shielded Crockett from the man-in-black's attention.[56]

His stealth was also aided by the distracted Kreuz. The man kept his head down, focused only on the steps ahead of him. At one point a heavy, intoxicated fellow grabbed his arm and spun him in a dance. Kreuz pulled away quickly, his face registering not annoyance, as Crockett would have expected, but panic, a deeply rooted fear. Once the reveler was thrust away, Kreuz doubled his pace, sprinting toward the door of the tavern.

Crockett waited several minutes before following Kreuz inside. He attached himself to a group of young businessmen who entered in a rowdy entourage. When the door of the tavern closed shut behind them, he peeled off from the group and made his way to the back of the room. In a stroke of

---

[56] Reader, you have probably caught on at this point, but, as Crockett and Brontë are now separating, Didiert and Earhart concocted another odd, split chapter. Again, you're welcome for shifting it into two separate chapters.

tremendous luck, he chose correctly—Kreuz was seated at the same booth as the previous day.

He was already huddled over, speaking to a group of similarly nervous gentlemen in frantic whispers.

The bar was full. Patrons hollered and laughed boisterously, getting into the holiday spirit. Crockett used this to his benefit; he slid behind a group of older gentlemen as if waiting to speak to the barkeep. He stayed close to the suspicious men and strained to listen.

His face fell as he realized they were speaking in an unknown language, a muddled vocalization he only recognized as not being German. His mind raced to find a solution; should he write down key words? Phrases? Would someone at the bar help him? How could he explain that he was attempting to overhear an organized crime syndicate in hopes of finding out if a giant elk-bear-puma creature was going after a secret, buried treasure? Would they find it plausible?[57]

But, in a wild, fortuitous twist, he heard a man speak up behind him. His tone was gruff and menacing, but his words were in beautiful, comprehensible English.

"Calm down," he said harshly. "Remember we are in a mixed company. English, please, while we are at the table. We all took the correspondence course."

Kreuz mumbled something. Crockett took a step backward toward the table to hear better.

"We have precious little time and must move forward quickly," the gruff man continued. "It is clear we must act tonight. What we seek is under scrutiny." There was a murmur of voices, to which the gruff man responded, "Scrutiny—it means people are looking for it and are closing in on it. Our time is running out."

A man with a squeaky voice whispered something. There was a murmur of agreement.

"Dinkle makes a good point. Not all of us can be on the move. We need

---

[57] The writer feels compelled to say, objectively, that they would not find it plausible.

agents to stay back and handle any interruptions or issues."

Someone else, this man with a booming, gravely tone, spoke up, "Yes. It goes without saying that we are sworn to secrecy and trust. You have already seen what becomes of those who betray us. Two corpses. If there is another who wishes to attempt a third betrayal, this next time the wood creature will be sure there is nothing left of you."

Crockett turned briefly to see the speaker of this comment. He noted that the threat caused a split reaction in the group. Half sniggered under their breaths. The others sat in stony silence.

No one spoke for several seconds.

Crockett, in the pause, looked a bit too long. One of the men, an especially unpleasant looking one with the face of a boar, made eye contact with him. The young lawyer blanched. The boar hissed at him.

Crockett spun and pushed further into the crowd to conceal himself. Once he was securely away, he strained to hear as the gruff man continued.

"Now Dinkle, Kreuz, and Hans, you will come with me. The rest of you will return to headquarters and await the others."

Chairs scraped and boots clomped on the floor as the party rose to separate. They were stalled by Kreuz, who spoke up. His voice was soft and snake-like.

"The others?" he asked.

The gruff man sniffed. "That is my business, Kreuz. Do not worry yourself with the logistics. You've ruined enough this time." The man and Kreuz locked eyes in a heated stare. Kreuz was the first to blink. When he did, the gruff man spun on his heel and stormed away.

Kreuz's eyes flashed. As the gruff man exited, he rose and followed behind. Crockett could feel the heat of the mobster's anger as he forced his way through the packed tavern.

With Kreuz absent, Crockett turned clandestinely and looked at the table to see who remained. The boar man was still there, picking his teeth with a knife. A small, skittish man sat beside him. They spoke in hushed tones, but the discussion appeared friendly. He put a hand to his mouth in surprise when he saw their lapels. What shocked him and caused his gaze to linger was that, although both wore handkerchiefs, one man's was green and the other's was gold.

Crockett caught himself staring. He spun and pushed further into the crowd just as the boar man looked toward him. Fearing he'd been spotted, and the man would use the knife for something more menacing than his teeth, Crockett rushed toward the other side of the bar.

When he felt he was out of harm's way, he leaned against the back wall and pondered the significance of the conversation. What would they do tonight? And who were the "two corpses"? Was it Bristol and the man who'd been killed the first night in town? Or was it someone else?

His thoughts were disrupted by one of the English businessmen from the group he'd followed in, who gripped his arm and pulled him to their table.

"Horse man!" he yelled.

Crockett assessed the group. He marveled that any of them were standing. They were exceedingly drunk. (He was both proud and embarrassed by his fellow countrymen.) Even Phipps in the throes of the Colonel's binge the day before was like a nun in comparison.

"Pals," the man who grabbed Crockett said staggering, "it's the horse guy who followed us in." The other men looked at him with bleary eyes. "We took bets. You English or Dutch?"

"English," Crockett said. He grew nervous watching his new companion sway back and forth. The speaker was spilling his drink and bumping into those around him, many of whom gave him searing looks.

One of the men who was seated took out a bill and tossed it at another drunk. "Aw! I said he had Dutch nostrils! Look at'em! They're Dutch! Dutch as the day is long. I was going to order him a Dutch Pour!"

A man in tweed nodded fervently. "That's what I was sayin', too!"

This caused a lot of general hmm'ing and harr'ing. Crockett used the window to attempt an escape. This was abruptly stopped by his swaying friend.

"My name's Roger," he said.

"Nice to meet you, Roger."

"Oh, wow!" The man spun, his drink falling completely out of his hand.

"You hear that, errybody? His name's Roger too!"

This caused an uproar at the table. One of the other men stood and patted Crockett's back.

"Second Roger," he said. "What brings you to Praktisch?"

Crockett was now doubly nervous watching Roger and these other men defying all odds by staying upright.

"I—" Crockett gingerly reached out and grabbed Roger before he fell into a group of Germans behind him. "Well, I came for the festival."

"Festival!"

This was shouted in unison by all the Englishmen. The man in tweed thumped his glass on the table. He grew so excited he threw back his chair and stood up.

"That's what I was sayin', too!" he shouted.

"We were passing through on business and thought we'd stop by," Roger said. He was now using Crockett as a support for his weight. "Then there's a rubbery."

"A rubbery?" Crockett could barely concentrate. The man in tweed was now standing and looking as if he was ready to fight someone.

"Yeah, they rubberied the records office. Right outside our hotel!" Roger leaned over to grab another drink at the table. Crockett had to grip the seat of his pants and pull him back before he fell. When he returned upright, he appeared to have forgotten his wanting a drink. He turned right to Crockett and belched.

One of the men seated laughed so hard he fell backward out of his chair. The chair crashed on the tweed man's foot, who let out a terrific shout.

The din swelled. Several voices in different languages started to yell. Roger appeared to notice none of this as he patted Crockett's jacket.

"Sorry about that. I get that sometimes with ale. The belches." He wiped his nose with his jacket. "What was I sayin'?"

"The rubbery?" Crockett's eyes went wide as he saw the tweed man throw a punch at his English friend. He missed and planted a fist right into a very large local man's stomach.

"Yeah!" Roger shouted. "They woke us up with all the coppers. They say it was some guy and another tiny guy."

"Tiny guy?" Crockett asked.

Roger's eyes narrowed. "You callin' me tiny, Second Roger?"

But Crockett was the least of Roger's worries. A chair flew and crashed just above his head. Roger awoke from his stupor and saw that Tweed and his other English friend were in a terrific brawl. Roger wasted no time leaping across the table, landing several feet away from the large local, who was pummeling both his friends at the same time.

Crockett used this brief intermission to sprint through the crowd and exit into the street. He gasped for breath once he was down the front steps. This respite was broken by the sound of shattered glass and a table being thrown from the tavern's window.

The cacophony from the pub was drawing people to the area. Shouts and jeers were heard as he stumbled through the growing mob and headed toward the inn.

A flurry of thoughts raced through his head as he escaped.

In the past several hours, the stakes and mysteries surrounding the inn had multiplied: What was the treasure? What did the mob and Bristol's death have to do with it? Greta was the baroness, but what did she want? And how were Collanhall and Phipps involved? Who were the mud people, not to mention the tiny man from the "rubbery"?

And *what was* the Caddywampus?

A chill was in the air as Crockett pushed through the growing throngs of people. With the intensifying shouts from the fight behind him, what would usually be a beautiful sight—the street amassed with individuals, their lanterns shining with golden light—instead took on an eerie feeling in the dark afternoon. Families pushed their way out of the street and toward shelter; those under the influence of alcoholic spirits were laughing and caterwauling as rain yet again began to fall. Crockett threw a backward glance and saw that the tavern fight had spilled into the street.

He picked up his pace. In the cold and deepening dark, he shivered thinking of the malevolent men in the tavern and the boar man's sinister hiss. Whatever conclusion this Caddywampus mystery was intended to come to, they were accelerating toward it like a brakeless minecart. And, whether he and Brontë knew the reason and the motives behind it or not, the mobster in the pub made it clear that a violent end was in sight.

29

Ursula at Home

On the road back to the lodge, Brontë tried to formulate a plan. This was derailed by Greta, however, who was also plodding along the path and proved to be a massive distraction. During their short jaunt together, the Dutchwoman berated Brontë about her "lack of feminine graces" and "the importance of regal headwear." The younger woman did eventually break away, but the tirade lasted nearly the entire trip back to the inn and kept her from preparing to meet with Klaude.

The old dame's thoughts buzzed in Brontë's head afterward as she stood at the entrance of the lodge. Her hand was poised on the door; her eyes were closed. It took everything in her power to stem the rage stirred by the old woman's criticisms. Her thoughts swarmed like bees and refused to calm. In desperation, her focus drifted skyward in a silent prayer. She asked for Ursula to be absent, Klaude to be in his room, and copious amounts of new information about the doctor and the key to be sprinkled upon her.

When she opened her eyes and pushed open the door, this prayer seemed to have been answered—the inn was perfectly silent.

She repressed a gleeful smile as she crossed the room and headed toward the stair. Her hand was on the banister, her right foot hovering over the bottom step, when she heard a great, garbled wail. The sound came from the billiard room. It was followed quickly by a clatter, which Brontë believed to be the sound of falling glasses. After this disruption, the room was quiet.

Brontë pressed her foot down on the stair. Silently she treaded upward.

With an exhalation of relief, she reached the top. She paused for a moment, turning toward the hallway that led to Klaude's room. She took a step forward and immediately paused when she heard her name echo in the main hall.

"Mrs. Cook?"

Blood rang in her ears as she turned toward the voice. The hulking figure of Ursula Deutschefaber looked up at her from the door between the billiard room and the sitting room. For the first time in their visit, she looked haggard. Her tightly pulled bun was full of splaying hairs. The tartan coat and white blouse, which were always tucked in and pressed to taut perfection, appeared as if they had spent the afternoon in a butter churn.

"Mrs. Cook, are you going to see Klaude?"

She did not sound angered or embittered. Brontë was sure she was coming to reprimand her for ascending to the second floor. But the large innkeeper's voice was heavy. It was almost pleading.

Brontë, uncertain what to do, and emboldened by Ursula's calm state, decided to speak the truth. "Yes," she said. "I want to ask him a few questions."

Ursula sighed in response. She took several long, labored steps across the room to the sofa and sat. The seat's springs let out a tremendous groan beneath her weight. Brontë noticed for the first time that she held a large bottle of gin in her hand. She lifted it to her lips and took an exceedingly long draught. Upon swallowing her drink, she put the bottle down on the table, precisely placing it in the lower corner. When this was done, she sat, staring blankly at the fireplace.

Brontë did not move during this dramatic event. When it was completed and Ursula sat in silence, she could not decide a course of action. Ursula was not hindering her from going to Klaude's room, yet in any book or even pamphlet of etiquette, she was required to go down and comfort the massive German woman.[58] She took a deep breath and then turned and treaded back down the staircase.

Ursula heard her movement and tilted her head slightly.

"You, perhaps, never feel like this," she said. "With your incredibly attractive husband deigning to marry you, I can't see why you would."

Brontë stopped her approach, swallowing a rising surge of anger.

"I assume you had a large dowry or have an arrangement where he can dabble with other maidens if he—"

"Ursula," Brontë's fists were balled, "let's put my feelings aside. What is the feeling *you* are currently experiencing?"

"In German we have a very specific word for it. It roughly translates as 'a state of desolation after one's brother is mauled by a fictitious creature, and you have just had to tell your other brother about it.' I think in English you may say 'sad.'"

"You Germans have such a wonderfully specific language."[59]

"It is far better than English." She said matter-of-factly then slumped further into the sofa. Her erect posture gave way to a half-erect slouch. "Bristol's death—that awful policeman tried to interrogate Klaude about it last night. I nearly had to fight him off. But I couldn't let him find out that way. I mean to me it's an inconvenience. But, while I'm unaffected, I knew poor Klaude would be horrified. I had to tell him tactfully about everything. He had to know *why* he died." Ursula closed her eyes and took a deep breath. "It's complicated, you know. We are running out of money, and Bristol was the one with the…" She hesitated briefly, finding the correct word. "He had the *business connections*."

"It's a lot to have to think about." Brontë reached into her trouser pocket and pulled out a handkerchief. However, when she remembered the earlier hankie incident, she put it away. The reminder of that odd event could only affect the woman in a negative way. It did not help that her and Crockett's

---

[58] For the sake of historical transparency, there was one etiquette digest written by Satanists in the 1910s that suggested it was purely optional to comfort forlorn Germans.

[59] The author agrees.

walk through the rain and mud had stained it a light brown.

Ursula noted none of this; instead, she groaned and took another drink of gin. "It *is* much to think about. Even my correspondence course on finance won't be able to pull us out of this budgetary collapse." She closed her eyes and rubbed the lids. "It's been nothing but tragedy for our family for years. My father, my mother, my two brothers, all, in some way, have been destroyed by this place. I am beginning to think we should leave Praktisch. It may be best for Klaude."

Brontë looked upward at the family portrait. In the years since the portrait, a hoard of unfortunate circumstances met the formerly happy Deutschefabers. Empathy replaced the seething anger she felt at Ursula's earlier mention of the dowry. She walked closer to the innkeeper and sat down beside her. Fighting her own fear of the large woman, she gripped Ursula's large, square hand.

As Brontë cupped it, Ursula shook it away. A look of revulsion crossed her countenance. "What *are* you doing?!" she hissed.

"I was trying to console you." Brontë awkwardly put her hands in her lap.

The innkeeper clutched at her heart. "My word! You must tell a German before you simply touch them."

"I'm…sorry," Brontë said.

Ursula took a deep breath and closed her eyes. "I do understand other cultures have different ways of doing things. I've been reading a book[60] about how to relate to other humans to help be more amicable with guests." She paused. "Speaking of," her voice shifted slightly. She appended a feminine lilt to her thundering voice. "How are you? How are you finding the weather?"

As if on cue, a blast of thunder shook the windows.

"It's," Brontë watched a tree branch fly through the air outside the lodge, "not the best weather for a festival."

---

[60] It's believed this book was Dr. Hans Schneider's 1910 book entitled *Erschrecken Sie Andere Nicht: Wie Man Sich Wie Eine Person Verhält*. The English title of which is *How to Stop Scaring Others and Feign Humanness*.

Ursula groaned. "The festival—it was our chance to return the inn to its former glory. After the murders, deaths, maimings, imprisonments…who could have foreseen this week would bring a mythical monster and more death?"

"I would agree," Brontë said. She moved closer to Ursula. "Crockett and I have been trying to figure out how so many odd things occurred all at once."

"And those are things you know about," Ursula said. She shook her head. "The Caddywhatwhat—or whatever Phipps calls it—the murder in town, the missing children…" Ursula's face turned red. "And Sylvia."

Brontë started. "Sylvia?"

Ursula ground her teeth together. "She told me after Bristol was eviscerated. They were planning to elope."

"What?!" It was Brontë's turn to clutch at her heart.

"She came to me this afternoon. I had just told Klaude about the events, so I was especially surly. She told me everything, the little tart. She thought I didn't know."

"I think your book on human relations would recommend not calling women 'tarts' in polite company, Miss Deutschefaber."

"I did say 'little.'"

Brontë decided to let this pass. "Did she tell you anything else?"

Ursula lifted herself forward. She smoothed her trousers. "She said she and Bristol were getting ready to run away together. Bristol was making arrangements. He planned to give Klaude and me a large sum of money and run off with her."

"You don't say…"

"Mrs. Gestahlt said the same thing earlier this afternoon. She overheard us yelling and came over. Not knowing much English or German, she proved to be an excellent listening companion, perfectly incapable of telling anyone Sylvia's secret. She also needed a break from her packing. It appears that the family is checking out earlier than expected."

It was difficult for Brontë to keep up with the waves of new information. Different lines of thought zipped through her brain. The Gestahlts…they were leaving as the mob planned their sudden move…and what was Bristol going to do to ensure his sister and brother's financial security?

"The children and Mr. Gestahlt are already gone. They left the poor woman to clean up everything, even that awful mess in their tub."

"Mess in the tub?"

"Ha!" Ursula crossed her arms. "Little Tart Sylvia said she thought it was blood. Black blood! Can you believe her incompetence? Tarty and idiotic."

"Again, perhaps less insults with loose acquaintances, Miss Deutschefaber."

"Tarty and a little idiotic then," she said. "But I assessed the mess, and it is much closer to the fabric dye my mother used to color my dresses when I was young."

"Fabric dye…" Brontë was now the one slouching on the couch. Her brain was reaching a point of saturation.

"Either way, we lose their payment for a night. It's hard to say which is the larger inconvenience, the loss of that coin or my brother's murder." Here she paused, as if in thought. She continued quickly, "I will say my brother; the blood clean-up alone was a massive distraction to the pre-festival fête."

Brontë said nothing. While her mind whirled with activity, she could find no central spoke that tied the thoughts together. The book Petrarch bought them for their honeymoon offered no concrete advice on their current predicament. What did it all have in common?

The Caddywampus.

The dye.

Green and gold handkerchiefs.

The baroness.

Phipps, Collanhall, and POOP.

The key, treasure, and sixth cabin.

"Ursula," Brontë spoke slowly, "do you have any inkling as to the root cause of the current chaos? Why would this be happening, and, more importantly, why now?"

Ursula clicked her tongue. She raised the large bottle of gin to her lips. After another long draught, she set it down in the exact same location from which she'd pulled it.

"I have no idea. And," she stood and picked up the bottle, "I can say I really don't care. My only thought is how to protect Klaude from any more of these disturbances."

She took a step forward. Her knees wobbled. She nearly collapsed to the ground. Brontë ran to her side and tried to support her. As she felt the woman's immense weight on her shoulder, she realized the futility of her action. While Ursula was able to stay upright, Brontë slunk and collapsed under the strength of the innkeeper's hand.

"Thank you, Mrs. Cook. I appreciate your help."

"Quite all right," Brontë said, supine on the carpet. "You should, however, go get some rest. I think you may have had a bit too much gin."

"I should," Ursula said. She tottered away, toward the stairs. "The gin is making my thoughts a bit confounded."

"Gin does that." Brontë pulled herself up.

"I'm beginning to wonder what your husband looks like disrobed."

Brontë felt the familiar flush of anger ripple through her heart. "Again, Miss Deutschefaber, not a thing one says in polite company."

Ursula did not respond but moved lethargically toward the staircase. When she had her foot on the bottom stair, she turned.

"And it's fine if you go see Klaude. He spoke of you this afternoon before I told him his brother was brutally murdered." Ursula smiled slightly. "He has a fraternal affection for you."

A blush illumined Brontë's cheeks.

"It appears the Deutschefabers favor the Cooks." After saying this, Ursula let out an odd, erratic aspiration from her mouth which Brontë assumed was an attempt at laughter. She continued making the sound as she crept up the stairs.

Brontë did not want to follow her directly but was forced to when the great tower of a woman nearly toppled backward as she approached the middle of the stairs.

Brontë raced behind her and, with all her might, managed to push her into an erect position. With the giant woman's arm over her shoulder, they ambled up the stairs. Rage and pain coursed through Brontë as they trudged down the hallway toward Ursula's chamber.

30

Klaude and the Key

They passed Klaude's room and approached the innkeeper's suite at the end of the hall. As they neared the door to her chambers, Ursula pushed Brontë away. It took all the large woman's concentration to stand without support.

"Thank you, Mrs. Cook, but I shall be all right."

"Let me at least make sure you get into the room."

"No. You have been too kind already."

"I really must insist," Brontë said, thinking of the etiquette pamphlet. "Let me help you lay down. I will feel considerably better to know you're in bed."

Ursula said nothing. Then, very suddenly, her gag reflex acted, and the large woman sprayed the wall with a thick coat of vomit. Brontë pressed herself against the opposite wall just as it happened. She escaped the force of the blast, but she could not hide the look of disgust that expressed itself in her curled lip and upturned nose.

"That," Ursula said at the conclusion of the spray, "was why I wanted you to go."

Brontë stood still for a moment, unsure if even the guilt of denying the pamphlet would be enough to force her to assist the innkeeper in undressing and bathing. There was no reason to contemplate further, however, as the bulky innkeeper slammed her fist against the wall.

"Mrs. Cook, if you do not mind, I'd like privacy."

Brontë nearly contested again but Ursula's gag reflex reared its head and a second, smaller spray collided with the wall. This was enough to send Brontë scurrying toward Klaude's room. When she arrived at his door, she did her best to block out the sound of the innkeeper's retching.

She had to have clear thoughts to plan a course of action.

Truly, there was not much she could do but say a second prayer, this time that Klaude would be forthcoming with information about the key. Emotionally, he would be fragile. How could he not be? Anyone would be reeling from the revelation that their brother was murdered.

But there was no time for delicacy.

She needed to get information and then find Collanhall. No matter what emotional state she found the young man in, she had to complete her mission.

She had to get the key.

She raised her hand and gently rapped on the door. After a few, unanswered knocks, she spoke through the keyhole. "Klaude? Klaude? It's Brontë. I've come back—there is something I need to discuss with you."

She pressed her ear to the door to try to hear an approach, but there was no sound. Ursula's retching had subsided. The hall was quiet.

"Klaude?" she spoke with more volume. "Klaude, it's urgent that—"

The door opened and the young man appeared in his chair. His eyes were red, his face pale. He attempted a smile at the sight of Brontë, but it was forced and fleeting.

"Hullo," he said quietly. "I assume my sister doesn't know you're up here."

"She does, actually." Brontë turned and closed the door. She crossed the room and stood near the small table. The mystery book which had been placed there earlier was gone, a fresh volume in its place. She took a deep breath and lowered her voice. "I need to speak with you very quickly, Klaude. I know you've just received the horrible news about your brother…"

Klaude choked. He closed his eyes forcefully and exhaled dramatically. "I have…it's…" He stopped and took a breath. He wiped his eyes with the sleeve of his shirt. "It's not important," he said finally. His voice shook.

"I—well—please, continue. My feelings are complex and will be dealt with."

Brontë's heart ached. "Klaude, I…"

"I assume this is not about my brother," he said softly. "And if you could distract me from the grief for a moment, I would be very grateful." He forced another smile. "So, is this about treasure? Or detective work?"

Brontë extended her hand and gripped Klaude's. She gave him a warm, compassionate smile. "You're very much correct. Crockett, my husband, and I think that the dramatic mystery surrounding the inn is coming to an end."

Klaude's eyebrows rose. "And who is it? Who's done it?"

Brontë swallowed. "Well…we don't know who it is, who has done a thing, or what the thing is…"

"I'm sorry?" Klaude smiled genuinely. "That sounds like shoddy detective work, Mrs. Cook."

"Well," Brontë's voice rose, "we haven't gotten through the detective manual…so…" She twisted her shirt collar. "But what we do know is that the treasure in Doctor Gutermord's cabin could be more central to the case than we originally thought."

"The treasure? I told you that wasn't real." Klaude wheeled closer to Brontë. His brow furrowed in thought. "What more do you know?"

"We think it could have something to do with…" Brontë winced, "with Bristol."

Klaude's eyes grew damp. He cleared his throat to remove emotion from his voice. "Ursula said he was involved with things…inappropriate things…"

"Regardless," Brontë tried to avert the topic from Bristol, "we are unsure. But we believe there is some valuable object in the doctor's cabin."

Klaude was incredulous. "The treasure can't be real! We searched!"

"From what your father told us…"

Klaude froze. His face, already a ghostly shade of white, lost any remaining color. "My father…?"

"We spoke to him at the prison."

The young man turned away from Brontë. His whole body shook.

"But—but—but—but my father is dead!"

Brontë staggered back. She was incredulous. Klaude didn't know his father was alive?

"Bristol and Ursula…they said he died years ago," he continued. "Ursula said he was killed by a man named Grendel. He killed him with a hot poker during the annual prison Christmas exchange. They were listening to 'King Wenceslas' and the prison guard turned his back to get more egg nog."

"Oh…" Brontë wished nothing more than to force herself into the depths of Klaude's closet again out of shame and discomfort. She also felt quite impressed at the detail of Ursula's lie. "I'm so sorry, Klaude. We also thought he was dead, but he's still in prison. We saw him. He's in the castle."

"Why would they lie?"

"I—" Brontë extended her hand and gently gripped Klaude's shoulder. "Klaude, I don't know. There is much unknown at the heart of this matter. Everything is in shadow with only pinpricks of light."

Klaude pulled away from her touch. He rolled his chair toward the window.

They sat in silence for a moment. There was a slight clatter downstairs. Brontë did not need Sylvia's bondage sheep to know that something was not right. She also heard noises in the hall, but she assumed it was Ursula trying to clean herself from the prior vomit incident.

"Klaude," she said as a louder noise sounded from outside the door, "I'm sorry to press you, but I feel our time is short. Did the doctor give you a key? Is there some special token which he bequeathed to you?"

Klaude turned toward her. He ran a hand through his short, blond hair. "Why should I trust you?" he asked. His gaze lifted and he looked pleadingly into Brontë's eyes. "My brother was a mobster; he and my sister lied to me about my father." Klaude shook his head. "A great many things aren't true that I thought were!" The young man wiped tears away with his sleeve. "Bristol was my best friend before the accident. He was protective and loyal and lovely. I don't know what happened. Why did he…lie? Why did he and Ursula conceal this from me—"

A sound, much louder than before, clattered in the hallway. Instinctively,

Brontë moved so that she was between Klaude and the door. The thought of the key fled her mind for a moment. Her primary instinct was to protect them both from whatever was lurking in the corridor.

"Brontë," he said softly. "Bristol also asked about the key a few days ago…I don't know anything, but the doctor—"

But Klaude did not have time to finish.

With a loud *thwack!* the door to his room flew open. Two large, glowering men stood in the threshold. And, to Brontë's great surprise, standing in the middle, arms crossed over her vomit-stained jacket, was Ursula.

"Mrs. Cook," she said in her booming voice, "I think you've said quite enough."

The innkeeper's shadow loomed large in the spacious room—the size of her corporeal form had never been more palpable or formidable as it seemed at that moment.

Brontë shrank back. She placed a hand on Klaude's chair and braced herself against the back window.

"Ursula…I thought…" Brontë did not know how to react. She assessed the men standing with Ursula. Both wore a green and gold handkerchief. Her imagination raced. Was Ursula behind the scheme of the Caddywampus? Was she involved with the gangs and mobsters gathering in Praktisch?

As she pondered this, she felt something rustle against her back. She turned and saw Klaude looking at her. His eyes were pools of terror.

"You think a great deal, Mrs. Cook," Ursula said. She motioned for the two goons to approach Brontë and Klaude. "But the time has come to act, and I need you to keep your meddling nose out of our lives."

One of the men grabbed Brontë's wrists. She fought against him, but the other took hold of her shoulder. They dragged her across the room and forced her to her knees in front of Ursula.

"Take Klaude somewhere safe," Ursula said to the men. "He's already seen more than I would have liked."

The goons shifted from behind Brontë toward Klaude. One of them grabbed Klaude's chair and wheeled it toward the door.

"Ursula…" Klaude was barely audible. He appeared to be in shock.

"Take him to the linen closet on the other side of the lodge and leave us." Ursula stepped away from the door to let the men through. They exited into the hall with Klaude.

When they were gone, Brontë stared into the innkeeper's eyes. Just as on the night of her brother's death, she looked as if the chaotic events surrounding them were a mild inconvenience. Aside from the pallor from her drinking sickness, she was the picture of control and poise.

"I am also not happy about this, Mrs. Cook," she said tersely. "I was vomiting in a mop bucket when the mob arrived. I thought there would be more time…"

"Are you going to kill me?" Brontë braced herself for the response. "Or… are *they* going to kill me?"

Ursula shrugged. "It's hard to say. If you are a good hostage and stay out of the way, nothing will happen to you. If you put up a fight…well…I cannot say what they will do to you."

Brontë examined the large woman's face for any sign of emotion. When she could read nothing, she continued her line of questioning.

"So, it's you then," she said. "The Caddywampus, Bristol's murder, the pursuit of the treasure…"

Ursula shook her head. "No. I have only been a small piece of this puzzle. I have no idea what the Caddywampus is…or why it is. I didn't kill Bristol, although, I didn't help his cause either."

"What happened?"

Ursula hesitated. "My correspondence course on villainy and chicanery would adamantly tell me not to divulge the secrets of my involvement, but I do feel moved to. You know most of the plot, anyway. I told you the edited version earlier."

"About Bristol and Sylvia?" Brontë tried feverishly to put the pieces together.

"Yes." Ursula's face twisted into what Brontë could only assume was one of the woman's rare smiles. "It is a joy to see you so low, Mrs. Cook." The innkeeper savored the words. "I have to say, there were moments when I was nearly jealous of you."

"Because of my husband, you mean?"

"Of course. But also, you—your ease." Ursula's smile collapsed into its usual tight, emotionless line. "You are confident and very clear-headed. My motivation to befriend you and to loathe you were nearly equal."

A slight ruckus broke out down below. There were some bumps and bangs.

"Incompetent mobsters." Ursula sniffed.

"What is your involvement?" Brontë was consumed by both fear and manic curiosity. Of all the characters at the Deutschefaber Inn, Ursula was the one she suspected least of any foul deeds—her priorities were solely the inn, Klaude, and her odd flirtations with Crockett. It never occurred to her that Ursula's love of the inn would intersect the ghastly events surrounding them. The innkeeper's clear disdain for the men who assisted her that evening only fueled Brontë's interest in Ursula's role.

"I am not one to favor long, embellished stories," Ursula said, "so I'll give you the simple facts. In only one case am I guilty of wrongdoing, and I believe that is more of a…theoretical moral issue." She smoothed her trousers and cleared her throat. "Bristol announced his intentions to marry Sylvia shortly after she arrived. Their romance was quick and idiotic—a 'whirlwind' as Sylvia described it to me earlier this evening in an effusive, embarrassing, emotional monologue." Ursula cringed. "It bore none of the signs of the deep, beautiful connection that I shared with your husband when he arrived."

Brontë moved to speak but then thought better of it. She bit the inside of her cheek to keep herself from making an angry retort.

"I had noticed their affection blooming. I asked Bristol about it, and he confirmed it was true. He was making plans that would 'protect the inn forever.'" Ursula let out a loud, pronounced "tsk!" She shook her head. "He was weak, Mrs. Cook. Leading up to the moment when he could secure our future, he wavered."

Brontë tasted blood. She released the bite from her cheek and spoke. "What was the scheme?"

"Bristol secured some knowledge about the supposed treasure in the doctor's cabin. He would not tell me the details of what it was, but one evening he was a desperate mess and told me part of the plot. You see he worked for the green and gold, a gang which operates out of Praktisch. In our region there is a truce between the green mob and the gold."

"The handkerchiefs…"

"Indeed. Very unfashionable if you ask me. I wouldn't join a mob unless they had a nice plaid or tartan color scheme."

Brontë looked down at Ursula's boxy, brown heelless shoes and thought fashion was not something she should opine about.

"Bristol, in his moment of panic," the innkeeper continued, "told me he planned to double-cross his green and gold gang and sell the secret to a rival mob, a group out of Eastern Europe and Russia with global connections. He'd give half the money to me and Klaude and take the other half to start a life with Sylvia."

"Did he do it?" Brontë asked. "Is that why he was killed?"

"Well…" A regretful tone crept into Ursula's flat voice. "You see, I didn't trust him. My brother was a bull—quick to temper, thoughtless, and ate a lot of grass. When I heard he might back out, I sought out the green and gold gang and told them the plot. I didn't think Bristol would get the money from the rival mob, and I was worried he caused a breach with the green and gold. I had to make sure our finances were taken care of and we were protected…even if it meant….well…"

Brontë's eyes went wide. "Betrayal."

Ursula gritted her teeth. A feverish glow lit up her eyes. "Yes! I would do anything, Mrs. Cook—anything—to protect the inn and Klaude. I knew this information could earn their trust and protection forever."

There was a moment of silence. Brontë thought Ursula would say nothing else, but to her surprise the innkeeper warily continued. "The…the man, Kreuz—"

"Kreuz!" Brontë jumped up. "He's the leader?"

Ursula was repulsed by Brontë's show of emotion. She took a step backward toward the door. As she did, there was another clatter below. Both women turned to look in the hallway.

"What—" The innkeeper grew anxious. Her breath became quick and shallow.

"Ursula," Brontë took a step toward the innkeeper. "What happened? What did Kreuz say?"

"We made a deal," Ursula said. The color drained from her face. "If I intercepted the spy who was meant to get the information from Bristol…" She stopped speaking.

Brontë's heart skipped. "You…"

"I wasn't going to. I didn't think Bristol would even commit the betrayal. As I said," droplets of sweat broke out on Ursula's forehead, "it's a gray moral issue. He was a criminal, and I never intended to."

"What happened?"

"Bristol *did* go to the rendezvous and told the contact the information." Ursula's voice was flatter and more emotionless than usual. "I knew where they were going to meet. He told me the whole plot the day of his emotional distress. I arrived at the rendezvous, and Bristol was there. I didn't think…" She paused. Once again, she smoothed her trousers. She cleared her throat. "I saw him speaking to a man. I panicked. I'd promised to take care of the situation, and I did it. I took care of it. I did it with my hands. The man tried to flee, but I…"

Brontë's eyes immediately fell on Ursula's huge hands. She shivered. They were definitely capable of, as Bunce would say, "garrgging" someone.

"It was chaos. Bristol told the man the information and fled. I panicked and ran after the man to keep my deal with Kreuz. I didn't see that there were two. By the time I came up to the informant, the second man disappeared into the shadows. The other man was right there. I did it…but I am not a killer, Mrs. Cook!" In the four days since Brontë had known her, it was the most emotion she'd ever seen from Ursula. "It was an accident, if anything," the innkeeper continued. "I did it out of sheer terror. It was self-defense…it was a worst-case scenario! I could not stop the second man, Bristol was guilty of confessing the secret, and I had…done it." Ursula took a deep breath. "Bristol didn't know I was involved, but even I couldn't hide my emotion when I returned home. He knew something was wrong that next morning. I hid it as best I could."

"Why did Bristol die, though?" Brontë searched her memory for any clue from the altercation she saw between Bristol and Kreuz. What had he said…? *If you didn't tell us, Deutschefaber, that is tantamount to treason.*

Ursula shifted uncomfortably. "Well," she said slowly, "I was fearful, but I returned to Kreuz to face my failure."

"What…what did he do?" Brontë could only imagine what the tall, haunted man was capable of if he was displeased.

"He told me that I had done well. I proved my worth to the organization. Even though the second contact escaped, I proved I could do…what was necessary." Ursula swallowed. "I begged him to let Bristol go. I said he was leaving with Sylvia. He wouldn't be around for long. Kreuz said he would let him live only if he confessed the truth. Bristol had his reward from selling the information, but he was trapped in Praktisch. If he left town, the mob threatened to kill him—fleeing would be an admonition of guilt that he had betrayed them. And then well, he…"

Brontë re-imagined the scene in the street. He saw Kreuz hovering over Bristol, the younger man quaking in fear. Bristol denied that he'd done anything wrong, but Kreuz knew all along he had.

"He didn't confess," Brontë whispered.

"My guess is that when Bristol failed to tell the truth and give Kreuz the information he passed onto the rival gang, they…" Ursula pursed her lips. "Well, you saw what happened on the stoop."

A crash sounded below. Ursula turned fully toward the hallway. Brontë used the opening to attempt a desperate escape. She ran toward the window. She threw open the trunk and searched for the sheet that aided her first escape.

It was gone.

Ursula pounded across the room. She "tsked" once more.

"Mrs. Cook, I fear you are making me act more the villain than I prefer. For your own safety, I shall secure you for the evening."

It took little effort for the giant innkeeper to throw Brontë over her shoulder and carry her into the hallway. Additional signs of mayhem erupted from below. Crashes, bangs, and the bellows of men echoed from the main hall.

A few steps from Klaude's door was a small broom closet. Ursula jerked it open and tossed Brontë inside.

"For safekeeping." She slammed the door and Brontë heard the key turn in the lock.

"Ursula," she said quickly. Her voice was shaking. She pounded lightly on the door. "I need to go; I need to meet my husband."

The urgency of the situation overwhelmed Brontë. She was being imprisoned. Crockett wouldn't meet with her. The arrival of the mob at the inn made her certain that they needed to get to the sixth cabin as soon as possible. Whatever forces aligned to seek the secret treasure must be moving rapidly. If the sounds below were any indication, the game had already begun.

"I'm afraid I cannot let that happen," Ursula said flatly.

Brontë's heart pounded as she heard the innkeeper turn away from the door and thunder down the hallway. She clenched her fists and fought a scream. Around her was nothing but darkness. She fell backward into the closet and found the wall. Despair consumed her as she slid to the floor. Ursula's boxy-shoed footsteps faded away, leaving Brontë alone in silence and shadows.

31

The Baroness' Story

On the way back to the Inn, Crockett's mental puzzle box whirred with activity. But after sifting through the complex web of clues, he couldn't find any threads that clarified the mystery. It was true the mob—green, gold, or green *and* gold—meant to seek whatever treasure was in the doctor's cabin, but he wasn't sure what that treasure might be or how the events of the past week precipitated the mob's pursuit of it now.

And who were the figures seen in town? The mud people? The tall man and the small man who broke into the records office? Could they be the same? If they were not the same, were they acting together?

And, for goodness' sake, what was the Caddywampus?

His pace slowed when he came upon the lodge.

Something felt wrong.

A steady drizzle fell from the sky; the occasional bolt of lightning or crack of thunder came at unpredictable intervals. This all was made more ominous by the empty, lightless cabins scattered throughout the grounds. Phipps, the Gestahlts, Greta, and Collanhall's windows were all devoid of any signs of life. The only flickers of illumination were visible in his own window, indicating Petrarch was at home and settled in reading or doing his exercises.

"Where is everyone?"

Crockett ceased walking. He rubbed his eyes to be sure that he was not imagining the lifeless grounds; when this failed to produce a change in scenery, he pinched himself to be sure he wasn't dreaming.

Both options failing, he ran with double speed up the path to his own cabin.

He threw open the door, his nerves nearly shot. His mental puzzle box spun—the mob said they would go to the cabin tonight; the grounds of the inn were abandoned… Where *was* everyone? No one would go to the festival on a dark and stormy night such as this.

These ideas evaporated when his eyes fell upon the scene in his cabin.

Greta van der Raaf sat on the sofa. Her skin was pale, her eyes cloudy. She gazed upward at the ceiling. Petrarch was kneeling beside her. He held a cup of water to her lips.

"Drink, my dear," he said. "You need some strength."

"Petrarch!" Crockett rushed to the sofa. He placed a hand on his master's back. He couldn't help but feel a slight joy in seeing Greta in a miserable state. While he did not wish dire illness on the miserly, old woman, he did enjoy seeing her uncomfortable. "What's going on?"

Greta moaned. Her cloudy eyes shut. The old woman raised her hand to her forehead. Crockett then saw a gash hidden by her hairline. Fresh blood oozed down her face. His eyes darted to Petrarch.

Petrarch nodded; the two men, having worked closely together for years, needed no words to infer the other's thoughts. He mimed for Crockett to be silent and indicated the bedroom. The men quietly stood and made their way to the private quarters.

Once inside, the door shut, Petrarch rubbed his eyes. He let out a long, doleful sigh.

Crockett's voice shook. "Was Madame van der Raaf attacked?"

Petrarch's throat was dry. Crockett could tell he was trying to keep his temper.

"It was Phipps," he said coldly. "When Greta returned from errands in town, she and I were to meet for tea. I waited for her arrival. I needed to do a bit of writing, which distracted me for a bit, but it soon grew late. I left the cabin to see if she was back yet, and I found her on the path in this state. She was coming to get me, staggering about. I immediately brought her inside. That was just moments before you arrived."

Crockett thought of the empty grounds. "When you left to find Greta, did you see anyone about? The grounds are now abandoned."

Petrarch's eyebrows raised. "No one is around?" he asked. "I didn't see anyone…I was very distracted by Madame van der Raaf…" The old man rubbed his temples.

Crockett could tell his master had dove into a deep pool of thought. "Would you like me to fetch your thinking pipe, Petrarch?" he asked.

Petrarch waved him off. "There's no time, my boy. This is a very curious evening."

"Did you see anyone before you found Madame van der Raaf?"

"I saw nearly everyone when I went for a walk in the late afternoon. All the lodgers took the break in the rain as an opportunity to get fresh air." Petrarch's face was grave. "Collanhall was chatting with Phipps. Mrs. Gestahlt said 'Love buggies!' as I passed. She appeared to be emptying the cabin, but she was accounted for. Sylvia was even about; she asked Phipps if she could clean his cabin while he was speaking with the colonel."

"Where did they go?" Crockett's mind whirled. He looked to the bed and saw *Detectivating for the Dunce*.

Petrarch followed his line of sight. "I think we're beyond the time for books, Crockett. If we don't know the solution now, we may be too late."

"It can't be too late, Petrarch!" Crockett's eyes shone with sparks of hope. "The only failure would be inaction."

For the first time since Crockett had entered the cabin, the old man smiled. "My boy, your courage continually impresses me. Even when you collapse at the sight of a young girl or colored bird, you always bounce right back up."

Crockett blushed. "What else is there to do but get back up?"

"Indeed." Petrarch stood taller. A rosy hue returned to his cheeks.

His young apprentice followed his lead and adjusted his posture. They both gained courage in the fading evening light.

"Now!" Petrarch continued. He cleared his throat and sniffed proudly. His voice resumed its normal, stentorian tone. "Once I returned home, I got to work in my journal and on my physical prowess."

"Did you notice anything outside?" Crockett asked. "Was there a noise? Any kind of event which would explain our co-lodgers' disappearances?"

The old man pursed his lips. "The sounds of their activities faded, but I assumed it was everyone going to dinner. I was deep in my work. I did keep my eye on the clock awaiting Greta's arrival. When she was a quarter hour late, I peered out the window. The sky was dark, rain was falling, and the grounds were empty."

"So, the others disappeared about dusk. That wasn't too long ago." Crockett ran a hand through his hair. "Did Greta give any more details about the altercation with Phipps?"

Petrarch scowled. "No, she…well, on the trail, she could barely hold herself up; blood was covering her face. I couldn't see the wound and was afraid it was mortal."

"Oh, Petrarch…" Crockett extended his hand and gently gripped his master's shoulder.

"I helped her inside," Petrarch continued quickly. "She was moaning and muttering, 'Phipps has it.' She said this repeatedly."

"Phipps." Crockett felt a broiling rage in his heart. "That no-good, American snickerboot!"[61]

"My boy!" Petrarch's shook his head. "There is no need for foul words. We aren't privy to what he took, why he took it, or what is at stake."

"Could Phipps be behind it all?" Crockett's thick eyebrows nearly shot off his face. "That awful gnat of a man. Could he be the one working with the mob and acting as the Caddywampus? Is that why he named it?!" Crockett felt his chest constrict. "He wanted to title his own monster! It makes perfect sense!"

---

[61] The author asked a linguist how "foul" the term "snickerboot" was in this time period. His response: "It was the atomic bomb of early twentieth-century insults. Imagine chaining 45 f%$ks, 11 wh$#@s, and 15 b&^$hes together and lobbing them at a baby duck. That was the general impact."

Petrarch smiled faintly. He shook his head. "Crockett, I don't think now is the time for our usual wild conjecture. We need to speak with Madame van der Raaf and gather the pertinent facts. From that point, we can plan our next steps."

"We're running out of time, Petrarch. The mob is on the move and the grounds are empty. We must act now!"

"Petrarch…" A faint, hushed voice called from the next room.

Petrarch and Crockett rushed to Greta. They found the old woman more awake than upon Crockett's entrance. Her face was pale, her eyes still unfocused and hazy.

"My dear," Petrarch said kneeling by her side. "How can we help you?"

Greta took a deep breath. She planted her frail hands onto the cushions and pulled herself up. When she was sitting upright, she tried to focus fully on the two men before her. Crockett handed her a glass of water that Petrarch had put on the table. Once she had taken a long drink, she spoke.

"There is much to share, but I feel that for the first time since I have known him, Crockett is correct. Our time is short. There are many dark forces on the move, and they are all converging on Himmel's cabin."

"Himmel?" Petrarch looked at Crockett. His apprentice shook his head, indicating shared confusion.

"Himmel Gutermord, the doctor of the woods, the supposed evil of Praktisch," she paused and steeled herself, "my estranged husband."

A quiet fell over the room. Petrarch, who had not been privy to the revelations of Mr. Deutschefaber in the prison, was completely lost.

"You're the baroness," Crockett said.

Greta sized up Crockett, almost as if she was proud of him. "Yes, Crockett. Two instances of you being correct then." She took a deep breath as if preparing for a Shakespearean soliloquy and turned to Petrarch. "Himmel and my marriage was tumultuous. We were young. It happened in secret when he was seventeen and I was fifteen. He came through my hometown doing research, and we immediately fell in love." Crockett was shocked to see small silver tears appear at the corner of the old woman's eyes. "We ran away. My family never would have allowed it." Her eyes drifted to the corner of the room, their wet gaze fixed on the distant past. "It's rare to find a love like that…to fully give yourself to someone without expectation or fear."

The old woman indicated the glass of water, which Crockett passed back to her. Rather than take a sip, she held it in her hands. She peered into the water; her aged reflection rippled as she gently shook the glass.

"We eloped to Praktisch and lived. Those were very happy days. Himmel ran his experiments, and I learned how to take care of a household." Greta turned to Crockett. "While your relationship with Mrs. Cook pales in comparison to my own, I did enjoy seeing you both this week. It reminded me of my own newlywed days. We had such wild and untamed—"

Crockett, fearing the old woman was going to possibly speak of her bedroom activities and sexual piping, interrupted. "Lovely. If we could skip ahead to the necessary backstory revelations, please."

"I wouldn't mind hearing about the wild, untamed part, Crockett," Petrarch said.

Crockett suppressed a rising sickness. "We are running against a tight timeline," he said quickly. "I'll let you two discuss that when I leave you."

"That's fair," Petrarch said. "I would prefer to take notes, anyway, so we can circle back to that."

"You may need a few notebooks, Mr. Bluster." Greta puckered her lips.

Crockett, fearing they were on the verge of losing the story's thread completely, spoke again, "Greta, you said the relationship was tumultuous. Was Himmel a good husband?"

"Yes!" Greta sneered at Crockett. "A better husband than you, Mr. Cook. Better looking at least." She took another sip of water and continued, "The tumultuous parts I spoke of were all external. He was very thoughtful. He built a small contraption for me. It fit in a piano and would play my favorite song without human hands. It struck the right notes on its own accord. Everything about those days was marvelous; they felt filled with magic." The old woman trailed off. She shut her eyes.

"My wife and I had similar days," Petrarch smiled encouragingly. "We never grew tired of each other, even when we were older, seasoned. Neither of us could play the piano, though, with or without a machine."

Greta and Petrarch shared a warm gaze. Crockett tried to suppress his look of confusion and distaste at, what appeared to be, his mentor falling for a rather rude and condescending woman.

The moment passed. Greta sighed. "Those days were short. My father tracked me down and arrived in the woods one morning a year after our marriage. My brother had died, and I was the sole heir of the family. He said that I could return home, bury this little excursion and not speak of it, and take my place as the future baroness."

"You chose your family over Himmel," Crockett said softly. "What a horrifying decision to have to make."

Greta clicked her tongue. "Wrong, Mr. Cook! Your correct streak is over. I chose Himmel! I told my father to leave me and do what he wished but that I had a home and was happy."

Petrarch's face fell. "They forced you…"

"They took me," Greta said emotionlessly. "I was carried out of the house screaming. Himmel tried to help. He…" She shook her head. "I was thrown in the back of a carriage and hauled away. I saw three of my father's men approach our home. Himmel was enraged, his clothes torn, facing them alone.

"When I returned home, my father told me he was dead. He said his men murdered him and buried him in the woods." Tears streamed down Greta's face. "I believed him."

The old woman broke with emotion. Slow, mournful sobs shook her frail body. Petrarch gently patted her knee. Crockett felt badly; he had judged the woman too harshly. He took the water from her so he could fill it back up.

After a time, she regained her composure. She cleared her throat. Her normal detached, chilled tone returned to her voice.

"A rising family approached my father, and he divulged my first marriage. They had a son who was willing to marry me for the power my barony offered, regardless of my past. It wasn't an unhappy life; we had children. I always thought of Himmel, but I believed him dead for so long…"

"How did you discover he was still alive?" Crockett asked.

A smile appeared on the old woman's lips. "Something inside me always wondered if he was truly dead. One of my servant girls and I grew very close after my children left. On one beautiful fall day I had an overwhelming memory of Himmel. I remembered how we use to pace through the fallen leaves in the forest. We'd spend hours out there—blissful hours.

"That day, I called my servant to me and offered to send her to Praktisch. I told her to ask in town for a doctor named Himmel Gutermord. He used to live in a cabin in the woods. My husband was gravely ill and not long for the world, so I…I suppose I hoped by some twist of fate we could be brought back together." Greta's eyes grew misty again.

"She sent me a letter two weeks later," she continued. "Himmel was dead. Killed," her voice grew ominous, "by a madman."

Petrarch blanched. "He had just died?"

"Yes," Greta said harshly. "A few weeks before my maid arrived." The old woman shook her head. "A cruel fate."

Crockett brought the water back in and set it on the table. He thought of Mr. Deutschefaber in the dark dungeon. "You were the one who made sure the perpetrator paid," he said softly. "You wanted to make sure your beloved was avenged."

Petrarch's eyebrows went up. He and Crockett briefly exchanged a glance.

Greta nodded. "I thought that's what I was meant to do. I believed that's why God gave me that fall day to think of Himmel. I sent a carriage with additional clothing and money to my servant. I told her to make sure that the man who killed Himmel was thrown in jail and never saw the light of day again."

Crockett thought back to the old man in prison. How many years had he lost due to this old woman's vengeance? He wondered if it was appropriate to tell her his side of the story, what he very much believed to be the truth: Dr. Gutermord took his own life in grief over Klaude's accident.

"After the trial," Greta continued, "I received a letter in the mail from a solicitor. It contained a note from Himmel and a map to a place beyond the cabin. He said it would guide me to a final goodbye. I was to find the youngest son of the Deutschefaber family and go out there together."

"Why…" Crockett grew pensive, "why hadn't he written to you before?"

Greta's tone hardened. "He wrote. Every month he wrote to me, but my father and husband burned the letters. My father knew he would try to reach out and so he stopped him."

"That's monstrous!" Petrarch's face grew purple with rage. "How dare they!"

Greta said nothing. She stared intensely into the fireplace. After a moment of silence, she wiped her eyes with her dress. Crockett, seeing her wound was beginning to ooze again, gently wiped a trail of blood from her forehead. The old woman, regaining some of her verve, slapped him away and took the handkerchief.

As she dabbed the wound herself, she continued, "I couldn't face the cabin or his memory, so I put the note aside. This spring my old servant said that people were talking about Himmel again in Praktisch. There were rumors of the cabin and treasure resurfacing. That's why I made my way here. I still…" She took a deep breath. "I still don't know if I want to remember. That cabin…" Her voice quavered. "I don't know if I can face it after all these years. I want to keep it as a blissful memory."

Crockett sat bolt upright. He had been lost in the tale and forgotten the urgency of their position.

"Phipps!" he exclaimed. "What did Phipps take from you?"

Greta bared her teeth. "He incapacitated me and searched my cabin. Throughout the week he tried to befriend me and get the truth out, but I wouldn't tell him anything. I awoke as he was shaking out my things." Greta grunted. "He's a poor mercenary. He barely knocked me out for thirty minutes. He had just found the note and map when I awoke and screamed for help. He struck me again and fled. That's when I left to find Petrarch."

"Do you know who he really is, Greta?" Petrarch asked. "How is he connected to this?"

The old woman scowled. "I don't know. All he did was blather about his writing and then probe me about the cabin. He somehow knew who I was."

"How could he?" Crockett asked.

"The only one who knew my identity was my servant. She stayed in Praktisch. Crockett, you saw me speaking to her this afternoon. She owns the candy shop."

The hairs on the back of Crockett's neck stood up. It appeared the web of connections in Praktisch was expanding at alarming speed. "I don't think we have time to speculate on Phipps's source of information. We do need to get moving. Greta, was there some kind of key with the note? We heard that you and Klaude both had one."

Greta looked truly surprised. "Key? No. It was a lovely note telling me to seek Klaude, but it didn't have a key of any kind. There was a puzzle on the back that yielded a sequence of numbers, but that wasn't…" Greta's brow furrowed. "I thought nothing of it. It was very like him to play with puzzles and games. I hadn't thought about it for some time."

Crockett ran a hand through his hair. "Numbers—they must mean something. What does Phipps know that we don't?"

"Well, my boy!" Petrarch stood up. He began doing stretches with a manic energy. "We have to go after him to find out. Time is of the essence. He's grown desperate if he attacked Madame van der Raaf. We have let far too much time elapse. He may already have secured the treasure."

Crockett's heart stopped. "Brontë…"

"What of her?" Petrarch sensed Crockett's dread.

"She should have returned. She went to speak to Klaude. Oh no. What if…?" The dread Crockett felt the entire week returned with intense force. "I didn't think she'd be in danger! Petrarch, what have I done?"

Petrarch thudded his belly and stood up. "I'll go after Brontë. You need to find Phipps before he tries to steal what is not rightfully his."

"It's probably too late!" Crockett felt hopeless. He was frozen with terror thinking of Brontë being in peril. "I need to find her. I have to go after Brontë."

"Crockett." Petrarch's voice grew stern. "Use your lawyerly brain. You need to go into the woods. You know where the cabin is and the secret room. The most that could have happened to Brontë is she got cornered by

Ursula and asked to look at some vomit in a harpsichord."

Crockett sighed. "What if it *is* too late, Petrarch?"

"The only failure," Petrarch said resolutely, "would be inaction."

The old lawyer approached Crockett and put a hand on his shoulder. Crockett looked into Petrarch's eyes. He nodded resolutely. The young man slowed his breathing and concentrated. There was little time and much to do.

"Petrarch, come with me," he said quickly, "we need to get into Collanhall's cabin and procure weapons. Then, I'll head to the woods, and you can go to the lodge to seek Brontë. Whatever happens, we'll do our best."

"Our very best." Petrarch swelled with pride. Only a few months ago, Crockett would have been on the floor shrieking in panic.

"I may have expected this bravery from Petrarch," Greta said, "but not from you, Crockett." A smile appeared on her lips. "Well done."

Crockett gave her a Collanhall-style salute and turned; he grabbed a lamp on the table and threw open the door of the cabin. Petrarch followed but was stopped by Madame van der Raaf. The old woman gripped the elder lawyer and leaned closely to him. Petrarch, for a moment thought he was under attack. This fear vanished when he felt the Dutchwoman's soft lips press against his cheek.

"For luck," she said.

Petrarch's face grew as red as a strawberry. A luminous smile filled his countenance. With a surge of virile energy and a gleeful shout, he burst from the cabin. The baroness-enamored lawyer felt so youthful, he nearly overtook Crockett on the way to Collanhall's lodging.

32

Crockett on the Case

There were still no lights on in the colonel's cabin. The front door was shut. Adrenaline surged through Crockett's body disallowing rationality into his decision-making processes. He closed his eyes, reared back, and charged up the steps of the cabin to force his way in. When he thrust against the wooden structure, there was no give. He bounced backward, launching off the front stoop. Petrarch found him dazed and covered in mud, collecting himself.

"I don't know if the door will budge," he said attempting to stand upright.

Petrarch helped him up. Energized by Greta's kiss and feeling thirty years younger, he said, "I'll take a second pass at it, my boy. I have a bit more mass to put behind the thrust."

The old man sprinted toward the door. To both his and his assistant's surprise, the portal was opened by Sylvia, just as he approached it. This caused the old man to race into the cabin unimpeded and collide with the table in the center of the room.

Sylvia was so flummoxed by the situation that she could only stare in wonder as Crockett ran to his master's side.

"Petrarch!" he cried. "Are you seriously injured?"

"Oh! No! No worse for the wear." The old man crawled onto the couch and lay still. "I simply need a moment to recuperate."

Crockett turned to Sylvia. "What are you doing in the colonel's cabin?"

The young maid, still reeling from the chaos of the recent arrival, stared blankly in response.

"Is everything okay?" Crockett looked between his collapsed friend and the frightened maid and thought it best to give them both a moment to regain their composure.

He lit another two lamps and fetched cups of water. Despite his concern for both, he knew he needed to stay focused on his mission. He set down the water and immediately made his way to Collanhall's arsenal. He assessed the weapons with complete ignorance. It came to his attention that a detective should acquire intelligence on a variety of maiming devices.[62]

Sylvia, having regained some of her wits, was surprised by the sight of Crockett digging through the assortment of weapons Collanhall kept in a pile on the floor.

"What," she asked softly, "is going on?"

"Perhaps we could ask the same of you, my dear." Petrarch had not let on to the true catastrophic impact his accident had on his head. Crockett's rattling of guns, maces, and other weaponry sounded like tiny explosions in his throbbing cranium.

"I was cleaning," Sylvia said quickly.

"In the dark?" Crockett threw a suspicious glance backward as he tossed aside a large revolver.

"Yes," Sylvia said. "Well, I *was* cleaning. But then…"

"But what?" Petrarch grunted.

"Well…"

Crockett ceased his rummaging and looked back at the young maid. Her face was red, and tears ran down her cheeks. Although normally an empathetic person, the sheer number of revelations and tears that evening had worn on him.

"Not to be rude, Miss Vindrikimmel, but could you perhaps share what is on your mind? Do you have some revelation? Are you the second cousin

---

[62] A chapter of the book they so rarely consulted was full of insights on the best weapons to use whilst detectivating.

of the doctor? Are you the murderer? Or a thief, perhaps?"

"I can answer that," Petrarch said, beginning to see spots. "She's Bristol's lover—was Bristol's lover."

Crockett raised a saber he found in the pile and pointed it at Sylvia. "I hate to be so forward, but does that mean you are part of the mob connection? Are you a secret murderer?"

The young maid shook her head fervently. "No! No! Bristol and I were together, but I know nothing else. He always kept me away from his criminal connections. He wanted to keep me safe…"

"So, my dear, do you know anything about the treasure and the cabin?" Petrarch asked, now suddenly seeing two Sylvia Vindrikimmel's moving around him.

"Not a thing, Mr. Bluster."

"Do you know where anyone is? Ow!" Crockett squealed. He'd closed his hand on an object that looked like a soup spoon wrapped in barbed wire.

Sylvia sighed. "I haven't seen anyone. Collanhall was on his way out in quite a hurry when I arrived. He was carrying a gun with him, but he didn't say where he was going. When he left me alone, I blew out the lamp and took a brief respite. My sense of impending doom grew debilitating this afternoon. This morning it was a small twitch—a twinge—of something dangerous on the horizon, but by the time I got to Master Collanhall's cabin, it was a roaring, alarming feeling. Mix that with the death of Bristol…"

"I can relate to roaring and alarming." Petrarch dabbed his tie in the water Crockett provided and put the damp material on his pounding head.

"To take my mind off everything, I was about to prepare a lamp and look at this book when I heard your body slam against the door."

Sylvia held up a tattered book. It once rested on the table, but, after Petrarch's assault, had fallen beneath the sofa.

Petrarch looked at it and nodded. "Looks like some American tripe," he said shutting his eyes. "*The Great Treasure of the Adirondacks*, a Phillip Ellsworth adventure log."

"What's an adventure log?" Crockett asked as he (more cautiously) dug through a third weapon pile.

"It's a story about a man who goes on all manner of adventures looking for treasure," Sylvia added.

"I'm sure it would make the time go faster." Crockett finally found a gun he believed he could manage. It was a smaller pistol with a fully loaded chamber. "I suppose this will do," he said turning toward the door.

"Where are you going?" The color immediately faded from Sylvia's cheeks. Her eyes grew wide and wild.

"Off…" Crockett said hesitantly. "I have to go see to something." He turned to his master. "Petrarch, find Brontë. Please, hurry."

The old lawyer stood and saluted his assistant. "Yes, my boy. I'll go see if Brontë is in danger—you go catch Phipps."

"Phipps…" Sylvia bit her lip. "Is he really as terrible as he seems? I was hoping he was simply arrogant and obnoxious." She clasped her hands and pressed them against her chest. "Did he kill Bristol?"

Crockett shook his head. "I don't know, Miss Vindrikimmel. What we do know would take too long to explain. But I believe our friends are in danger, and a large element of that danger is Mr. Phipps."

As his attention turned back to the maid and the collapsed table, he noticed a metallic, golden object on the floor. It was a crest emblazoned with the acronym POOP.

"Petrarch," the young man motioned to the object, "I think I may have been right about that."

"Indeed, my boy. If anything, this adventure has proved that you are an expert in matters of both POOP and ARSE." Petrarch bent over and picked up the gold object. It glinted in the glow of the lamps.

"Mr. Cook," Sylvia rose and came toward Crockett. "Please be careful. My premonitions are overwhelming. Something dangerous is on the grounds of the inn. Take every precaution."

She gripped the young lawyer's hands and looked deeply into his eyes. Crockett was touched.

"I'll exercise every bit of caution, Miss Vindrikimmel. Please go with Petrarch to check on Brontë. I must away to stop Phipps. There isn't much time."

Sylvia dropped his hands. Without another fleeting glance into the room, he vanished outside. His footsteps disappeared toward the wood.

Petrarch, trying to keep up the appearance of health while Crockett was present, collapsed the minute he disappeared. Sylvia went to him, kneeling by his side and gently rubbing his arm.

"Miss Vindrikimmel," Petrarch said plaintively, "fetch me some whiskey. I shall jolt my senses and then head off to assist Brontë."

#

The pathway down to the ravine was more treacherous after the recent storm, and although the tempest's gathering menace had passed, a light rain was still falling, and thunder rolled in the distance. Crockett attempted to move gracefully down the hillside, not only for the sake of his own corporeal security, but because the lamp he held was vital to him getting into the secret room.

His mind was fully concentrated on all of the developments in the mystery; he felt as if he were on the verge of understanding the whole messy case. Each revelation and clue from the previous day rattled through his brain. His detective puzzle box spun.

There was some relief that after days of the figures at the inn being disparate, confusing entities, they were finally coalescing. Greta was present to find out what her husband left her. Phipps knew something about the treasure and tried to use Greta to find out more information. Collanhall was involved in a police organization, most likely in pursuit of Bristol or the mob. The Gestahlts' involvement was probably a smaller part of the puzzle, if any; perhaps they truly were there for Mrs. Gestahlt's love of "buggies." Anyhow, they were probably already gone. The Caddywampus remained a baffling figure of unknown origin, but there was no doubt it was serving as an accessory to some of the vandals involved in the mayhem. Petrarch's observations about the appearance of the creature alongside the events made that seem a likely connection.

Crockett ran down the last ten feet of the hillside and onto the trail to the sixth cabin. His heart beat faster as he turned his attention to the ground. Brontë's note about the value of footprints was foremost in his mind. In this instance, they told everything. Not only were there tracks of many men, but alongside them were the huge, claw-like marks of the Caddywampus.

"Who are you, Mr. Wampus?"[63] Crockett asked the dark. "And what is the thread that binds you to what's happening here?"

The forest was silent except for the sound of the pattering rain. All wildlife had sought refuge from the shower.

The young lawyer felt his nerves rattle the closer he drew to the abandoned cabin. While he had been fearless earlier, now that he was approaching the point of climax, he felt his courage start to flee.

It was a relief that the cabin showed no signs of life upon his approach; no lamps were lit, no shadows scurried about, no sounds could be heard. On the ground, he still recognized the presence of footsteps, both human and creature, but they led exactly where he thought they would—toward the back of the cabin and the secret trail through the brush.

Crockett edged around the side of the cabin and peered toward the hidden trail that he had taken before. Again, relief flooded him as he realized that no one was about. He was about to push forward, when he stopped and pressed his back against the side of the cabin.

"What if it's a trap?" he asked himself.

The only sound was the dripping of rain.

"The entrance to the tree is closed. There is only one way in and one way out." A warm tingling of hope tickled his scalp. "Or is there?"

He looked around the corner again and studied the bush which led to the secret tree.

"I should scout the area."

He moved toward the brambles. As he assessed the entrance to the trail, he saw clear signs it was the center of new activity. No longer was Phipps's

---

[63] My lawyer wanted me to make it clear this *is not* a reference to the 1928 West End show *Mr. Wampus & Me*, the story of a child overcoming trauma-induced astigmatism to win a horse race in rural Scotland. (The child was a jockey—he was not racing against the horses.)

feather the only indication of someone being present. The branches were shaken and broken. The small tunnel path was nearly visible, even in the dark.

"Who else has found you, little tunnel?" Crockett whispered to himself.

A low, menacing growl responded to his query.

Crockett turned and froze. His joints locked as fear surged through his extremities. He tottered over, hitting the ground and rolling onto his back. Standing over him in the darkness was the Caddywampus.

The towering beast raised its claws and growled once more. In the dark it looked massive, its bestial form merging with the shadows around it. Its red eyes shone like coals in a phantom furnace.

The young detective could make no sound with his frozen voice. He simply watched as the beast lunged toward him. The image of the monster prepared to strike was the last thing Crockett saw before he fainted, the world fading to black.

33

Brontë behind the Door

The initial moments of Brontë's entrapment were a mercurial mess of emotion. At first, panic overwhelmed her; this gave way to an explosion of anger. In a fit of rage, she smashed her fists against the door screaming very unladylike (and unpamphletlike) phrases at Ursula. When she was out of breath and energy, she sagged to the floor in despair.

With her feelings freed, she focused her mental faculties on a plan of escape.

She first used her hands to explore the closet. They roamed over brooms, buckets, jars, and unknown objects of various sizes and compositions. There appeared to be a large cloth, which Brontë assumed was used to cover furniture as one painted. This hypothesis was based on her feeling several canisters with congealed substances on their sides and tops near the back of the closet. She accidentally knocked the lid from one of these. Her hand slipped in, causing a brief second bout of panic.

After this paint-based terror and a haphazard cleaning of her hands with a wipe on the paint cloth, she turned her attention to the door of the closet. Her hands found the knob, which she explored with keen interest. It was made of a smooth brass material. The keyhole was large.

"What can I use to open it?" she asked herself. "Lock picking is probably covered somewhere in that detectivation book we're always finding time not to read."

She got on her knees and resumed her search. She sought any kind of instrument that would allow her to pick the lock. While the small space was filled with an odd assortment of clutter, it appeared none of it was small enough to insert into the latch.

Brontë, however, didn't give up hope and explored every inch of space. It was in the back right corner in which she found a crevice in the wooden floor. Inside it was a small nail.

"This could do." She took it and crawled back to the door.

The nail slid easily into the keyhole, and Brontë swirled it inside in hope of catching the mechanism. It was during this endeavor that the voices below her grew louder. At first, she'd barely noticed them. She assumed it was Ursula speaking to her coterie of mobsters, but the conversation had grown angrier. Some of the words were nearly intelligible through the thin door and floor.

With what little attention wasn't focused on the lock, she tried to overhear, but the voices were still too muffled to understand. The most she could make out was that one of the voices bore the loud, bawling tones of Ursula Deutschefaber. The other was a man. While they both began with a mildly combative timbre, the tones quickly escalated to a shouting match.

"Conflict inevitably comes from dealings with non-Danube mobsters," she muttered to herself. "Serves her right."

The fight below intensified as Brontë dug the nail around in the hole, hoping to catch the latch. The voices ceased and then erratic bangs and bumps resonated through the floorboards.

Brontë felt sweat trickle down her brow. Her throat grew dry.

"I only need to escape," she whispered to herself. "Once I'm outside of this closet, I will go to Klaude's room and make my way to Crockett."

The explosion of a gun echoed throughout the lodge. The shock of the blast caused Brontë to fall back from the keyhole; her nail flew from her hand and clattered away in the dark.

"Diggleshroot!" she said, choosing the familiar ejaculation of Petrarch's more to calm her nerves than express frustration.

This composure was very necessary as clashes and bangs below came with renewed vigor. Ursula's voice was joined by the garbled tones of several mobsters.

Brontë blinked. She was determined that, rather than growing disoriented or fearful, she would become focused. People below her were fighting; one of the characters had a violent weapon. The most she was capable of was finding her nail and making as much progress as possible toward escape. That was all she could control—it would be the nexus of her attention.

Slowly and methodically, she searched again with her hands to find the nail. When it slipped away from her, the clatter was from her near left side, so she was sure it would not take long to locate. During her search, she kept some of her focus on the voices below her. She could no longer distinguish between distinct vocalizations. There were odd shouts and groans mixed with mumbling and banging.

She was sure the mobsters and Ursula were physically fighting. Although she cared little for the broad, backstabbing innkeeper, she did hope Ursula was not at the end of the gun blast.

She had just found the nail, her heart lifting with hope, when the small closet was flooded with light.

Brontë, shocked by the sudden immersion into illumination, shrieked in terror and fell backwards, colliding with the cans of paint.

"Shhh!" Her rescuer raised his hands to his lips. His bright blue eyes shone with both fear and excitement. "Mrs. Cook! We have to act quickly."

Brontë looked up into the pale, welcoming countenance of the youngest Deutschefaber. "Klaude?" She removed her hand from a bucket of paint. She unthinkingly wiped off the mess on the front of her blouse. "How did you—?"

"I've been able to escape these rooms for years with creative lock picking, but," he motioned to his chair, "there's not much motivation to escape due to the steepness of the stairs." He wheeled his chair around and pushed himself away from the closet.

Brontë, still dazed in the light, rose and followed him.

Her shriek caused the voices below to cease for an infinitesimal moment, but they had resumed with renewed fervor. Now that she was free, she could hear that it was a cacophony of languages and dialects. The bangs, shouts, and crashes echoed throughout the lodge.

"Klaude, what is going on?" Brontë asked.

The young man shivered. "It's pure chaos, Brontë. The mobsters have broken into a near riot. They are all fighting each other."

Klaude whipped his chair into his room. Brontë followed behind. Once the door was closed behind them, Klaude motioned to his bed.

"The sheets," he said quickly. "Start tying them together. We'll make a new rope to get you out my window."

Brontë ripped the top sheet free and braided it to strengthen its hold. Klaude did the same on the undersheet.

"I wonder what caused the escalation with the mobsters," Brontë said, her fingers moving furiously.

"I didn't have time to look. I do know the root cause was the arrival of someone new. I heard my sister greet someone at the door and then…well, it didn't take long to erupt into the chaos you heard from the closet." Klaude pulled a knot into the sheet.

"I'm so glad you came," Brontë said. She grabbed Klaude's knotted sheet and twisted it to her own. "I don't know if I would have managed to get the door open with the nail I'd found on the floor."

Klaude wheeled closer to see if he could assist with the sheet work. "Lock picking is a complex skill," he said. "You know Charlemagne—"

"I don't," Brontë said quickly, "need to know what Charlemagne says about lock picking."

The two worked on in a tense silence. Brontë finished twisting the two sheets together and looked at Klaude. The young man gave her a smile.

"You know, I never thought I'd be pulled into an adventure like this. It's just like in my mystery books."

Brontë laughed nervously. "It is. Although, even with Crockett and my adventures, I don't think the stakes were nearly this high. There is true danger—"

Just as Brontë said this, the gun went off again.

Klaude and Brontë exchanged panicked looks.

"We need to get you out of the lodge," Klaude said.

He wheeled over to the window and undid the latch. A cool breeze blew in. The rain had ceased, and the night air was damp.

Brontë brought the makeshift rope over to him. "I should apologize again," she said. "Not just about ignoring Charlemagne but in bringing all this madness to you. I know some of it is good news and some of it bad, but it should have been shared with more care and compassion. Your father...I had no idea you thought he was dead."

Klaude took the sheet from her and tossed it out the window. The crashes and bangs below grew louder.

"Most of the things I should have known," Klaude said. "There were holes in our history that I never sought to fill. Ursula, as hard as she tries to take care of me, thinks the truth, in all its forms, is damaging. I appreciate your candor. And your warmth. You could never replace my brother, but I'm glad I had someone here when it all happened. I've missed having friends."

He smiled at Brontë. The young woman gently squeezed his hand. She then lifted her leg to begin her descent out the window.

"Brontë," Klaude said quickly, "did you find the note I gave you?"

The young woman shook her head. "What note?"

"I slipped it in your trouser pocket when Ursula approached us."

Brontë put her hand in her pocket. She pulled out a small slip of paper. On it was written a sequence of five numbers.

"What is this?" she asked.

Klaude shrugged. "I don't know. In Dr. Gutermord's last note to me, he put a puzzle in the back. I never thought anything of it—he loved those kinds of games. The solution was a message and this string of numbers." Klaude eyes grew moist. "My brother, before all this happened, asked after the note. He was very interested in it."

"Could the numbers be the key?" Brontë asked. She flipped over the paper.

"I don't know."

Brontë looked into Klaude's eyes. "Well, I can assure you, if there is something that belongs to you left by the doctor, Crockett and I will do our best to retrieve it."

"I've no doubt you will."

She hesitated near the window. There were few words to say to Klaude, someone who had shown such bravery and fortitude in the face of the insane events of the past week. "I can't thank you enough for your help," she said. "After this is over, we are having a cup of tea and a proper, polite conversation. I promise absolutely no intrusions, gun blasts, or dramatic exits from windows."

"Of course."

Klaude tied his end of the rope to his chair and braced it against the wall. Brontë peered over the edge of the building and into the darkness below. She fully expected another crash into the bushes. She was about to take the leap when there was another blast of a gun.

This time it was much closer.

Brontë, shocked by the noise, fell back from the window.

Klaude turned to the doorway and gasped. Brontë's eyes followed his gaze. They were locked on a tall, shadowy figure standing in the doorway.

"Are entrances into your room always this dramatic?" Brontë whispered to Klaude.

He didn't have time to respond. The menacing figure drew closer to them.

"No need for that escape route," a familiar voice proclaimed.

Collanhall stepped forward. His hair was disheveled, and his usually starched and ironed clothes rumpled. Spots of blood covered his left arm. Klaude and Brontë eyed him warily. The colonel did his best to assuage their fear with a polite smile. He spoke once more.

"Sorry for the dramatics, but, Mrs. Cook, I need you to come with me."

34

The Secret Cell

Crockett now understood the agony of Petrarch's accident in Collanhall's cabin. The young lawyer's skull felt as if it had been shattered and the pieces lodged into his throbbing brain. The effort of opening his eyes was painful and taxing. Even the dim light thrown from a single lamp made his head quake with renewed pain. As he started to gain feeling back in his limbs, he noted that his hands were shackled.

It appeared he was in a cave. The floor was damp and wet. Above him stalactites hung from the ceiling. He breathed in the crisp, cold air of the cave; a faint smell of kerosene from the lamp was the only distinguishable smell. Water dripped slowly from above, each drop reverberating throughout the chamber.

The sound was agonizing to Crockett, who let out a groan in response to his surroundings, "Uggghhh."

"Oh, don't be such an English pansy."

The young lawyer turned toward the voice. A feeling of revulsion overcame him as he saw the rotund form of Elsinore Phipps.

"Phipps..." Crockett wanted to imbue his tone with more acrimony, but the pain limited his emotional sentiment. The most powerful feeling he could convey was that of someone suffering with light indigestion.

"The one and only, dear sir." Phipps piggish mouth turned up in a smile.

"Or should I say American pulp adventure writer, Phillip Ellsworth."

Crockett looked at Phipps intensely (or as intensely as his growing migraine would allow).

"Oh," Phipps giggled slightly. "Very impressive, Mr. Cook. I owe the colonel a handful of gold marks; I thought your bungling detective work would get you nowhere, but he thought you'd find success. It does appear you got somewhere with the help of that idiotic detective book."

When Crockett's eyes fully opened, he realized Phipps was in the same predicament that he was in (albeit without an egregious head wound). Like Crockett, Phipps was shackled and seated on the floor.

"You're a prisoner," Crockett said, quickly connecting the dots, "You're innocent. You're not the Caddywampus."

Phipps sniggered. "Certainly not innocent, but, no, I am not the one marching around in that despicable suit. It must smell horrendously; I don't know how anyone stands it. Add to that the machinery running inside, and it must reek of musty human and oil."

"It is a machine..." Crockett closed his eyes and tried to think.

"Yes, you dolt. You thought it was real? You were afraid of the half puma, half elk, half bear?"

"No." Crockett grew petulant. "I knew it wasn't real, but I was unsure what it was...precisely."

"Well, bravo, detective." Phipps sniffed slightly.

Crockett, furious and disinterested in Phipps (regardless of the information he could provide), began rolling away from the little writer toward the exit.

"It's no use," Phipps said. "They're watching the door."

"Who's they?"

"That," Phipps said with a sneer, "is what I don't precisely know. This is an entire *series* of caves." Phipps's sneer faded as he found joy in launching into a long, rambling description. "If you walk out of this one, you'll travel through a tunnel to find another and then another before you can escape. Three open caverns—*trois*, as the French would say. And every small one is *filled* with nefarious mobsters—"

"*Ruhig sein!*"

Crockett had never been more delighted to see an unpleasant man with a gun. A mobster in black had entered the room and pointed his weapon at Phipps to get him to be quiet. He growled a second threat before turning away.

He had barely left the room when Phipps spoke again.

"Cave architecture aside, aren't you at least curious how I knew about the Caddywampus being a machine?" he asked.

Crockett stayed silent in hopes of avoiding more annoying diatribes.

It was not successful. The writer continued. "Well, there's nothing else going on at the moment, so I'll tell you." Phipps let out a coarse grock then took a deep breath. (This deep breath was growing ever too identifiable to Crockett as the standard inhalation before a long-winded revelation or backstory is told.) "I found the costume. It was placed, very haphazardly, in the secret room behind the abandoned cabin."

Crockett continued to stay silent, although his resolve to remain mute was breaking down with this first revelation from Phipps.

"I don't know why it was left there or by whom, but it was there. It's an ingenious contraption—a metal carapace powered by some sort of micro-steam-engine technology. The operator can climb into the metal structure and run around creating monster tracks wherever he pleases."

"You don't know who created it?"

Phipps's eyes glittered with delight at having won over Crockett's interest. "It wasn't my concern. I was after the treasure."

"So you could write about it." Crockett sighed. "I do find some relief that you were writing an adventure story rather than some swill about walking in the woods."

The small writer's face grew red. "Well, that will be the title of my *memoowuz*, but, no, it's not why I'm here."

"Your what?"

"My *memoowuz*."

"Is that American English for something? I'm not familiar."

"My life story—my *memoowuz*."

"Your memoir?" Crockett stared. "You're trying to say 'memoir'?"

"If you're an illiterate idiot, I suppose you may say it like that."

Crockett again contemplated rolling away from the writer—being murdered by a mysterious foreign mobster with a weapon seemed a better alternative than the present conversation.

"If you're going to keep probing, then I'll just tell you—"

"I'm not probing," Crockett said heatedly.

"Well, you're a poor detective then. Charlemagne would have had loads of questions for me."

"Phipps—"

"Yes," Phipps said emphatically. "I am Phillip Ellsworth, the famous, dashing American author behind the series of adventure books about lost treasures. I have been disguised this whole time to be sure you wouldn't recognize me." The little man removed his glasses and ran a hand through his hair, slightly mussing it. "Now you should be able to see it."

"I have no idea who you are, Phipps," Crockett said resignedly. "In England we tend to read actual literature rather than your American adventuring nonsense."

"Say what you will, but I suppose you've never written a book which has been hailed as, 'A book of many pages.'"

Crockett did not respond. He leaned his head back against the wall of the cave and sighed loudly. While Phipps was helping his understanding of the mystery, he was doing nothing to assuage his cranial pain.

"In my adventures I've built quite the network of spies and informants, one of whom was connected to the owner of the candy shop. She told my spy about what was happening in Praktisch. Needless to say, I dropped everything to get here. I didn't know everyone staying at this decrepit inn would be involved."

Crockett's ears perked up. "Everyone was involved?"

Phipps smiled his piggish smile again. "Nearly. Greta was none other than the—"

"I know about Greta," Crockett interjected, hoping it would temper the length of Phipps's explanation. "She's the doctor's wife, the baroness."

"Ooh!" Phipps giggled delightedly. "Two points for Crockett! Yes, I found out about her from the candy shop owner. She loves to chat; I'm glad my mother taught me German as a child. She told me all about the note Greta had from the doctor. This week she served as a ripe plum from which I could extract juicy information."

"Is that the kind of metaphor I can look forward to in your books?"

Phipps scoffed. "Better than anything you and Brontë wrote in your silly notebook."

Crockett blanched. "You…you were in our cabin?"

"I was in everyone's cabin. And around everyone's cabin. People really need to check out their windows to see who may be eavesdropping. It was all in the service of art, however; a writer must know everything that's going on."[64]

"How dare you!"

"Please, Crockett. I'll keep your secrets. You had interesting theories about it all. I appreciated the log of activity. It may appear in print someday across the pond."

Out of frustration, Crockett struck his head against the wall of the cave, upping the level of pain within his skull. He blew a strand of his damp hair out of his eyes.

The little writer was glowing. He knew he could simply slip out another clue to get Crockett back into his clutches. He continued, "Collanhall was here investigating the murder that took place in town; the strangling incident earlier this week."

"So he is POOP?" Crockett asked.

"Indeed! Cheers again! Events leading up to this whole mess in Praktisch intersected with his police work in Australia. It is rumored some individuals involved in this are from an international crime syndicate. Our drunken colonel is, in fact, an international man of mystery." Phipps, annoyed by his revelatory mussed hair, smoothed it down. "Collanhall believes the man killed in town this week was murdered by these international bandits."

---

[64] The author feels he should interject that he has never once listened at a window for information for his books.

Crockett's puzzle box whirred. Although he kept getting deluged with facts, he couldn't piece them together into a complete solution. In both the Beatrice case and the Mayweather incident, there was a startling, revelatory lightning bolt that brought it all together. In this instance there was none.

He had so many questions that needed answers, but with his thoughts in such a state of chaos, he ended up asking Phipps the first and most banal question that came to mind, "Does Perth really lead the international policing effort in Australia? I would think Sydney or even Brisbane."

"Collanhall is actually in a smaller division of POOP. He belongs to the Northern Intelligence Network Community of Melbourne. He's NINCOMPOOP."

Crockett was both surprised and unsurprised by naming conventions in Australia. "So," he said, hoping to drive the discussion away from acronyms, "I'm guessing you joined forces with Collanhall. That's why your cabin was marked with POOP."

"Hooray!" Phipps jeered. "I made an alliance and gave him one of my books. I shared as much information as I could. I didn't tell him about the secret room behind the sixth cabin. I didn't want him interfering with my own interests."

"So…" Crockett's headache was finally fading. He began assembling more complex thoughts together. "Greta is the baroness, Collanhall is the police, you were writing about the treasure—what about the Gestahlts?"

Phipps's glow faded. "Neither Collanhall nor I know. Collanhall couldn't tie them to the green and gold gang."

"What did you find in their cabin?"

"It was very odd. It was spartan—no toys, books, or items for the children. That's why they were always running about the grounds like wild turkeys. But even the mister and missus didn't have many clothes. I believe that's why Mrs. Gestahlt was always washing. It didn't make sense for a holiday."

It was not a lightning bolt but a small spark which struck Crockett at that moment. He was about to confer with Phipps about his theory when there was the sound of heavy footsteps approaching.

The man in black returned. He barked in his same violent manner as before. He then pulled Crockett to his feet. Once the young man was up, the guard forced Phipps to stand. Both Phipps and Crockett were shackled to heavy boulders in the cave. The guard freed them and prodded them forward.

"Go!" he bellowed in a heavy accent.

Crockett felt panicked but followed the orders. The three men marched out of the small, prison cave and into a dark tunnel.

The path ahead of them was treacherous. The only light on the dim trail was thrown from a lamp held by the man in black. Both Crockett and Phipps tripped several times as they wound through the cave. Eventually, they entered a small room—if the small cavern could be called that. It appeared to be the second of the *trois* caves that Phipps told him about. There was enough space for a few people. Crockett could not make out the other shadowy figures, but seated in front of them, his face illuminated by a bright lantern, was Kreuz. The chiaroscuro effect of the lighting made his gaunt face look like a horrifying mask. His sleeves were rolled up and Crockett noted a small, black tattoo on his forearm. He could not make out the shape; Kreuz's sleeve slipped and covered it just as he noticed its presence.

The head mobster's dark, placid eyes shifted their attention to Crockett and Phipps.

"Put them beside the others," he said coldly. He waved to the floor near two unseen figures and turned away from them, deep in thought.

The man behind Phipps and Crockett shoved them to the floor. They collapsed and nearly rolled on top of the other two shadows. As Crockett attempted to pull himself into a seated position, he lifted his head and found he was looking into the faces of Mr. and Mrs. Gestahlt.

"Hullo," Mr. Gestahlt said. "Good you not dead."

Crockett was about to ask a question, but he was beaten to the punch by Phipps.

"What are *you* doing here?"

The mobsters loathed the little man as much as the rest of the lodgers at the inn did. With a swift movement, Kreuz extended his long arm and struck Phipps in the back of his head with the revolver. The plump writer collapsed, knocked out.

"Thank you," Crockett said instinctually.

The guard shoved Crockett. Phipps, apparently always getting in the final word even when unconscious, began to snore.

"Take him back to the cell," Kreuz said softly. "How is he always a nuisance?" In the dark cavern, the mobster's voice was more chilling than in the pub.

He turned to Mr. and Mrs. Gestahlt. He was clearly agitated, his voice a razor-sharp point. "Where are they?" he asked coldly.

Mr. Gestahlt, who appeared completely unimpacted by their current incarcerated state, shrugged. "I don't know. Caves confuse."

"Love buggies," added Mrs. Gestahlt.

"They have the map." Kreuz's voice sharpened.

Mr. Gestahlt said nothing.

Kreuz's skeletal form twisted away from them. For the first time, Crockett saw a small hole near his feet. It looked small, barely the size of—

Crockett spun and faced Mr. Gestahlt. "The children?"

A mobster hissed something in a foreign language and aimed his gun at Crockett.

Mr. Gestahlt nodded placidly, again unbothered by the terror around them. He responded in a low, barely audible tone, "They in hole."

Kreuz turned to Mrs. Gestahlt and said something in her native tongue. The young woman looked to Mr. Gestahlt nervously. It appeared as if she were trying to think of something. The two then whispered back and forth; this greatly frustrated Kreuz.

"You don't know the children's names?" Kreuz was incredulous. He had switched from the Gestahlt language back to English out of shock.

"Now that's plain rude," a mobster who spoke English said. "Children are our future."

"We make up the Adon and Ava names, but we no know real ones. Children and us have business partnership; we don't discuss personal." Mr. Gestahlt said this matter-of-factly. Mrs. Gestahlt nodded in agreement.

"I would shoot you right now, if we didn't need you alive until they return," the English-speaking mobster said, raising his gun in the direction of Mr. Gestahlt.

"It does not matter, Frederick." Kreuz waved him off. "Just call for the boy and girl. We have the numbers from Bristol, it must work."

Frederick stepped forward and called for them in German.

There was no response from the dark. A tense moment unfolded as they listened. Crockett suddenly realized the implications of the two young children wandering in the dark caves alone. He and Phipps had nearly fallen dozens of times on the short walk from their cell.

Kreuz looked to Frederick and indicated he should call again. The guard opened his mouth, prepared to yell louder, when there was a shout in the distance.

It was deep and masculine—clearly not from a child.

"What is that?" Frederick trembled. "That wasn't a child…"

"Could be," Mr. Gestahlt said calmly. "They grow up so fast."

Kreuz's eyes flickered to a corner of the room. Crockett, his vision nearly adjusted to the dark, noticed a second passage, separate from the one they had followed from their prison cave. If the duplicitous writer was correct, it led to the third and final cave: the only exit.

There was another shriek, this time louder and closer.

"What's going on?" Frederick raised his gun. His hands were shaking so badly that the gun slipped from his grasp and clattered onto the stone floor.

Kreuz's face showed no emotion. He pointed to another henchman, who still held his weapon, and indicated for him to go investigate.

"That the only way out," Mr. Gestahlt whispered to Crockett. Even he was beginning to grow fearful. Mrs. Gestahlt leaned closely to her husband and laid her hand on his leg.

They heard the guard leave the room, his footsteps trailing in the distance. The second passage twisted so that once the guard moved ten yards away, he turned and disappeared from their view. Eventually, the halo of light from his lamp vanished completely.

After only a few moments, the man's footsteps ceased. Crockett's eyes flashed to Kreuz, who sat pensively. His fingers were steepled and pressed to his mouth. Mr. and Mrs. Gestahlt huddled together; they gazed nervously at the tunnel into which the guard disappeared.

Time slowed. Crockett could hear the breathing of the others in the room. Frederick's was the most ragged. He had collected his gun and sat in terrified silence near Kreuz. In a moment of weakness, he attempted a similar fearful pose as Mrs. Gestahlt. He leaned on Kreuz's leg for support. The gaunt leader, however, met this with a firm rebuke and shoved him to the ground.

It was then that chaos broke out.

There was a blast of a gun and more bellowing. Voices shook through the caves—screams, shouts, and battle cries echoed through the stony walls. Frederick, in terror, toppled over their lamp, sending the room into absolute darkness.

A dim light appeared in the passage to the third cave. There continued to be the sound of screams, punctuated by more discharges from a firearm.

Beside him, Crockett heard the chaotic shuffling of feet and the jostling of bodies. He was unsure if it was Kreuz, Frederick, another henchman, or the Gestahlts, but individuals were moving. Shadows rushed down the second tunnel toward the room with the outbreak of violence.

Crockett, as was his usual reaction to terror, froze. His heart raced; his palms sweated. He tried his best to collect himself, but each time he would begin to wrangle his emotions, there would be an additional scream or another gun blast.

There was a brief silence and then he heard a rumble come from the tunnel before him. Two, glowing red eyes appeared in the dark.

"No..." Crockett's voice was a coarse whisper. Adrenaline flooded his veins. He tried to stand.

The eyes grew closer, the beast was crawling through the tunnel. He could hear its claws grate against the stone walls. A fierce, guttural growl came from its open jaws as it pressed through the narrow passage.

"Phipps said you weren't real! You're simply a machine!" Crockett yelled.

The young lawyer had no time to reflect on the stupidity of this statement.

The beast shoved into the open room and was upon him. In the complete dark, its red eyes were the only light. It growled again and slammed one of its claws against the wall.

It leaned down so closely that Crockett could smell the stale odor of its musty fur. He slipped out of consciousness as the beast growled, mere inches from his pale face.[65]

---

[65] Apologies for the long footnote, but as we approach the climax, I think a long explanation will keep the last pages free of authorial interjection. *Ahem* This section was the last written by Didiert and Earhart. It grieves me to say that they met their end on the da Vinci Society "flying" machine. Strong winds and renegade seagulls caused their end. Despite not being airborne, winds drove them to the edge of a cliff where the seagulls mistook them for two large loaves of bread and violently attacked them (the hazards of wearing white linen suits). The ensuing chaos led to them losing control and hurtling off the cliff. Adelaide (Earhart's mother) inherited their notes. She also created a monument to them in her garden in rural England. The loss of her son, evidently, made the elderly woman soften on her disdain for sodomy. The notes for this novel, along with many others, were passed on to me by the shopkeeper, whom I met in London. The remainder of this novel was patched together from what was left in notebooks, journals, and letters between Didiert and Earhart. As the reader may feel sad for the two struggling artists who put this book together, I feel I should conclude this footnote with the inscription Adelaide Earhart put on their monument: *"While both odd ducks in life, they found each other. They ended life, just as they lived it, embracing discovery and imagination, taking chances no one else dared."*

35

The Rescue Party

An hour before Crockett's encounter with the Caddywampus in the cave, Brontë was still at the end of Collanhall's gun in Klaude's room.

The colonel asked for her assistance and then lowered his weapon. He saw the unbridled terror in both Klaude and Brontë's eyes. He also felt an intense panic when he realized that Brontë was covered in blood.

"Did I shoot you?" he squealed. "I don't think I shot you. How would that happen?"

Brontë and Klaude looked at each other confusedly. It was then that Klaude noted that the paint Brontë accidentally smeared on herself in the closet was sanguine.

"It's paint," Klaude said.

Collanhall, normally a pillar of fortitude, was on the verge of tears. "Thank goodness!" he said. He wiped his eyes, trying to erase any sign of emotion. "I sometimes act rashly—it wouldn't be unlike me to shoot an ally out of excitement; I lost seven poddybillows on my last officer review because of my dramatics."

Neither Klaude nor Brontë knew where to start with questions. There were too many options: the whereabouts of Ursula; a clear, quick definition of a poddybillow; or the fact that the colonel had, quite obviously, shot several people he was allied to.

"Poddybillows aside, sir, what is going on?" It was Klaude who spoke first. The young man was both thrilled and terrorized.

"I've come to help," Collanhall said brusquely. "POOP never leaves you unattended, even when it's unwanted."

"POOP!" Brontë's eyes shone. "Crockett was right!"

"Actually, a NINCOMPOOP." Collanhall took for granted that neither Klaude nor Brontë would know the meaning of the acronym.

The non-Australians didn't care. They looked to context clues rather than inquire further; as things were going, with the large man in tears confessing to accidentally shooting multiple people, their priority was getting on the other side of the gun. Collanhall was wearing his POOP star on his chest. They inferred he had legal authority.

"Well," Brontë said, moving from the window to get behind Collanhall, "you said I'm to come with you. Where…are we going?"

"To save everyone, of course." He lowered his gun. "I owe Phipps some gold marks. I thought you and your scrawny husband knew what was going on. That book is rather extensive. I assumed it would help you get to the resolution."

Brontë grew irritable, but she had to acknowledge the truth; she and Crockett didn't have any idea what was going on. "It's true. We have loose threads and scraps but no understanding of who is after what and why," she said defeatedly.

"It's all right! As we say in Australia, 'A koala doesn't kip unless you catapult the crinklewheel.'"[66]

Brontë and Klaude nodded enthusiastically, hoping it would facilitate a movement forward in the conversation.

"Now!" Collanhall returned to his normal bearing. His tears were gone and his tone loud and bellowing. "Let's go to the hidden cabin!"

He marched out the door, leaving Brontë and Klaude behind.

Brontë took a moment to reflect on the current trajectory of the night. It

---

[66] I realize I'm already breaking my vow to end authorial interjections, but in regard to this Australian aphorism…Reader, your guess is as good as mine.

was true that they needed to get to the cabin quickly, but they also need to act strategically. She and Crockett had both been in dire situations before; she knew Crockett could hold on and fight Caddywampuses and green and gold mobsters. Her husband, despite his excitability, always rose to the occasion. She smiled thinking of him, a man who danced on a knife blade of bravery and cowardice.

Klaude interrupted her thoughts, "Brontë, can you assist me downstairs?" The young man's eyes shone with determination.

Brontë nodded quickly. "Of course!"

"Good. You can go with Collanhall. I'll call the local police and meet them when they arrive." His pale cheeks were flushed with excitement. "I feel I've stayed up in this room long enough."

They moved quickly out into the hall following Collanhall. The colonel was in the middle of a diatribe about hunting. He had not noticed Klaude and Brontë had not been behind him.

"And that, of course, is why you can't play the flute around a ninnybludgeon—"

"Colonel!" Klaude yelled to get the large man's attention. "Where is my sister?"

"Oh!" Collanhall turned. He blushed slightly. "She's safe. She was getting very combative, so I had to tie her down to the sofa." His face grew steely, "Many of the fugitives, ne'er do wells, and criminals with her, however, did not make it."

Brontë and Klaude gasped. While Collanhall confessed to accidentally shooting his partner and others, they couldn't see him murdering anyone on purpose, even if they were nameless mobsters.

"Oh!" Collanhall started, "I said, 'They did not make it,' but they're not dead. I asked them to pour me a whiskey and they refused. I had to knock them around a bit and then make my own drink. Mobsters have no manners. They're alive and well, tied up in the billiard room."

"Good," Brontë said, relieved. Attempting to lighten the mood, she looked to Klaude and continued, "I was worried with your lack of poddybillows that you may have shot Miss Deutschefaber."

Collanhall's face dropped slightly. Brontë's mouth fell open.

"You didn't shoot her, did you?!"

"I didn't…" They were now almost to the stair. Collanhall stopped and turned. His eyes looked upward, as if he were a child caught for having his hand in the cookie jar. "I didn't *not* shoot her, if that's the question."

Brontë's eyes were wide. "But she's alive?"

"Breathing! And I bandaged the wound myself. Not even a little mortal!"

Klaude and Brontë both went pale. They were very concerned with the "help" they were receiving from Collanhall.

They had no time to ruminate, however, as they were at the stairs. It took little effort between the colonel and Brontë to get Klaude down the steps. When they arrived at the bottom, they saw Ursula. Her arm was bloodied and her face an ashy gray. She was bound and gagged. Upon seeing Klaude, her eyes went wide. She frantically tried to roll herself off the sofa.

"It's all right," Brontë said. "We're getting help!"

Ursula's face reddened. Spittle ran down her chin from the gag.

"She's very excitable," Klaude said. He wheeled to the front desk and grabbed the telephone. "I'll make the call to the police—you two, go!"

"Ask for Bunce and Bosch," Brontë said. "They'll be able to help—"

Her directive was interrupted by a tremendous crash.

Petrarch barreled through the front door. The old man could barely stand. His pupils were wide and dilated.

"Petrarch?" Brontë ran forward and grabbed the old man. He was in the process of toppling forward.

"Brontë?" he asked, his eyes unable to focus. "I came to help!"

Brontë looked to Collanhall, who clicked his tongue.

"I took a medical course in the service." He took a dramatic step forward and pressed his hand to Petrarch's wrist to get a pulse. "It was focused on shark bites, but I'm sure this is similar. Does anyone have a harpoon?"

Brontë reached out and shoved Collanhall backward, trying to keep him as far from Petrarch as possible. She was greatly relieved when Sylvia entered the lodge in quick pursuit of the old man.

"I'm so sorry," she said softly. "He's been running amuck since Crockett fled. I got him some whiskey and then he tore off into the woods. It took the better part of a half hour to direct him back here."

To everyone's surprise, Petrarch had begun snoring while standing up. Sylvia gently helped him to the sofa and set him beside Ursula.

"Klaude," Brontë said quickly, "could you also call out for a doctor? I don't think Petrarch is well."

"He had a tremendous crash," Sylvia said. She warmly laid the old solicitor back and adjusted his hands so they were on his stomach. "He and your husband were in quite the state. I think whatever has been going on at the lodge…" A tear formed at the edge of her eye. She wiped it away quickly. "Well, it appears as if it is coming to a head this evening."

"It is!" Collanhall took a step forward. "Murders, thieves, mobsters—it's quite the predicament. As we'd say down under—"

Brontë interrupted to avoid another Australian aphorism, "Sylvia, where is Crockett? Did he go to the cabin?"

"Yes. He was fetching a weapon from Collanhall's lodging. I'd just seen the colonel leave and was distressed. My own premotions have been wild all day. They've grown in intensity. When I saw you," she indicated Collanhall, "leave with a gun, I assumed the worst."

"It may be even more dire than that." Brontë looked at Ursula, who was still foaming at the mouth. She stepped forward and gently took Sylvia's hand. "You stay here with Klaude, Ursula, and Petrarch. We have help coming."

Sylvia nodded. "I will. You…" Her eyes grew larger, "you aren't going with Collanhall are you? That's madness!"

"Believe it or not," Brontë smiled, "I've been in similar situations before."

"And she will make excellent bait," Collanhall added. "I'll throw her out to draw the mobsters in. Should be able to do it without too much bloodshed."

Sylvia's face went white with fear. Brontë gripped her hand tightly and whispered, "I'll be fine. Take care of everyone here. And," she indicated the other room, "lock the door to the parlor. There is an assortment of angry, violent characters tied up in there."

Sylvia swallowed hard. Brontë patted her shoulder and turned to

Collanhall. The two exchanged a nod and then left the main lodge.

They stopped briefly at Collanhall's cabin to secure another lamp and a weapon for Brontë. The young woman felt much better with a firearm in the presence of Collanhall, even without the knowledge of how to use it.

When they were prepared, they began their descent into the ravine and toward the cabin.

Collanhall spent the trek explaining his role in the mysterious goings-on at the Deutschefaber Inn.[67] His hunter persona had been a bizarre, elaborate cover story.

He was actually a police officer in pursuit of a crime duo who spent time in Australia the previous year. The pair of criminals hit ten Australian banks in the span of eight months; not much was known about them other than that they were part of a larger, international syndicate that had deep ties in Russia. It was believed they were a husband-and-wife team, as they often smooched[68] one another during the robberies (a trait that led them to be identified in Australia as the Smooch Moochers).

The criminals were eventually found in a small hotel outside of Perth, but they narrowly escaped, leaving behind a stack of fraudulent passports.

Collanhall was dispatched internationally to pursue them; after nearly a year of detective work, a breakthrough clue indicated that they were on their way to Praktisch on a secret mission. Collanhall got this information entirely by accident—he arrested a café owner because he didn't like his anti-Australian sentiments; however, it turned out the man was an accessory to the Russian mafia and sold out the husband-and-wife team in order to

---

[67] This was one of the only remaining sections fully drafted in Didiert's journal. He used it to "practice the Australian discourse." In an editorial decision, Collanhall's dialogue has been condensed to prose. The original section held so many Australian turns of phrase and slang, it was largely unintelligible. For example: "But you really cannit pubby, if you don't, so that's what brought it up'n about to the risin' of my own kippin' in the conswabble." For the record, it was worse than Cubesy McGillicuddy's backwards speech.

[68] While the term "smooch" didn't come into use until the 1930's, I have tweaked it from the original text which used "buss." This term seemed too archaic and too likely to cause giggles for the friends of Dorothy reading the text.

keep his café.

The tip proved to be correct. The murder of the mysterious mobster in Praktisch occurred just days before Collanhall was set to arrive. The information also indicated that the Russian duo was involved in an intermafia war in the little German town. Collanhall was sure that the couple had to be involved in the murder in some way.

"So," Brontë said, "you still don't know who they are or what they're after here?"

Collanhall's ears purpled slightly. "Not entirely. I've been trying to find out information from those here and in the lodgings throughout town. I assumed the couple would be staying somewhere in the vicinity. I've been looking closely at any couple in the act of a smooch. My first full day here I also tried to get the men at the inn drunk. It's the most powerful interrogation technique we have in NINCOMPOOP. Unfortunately, Gestahlt and your husband divulged nothing. Phipps was useful."

"Phipps and 'useful' being contained in the same sentence *is* cause for surprise," Brontë said.

"Phipps is a bit odd, but he was very helpful. He nosed about in everyone's cabins for me. He's researching a book about the secret cabin and the mysterious treasure, so he was invested. You may have seen his other book floating around this week. I guess in America he goes by Phillip Ellsworth. Anyway, for his help, I gave him immunity in case I had to call in my own team for backup."

Brontë suddenly remembered the marks on the stoop. "That's why you put your," she refused to say the term out loud, "organization's name on Phipps's stoop."

"Yes. While he snooped about the inn, I went into town and looked at lodges and found out what the local constabulary knew about the mob activity. It turns out," Collanhall's voice grew softer as they came to the bottom of the ravine and found the trail to the sixth cabin, "Praktisch is a meeting point for multiple nefarious groups. There used to be a green and a gold gang, but they have since merged to create the green *and* gold. But!

Some green and some gold didn't like the merger and stayed separate. Add to all that the fact that there were other warring factions—including a few gentlemen in a puce sect—and you have the recipe for an international mob war. This morning I went to Praktisch prison and did further research. There were a few criminals from the different factions being held there. They all hate each other, as you can imagine."

"So that's why you went to the prison." Brontë was grateful another open mystery was closed. "But where are all these colorful criminals from? Did you find that out in your research?" Brontë also lowered her voice. Ahead was empty darkness, but she had the feeling of a menacing presence drawing near.

"That's the interesting part—" Collanhall stopped. He raised his gun and did a sweep of the area looking through its sight. When he was satisfied, he continued forward slowly. "They are from all over Europe. Our friends, the married couple, used to be part of a Russian group, a green faction, but the ties were severed. The café owner said that they were going to Praktisch to begin again."

"Begin again?"

There was a rustle in the woods.

Collanhall motioned for her to stop. "Put your light out," he whispered.

Brontë blew out her lamp and huddled closer to the colonel. Her hands shook violently. Slowly, she scanned the dark, looking and listening for signs of light or activity.

Had it not been for the impending threat of an international mob, the night would have felt idyllic and tranquil. The rain finally passed on, revealing a wide, deep sky full of stars. They didn't need lamps, as the moon shone like the front light of a train above them.

A twig snapped behind Brontë.

She turned and saw a dim figure before her. She gasped.

There was a moment of silence before the melee broke out. It was pure, Australian-fueled chaos.

Collanhall whirled around, punching the figure who was close to Brontë. The man sputtered and launched backward, howling in pain. This rang the alarm for the others who were hidden in the woods. Shots rang out in the night.

Brontë dove to the ground while Collanhall went to mesmerizing work. Despite his lack of poddybillows, the man was a master fighter. His movements could only be described as water-like; he flowed effortlessly between trees, enemies, and explosive gunfire. When Brontë regained her courage, she raised her head and took in the scene.

As Collanhall danced through the trees in a khaki-colored whirl, men in black ran from the shadows to attack. No one paid much attention to the young woman on the trail (she clearly wasn't the bait Collanhall hoped for). This gave her an opening to assist.

Near her, a large tree had collapsed leaving an assortment of downed branches that could make excellent cudgels. Brontë did not like the thought of shooting anyone, so the makeshift clubs were enticing. She set her gun down near the trail in a spot she could easily find then raised a branch and joined the fray.

The mobsters, unintimidated by her sex, chose to ignore her, which allowed her to follow Collanhall's lead and whirl with her club, knocking many mobsters about their heads and rendering them unconscious.

The battle raged for the better part of five minutes. Brontë realized the "army" she believed to be around them when the attack began was only a coterie of five or six. She and Collanhall took them out swiftly.

In the end, Brontë was breathing heavily just off the trail, while Collanhall punched the final mobster in the face.

"Ho ho!" he called. "Excellent work, Mrs. Cook. When bait becomes beast!"

She raised her tree branch in salute.

The celebration was short-lived, however, as she felt a cold, metallic object press into the back of her skull. Her blood froze. The mysterious person used their gunless hand to grip her around the waist. He yelled in a foreign language and shook her.

Collanhall raised his hands in surrender.

"Oi!" he yelled. "It's okay!"

The mobster screamed back at him in his mother tongue. Collanhall nodded.

"Yes, yes. Well, let's get on with it."

The colonel marched toward them, hands in the air. Brontë shook violently, unsure what they could do. Her tree branch had fallen to the ground, and by the strength of the man's grip, she knew he was a formidable foe.

Collanhall, on his approach to them, suddenly tripped.

Brontë never knew how what happened next was accomplished, but in later years she would tell everyone that they must always trust the skills and intuition of an Australian, regardless of the Australian's seeming lack of skills and intuition.

During his tripping motion, Collanhall flicked into his back pocket and pulled out an arch-shaped piece of wood. It flew from his grip and struck the mobster in the face, missing Brontë by an inch.

The man reeled backward. Brontë, wasting no time, turned and threw the first punch of her life, colliding with the man's nose and sending him sprawling farther backwards, unconscious.

When he was on the ground, the young woman could only stare at the incapacitated gentleman in wonder at her own power.

"I—" Her voice shook.

Collanhall bounded toward her. He patted her on the back and laughed loudly.

"Tremendous!" he bellowed. "That is why you always keep a boomerang in your backie. And," he took Brontë's hand and kissed it, "why you never underestimate a woman."

The impact and terror of what occurred hit Brontë with the force of a train. She slumped over, leaning against a tree.

"We could have died," she rasped. Her breath came in quick, panicked bursts.

Collanhall nodded. "And we still may," he said nonchalantly. "We now move into phase two."

"Phase two?" Brontë gasped. "I wasn't aware we were in phase one."

"Phases occur quickly in the heat of battle."

Collanhall extended his hand and helped Brontë away from the support of the tree.

"Phase two emerged when I saw something on the ground. It's just down the trail and near the cabin."

Brontë's eyes went wide. "What did you find?"

Collanhall guffawed. "Something ingenious. And it's going to help us end this."

36

Phipps Proves Useful (Again)

Crockett awoke just moments after passing out. His situation had worsened.

He was being held in the air and shaken violently by the Caddywampus. The odor of the monster was thick, a cocktail of musk, dirt, and oil that turned the young lawyer's face green. Although he tried to writhe free, the beast's grip on his shoulders was tight as steel. Its massive teeth glimmered in the dim light of the cave.

Crockett was sure this was the end. His life flashed before his eyes—a short narrative highlighted by his love of Brontë and the great times with Petrarch, but, aside from that, fairly dull. (There were far too many scenes of him doing paperwork in the law office.) As the Caddywampus held him aloft, its grunts turned to a staccato rhythm. It sounded as if it was laughing.

His torture was interrupted by a cry of "Demon dingoes!" from the other part of the cave.

The beast grunted in response. It was not the staccato grunt-laugh from before, but a startled groan of surprise. It turned its attention away from Crockett, setting him on the ground and stomping back in the direction from which it came.

Crockett stood and shook his head to gather his senses. "It's okay, Crockett," he whispered to himself. "Stand up. Get one foot in front of the other."

When his eyes opened, there was a light ahead of him. Standing before him were the two Gestahlt children, their eyes wide.

"You're all right!" Crockett sat on his knees. He reached out and gripped the young boy and girl closely to him. He gently wiped the grime away from their small faces.

The non-English-speaking children stared at him confusedly.

"Are you," Crockett pointed to their bodies, "feeling well?" The second half of the question was less intuitive to make via sign language, so he smiled hugely and (for some reason) swung his arms as if he were marching.

The children's emotions changed from confused to concerned quickly. Crockett tried to think of another way to communicate, when his thoughts were interrupted by a Caddywampus roar from the other room; this time, however, it was short, and, if Crockett could ascertain the mood of monsters, distressed. Cries and shouts also echoed down the rock hallway from the other part of the cave.

Crockett attempted to pull the two children closer to him for safety, but they were unbothered by any of the horrors around them: the dark cave, the growling of a beast, the shouts of men in battle. They said something to each other in their foreign tongue and then bolted away from the young lawyer, down the second corridor toward all the mayhem.

Crockett was left in darkness.

"What to do?" he asked himself aloud.

He was embarrassed to admit that, at the climax of the mystery of the Deutschefaber Inn, he had no idea what was going on. The Caddywampus was roaring about, Collanhall appeared to be alive and frightened in the other chamber, and the Gestahlts and their children were shockingly nonplussed about any of the disastrous events surrounding them. The mobster link in the convoluted chain was also unclear in the current moment.

At the very least, he had not seen or heard Brontë, so hopefully she was outside the danger of this maelstrom of mobs, monsters, and malevolent writers.

He also felt helpless, not knowing how to assist anyone caught in this tempest. The most reasonable plan of attack would be to enter the other chamber secretively to gain an understanding of the unfolding crisis. He, however, could only see a dim pinpoint of light down the long hall and was concerned he could end up injured by bumbling down the dark corridor. There was also the possibility that said bumbling would be so noisy that he would give himself up.

The shouting began to diminish. Even the Caddywampus' bellowing became tamer. The appearance of the children could have caused the voices emanating from the mysterious room to calm.

His eyes flicked to the left and he realized, for the first time, that there was also a dim spark of light coming from the other passage. Phipps was still in the prison cavern.

In an instant, a fully developed plan birthed itself into Crockett's consciousness. Throwing caution to the wind, he turned to the left and headed toward Phipps's cell.

The journey down the rocky path proved more difficult than his first sojourn, when he and Phipps were marched there. He tried his best to keep his exclamations of pain to a minimum, but every step brought Crockett's head into a collision with a stone or his knee into contact with sharp boulders. He felt warm blood trickle down his forehead; his vision blurred and doubled. By the time he emerged into Phipps's prison chamber, he was staggering slightly and had trouble locating the pudgy author.

"Are you all right?" Phipps looked terrified. Crockett realized he may be bloodier and more bruised than he thought.

"Very fine," he said quickly. "But I need you and your lamp."

Phipps looked at him suspiciously. "What is going on? I heard screaming, disorder, and then silence."

Crockett thought briefly of posturing that he knew what was happening, but he believed his beaten face would undermine that charade. "I don't know what's going on Phipps," he said finally. "The Caddywampus appeared; it nearly strangled me, but then I believe Collanhall appeared, causing it to flee."

Phipps looked slightly relieved. "Collanhall is here? Did he bring his reinforcements?"

"I heard him," Crockett said. He picked up the lamp. "I don't think there are any reinforcements. We need to go help…whoever…and…well, bring resolution."

The scheming writer looked at Crockett with a glint in his eyes. "You still have no idea what is going on, so what could you possibly mean by 'resolution'?"

"Truthfully," Crockett wiped a trail of blood from his forehead, "I don't know what I mean. I just know that Collanhall is in trouble and that we need to try to help him." He sighed. "The most important thing for us to do right now is get into the other chamber and see what's going on."

Phipps clicked his tongue. "I suppose so."

Crockett extended his hand to shake with Phipps. "We'll enter together. We'll help where we can."

The American stared at Crockett's hand for a moment. His eyes then shifted to look directly at the young lawyer.

"Agree that I get sole rights to the novelization of this story. I don't need British competition mucking up my sales."

Crockett rolled his eyes. "Of course, yes. You can write whatever you want, Phipps. I'll look forward to reading *Being an Arse in the Woods While Being an Arse*."

Phipps smiled gleefully and raised his shackled hand to shake Crockett's. As their two hands pumped up and down, they both smiled stupidly in hopes it would calm any suspicions of the other.

Both planned a betrayal.

"Excellent." Phipps motioned to an object by the lantern. "He left the key there. Open these shackles and let's go forward."

Crockett made quick work of Phipps's restraints. When he was free, Crockett picked up the lamp and headed down the stony path.

With the lamp, the journey through the corridor was much easier. In just a few moments, they reentered the second room with the secret hole. Crockett did not hesitate but turned the corner and made his way down the passage toward the third cavern.

As they entered the passage, Phipps kicked the back of Crockett's leg.

"Crockett," he hissed, "we can't be running ahead without knowing what's going on. And they'll see the lamp! Put it out!"

Crockett turned and nodded. He blew out his lamp.

They crept forward until they could see into the other chamber. It was unclear what was happening or who was involved. Hushed voices could be heard but no words. From their vantage point, they could only make out a few shapes in the dim light. The space itself was far larger than either of the other two caves. Crockett's neck craned upward to see if he could make out how high the ceiling extended. As he assessed the room, Phipps began to push past him. Crockett held out his hand to stop the writer from moving forward.

"Let's evaluate before we lose our heads," he whispered. "There is a boulder up ahead that can conceal us while giving us a better view of what's happening."

Phipps nodded.

Crockett crept quietly toward the boulder. He kept his eye on Phipps, who behaved as selfishly as he expected. The piggish author shoved him out of the way to get behind the boulder and procure concealment for himself first (the writer's planned betrayal). As he scrambled to hide, Crockett initiated his plan (the amateur detective's own more dramatic act of treachery).

To say it was clever or well thought out would be a lie. It was partly an act of desperation, but mostly it was a classic Crockettian response to a fear stimulus. The young lawyer performed two quick actions, which he believed would cause a distraction and allow him to better assess the situation in the third cavern.

First, he hurled the extinguished lamp to the left side of the larger chamber. It flew and shattered against a large stalactite. The noise from its destruction echoed throughout the large cavern.

Phipps turned back to him, alarmed. Crockett savored his distress for half a second before rearing back and initiating his second action: kicking the portly writer so that he launched, face forward into the large chamber. The feel of his shoe against the ample buttocks of the American, as well as the grunt of "Ooofff!" that followed it, were unbelievably satisfying to the young detective.

Once these two actions were completed, Crockett ducked behind the boulder and watched the reactions take place. It was his hope that the lamp's crash and the emergence of Phipps would mask his own presence, giving opportunity for him to gather intelligence on the mysterious party.

The plan proved successful, although perhaps not as Crockett intended: a surge of violence erupted that benefitted the non-mobster contingent.

Kreuz, who had Collanhall at gunpoint, turned toward the noise. The colonel seized the opening and spun, kicking the gaunt mobster to the ground. Kreuz's weapon flew from his grasp, striking Phipps in the head and causing Crockett a second wave of satisfaction.

The Caddywampus, which had bizarrely been standing back with its immense paws raised into the air, used the disruption to leap forward and strike the remaining two mobsters, knocking them to the ground.

In the shuffle, Crockett saw Mr. and Mrs. Gestahlt flee; they rushed toward a stony ramp at the other end of the cavernous room. They paid no attention to their children, who, in the chaos, excitedly whooped while running and kicking the mobsters who lay on the floor. The little girl felt the urge to kick Phipps as well, which Crockett supported enthusiastically.

As the dust settled, Collanhall held a weapon pointed directly at Kreuz, while the Caddywampus used the mobsters as a seat. The two mafiosos groaned under the weight of the furry creature. The children jeered and Phipps whimpered.

"Well," Collanhall said, "I suppose that's the end of it."

The gaunt man sneered. His steely, emotionless tone disappeared; his voice became a feral rasp.

"You have no idea what you're up against."

"A skinny, whining mobster, I would say." Collanhall chuckled. The Caddywampus let out an odd, giggle-like growl.

The gaunt man's eyes suddenly grew placid. He stood still.

"You can believe that," he said.

He kept his arms raised but took a step backward. There was a slight, nearly inaudible click and then the man crumpled to the ground.

Collanhall jumped. "What?"

The Australian ran over to the fallen man and felt for a pulse. The mobster convulsed for a moment and then fell limp.

"Cyanide." Collanhall stood up and looked down at the fresh corpse. "Mobsters like to pretend they're not dramatic but look at this. They are worse than theater folk, if you ask me."

The Caddywampus growled in agreement.

"I'm sorry for causing all that commotion, but it appears to have helped," Crockett said fully entering the room.

Collanhall caught sight of Crockett and gasped. "My word, old boy, are you all right? Your face looks like it's been to war without the rest of you."

"Oh." Crockett felt the lumps on his forehead. "I had a bit of trouble in the hall. It's difficult maneuvering in the dark."

The Caddywampus growled.

"Who is that?!" Crockett asked. "Is it…I mean who is the Caddywampus?"

With a few huge strides, the monster was upon Crockett. It leaned down and picked him up, capturing him in a smelly, uncomfortable hug.

While Crockett was embraced, Collanhall helped Phipps to his feet. The Gestahlt daughter gave the writer one final kick before laughing and running to her brother.

The beast sat Crockett down. It took a few steps back and then stopped. There was a soft hiss and a crack as if bones were being broken. The monster's ribcage separated, and he saw the sweaty, ragged body of his wife.

"Brontë." He smiled hugely. "But…what…are you all right?" His heart raced when he saw the red paint smeared on her blouse.

His concerns were alleviated, however, when Brontë stepped out of the Caddywampus machine and ran to him. She pressed her lips against his. Although she smelled of sweat and oil from the suit, Crockett enjoyed the moment immensely.

Phipps groaned disgustedly.

Crockett pulled away and looked deeply into his wife's hazel eyes. "But what? What happened? And who…?" He pressed his hand to the red stain on her shirt.

"Paint," she whispered conspiratorially. She kissed his hand.

"It's a very long story," Collanhall interrupted. "We will explain in a moment, but, for now, we have a treasure to collect."

37

Dr. Gutermord's Secret

The next few moments found Collanhall struggling to explain to the children that they needed to climb back into the darkened nook in the other cave to secure the treasure. His mixture of sign language and broken German proved only modestly successful. The children stomped around and tried to explain something back to him. It was Brontë who finally understood.

"They need both sets of codes," she said turning to Phipps. "They have the ones Kreuz secured from Bristol before they…" Brontë shivered remembering the shadow hanging on the stoop. "Well, anyway, do you have the numbers from Greta's letter?'

The little writer's eyebrows went up. "Oh! I…" He dug into his trouser pockets and pulled out a crumpled note. "I didn't…well, this is a surprise. I didn't know the numbers meant anything." He turned to the children. In perfect German, he announced the string of five numbers written on Greta's note.

They understood immediately. With gleeful shouts, they bounded down the corridor to the second cave.

Brontë couldn't hide the gloating in her voice as she addressed Phipps. "Both Klaude and Greta had codes in their final notes from Dr. Gutermord. Bristol sold his brother's to Kreuz, but Greta still had hers."

Phipps pursed his lips. "Well, I suppose getting secondhand rumors from candy shopkeepers isn't failproof." He let out a terse grock. "At least she knew the old woman's note had something useful in it."

"No use blabbing about it!" Collanhall twisted his mustache. "Let's wait and see what the children discover to unravel the final kinks in this kookaburra!" He bounded away from the small party.

Brontë picked up two lamps and motioned for Crockett and Phipps to follow.

As they entered the tunnel, Phipps proved startlingly quiet. The beating he'd taken falling into the cave, the shame of not understanding the code in Greta's letter, and the rage of paying the candy shopkeeper for semi-useless information, had shaken him. He only mumbled, "Kookaburra...ridiculous word," and then stayed silent.

They entered the second chamber. The children grabbed one of the lamps from Brontë and then dove into the little hole. Their giggles echoed through the caves as they vanished from sight.

As the rest of the party stood in the cave, anxiously waiting, Crockett looked upon his wife with deep admiration and relief.

"Brontë," he said, "this was quite the climax. What have you and Collanhall been up to? How did you get in that suit? Who is the mobster? What is the Caddywampus?"

His wife looked to Collanhall, who winked back at her. "Well," he said, "I suppose I can start, and your wife will fill in gaps where she can."

"Please do," Crockett said. He took a seat on the stone floor. Certain that the tale would have a great many twists and turns, he wanted to be comfortable.

"It may surprise you," Collanhall began, "but I am a first-rate NINCOM-POOP from Australia."

"I would never have guessed," Crockett said. His throat hurt from the swell of laughter which threatened to burst forth. Even the taciturn Phipps looked as if he was about to combust into giggles.

"As I said, first-rate, so of course you wouldn't have guessed a thing." The colonel cleared his throat and carried on, "My job was to track down a pair of Russian mobsters who had done a great deal of damage in Australia. The quest led me to Europe and then to Praktisch where they were suspected to have fled. The dastardly folks were always in disguise. I had passport photos, but they had more wigs and false noses then I have poddybillows. My work was cut out for me."

"They came here on a covert mission," Brontë added.

"The Gestahlts," Crockett said nodding.

"Oh!" Collanhall looked slightly embarrassed. "Yes…of course. The Gestahlts."

"I knew that bit," Phipps scoffed.

Everyone ignored him.

"I put it together while trapped in here." Crockett had remembered the morning before the storm when he'd heard the mysterious voices near the cabins. He'd finally understood it was the whole Gestahlt family returning from their scheming in the caves. This helped him put the rest of the pieces together. "The Gestahlts didn't know the names of the children or of their false home country. Their cover story had several Soborbian-sized holes in it. They obviously picked the children up in town. That explains the two missing orphans before we arrived. I'm sure the poor things were thrilled with some food, shelter, and some adventure with the Russians."

Brontë nodded, her own brain shuffling together the odd events of the week. "Yes. And that's why Ursula mentioned that the Gestahlts suddenly remembered to bring their children when we checked in! Their 'poor planning.'" She smiled proudly and continued, "Mr. Gestahlt is also a machinist, so he constructed the Caddywampus suit. They wanted to use it to frighten people away from the sixth cabin and the ravine so they could seek the treasure."

Phipps let out a disruptive "GROCK!" When all eyes turned to him, he stuck up his nose and spoke. "That explains Mr. Gestahlt's itching. That suit must have given him a rash."

"I can attest to that," Brontë said, scratching her neck. "I think that also explains the dancing footprints on the side of the ravine. The Caddywampus wasn't doing a reel but was very uncomfortable."

"Ah!" Crockett smiled. "And the black substances in their bathroom!

That was dye for the children's hair. They stole two blond children and had to cover their tracks."

"And," Phipps puffed out his belly, "the single trunk. They didn't have any room for clothes for the children. It explains their dirty, ragged appearances."

"It could have been how they smuggled that monstrous suit around Europe." Collanhall laughed. "My my! It was all in front of us, wasn't it?"

"But," Crockett grew animated, "what happened to them? How did they find the information about the cave and the treasure? And if they had it, why didn't they grab the treasure and run?"

"I can provide insight there," Brontë said. "When Sylvia arrived at the inn and Bristol fell in love with her, he hatched a plan. He thought he could use the information from Klaude and the rumors of the treasure to fund his and Sylvia's escape to a new life together and also provide security for Klaude and Ursula's future. He knew the doctor gave Klaude a note that had a sequence of numbers on it. He also knew about the secret room beyond the sixth cabin. And while he wasn't sure if all that would lead to treasure, he thought he could make a greedy buyer believe that it would." Brontë sighed. "He was right, of course. He sold the information about the code and the secret room to the Gestahlts' Russian mob. But he made a grave error in his calculations—he thought that he and Sylvia would be long gone before any mobsters got stuck trying to find the treasure." She hesitated, unsure if she should mention Ursula's involvement. Despite her loathing of the innkeeper, there was no sense in tarnishing her reputation if it was not called for. "But he was betrayed and forced to stay in Praktisch under pressure from the green and gold gang. When he wouldn't confess to his betrayal, they killed him and got the code from him. This caused both the Russians and the green and gold to only have the information from Klaude. No one knew about Greta's code, so the information was incomplete. The Gestahlts didn't yet know they lacked information. They were simply trying to find the treasure's location in the caves."

"Precisely," Phipps was nearly twitching he had not spoken in so long.

"The shopkeeper informed me about the break-in at the records house. That's when I put it together that someone was stuck looking for the treasure." Phipps stopped. He let out one of his tortoise-like chortles. "Oh! Stuck! Cave systems! My word, pun intended!"

Collanhall, Brontë, and Crockett stared at him, unamused.

The writer blanched. "No senses of humor at all! I can't wait to get back to America where people will laugh at anything." He straightened his waistcoat. "Anyway, the Gestahlts didn't know where to go, so they hoped information about the land would clarify what else was around the cabin. They knew they were missing something. Gestahlt enlisted the boy to help him sneak through the window."

"The tiny person we heard mentioned, Crockett!" Brontë's eyes went wide.

"The Gestahlts were not as covert as they thought," Phipps added. "The shopkeeper told me all about the mud people and the tiny man. I guess they got into the caves first thing and discovered they needed the help of small bodies, so they galloped into town covered in filth and grabbed those children."

"They definitely solved the problem," Crockett said awkwardly.

"Hmmm." Collanhall scratched his chin. "This records business clarifies what I found out in my investigation, too. I asked the recordkeeper about the break-in. He mentioned the information about the Deutschefaber Inn, but he also said they looked at mining records."

"So, they discovered the interior cave system and the entrance to the treasure." Crockett tapped his chin with his finger. "Well, Brontë," he smiled, "I think we need to go back to the detective book. We need far more information than simply how to look at footprints."

Brontë suddenly laughed. "Crockett! The footprints! That also explains Gestahlt and the children marching around with those odd contraptions on their feet that first rainy morning."

"They were covering footprints from our sighting the night before!" Collanhall clapped his hands.

"Indeed." Phipps interjected himself again. "I bet after the morning you and Collanhall discovered those prints, Gestahlt stayed away from the cabins and stuck to the territory below the ridge. He knew he couldn't walk home in that suit. The tracks would lead right to his cabin."

Crockett nodded, satisfied with this train of thought. He suddenly leapt up from his seat on the floor. "The Gestahlts got away, though! I bet they're already on a train away from Praktisch!"

Collanhall crossed his arms over his chest. "Not on my watch. Those Smooch Moochers will pay for their crimes. When things started to go sideways, I called in an additional TURD from POOP. TURD is the Taskforce of Undercover—"

"There's really no need," Brontë said. "We can use context clues, Colonel."

"Well," Collanhall proceeded, "they arrived right on time. Brontë and I incapacitated a cordon of green and gold mobsters, and TURD came surging over the hill. I had them wait outside the cave while we infiltrated. I assume they have Mr. and Mrs. Gestahlt in custody as we speak."

"Well, I'm quite impressed," said Phipps. "I really thought the lot of you were entirely incompetent, but it appears as if it's just general idiocy."

Again, the rest of the party ignored Phipps.

"So," Crockett's thick eyebrows knitted together, "the Gestahlts were sent by their mob to collect the lost treasure of Dr. Gutermord. I think we've pieced that bit together, but...where did Kreuz come from?"

"That bit got very interesting," Brontë said. "While you and Phipps were in the other cave chambers, Collanhall and I tried to interrogate Kreuz." She threw a glance at Collanhall.

The old soldier chuckled. "He was not a verbose villain willing to share his diabolical plot, but his associates were very chatty. Before you and Phipps came bumbling in, we found out some important information. You see we were at the intersection of an odd sort of war which centers in Praktisch. It's still unclear the shape of it all."

"The green and gold gangs both operate out of Praktisch," Brontë said, "but there is an odd alignment of different groups. They merged into the green and gold, rivals becoming allies, to fight against outside enemies, which included the syndicate the Gestahlts belong to."

"But, oddly," Collanhall added, "Kreuz doesn't belong to either one of those groups. He is serving as a kind of overlord of this region holding together this unholy alliance."

Crockett thought of the tattoo he'd seen on Kreuz's wrist and the group of mobsters he saw at the pub. Who were these people? How far did their network of nefarious mobsters go?

Phipps pursed his lips. "Who is Kreuz then?"

"It appears he works for a very large, infamous organization in Europe. They have allegiances with a number of iniquitous groups all over the continent."

"Bristol was trying to get out of it," Brontë sighed.

"He betrayed the green and gold for the same group that the Gestahlts were working with," Collanhall added.

Brontë swallowed. She knew that the information about Ursula would now be found out. She felt slightly bad about it. But only slightly. "That is the mystery around the dead man in town upon our arrival. There was a hodgepodge of betrayals connected with Bristol's rendezvous with the Gestahlt gang, including one committed by Ursula."

Phipps gasped at this realization. "Ursula?!"

"Yes." Brontë tucked some hair behind her ear. "As I said, Bristol thought the information would secure a financial future for all of them: him, Sylvia, his sister, and brother. Ursula found out about it and got involved."

"I'll never understand the ridiculous things people do for love." Phipps said this as he admired his own reflection in the brass fixture of a lamp.

"Ursula thought Bristol was going to back out of the deal with the Gestahlts' gang and leave Klaude and her with no protection," Brontë said, "so *she* made a deal with Kreuz and the green and gold gang to betray the Gestahlts' Russian gang....and Bristol."

Crockett's rubbed his temples. His brain was nearly mush.

"But," Brontë continued, "Bristol went through with his planned betrayal. Ursula was then stuck in the middle. She saw Bristol sell the information and caught one of the Russians, but another one was present and got away. The second mobster was able to tell the Gestahlts the information."

"Not a bit surprised the innkeeper could kill a man." Collanhall nodded. "Did you ever see her open a bottle of wine?"

"Of course," Brontë continued, "Kreuz eventually did get the information Bristol sold to the Russians. The night he was murdered, the green and gold tortured it out of him."

Crockett wiped the sweat from his brow. Despite the cool air of the cave, he was realizing how dangerous this adventure had been. Four groups of criminals converged on the little town in which they chose to honeymoon. That's not even to mention the murderous innkeeper, the raucous military man, and the duplicitous writer. He looked at Brontë, grateful they were alive.

"I suppose the last piece is Greta." Brontë thought aloud. "Why did she reappear after all these years?"

"The shopkeeper," Phipps said finally turning away from his reflection. "She is an informant between the different warring groups in Praktisch. When she received word that Bristol planned to sell a rumored code tied to the old doctor, she contacted Greta immediately. She also informed one of my little birds. Word travels very fast when you know the right people."

"So," Crockett turned to Brontë with a crooked grin, "that explains Phipps, the Gestahlts, Greta, and Collanhall. We were the only ones here out of coincidence."

Collanhall laughed. "Well, if you read my article in *Aussie Wine and Hunting,* you'll know I don't believe in coincidences."

"Fate then," Brontë said resolutely.

"We thought we saw crossroads, but there was only one path forward." Crockett walked over to his wife. He gripped her waist and kissed her on the lips.

Phipps groaned.

Collanhall smiled approvingly. "Ah, love. As we say in Australia, if you love a loon and you can kanga a roo, you can overcome the dune."

There was a wave of polite nods in response to this. The collective hope was that Collanhall would not feel the need to further explain this Australian saying.

"It's all rather convoluted, isn't it?" Phipps said after the silence.

"Love?" Collanhall asked.

"No, you idiot," Phipps snorted. "The plot. I assume it's not over. You'll need to find out more about this Kreuz fellow. It was very dramatic of him to use that cyanide."

"If *you* are calling someone dramatic, Phippsy, it qualifies as one hell of a show." Collanhall roared with laughter. To punctuate his mirth, he slapped the piggish writer on the back. To everyone's surprise, Phipps joined in. His laugh was a soft, earthy wheezing sound that, at first, alarmed everyone.

"But you are correct," Collanhall continued, "Praktisch is a den of moles, mobsters, informants, gangsters, and spies. TURD and I have our work cut out for us."

After this thought from Collanhall, everyone grew silent. There was still no sign of the children. As they waited, each of the gathered party pondered on the events of the week. Crockett sighed and sat back down on the cold floor. He steepled his fingers together and thought deeply.

"But I do wonder what precipitated tonight." Brontë's eyes were unfocused. She appeared to be looking for an answer in a dark corner of the small chamber. "It seems as if things came to a sudden head."

"Well," Phipps was all too eager to jump in, "I can add understanding to that, my dear. You see, I had gone into town to meet the shopkeeper. When I found her, she was in a state of distress. She knew you were on your way to the prison, so she believed—"

"How?" Brontë stared intently at Phipps. "We told no one. She must be the best spy in the world if she assumed we would go to the prison after Bristol's death."

Phipps's face contorted into a malevolent smile. "The shopkeeper isn't the only spy in Praktisch."

Crockett gasped. His cranial puzzle box whirred. "The man-fairy! We talked to him, Brontë! We saw his handkerchief."

Brontë gawked.

"He passed on word to the shopkeeper, then the shopkeeper told me. I saw them chatting as I approached her store. She told me things were coming to a head. I knew Greta had important information…" He let out a light grock. "Not about the codes…but, well, anyway, I did what I needed to get the letter from Greta. I do feel a bit badly about knocking her out, but, as we say in America, eggs are broken whencewhile making omelets." Phipps turned to Collanhall. "There's probably a better saying in Australia for it."

"No. We'd just say you're an arse."

Crockett couldn't help but laugh. Phipps, for the first time that week, looked the slightest bit embarrassed.

"So," Brontë said ignoring the exchange, "the fairy and shopkeeper passed on word to the mobsters in town."

"I think the Gestahlts also knew something was coming," Collanhall said. "They probably had their own spy network which explains why they were on their way out. Their information was better than the shopkeeper's."

"They were ready for me." Phipps crossed his arms. "After I surprised Greta and moved into the woods, Gestahlt, in his monster costume, assaulted me at the bottom of the ravine. He smacked me over the head and carried me down to the cabin."

"I also fell victim to a smack from Gestahlt." Crockett rubbed the back of his head.

"Little did he know that the whole green and gold gang was waiting for *him*," Collanhall said. "They subdued him and left the suit in the sixth cabin, unattended, which," the colonel looked at Brontë with pride, "Brontë and I used in our infiltration of the cave."

Brontë screwed her face up in thought. "You know, it's a bit serendipitous how it all turned out. Phipps, you only gained the code from Greta by accident because of the shopkeeper, and the gangs only knew of the existence of one code—Klaude's. Each only had half and believed that to be all. If all of us hadn't converged tonight, we may have never discovered the treasure."

"Hmph!" Collanhall placed his hands behind his back. "It's true! It took everyone involved to bring it to a conclusion, even Bristol, Sylvia, and the children."

Crockett laughed. "Sometimes it takes a complicated plot to get to a seemingly simple solution. Spies, mobsters, double agents, and missing children—Brontë, it's been a good learning experience. I doubt even the book has much on this kind of mystery."

Brontë crossed her arms. "Indeed. I think we're all lucky to be alive."

At that moment, there were noises heard from the small hole. The lamp emerged first, followed by the tiny body of the little girl (who they had still never learned the name of). She was followed by the boy, who, as a sibling would, shoved her out of the hole and made her trip and bump her head on the floor.

They both cursed at each other in German and began to fight. Collanhall interrupted the clash. He found separating the two young children as taxing as his battle with the pack of mobsters in the forest.

When they were finally calmed, Brontë, Phipps, Crockett, and Collanhall stared at them eagerly.

"The treasure?" Phipps squeaked. His eyes filled with a gluttonous glow.

The children looked at each other and shrugged. They handed Collanhall a scroll of parchment the size of an architectural drawing, and a small, velvet jewelry box. When this was done, they proceeded to brawl again.

Phipps's face fell as he looked at the tokens in Collanhall's hands. Even in the low light, he could tell the scroll of parchment was more of the doctor's unhinged schematic drawings. His only hope was the small box. "Open it, Collanhall!" he bellowed.

The Australian gently pried open the box. Other than a piece of paper that fell out of it, the inside of the box had only a simple ring made of metal.

"That's it?" Brontë looked at Crockett.

"The treasure is…a drawing and a ring that looks like it came from a joke shop?"

Collanhall examined the ring closely. "It…does have a gem in it. It looks like a small ruby."

"Emphasis on *small*," Phipps groaned. "Dozens of years, murders, and mobsters looking for this, and it's a speck of sad, German garbage."

"The note," Collanhall said picking up the piece of paper, "looks to be for

Greta."

"It must be his final words to her." Brontë's eyes teared up. She drew near Crockett and put her head on his shoulder.

Crockett gently reached out and put his hand on the scroll with the drawings on it. "May I?" he asked.

Collanhall gave it over. The young lawyer gingerly unrolled it. In the dim light it took a moment, but he soon decoded the image.

"Brontë…" He couldn't suppress a smile as he realized what the doctor had done.

His wife peered over his shoulder; she, too, took a moment to realize the purpose of the document. When she understood, she gasped. A tear came to her eye.

"Oh, that's beautiful," she said. "What a lovely gift."

<h1 style="text-align:center">38</h1>

Things Set Right

Crockett finally got to see the last cave's architecture on their exit. The single entrance was a stone ramp carved along the easternmost wall. This led up to a door, which was concealed by a bookcase in the cozy little chamber Crockett discovered on his excursion past the sixth cabin. Had the Gestahlts not known of it from the information from Bristol, he doubted anyone would have ever stumbled into the secret caves beyond. He remembered the voices he heard on his first journey into the little chamber. The Gestahlts must have slipped behind the bookcase when they heard him approaching through the brush.

"It really is ingenious," Crockett said admiring the latch behind the bookcase. "Dr. Gutermord was brilliant."

"He was too brilliant." Brontë smirked. "If this treasure lay buried for nearly a decade, he should have given more clues."

Outside the cave and in front of the sixth cabin, Collanhall was proved correct about TURD. The force apprehended the Gestahlts (or the couple everyone knew as the Gestahlts), who were sitting, with some agitation, between a cluster of the Australians. One of the men had a very large, intimidating nose; if Collanhall's earlier facts had been correct about Australian hands, noses, and feet being classified as weapons, this man's must have been in a killing class.

"They agreed to the bargain," a stout man in a military uniform (with a modest nose but large feet) said proudly. "They'll inform if we let them go. They're smart people—crafty as cockatoos, but they can negotiate like a right wallaby."

After a brief introduction to the small fighting force of five soldiers, Collanhall led all those gathered back to the main lodge.

The trek proved joyful. The events of the evening had taken so long that a sliver of dawn light appeared on the horizon, bathing the whole world in hues of pink and gold. The other members of TURD were gregarious. They were friends with the Gestahlts by the time they emerged out of the ravine. The children also had a fantastic time, being lifted and passed between the Australian military men with alacrity. One of the Australians smuggled a massive container of whiskey, which was nearly finished during the short journey. Crockett was relieved that they arrived at his and Brontë's cabin right when one of the younger officers suggested a game of Dingo Dip Dip.

"We'll take our leave of you here, Colonel," he said warily.

Brontë dodged the hand of an officer who extended her the whiskey. "Yes, I think it's best we get back to Petrarch. Do you mind if we take the note and ring to Greta?"

"Of course not!" Collanhall stood erect. "You appear to be the closest to her." He handed over the ring and paper. "And what about this drawing? You said you know who it's for?"

"Yes!" Brontë nearly ripped the parchment from Collanhall's hands. "I can give it to him."

"Excellent! Well, the men and I will retire to the lodge and work with Ursula. I think she'll be happy to know the whole plot. I believe we can also negotiate a deal on her involvement in all this—an accidental mobster murder wouldn't even get you a ticket from a constable in Australia."

Collanhall marched off with the group of soldiers. Crockett laughed when he saw Mr. and Mrs. Gestahlt hoisted on two of the TURD members' shoulders. The children skipped alongside them laughing and singing a song in German.

"Australians are a bit odd, but they certainly are friendly, aren't they?" Phipps said. He lingered after the party left. Crockett was surprised that the smug writer wore a look of contrition. He let out a soft grock and continued, "I want to give my apologies to Madame van der Raaf. In the heat of the moment, I was far too destructive. Women need a light slap on occasion, but I crossed the line."

Brontë's face reddened. In the recent past, her own family had her trapped on a couch and doused her with water in the name of female hysteria. "Mr. Phipps, I believe *you* could use a light slap on occasion." She suddenly stopped, her anger fading due to the rise of a sudden thought. "I suppose we should call you Mr. Ellsworth now, shouldn't we?"

"Phipps is fine," the little man said. "I still consider myself in character. And," he wiped his nose sheepishly, "I've rather liked some of you. I've enjoyed being Mr. Phipps."

Crockett's expression softened. He motioned for Phipps to enter their cabin.

Inside, Petrarch was engaged in his morning exercise routine. His rotund belly quaked as he dipped to touch his toes.

"Good morning, Petrarch!" Crockett rushed forward and extended his hand to the older solicitor. "We did it, old man. Everything is solved!"

"My boy!" Petrarch's ruddy cheeks glowed even more richly in the morning light. "We must hear! I'll prepare tea and snacks. You both can rest. Greta is sleeping soundly in the bedroom, so please keep it down a bit."

Petrarch shuffled over to the attached kitchen. While toe touches were easily accomplished, it appeared he could barely walk. "Sleeping on the couch has proved more debilitating than I originally foresaw," he said in a whisper. "It may also have been the copious injuries I received last night. Either way, I may need to see if Bristol's room is available in the main lodge."

Brontë and Crockett rushed to help the solicitor, while Phipps grocked and took a seat on the sofa. Once tea and biscuits were prepared, those present at the Climax of the Cave—as Phipps continuously referred to it—told the long story of the mob activity, the Gestahlts, and the truth behind the Caddywampus.

"My goodness," Petrarch said setting his tea down. "It's very complicated, isn't it? To think that this small town was linked to a large, international confederation of criminals."

Crockett's eyebrows rose. "I still find it odd that Kreuz and a larger criminal organization would be called in for a turf war and a rumored treasure."

"Well, Collanhall said it was because of the conflict," Brontë said. "Kreuz needed to make sure that they were getting along."

Crockett pursed his lips. He couldn't get Kreuz's odd tattoo out of his mind. "I suppose so…but this seems like an odd territory to fight over."

"Indeed!" Petrarch took a sip of tea.

It was then Brontë noticed a large welt on the old lawyer's forehead.

"Petrarch! How are you?! When I left the lodge, you were supine on the couch."

"Oh!" The old lawyer laughed. "After a bit of a rest, I was awakened by the arrival of Bunce and Bosch and the doctor. No worse for the wear. The policemen cleared the trapped mobsters out of the billiard room and hauled them off to the prison. They are probably still preoccupied by interrogations and policing procedures. Many of the mobsters were quite unruly. Once freed, Ursula had to beat one back who was attempting to defecate in the piano."

"I guess it happens more often than one would think," Crockett said stupefied.

"Criminals!" Phipps interjected, happy for a chance to editorialize. "You really can't use logic to understand their actions, Crockett. As our friend Collanhall would say, 'They're as capricious as crocodiles.'"

Crockett snickered. "That's true, Phipps. We may, for the first time, agree."

Phipps's jowls shook before stretching upward into a smile.

It was then that Madame van der Raaf appeared in the doorway of the bedroom. She somehow found the time to do her hair and apply a light dusting of powder to her face. She also wore a hat covered in flowers and a few papier-mâché bees. Petrarch immediately rose and assisted her approach to the couch.

Brontë and Crockett told a condensed version of the events in the cave to catch the old woman up. Phipps sat silently, preparing to make his apology.

As the story unfolded, the dour Greta grew almost joyful. Her rouged face flushed with, what appeared to be, pride.

"That was how Himmel was," she said. "Brilliant and brazen. The cave, the secret passages, the twin secret codes—that is very much something he would do."

"A true genius," Phipps interjected awkwardly. The writer grew uncomfortable. He played with his hands and stared at the floor. "And, Madame, if you'll…you see, I wanted to say that in the course of last night's events, I think some may construe my actions as, perhaps…that is to say, I'd really want to acknowledge for you that I, in some manner of speaking—"

"He's sorry," Brontë said flatly.

Phipps looked relieved. "Yes, that."

Greta scoffed. "You, Mr. Phipps, are an arse."

"Collanhall said the same thing," Brontë added idly.

"But because I am old," the elder woman continued, "I will forgive you. With what's left of my last years, I have no time for grudges."

"And I feel the same," Phipps said happily, "although much younger than yourself."

Crockett had to control the impulse to leap across the room and give Phipps a slap.

Brontë diffused his anger by speaking, "Greta, we are delighted to give you the gift that your husband left for you." She extended her hand and presented the old woman with the small box and note. Greta held it as if it were fragile. Her gray eyes sparkled.

"Oh my," she murmured. Her face was slightly red. "This was what all the to-do was about, then?

"Klaude also got a gift. A blueprint of one of the doctor's machines," Crockett said.

This seemed to make Greta even happier. She turned her attention back to the box. "It's like he's here. Seeing his—"

She peeled open the note and devoured its contents. It was a few pages long and the rest of the gathered party waited with bated breath as her eyes looked through it in its entirety. When she finished, she returned to the beginning and read it all again. After the second perusal, she folded the note and put it in her lap.

"He's such a kind man," she said softly. She swallowed. It looked as if her emotions were mixed and confounded—she could break into tears or fly into a rage. She returned her attention to the box that accompanied the letter and pulled out the small ring with the ruby. Her hands shook as she slid it on her right ring finger and looked upon it. "It's very much like Himmel, practical and thoughtful. He made it with odds and ends in the cabin that reminded him of me: cookware, a photo frame, a necklace I left behind…"

Phipps could not stop his nose from turning upward. "Very…nice," he finally said.

"Not to pry, Madame van der Raaf," Crockett said, "but is there anything of interest to us in the letter? Are there more secrets to be uncovered?"

The old woman shook her head. "No, this appears to be the final one. I'm sorry it took me all these years to find it. But," she cleared her throat, then stood and adjusted her hat, "I'm also looking forward to seeing what he designed for Klaude."

Brontë turned to Crockett and gripped his hand. The two newlyweds locked eyes and fell into an instant, love-filled reverie. They were not the only couple in a state of silent joy; Petrarch was admiring Madame van der Raaf as she looked at the ring once more.

"Well!" Phipps said disdainfully, suppressing the urge to vomit. "I suppose we should get back to the main lodge. We better go see what the Australians are up to."

He spun quickly and marched toward the door. When he approached the threshold and realized he was alone, he turned back around to see if the happy couples were in pursuit. They weren't.

The writer exited the cabin alone.

#

When Brontë, Crockett, Madame van der Raaf, and Petrarch arrived at the main lodge, they found a third and final fête at the Deutschefaber Inn had erupted spontaneously. Even Ursula, who throughout the week tempered the emotions allowed at any gathering, was seated on an Australian's lap (belonging to a man who looked very similar to Crockett with a non-lethal nose), entranced by a story. Most of the soldiers were drunk, serving as obstacles for the Gestahlt children to run between as they screamed and played.

Even Sylvia joined the party. She tried at first to clean as the Australians tore through the main sitting room, but once offered a drink and teased by a large, portly soldier, she put down her broom and joined a group on the sofa. Brontë smiled, noting that the young maid looked considerably healthier than she had during the rest of the events at the inn. The horrible premonitions stoking her *besonderer Sinn* must have finally come to an end.

Klaude was rolling his chair about; Crockett wondered at the erratic nature of his course until he saw one of the soldiers reach over and give him a long drought of whiskey from a bottle.

"It appears there is a party," Petrarch's eyes sparkled. "I haven't seen this kind of revelry since I served in the infantry under Queen Victoria."

"Oh, Petrarch," Greta said. "I'd be delighted to hear about your time in the service." The elderly lovebirds immediately fell into animated discourse. They were nearly to the billiard room when Greta turned around quickly. "Oh! Brontë and Crockett! Let me know after you give Klaude his gift. I would love to see what my Himmel did for him!"

The young couple nodded. Then Crockett pulled Brontë close to him and hugged her. "I feel Petrarch and Greta may soon join us as newlyweds."

"I think that's fine detective work, Mr. Cook."

"Well, that still only makes me the second-best detective in our family."

Brontë laughed. She looked toward the billiard room. Her mirth subsided. "Although Greta's a pill, it will be nice for Petrarch to have someone."

"I think so. The old man isn't done with adventure yet. I think she may be an excellent accomplice."

"Well, I took the best accomplice, so I suppose others will have to settle with what's left." Brontë smiled at Crockett.

Her husband kissed her out of an affectionate impulse. They were both slightly red, eyes shining when Klaude approached them. The mix of excitement and spirits caused him to accidentally run over Crockett's foot.

"Oh dear! So sorry," he said, his words slurring together. The alcohol made the formerly shy boy chatty. "You must be the husband!"

Crockett extended his hand. "I am indeed. And you must be the hero who helped my wife escape the house."

Klaude's eyebrows went up. "Well," he said, "I guess…well, yes! I am."

Brontë knelt beside his chair. "A hero indeed! We did it Klaude; I think we can call you an official detective now."

The young man, filled with compliments, swelled out his chest. "Had to do my part. It's what an apprentice in any of my detective books would do." He took a moment to bask in the glow of his success before he proceeded, "Collanhall says you routed them—the mob! And it appears Bristol wasn't a villain at all!" The young man smiled hugely. "He was in love with Sylvia and trying to do some good with his mob connections."

"Well, he was still a villain—" Crockett began to counter the young man's claim but was interrupted by a sharp jab to the ribs from Brontë's elbow.

"He was doing what he thought best for the family," she said staring daggers at Crockett. "You should be proud of him, Klaude."

The young man nodded. "I am. We, perhaps, would never have been as close as we were when we were children, but I think he would have been a good man if things didn't end as they did."

The young man's countenance drooped. Crockett, not wanting to let him wallow in melancholy, reached out and grabbed a bottle of spirits one of the Australians was waving about.

"To Bristol!" He raised the bottle, took a drink, and passed it to Klaude. The young man smiled slightly and took a sip.

Brontë finished her sip and then brought out the roll of parchment and placed it before Klaude.

"Klaude, Dr. Gutermord left this for you."

The young man lifted the parchment and examined it. His eyebrows contracted together as he read the small print.

"What is it?" he asked.

Brontë pointed to an image at the bottom of the page. "It's an invention."

Klaude stared at the page a few moments more before the realization set in. His eyes widened and his lips parted into a smile.

"It's…oh! But…I don't know if I can do it all myself…" The glimmer in his eyes faded. "It is such a wonderful idea, though."

The blueprints were for a design of an assisted walking machine. Built out of a mechanical shell similar to the Caddywampus, the contraption was meant to give the youngest Deutschefaber the means to move without the necessity of his chair.

"Weeeeeelllllll!"

The party was interrupted by an intoxicated Collanhall supporting an even more intoxicated Gestahlt.

Brontë gently gripped Crockett's arm as she saw their approach. She handed him the liquor bottle. "I'll just go get Greta so she can see Klaude's machine," she said amusedly. "You can engage with our spirited cohorts."

She winked at Crockett and left the room.

"Hullo there!" Collanhall extended his hand to Klaude. The shift in gravity caused Mr. Gestahlt to topple to the floor. His body was immediately leapt over by both of his fake progeny.

"Oops," Crockett knelt to help Gestahlt. The Russian smiled at the young lawyer and waved him off.

"I okay," he said. "Sleepy."

Crockett nodded and then stood. Collanhall shoved his hands into his trouser pockets and cleared his throat.

"So," he said, "you showed the boy the drawings."

"Yes," Klaude said. He took a breath. "I…it's lovely, but I don't think I have the skills to assemble something of this magnitude."

"You won't be doing it alone!" The colonel shot his index finger high into the air. "We made a deal with this machinist." He kicked Gestahlt's (now snoring) body to add emphasis. "He will provide us with intelligence and help you complete the plans for this machine. In return, he'll receive some leniency on his sentence. That and he's promised to give us some more information about his little mob."

Klaude's mouth fell open in disbelief. "Oh…that's wonderful! I can't wait to start!"

"You, my boy," Collanhall said patting his belly, "will be walking in a fortnight."

Klaude's eyes filled with tears. He attempted to say something, but the words came out as short, choked pockets of air. Once he had wiped his eyes and taken a deep breath, he was finally able to speak.

"This is too much," he said. His soft voice broke into a bubbling laugh as he spoke. "After years of secrets, lies, and fear, it's like waking up to a beautiful new morning."

"Indeed, it is," Ursula Deutschefaber added, joining them. Her hair was out of place and her blouse was untucked from her skirt.

"Sister," Klaude said, his voice quivering slightly with apprehension.

The innkeeper looked at her brother, her countenance softening. "Klaude…I do…there are apologies to be made."

Klaude breathed a sigh of relief. "It's all forgotten, Ursula. I think we should begin again. I can help with the inn—no more secrets or protections. And," a flush came to the young man's cheeks; had it not been for the spirits, Crockett felt he would not have continued, "I want to see father."

Ursula blanched. "I…"

"You will." Greta confirmed, as she and Petrarch joined them. Their two arms were linked.

"Madame van der Raaf…" Ursula's mouth dropped open. "What do you—?"

"It's a long story," the old woman said. "But, after hearing the story of the Caddywampus, and, on the advice of my lawyer," she turned and winked at Petrarch, "we will go about getting the charges lifted on Mr. Deutschefaber. I had a part to play in what has happened to your family, and I will make sure that it is amended."

Klaude's face glowed. "Well, this truly is a miraculous day."

Collanhall jumped into the middle of the small circle. Crockett and

Brontë were certain he was preparing to make a grand speech. They were surprised when he reached for the bottle in Crockett's hand.

"Dingo!" he yelled loudly.

Crockett, finally feeling some appreciation for the Australian game, reached out and took the bottle back from Collanhall. "Dip," he said resolutely.

"That's my boy," roared Collanhall. He then took the bottle from Crockett and picked up Mr. Gestahlt, now awake, opened his mouth, and poured a measure of whiskey down his throat.

"Tillywiggles!" The machinist proclaimed once the bottle was removed from his lips.

The entire gathered party broke out in a peal of raucous laughter.

39

Golden Lights

The joyful celebration made the morning go quickly. Brontë and Crockett decided to leave the festivities in the main lodge near noon to go back to their cabin to rest, bathe, and recover before going to the festival.

"Be ready to leave at five o'clock!" Madame van der Raaf called to them as they exited the lodge. "We must not miss the lights!"

Once inside their own cabin, the young couple felt the full fury of their fatigue fall upon them. Brontë's eyes kept forcing themselves shut.

"Crockett, what an adventure!" she said as she fell into bed. "I think it may outdo the Mayweather incident."

Crockett sat upon the bed and smiled at his prostrate wife. "I should think so: demon bear, machines, secret caves, a mob—" The young man suddenly stopped. "You know," he said quickly, "I should think the Danube Mob would have played some part in this. Being so close to Austria and in the middle of an international organized crime war—"

"Ah," Brontë said, sleep already descending on her, "that was explained as well while you were retrieving Phipps. It appears that the Danube Mob sat out on this one; the green and gold gang has ties to the Rhine Mob, which is a strong rival. The Danubes stay away from the Rhines' territory…"

Crockett stifled a laugh when his wife's speech transformed into snores. He adjusted the pillow under her head and then pulled a blanket over her shoulders. Despite the lack of sleep, the trek through the woods, his battle with a monster, and the glasses of whiskey he consumed in the lodge, he didn't feel fatigued in the least. He went back into the kitchen and prepared a cup of tea.

Petrarch soon joined him in the cabin. He threw open the front door and staggered to the couch.

"Crockett! My apprentice, my boy!" He hiccupped and fell onto the couch. "This holiday may be too holdious.[69] I haven't had this much excitement since a trip with my wife to Glasgow in '98."

"You'll have to tell me that story sometime." Crockett entered the living room. He pointed to the bedroom where Brontë slept and motioned for Petrarch to be quiet.

"Ah! So sorry!" The old lawyer's hushed voice was still rather loud. "I may soon join her in slumber."

Crockett prepared another cup of tea and then joined his master on the couch. Once his apprentice was seated, Petrarch lifted himself up. His eyes twinkled as he appraised Crockett.

"You've done quite well, Crockett. You've managed to solve three labyrinthine mysteries in the space of a season."

"I suppose," Crockett sighed. "I'm rather disappointed in us on this one. I felt as if I never did get to the conclusion. The end was a chaotic affair, no tidy solution at all."

"Hmmm." Petrarch took a long sip of tea. "Well, you can't always expect to figure out every angle, Crockett. There are many times factors come into play which are a bit beyond the veil. You couldn't have known about Kreuz. And the magnitude of everyone's involvement was difficult to discern."

"I suppose so." Crockett's thoughts drifted to *Detectivating for the Dunce*. "I believe Brontë and I both need to spend some more time in research." He laughed slightly. "We still know nothing about Charlemagne."

"Well, my boy," Petrarch's eyes fluttered close, "you'll soon learn that all detective solutions are six steps from Charlemagne."

---

[69] This word is another Earhart invention; again, it fits, so I'll let the man have his day.

"Really?"

"In this case, three. You see," the old man yawned, "Greta was married to Dr. Gutermord and she is a fifty-first cousin of Charlemagne's aunt twice removed."

"I don't," Crockett stroked his chin, "I don't see the utility in it, but I suppose it's a theoretical principle that must be learned."

"Quite right." Petrarch had barely uttered these words before his head fell forward and he was sound asleep.

Crockett laughed to himself and then snuck quietly into his room to retrieve the detective instruction manual. Unlike his previous attempt at perusing the tome, this time he opened it and began on page one.

#

At five o'clock Crockett and Brontë, freshly fed, bathed, and rested, joined everyone at the main lodge to head to the festival. All were present except the members of TURD and Phipps. The Australian army men were forced to stay in a hotel in the city of Praktisch; Phipps, staying true to his busybody lifestyle, went into town early to flit about and honk about his books to a larger, more general population.

When they arrived at the gathering, Crockett was surprised to see Ursula holding the hands of the two Gestahlt children, while Sylvia pushed Klaude behind her.

"Ursula, you seem to have formed a bond with the children," Crockett said.

The innkeeper nodded. "They're both emotionally enjoyable and practical," she said. "Their tiny hands are incredible for cleaning."

The girl child held up her hands which were covered in scrapes. She clucked something in German.

"She's very proud of those scars," Ursula beamed. "They enjoyed cleaning out the fireplace this afternoon."

"They're very talented," Sylvia added. "Madame Deutschefaber is going to report them being found and then offer to adopt them."

"With father coming home, we'll need all the help we can get," Klaude smiled.

"You spoke with him?" Brontë asked with delight. "How was he?"

Both Ursula and Klaude grew emotional for a moment. Had Crockett and Brontë not known Ursula better, they would have believed the passing expression was due to her eating a bad walnut.

Klaude, happy tears in his eyes, was the first to speak. "Yes. He's very happy to be coming home. Master Bluster wrote out a quick note, which we gave to him regarding Madame van der Raaf and the confessions which will clear his name."

"I started the proper paperwork today after my nap," Petrarch added. His face was pale, the signs of an early hangover writ on his features. "Greta and I shall go to the prison first thing tomorrow."

Ursula sighed. "I had to make many apologies when I saw him. I…well, I should not have so readily believed him to be a killer." Her face fell. She looked at Klaude. "And I told them everything: my betrayal of Bristol, the murder, and my deep and obsessive affection for you, Mr. Cook."

Crockett instinctively shuddered.

Brontë flushed with anger. She was about to speak, when Petrarch politely pushed her ahead and directed her attention to a large tree on the forest path.

"Let's let conflicts rest for the remainder of today, Brontë," he whispered.

Klaude looked warmly at Ursula. The little Gestahlt boy jumped into his lap. The youngest Deutschefaber giggled. "We will be a family again very soon," he said.

"Even," Ursula said, trying to sound happy, "the maid."

Sylvia couldn't keep emotion from her voice. "When Master Deutschefaber returns from prison, we're going to hold a memorial for Bristol, bury him properly."

"Why are we dawdling?" Madame van der Raaf called from ahead of them. "I don't want to miss the lights because of your emotional nonsense!"

The mostly happy party (Brontë's rage abetting and Sylvia's grief settling) continued into the town. Crockett, his bondage sheep freed, could finally fully enjoy it.

And it was truly something in which to revel. The mystery resolved and the storms passed, it was a scene from a picture book.

The sun was descending to the horizon, its broad beams shades of gold and red. Children frolicked in the streets, dodging between tourists and locals, and lanterns and signs strung across the main boulevard leapt and danced in the early autumn breeze. On the air was a combination of delightful scents: roasted meat, popcorn, and freshly baked cakes. The soft sounds of a German oompah band drifted through the air and started a few revelers dancing.

Phipps, who had been waiting at the end of the road into town, leapt to life upon their approach. He was accompanied by Bosch and Bunce.

"Hullo," Phipps said pompously. "Wondered when you all would come."

"Patience is a virtue, Phipps," Collanhall said. "We all deserve some leisure after the tribulations of this week."

"I suppose," Phipps's nose turned up. "You all will be grateful to know that I reported the happenings to the police. They knew some things from the hooligans they brought back from the lodge last night, but not *everything*, of course." He motioned at the officers. "They're going to send up some individuals in the morning and go through the cabin and the caves. I believe one or two mobsters didn't make it out in all the shooting and clawing."

Bosch stared directly at Crockett and Brontë. "It seems you figured it all out," he said through gritted teeth.

"Good work Booky and Cauliflower!" Bunce added.

"Yes...I mean, well, it was a collaborative effort. Collanhall was indispensable," Crockett said.

"I very much was also more indispensable. Superlatively so," Phipps added, straightening his waistcoat.

"We shall be very excited to interview you tomorrow, then," Bosch said, ignoring Phipps. "Enjoy the festival."

Bosch and Bunce slipped into the crowd, their eyes scanning for any signs of trouble or malfeasance. As Crockett watched them disappear, he clicked his tongue.

"You know," he said, "I wonder if they know any more details about Kreuz and his organization. He had the oddest mark on his wrist. I wonder if it means anything."

Collanhall slapped Crockett's back. "You worry too much, Crockett, my boy. The TURD fellows know something about him. Evidently, he's tied to a large crime syndicate from southern Europe. They think he's in cahoots with this scary, shadowy bloke named the Raven. He's quite a murderous dastardly fellow, I've heard. He once tied a man to a horse stuffed with dynamite and—"

"That will be all!" Greta had her arms crossed and was glaring at Collanhall. "We just survived one monster mastermind. I think we have time for a respite before discussing another."

Brontë linked her arm with Crockett's. "I agree wholeheartedly," she said quickly. "Let's be fully present here! It's gorgeous!"

In the gathering dusk, the world trembled with magic. Children's laughter rang on the gentle breeze, lights twinkled, and the sounds of music and laughter swirled around them.

The entourage did not stay together much longer after their encounter with Bunce and Bosch. Klaude, Sylvia, Ursula, and the children entered the candy shop to get treats. The shopkeeper and the man-fairy were both on the front porch when they arrived. The shopkeeper smiled and waved to Greta, while the man-fairy nodded and tossed Crockett a bottle of his moonshine (which he promptly slipped to Collanhall).

Further down the road, Phipps and Collanhall vanished into the pub. It appeared TURD had gathered there to continue their drinking. Crockett saw one of the Australians smoking a cigarette outside the tavern with the leader of the British blokes he'd met earlier. The Englishman had a black eye and a missing tooth.

He raised his hand and waved to Crockett as they passed.

"Hey, Second Roger!" he called.

Crockett politely waved back. Brontë gave him a questioning look, but he simply kissed her hand and shook his head. "Another time," he said softly.

The stream of people led to the outskirts of Praktisch. At that end of town there was a large clearing in the trees. Surrounding it were several vendors and sweets stands. Brontë pointed to one cart advertising Supreme Cheeses from Switzerland.

"I am always surprised when so much of what your sister says turns out to be true," Crockett laughed and pulled Brontë close. They continued along the row of vendor stands of art pieces, sausages, beer, and chocolate.

At the far end, they stumbled upon a milliner's tent. Crockett and Brontë insisted that they finally repay Madame van der Raaf for the hat that Crockett destroyed. The old woman pretended to refuse, but once several exchanges of "Oh, I couldn't!" and "We must!" were volleyed back and forth, she ran straight to an immense headpiece with a vulture upon it and handed it to the shopkeeper.

Debts repaid, the little coterie drifted to the center of the clearing where there was a small gazebo. People had already begun to swarm the field, taking seats to see the glow bugs' arrival at dusk. Crockett noted that some of the insects were already out and about, their small phosphorescent tails shining in the waning afternoon light.

Brontë found a spot near the tree line that would allow them to see the show in the gazebo and enjoy the insects. Upon sitting, the group fell into natural discussion, not of the horrors and mysteries of the week, but of their pleasures and joys.

Dusk fell as Madame van der Raaf turned her gaze up to the sky. The terrifying woman who first met them in the lodge seemed almost triumphant in the calm twilight.

"And what will you all do next?" she asked. "Personally, I need to return home and get some rest after the events of this week. After many years of restlessness, I feel I shall finally be able to sleep easily." She stroked Dr. Gutermord's ring on her finger.

Petrarch cleared his throat. "You *could* go home, I suppose," he said shyly, "but what if we pursued the plans you and I discussed earlier?"

Greta turned and tried to suppress a smile. "Well, I suppose I don't have to return home," she barked. "We may as well start writing our love story immediately."

"Yes," Petrarch thudded his belly. "I should say 'immediately' is the perfect time."

"I shall be Madame Bluster," the old woman said adjusting her large, ostentatious hat. "It is a fitting name for my final act." She leaned over and pecked Petrarch on the cheek. All appearances of a hangover fell away from the old man. His face filled with contentment.

"Congratulations," Crockett said. He tried to sound as joyful as he could, which was made difficult by the threatening expression Greta was directing at him. "We're not surprised."

Petrarch laughed. "Good detectives wouldn't be."

"Will you return to London for the wedding?" Brontë asked.

Greta and Petrarch exchanged a glance. The old solicitor and the baroness appeared to have discussed their unofficial plans in great detail.

"Well," Petrarch looked at Brontë and Crockett, "you see, a friend of mine brought up the prospect of settling for my retirement in Brogodovia."

"Brogodovia?" Brontë looked at Crockett confusedly.

"It's a small country on the coast," Petrarch said.

"It's lovely," added Greta. "There are beaches and blue waters, but the city is cosmopolitan, rich in culture."

"It sounds beautiful," Brontë said.

"Well," Petrarch went on slowly, "you see my friend is a detective. He was asking if I'd serve in a consultancy position in the law. A great many criminals pass through the small country en route to other places in Europe. It's a small hub for…complex illegal activities."

Both Brontë and Crockett's eyes widened.

"I don't think it's a task I'd be capable of all on my own," Petrarch added.

Crockett's face was caught somewhere between joy and confusion. His heart beat a modicum faster. "Petrarch, I don't quite know what you're insinuating."

"Well, my boy, what if we put your and Brontë's detective skills to use on a more permanent basis? We could do legal consultancy but also assist when an investigation requires it."

Brontë could barely contain her enthusiasm. "Yes, Petrarch! Of course!"

She stopped suddenly and looked at Crockett. "I mean, sorry, if—"

Crockett laughed. He squeezed Brontë's hand. "Yes, Petrarch. We'd be very interested."

Brontë grew serious. "You're sure, Crockett? You don't have a desperate feeling of angst from your imprisoned sheep, do you?"

Crockett hugged her tightly. "I believe my bondage sheep has escaped. After all, now that we have the Caddywampus captured, we'll be perfectly bored. I hope you've ordered a murder for our arrival, Petrarch."

Petrarch cleared his throat. "There is no need to worry about that. There are always a few being investigated at any given time."

"Oh..." Brontë and Crockett tried to suppress the elation in their voices.

"You'll need training, of course," Petrarch continued, "but I think Brogodovia would be a wonderful next stop for all of us." At the conclusion of this statement, he looked at Greta.

The old woman smiled.

It was at that moment that the sun finally slipped below the horizon and the insects shone fully in the dark. More people had gathered, bringing lanterns, which filled the space with a heavenly glow. The insects swarmed in fluid clouds of light around the outside of the clearing.[70]

Conversation ceased for the small party as the full, intimate beauty of the night surrounded them. Greta lifted a pair of opera glasses to her eyes and admired the shimmering waves of insects. Petrarch smiled warmly and gently patted Crockett's shoulder. Brontë leaned in closer to her husband. She pressed her lips to his ears and spoke soft words that made the young lawyer laugh quietly. The newlyweds then kissed and lifted their gazes to the sky. They watched lights pulse and glow. Crockett allowed his gaze to drift above to the stars—the millions of glittering lights both contented and excited him; it was as if he were looking into his own future, an expansive space of infinite possibility.

---

[70] The reader will be delighted to know that this bucolic scene was partly inspired by the resting place of Earhart and Didiert. It's a beautiful little hill that faces the west on Aunt Masslebaum's *primary* country estate (she appears to have lost some of her rancor after the couple's passing as well).

He squeezed Brontë's hand and returned his attention to the insects and lanterns. Very slowly, his thoughts drifted away. Consumed by the peace and radiance of the natural world, his imagination opened. In the placid twilight, his mind formed glittering images of the coming trip to Brogodovia, of the wild new adventures he would face with Brontë and Petrarch by his side.

Afterword

Dear Reader,

I hope this adventure of Crockett and Brontë's has been entertaining. It is a bittersweet conclusion in many ways. Saying goodbye to Earhart and Didiert was sadder than I expected. Although it required heavy editing to make this novel and *Beatrice* readable, I think there was a certain magic imbued in the text through their influence. Few writers—of any skill level—would attempt a cubist-inspired character who speaks in reverse; the line between lunacy and brilliance is very thin. I'd say Didi and Earhart walked it beautifully.

I can also now say that after an exchange between lawyers, @badgrrlkinzay47 and I have settled…well, whatever was going on. She has agreed to cease calling me a "#poophead" in public forums, and I have agreed to stop "annoying [her] with my face." I don't know what the future has in store for our collaboration, but I'm sure it will be *interesting*. I did assist her with some new edits on her book *Space Vampires from Outer Space* (which she describes as a "diet novel" due to its thinness), so if you have $1.99 and the Kindle app, you can check it out. I make no promises about how good it is. Her cousin Greg did call it "fine," so I think you could spend $1.99 in much worse ways.[71]

When Earhart originally wrote *Beatrice*, he planned the first four books in the series. He was able to write the first three (RIP to *The Mayweather Murders*, which is lost forever; you may still contribute your version of the events by visiting beatriceunbound.com.), but all that I have of the fourth is the detailed outline I found in his notes and papers. It is called *The Heart*

---

[71] Yes, Reader, this is a shameless plug. It was part of Kinzay and my "amicability agreement."

Thief and I am currently working on it now. It is a bit intimidating to be venturing into Brontë and Crockett's world without the full guidance of Earhart, but I believe there is still some residual magic from him and Didiert presiding over the effort.

Petrarch, Brontë, Crockett, and I will see you all soon. Remember to check out Kinzay's novella, if not for me then for my contractual obligation to her.

All the best,
Tedd Hawks

Coming Soon!

Crockett and Brontë will return! *The Heart Thief* is coming in 2024!